NEVER *expected* YOU

NEVER expected YOU

JODY HOLFORD

Entangled Publishing, LLC
2614 South Timberline Road
Suite 105, PMB 159
Fort Collins, CO 80525
rights@entangledpublishing.com

Amara is an imprint of Entangled Publishing, LLC.

Edited by Stacy Abrams
Cover design by Cora Graphics
Cover photography by izusek/iStock

Manufactured in the United States of America

First Edition September 2018

To Lola, we miss you.

"You don't find love, it finds you."
Anais Nin

Chapter One

With all the things she'd been through in the last year, Stella Lane had no intention of letting a bird get the best of her. She stared up at the pain-in-the-ass-albeit-kinda-cute parakeet trying to poke holes in her good intentions. It was just after ten a.m. and she was ready to call it a day. She wasn't even supposed to be working today, and she'd already helped a Great Dane through a tricky delivery, given shots to a very sweet kitty, and had her purple Converse puked on by a nervous labradoodle. *Just another day at the office.* She grinned, thinking it could be worse. Right now, the bird was just flying around. At least he wasn't dive bombing her or leaving messes everywhere.

The bird chirped, mocking her as it flew a little higher in the reception area.

"Come down here and say that," Stella sang out in a syrupy voice. She crooked her finger, like somehow that was a magic spell. She snorted out a laugh. Didn't work on men, it wasn't likely to work on a damn bird.

As she inched toward the other side of her waiting room

counter, she kept her sight glued to Pedro, certain those marble-sized eyes were sparkling with mischief. Stifling a yawn, Stella reached up and held out a hand, willing the bird to perch on her fingers.

When the door behind her swung open, she whirled. She was not the bird's biggest fan at the moment, but she was pretty sure her owner wanted her back. Seeing as this particular owner actually paid in cold hard cash rather than most of Brockton Point's preferred currency of casseroles and favors, Stella needed to keep the animal safe.

"Close the door. Quick," Stella called, looking up into a gorgeous set of eyes that were somewhere between gray and blue.

Wow. When she'd signed up for another veterinarian practicum student, she hadn't considered he might be smoking hot. Truthfully, she hadn't thought much about it at all, since it was routine. But this guy was enough to make her forget she was on a mission to catch a bird. *Business and pleasure do not mix.* The lesson might as well have been tattooed on her skin. Plus, Hot Guy was late, and that was as irritating as Pedro's taunting. *Okay, squawking, but it feels like taunting.*

The heat of summer and the scent of cologne wafted through the door before he could get it closed. It was a powerful combination, but Stella regrouped and turned back to the bird.

"Bird trouble?" the man asked, his voice low and amused.

She sent another quick glance his way. He was easily a foot taller than her, but that was nothing new. At five feet, most people towered over her. Those smoky blue-gray eyes stared back, crinkling around the corners. His dark hair was cut short on the sides and perfectly styled on the top—like the thirteen minutes he was running behind had been used to sculpt it into submission.

"You could say that. You're a bit late," she answered. *Cut him some slack. It's not Dexter's fault Pedro's owner thought he could walk right in and drop off his pesky pet.*

The student's brows rose. "I'm sorry?"

Stella noted the light gray T-shirt and jeans, thinking that while they looked damn good on him, it wasn't the typical student attire for the first day. Most practicum students—especially those in their final leg—were eager to impress the veterinarian they worked with in hopes of securing a position. Not that she was hiring. Unfortunately, free labor was all she could afford.

She had a solid relationship with the University of Maine and didn't want to wreck that by snapping at her newest recruit. Or hitting on him. It was hard to ignore the fact that he looked more like he'd walked off a movie set than a college campus. *Focus.* The last thing she needed was to cut off the supply of free, educated help.

Pedro eyed the new guy, who took small, soft steps and made a clicking noise with his tongue. Stella appreciated the initiative.

"She startles easily. Have you worked with many birds?" Stella asked, moving with a stealthy slowness to shut one of the open exam room doors.

"I've worked with a few different breeds. Mostly tropical."

Interesting. She wondered if he'd done any of his earlier schooling overseas. She would have loved an opportunity like that, but her goal had been to come back and work with her dad. That had trumped any other job offers. The bird fluttered her wings. *Oh no you don't.* With the doors all shut, Stella knew it was just a matter of time. She hadn't been able to give Pedro an injection, but the bird was older and likely to tire soon.

Pedro cooed at Stella's new student. Actually cooed. *Traitor.* "She likes you," Stella said, trying not to scowl.

Maybe Pedro could sense Dexter Braun's—which was the

name on the files she'd received earlier that week—patience. Animals sensed emotions and Stella's were riding high. Running on too little sleep and knowing she had to ask a big favor of a petty person later today had stretched her nerves thin. When Dexter shot her a lopsided smile, her belly rolled over like an easy-to-please puppy. *You're as bad as Pedro. You might as well coo. Nope. No. No.* Not only would she be his boss, but she didn't do relationships. Ever. Not anymore. Flings, sure. Though even those had become a thing of the past. For the last several months, all she did was work. *A work fling would be convenient, except for the multitude of gray areas.* Gray was an off-limits color in Stella's world. Black and white suited her just fine.

She thought about his eyes again but didn't let herself look. She needed more caffeine. Her brain didn't usually travel so many tangents at once.

"Did you hear me?" Dexter asked.

Stella widened her eyes and realized she'd completely zoned out—and it wasn't even about work.

"No. Sorry. What did you say?"

"If you sit in one of the chairs, she might feel less threatened. Both of us shuffling her into a corner probably makes her nervous," he cautioned. Holding a muscled, tanned arm out in a way that showed a hint of dark ink near the cuff of his short sleeve, he placed his palm upward.

Stella sat and watched. "She's not nervous. She doesn't want a shot."

Dexter smiled. "Parakeets are quite intelligent. Perhaps he senses your underlying disdain for her."

Stella arched a brow, unsure if she was amused or annoyed. Mr. University of Maine Veterinarian School certainly wasn't shy. "Well, Dexter, if she's that smart, she'll realize drawing blood is immediate grounds for disdain. If *you're* smart, which I'm guessing you are, you'll realize the combination of being bitten by our clever pal, not having enough coffee, and having a practicum student arrive late are grounds for irritable outbursts."

Dexter's eyes widened. "Actually, I'm not—"

Stella held up her hand. "Shh!" Did Pedro just move closer? The parakeet seemed to have shifted down the wall. Dexter grabbed a dog treat from a bowl on the counter and crumbled some of it into his palm, once again holding it face up.

"Come here, girl. You've caused enough havoc for one day. Come on down and say sorry to the pretty doctor before she gives in to one of those outburst urges."

Despite herself, Stella grinned. "Right. She's so not coming down for me."

Stella had a feeling females of all species listened when the sexy-doctor to be spoke in that low, gravelly voice he'd just used.

Pedro inched along the wall at a diagonal, coming closer without a lot of wing movement. Dexter patiently held his hand aloft and leaned against the reception counter.

"Is it always this quiet in here?"

Stella laughed. "No. Honestly, it hasn't been this quiet in months. But I was supposed to be closed today." *So I could meet you and then go grovel to the bank.*

Dexter crossed his ankles over each other and turned his gaze to her instead of the bird. "Is Pedro an overnight visitor?"

"No. I was coming in to check on some of the animals and Mr. Sutter caught me outside before I could tell him I was closed. I rarely am."

Since they were waiting on the whims of the bird, Stella decided to use the time to her benefit. She had a standard routine with new students, starting with getting to know them. "Why vet school?"

He glanced at her, seemingly weighing his words.

"I kind of fell into it actually. I always wanted to work with animals, but I joined the army and realized the number of animals impacted by combat is disgustingly high. It didn't seem right, so it became my focus."

Admiration and warmth filled her chest. He'd done a lot in a short period of time. She'd had lots of late bloomer students, but she'd thought his paperwork said early twenties. That was a lot of experience for someone so young. The idea that he'd put his heart and talent into animals in such conditions was more swoon worthy than the flex of his biceps when he stretched out his arm and rubbed two fingers together, calling to the bird again.

"Have any of your rotations included surgery?" Stella asked, afraid to move when Pedro lowered his position about a foot.

Before he could answer, Pedro swooped down toward Dexter's outstretched palm and actually settled on his arm.

"Son of a bitch," Stella muttered under her breath.

"Hi, sweetie. Hungry?" The bird pecked at his hand.

Stella rose slowly as her show-off student stroked the bird's feathers. The stupid bird actually preened. Dexter's hands were large, with long fingers that easily wrapped around the Pedro's body, preventing the bird from spreading her wings.

When he looked at Stella, his smile made her stomach somersault again. With a cocky nod of his head, he asked, "What now?"

Stella laughed quietly. Gesturing for him to follow her into the exam room Pedro had escaped from, she glanced over her shoulder. "Let's see how docile she is for you while I give her a shot."

Dexter's chuckle vibrated in the small, sterile room and sent shivers over Stella's skin. *Or maybe it's just cold in here.*

Right. It was cold.

They made it through the shot a lot easier with four hands, and when Pedro was back in her cage, dozing off, Stella breathed a sigh of relief.

Dexter was making himself comfortable, looking around the open reception room while Stella wrote up her notes. She'd never had a student with such…*sex appeal? A sculpted body? Mesmerizing eyes?*

"Confidence!" Stella closed her eyes when she realized she'd blurted the word out loud.

"Pardon me?" Dexter moved closer, but she refused to look at him.

"Uh, nothing. I'm just making notes."

"You're putting something in your notes about Pedro's confidence?"

Stella looked up, and sure enough, Dexter had crowded way too close, his eyes locked on hers doing strange things to Stella's sorely deprived libido. "I am. Yes."

Right. Stick to your story. The look on his face proved he didn't believe her.

Straightening, she closed the file and walked to the cabinet to put it away. She needed to reattach her walls of professionalism. This guy had definitely caught her at a weak moment, and she prided herself on not having many.

"There are no other patients in clinic today, so I'll show you around, but I do have some errands I need to run in a bit. Plus, I have farm visits. You can fill out some paperwork and then we'll head down to the stables. I need to check on my horse." Just the thought of spending a few minutes with Chocolate Chip made the tension slip from her shoulders. Too bad she didn't have time for a ride today.

Grabbing her boots from under the counter, she switched her Converse for them, then grabbed the clipboard with the paperwork.

"So, listen," Dexter said, taking the clipboard from her after looking at it like it might bite him.

Now he was nervous? Stella headed for the door with him on her heels. It would be easier to rebuild those sex-starved barriers if she wasn't breathing in the delicious smell of *him*. Six weeks. She could handle six weeks with a sexy, smirky student if he was as competent as he appeared. They'd barely stepped off the porch of the clinic her father had built before she was born when a tow truck came rumbling up the drive.

Stella shielded her eyes to block the already hot sun. Dexter shoved his hands into his pockets and rocked back on his heels.

"You fix cars as well as animals?"

"Not so much," she replied, not recognizing the tow truck driver or the passenger.

The big truck pulled a small, beat up two-door vehicle behind it. Her own dogs, Nacho and Soda, howled from the wraparound porch of the farmhouse she'd grown up in. It sat a short walk away on a small incline.

The tow truck driver parked, and the guy in the passenger side rushed out, almost bailing on the gravel drive.

"Slow down, guy," Dexter mumbled.

Stella winced, amused at Dexter's commentary but worried the person rushing them would face-plant in her clinic parking lot. He reminded her of one of her labs as puppies, all feet and ears.

"Something I can do for you?" Stella called as he continued to rush over to her.

Dressed in light chinos and a button up shirt, he straightened his shoulders like he was just now thinking of making a good impression.

"Hi. I'm so sorry for being late. Are you Doctor Lane?"

Stella's brows scrunched together. Dexter mumbled something under his breath that sounded a lot like "uh-oh."

"I am. And you are?"

He stopped in front of her, his breath choppy and his smile crooked. He had curly dark hair and the slightest hint of stubble on his young-looking face.

"I'm Dexter Braun, ma'am. From the University of Maine Veterinarian Program. My faculty associate arranged my practicum with you. I truly apologize for being late. My car broke down about fifteen miles from here. I tried to call but it went to voicemail."

Stella's heart hammered uncomfortably. Turning slowly, she saw who she thought was Dexter staring at her with an abashed forgive-me grin.

This ought to be good. This is exactly what happens when you get sucked in by sexy eyes and a killer smile.

She covered her chagrin with a glare. "Who the hell are you?"

Chapter Two

Zach watched Stella's gorgeous brown eyes go nearly black. He was sorry to see the moment end. He hadn't known what to expect, but it sure as hell wasn't the bone deep slap of attraction that sucker punched him from the second he laid eyes on her. *Also didn't expect her to mistake me for someone else.* He'd tried to correct her, but she'd cut him off both times. Her stare was pure fire, and damn if it didn't light a matching one in his gut. She wore her backbone as easily as her flower-patterned rubber boots, and that was sexy in spades. But he wasn't looking for sexy. Or sex. He was looking for a long-term relationship. *Business* relationship.

This surprising snap of lust was a complication, but it wouldn't derail him. He'd been waiting too long to be exactly where he was standing. Truthfully, Zach had hoped to be standing in front of Stella's father. News of his passing had only made him more determined to come home and do right by one of the few men who'd treated Zach with dignity and respect as a kid. Shouldn't surprise him that Doctor Lane's daughter had grown right into her father's shoes.

Stella Lane was appealing in ways he hadn't even known were possible. *Business and pleasure do not mix. And business is your only focus right now.* As a former army sergeant, discipline was as second nature as breathing. He could ignore a little attraction.

Reaching out a hand, he introduced himself. "Zach. Zach Mason. Veterinarian." Jesus. He wanted to smack himself. Who did he think he was? The James Bond of animal doctors?

Those long, inky lashes lowered, and he watched as she visibly breathed in and out to pull herself together. When she opened her eyes, she turned away from him and his extended hand to face the real Dexter.

"Please don't worry about being late, Dexter. Why don't you deal with your car, and we'll start again tomorrow?"

She looked and sounded cordial, but Zach had a feeling she was simmering under the surface.

"Are you sure? My uncle lives in town. I'll be staying with him, but I thought it was best to get here as quickly as I could," Dexter said. He brushed his hair out of his eyes and shifted his feet.

The tow truck driver glanced over, his eyes sticking long enough Zach thought he might remember him from high school. It was bound to happen despite the ten years he'd been gone and the thirty pounds of muscle he'd added.

Stella stepped forward, all sweetness and charm. "I'm positive."

She glanced back at Zach, and it was like Jekyll and Hyde—the look she gave him had fangs with a side of suspicion. Even his Army unit would have shriveled under that look. Zach grinned at her, making her whip back to the kid, smiling anew.

"I have more than enough to take care of today. You go do what you need to do. Come at eight tomorrow so we can chat before the first patient."

"Thank you, Doctor Lane. I really appreciate it."

"So now I'm hauling this thing somewhere else?" the tow driver asked, scowling.

"It would seem so," Stella said, straightening her spine.

Zach didn't like the lust that was coiling low in his gut, but she was gorgeous *and* ready to go to bat for some kid she'd just met? That was a combination no one could ignore. At least not a guy like Zach, who, more than once, had desperately needed someone to go to bat for him.

While Stella affirmed that she was sure about it, Zach looked around. Hell of a property—just like he remembered. Gorgeous and vast, acres upon acres. Rolling green lawns, some of it overgrown, some of it treed, lots of it fenced. The tree line was nearly miniature from where he stood. The farmhouse where he'd sat on the back porch with her dad was weathered with age but still standing strong. The new porch railings suggested it was cared for, as did the brick edging that closed in a small flower bed next to the porch. Ms. Lane didn't strike him as the type to let things fall into disrepair. She didn't look like she planted flowers, either. Looks more like they should be thrown at her feet.

He studied the smile she gave the young student, and the kid's eager nod made Zach feel older than his thirty-two years. If he thought hard, he sort of remembered Doc Lane's little dark-eyed girl running around with some of the animals. Mostly, he'd come to the clinic to get away from everything else. Back in the day, the land and the pets soothed a part of Zach that nothing else could. Calculating, Zach guessed he had about five years on Stella. He barely remembered her, but she probably didn't remember him at all. When he'd started feeling ready to come home, he'd read what he could about Stella online, but truthfully, there wasn't a lot. He'd done a little digging in phone calls with his mom, asking if the practice was busy, if she had a partner, but he had to be careful there or she'd be knitting baby booties.

The idea her son was coming home to stay was enough to put his mom in a perpetual state of happy. *Shouldn't have left her for so long.* It had been the best thing for both of them. Going away let him become something, and being a man who could provide for his mother had mattered. It wouldn't have happened if he'd stayed in Brockton Point.

Hopefully he could change Stella's current opinion of him, otherwise he'd be relying on a years old connection to her father that she probably didn't even know about. If nothing else worked, he'd be dusting off his knees to do some begging. Zach chuckled to himself at the thought. A part of him wouldn't even mind that task. *And you're ignoring that part completely.*

The driver and student headed back toward the truck, and Stella walked over to Zach. She didn't look happy, but he'd certainly faced worse. She wouldn't be one he could charm or out-maneuver, and knowing that made him want her—*it, you want it*—more.

"Why did you lie?" she asked. She whistled, and her dogs came running, circling them both, trying to check him out and get her attention at the same time.

He leaned down, let the first of the two labs smell his hand, and then crouched to rub their sides. He looked up at Stella. With the morning sun lighting the sky, she looked like a dark-haired angel. If he was ever overseas again, this was the image that would haunt his brain. All that quiet, somewhat fragile, beauty.

She arched a brow and crossed her arms under her breasts.

Right. She wasn't letting him off on a technicality. He rose, smiling when the darker of the two labs kept nudging his nose against him. "You caught me off guard. It wasn't my intention to mislead you. I did try to tell you, but Pedro started moving and you shushed me." So, not entirely his fault.

She started to protest, but he held up a hand and cut her off. "I did help you with Pedro."

Her shoulders relaxed some. "True. What can I do for you, Zach. Zach Mason?" He laughed at her teasing and noted her tone seemed friendly enough, but her gaze suggested she was waiting for him to drop a second shoe.

The wariness she didn't hide well made him wonder if she'd already been approached about partnership. Last he'd talked to his mom, she'd told him Stella Lane was working herself to the bone for casseroles and cupcakes. Brockton Point was growing bigger and she couldn't possibly serve the entire area as her father had once done. Zach could go anywhere, practice anywhere, settle anywhere. But home was where he wanted—needed—to be. So Stella Lane was his best option for the professional future he was counting on. The first step in a series of them that would firmly root him back to the very place he'd always wanted to belong.

Zach put his hands back in his pockets and gestured toward the barn with his chin. "Weren't you going to check on your horse?"

Stella looked down at her watch. "Shit. I have an appointment in forty-five minutes. You might as well come with me and tell me why you stopped by. Without an animal to be checked."

They walked down the sloping gravel lot to a path that led to the barn. It looked newer than the rest. The air was sweeter in Maine than the many places he'd been lately, and not just because of the woman beside him. Hell, a basement with no windows and no ventilation was nicer than some of the places he'd been in the last ten years. The more recent years had been better, but some memories never entirely faded.

"You're actually a vet?" Stella asked.

He glanced over at her, his brow arching. Some trust issues there.

"You don't believe me?"

She held his gaze, and once again, he admired her backbone. "People lie all the time."

True. Her tone suggested she spoke from personal experience. "Did I not just help you with your bird?"

She shrugged, faced forward, and kept walking. "For all I know, you watch a lot of Animal Planet."

Zach laughed. "I prefer National Geographic, but I can assure you, I'm not a phony. Wanna see my license?"

She smirked but didn't smile. "Have you been to Brockton before?"

"Grew up here, actually. I've been gone a long time, but I'm back to stay now. It's time to put down roots." He'd moved on from being the shy, poor kid with the well-known, jackass of a dad. The army had done something staying in town never could—made a man out of Zach. One he was proud to be, but it had taken some time.

Stella considered him a moment, then asked, "You have family here?"

Zach nodded, carefully stepping around the overgrown roots on the path. "My mom and aunt. A few cousins. My mom brings her dog to you."

Stopping, she tilted her head. "Wait. Sheila Mason?"

Zach grinned. He'd missed small towns where a person could guess someone's family members based on a last name. "She is."

A strange look passed over her features, but before he could question her, she continued down the path. "Your mom is a nice woman. Her border collie keeps her active. She's heading up Brockton Days this year. She's very persuasive and managed to rope me into setting up a clinic at the festival."

That sounded like his mom. Zach had inherited his mom's persuasive charm. Hopefully Stella wouldn't be immune to it.

"I would imagine, since I'm home, she'll be tagging me to pitch in. She loves dogs. Calls this one the son she never had. She's had them as long as I can remember."

Zach grinned because Stella looked like she didn't know whether he was joking or not. He was looking forward to doing more than just talking to his mom over the internet. There hadn't been a lot of time during his tours with the army to visit. Following the army, he'd finished his education and, in the last few years, he'd been working hard to stockpile money and come home. He hated knowing his mom was probably lonely. It was never his intention to ignore his mom. It was just a natural consequence of working his ass off. He called whenever he could, more so in the last several months while he was planning his return.

"She talks about you. Said you were an army sergeant," Stella said. He didn't know why, but the skeptical look in her eyes made him want to bring out the reluctant smile he'd seen a couple of times now. Or make her laugh.

"I was. Did two tours, only one as sergeant. I stayed overseas while doing my vet training. We worked with military animals, but also those in surrounding areas that were wounded from war."

It was a job he both loved and hated in equal degrees. Helping was in him—he'd been born an animal lover, but seeing their pain ripped him to shreds. People didn't realize that war had a domino effect on animals as well as people.

Stopping at the barn door, she looked his way and he felt her measuring him—assessing him. The less aggressive set of her shoulders was the only indication that his work history dented her shield at all. He'd bet money Stella Lane had been hurt. That kind of wariness—the kind that settled deep inside and shone through the eyes—was something he could identify with, but he was better at covering it up. Either that, or he'd just grown comfortable enough in his own skin not to give a damn what others thought of him.

"I never thought much about how war affects animals, or even service animals in general," she said, confirming his beliefs. She surprised him when her features softened. "That's pretty amazing. So you're back to stay?"

She'd softened a little, but she was still going to be a tough sell if he was reading her mistrust correctly. "For good. It was always the plan." She didn't need to know that part of the plan, in his mind, had been working with her dad. A stitch of sadness poked at his heart.

Stella eased into her smile and his stomach tightened. *Jesus.* A smile like that could make a man forget his name right along with his goals. But not Zach. He had discipline. *Keep telling yourself that, man.*

Stella pulled open one of the heavy, wooden red doors, making her biceps tighten. Whether it was natural or she worked at it, she was visibly fit. Tiny but strong. His lips quirked, thinking she probably wouldn't like the description. He stepped in, checking out the barn. There were several stalls but only one horse, who whinnied immediately.

"Hey there, Chocolate Chip. How's my sweet girl?"

A shiver ran over his skin at the sweet, nearly sensual way she spoke to the animal. Holy hell. He'd need to find a way to ignore the sexiness of everything she said and did. Maybe he was just jetlagged or had been too long without the company of a woman, but her voice danced over him in a slow, seductive waltz.

He cleared his throat. "Cute name. She's gorgeous." He was rewarded with a heart-stopping smile from Stella. *Damn.*

"Isn't she?" She nuzzled the horse with an affection that couldn't be faked. "You absolutely are. But she hasn't been eating much lately. Not sure if it's the temperature or change of scenery or something else entirely."

He wandered close. Between Pet Central, the mega clinic he'd been running, and being in remote places, he'd encountered a vast range of animals and illnesses or injuries that weren't typical in North America. *Good chance to test your skills on home soil.* Letting the horse sniff his hand, much like he had the dogs, he spoke softly.

"Hey girl. You sure are pretty." The horse nudged him. "She's yours?"

Stella nodded, running her hand down the horse's flank. "Yeah. She's fairly new. I only brought her home about a month ago."

Stella's obvious love for the animal in both word and deed made it easy to see she was a good doctor. Zach moved closer and continued to pet the animal, letting her get used to his scent. "Any changes other than the move? Diet? Was she with other horses at her last place?"

He started to unlatch the gate, and Stella put a hand over his. Heat flashed from her touch all the way up his arm, and his eyes locked on hers. He wasn't sure if the spark in her eyes was from lust or anger, but whatever simmered between them was tangible. Nearly visible, shimmering around them like a cloud.

"What are you doing? If you're not here to visit, why are you *here,* at my home and work?"

He hesitated. He knew that timing was crucial to any good plan. But she was asking now, and if he wanted her trust, he'd have to earn it. "I'd like to join forces with you, actually. I thought of hanging my own shingle, but this place has been the go-to for this town as long as I can remember. I want to be part of that. I have a lot to offer." *Okay, okay. Retreat. Give her a minute. Stop thinking about how damn sweet she smells.* He'd had his financials printed in case things went well. He wanted to show her, in print and word, that he was serious.

Wariness stole over her features and the horse neighed, like she sensed the shift in mood. "I'm not looking for a partner." Her jaw clenched, and she looked away.

He hadn't expected her to jump at the offer, but he hadn't expected the hard edge beneath her tone either. He kept his voice gentle, like he'd done with the horse. "I have a lot of experience and a lot to offer your practice. As a doctor and as a business partner."

Her eyes darted in his direction for barely a second and her lips pressed into a tight pout.

Maybe he was fooling himself to think she'd just take him on. His mom had said, more than once, that since she'd come home, Stella Lane was running on empty—catering to her father's patients whether they came to the clinic or they needed her twenty miles out. She was servicing the entire county, and that just couldn't be going as smoothly as she'd apparently like him to believe.

Stella sighed, and he couldn't tell if it was with irritation or boredom. "I'm not hiring."

Her spine rivaled that of soldiers in his unit. *That's good, because I want a partner who will have my back.* "Perfect. Because I'm not a high school kid looking for a part-time job. I'm a well-trained, very experienced vet, and I can offer a lot to your practice. Tell me you're not running ragged or tired of getting paid in Hamburger Helper and I'll walk away now. But if that's even slightly true, you should take more than five seconds to consider what I'm saying."

Her scowl bordered on cute. He noticed that even though her mood toward him had shifted, she kept her touch gentle for the horse. She leaned in, rubbed the horse's flank, and he caught the fatigue in her eyes. It got under his skin, but he could help that if she'd let him. He *needed* her to let him.

"I hate Hamburger Helper. But how do you tell an eighty-year-old woman that you'd rather have cash? Or, at least, cinnamon buns?"

A laugh burst from his chest at the sweet admission. "I can help you with the financial aspect as well. Having an outsider—especially one who isn't *really* an outsider—set some boundaries would take that weight off you."

Brockton Point might be growing, but they were still old school in their ideas of loyalty. Starting his own practice would be the long route to getting what he wanted, and Zach didn't want to wait any longer. Besides, this place—Stella's place—held happy memories for him and there weren't a lot of places in Brockton he could say that about. He needed action and to keep ploughing forward.

Watching her closely, he saw her jaw clench and her eyes met his. She tried not to show it, but he caught the flicker of... interest? He hoped so. Pressing the advantage, he stepped forward, letting his hand stay on the horse's flank, soothing her, almost as a way to show Stella he could.

"It can't be easy running this place by yourself. Brockton has only gotten bigger, and more people means more pets. We could keep all of them healthy and local. We'd be good together. A good team."

Stella's gaze shuttered and became unreadable and her back stiffened visibly. "I don't need to partner with anyone. Especially someone I don't even know. And I don't want to be part of a team."

Interesting. Hackles all the way up. Being part of a team grounded him. He needed it like air, but he sensed he shouldn't push just now. There was more to Stella's story, and he might have to figure out what before she'd let him in. He'd heard rumblings that the clinic had shut down for a while after Doc Lane's passing, which had hit him harder than he'd expected. For a bit, he'd wondered if he could buy the practice from her entirely, but then he'd heard she opened back up to taking patients, old and new. According to his mother, Stella had taken in only emergency patients while she sorted through paperwork and grieved. *Wonder who she leaned on through it.* The thought popped into his head without warning. Now, she looked like she'd rather rely on a pissed-off porcupine than Zach.

Dropping his hands to his side, he gave her the truth. "Be that as it may, I know your reputation and I knew your father. I want to be part of what you have here," he said.

The horse nuzzled Stella's palm. "You knew my father, as in, he was your vet?"

Zach smiled. "He was a hell of a lot more than that to me, if I'm being honest. But that's a story for another day."

"This has been a family run clinic for fifty years, and it's going to stay that way."

He stared at her, taking his turn to assess. "Brockton is my home. I grew up here. I think I'm a few years older than you, so we never went to school together. You don't look familiar and I damn sure wouldn't have forgotten if we'd met. But your dad…he used to let me spend time with him when I was a kid. He was a great doctor. I'm really sorry to hear he passed away."

With the close proximity, he saw the way her lip quivered and easily heard the shuddery breath she took. Before he could reach out, say something, or offer comfort, she took another step back.

"Thanks for asking, but I'm not interested. I have to get going."

In case he didn't catch on to the verbal dismissal, she turned her body, focusing only on the horse.

There was nothing more he could do today. She'd withdrawn, and he didn't know her enough, *yet*, to push past that. They had more in common than she thought. More than he'd thought. Stella wanted to carry on her father's legacy, and clearly she was still hurting. For now, he'd let her think about the idea, maybe come to the realization that she could use him—that they could build something bigger and better together.

"I'll see you around, Stella."

She glanced back at him. "Welcome home, Zach."

He nodded, turned, and went to his truck. He didn't dwell on the disappointment swirling in his gut. This was not defeat. He'd bring her around to his way of thinking, because she might not know it yet, but she needed him every bit as much as he needed her. He had plans, and he'd waited a hell of a long time to come home and put them into play. If he needed to adjust his strategy, he could do that. Leaving on the heels of Travis's death hadn't helped numb the pain, but being away had given him perspective. Since then, he'd gained a hell of a lot more.

With patience, Zach knew he could convince one sexier-than-sin vet that they could do great things together. *Professionally.* Right. Best keep that in mind. Zach backed his vehicle up and turned around in the gravel parking lot in front of her clinic, heading out of the driveway. In the rearview mirror, he saw her watching him leave. Her dogs flanked her on either side—her own little unit.

Zach vowed, right then, he'd work his way in, and they'd both be glad he did.

Chapter Three

Stella pulled out of the bank parking lot, forcing herself not to slam her foot on the gas as a visceral way to express the anger coursing through her. Who did Lydia-Rae Simpson think she was?

"Stand-in bank manager, a.k.a. former prom queen who doesn't realize she's no longer wearing a crown," Stella mumbled into the cab of her aging Cherokee. At sixteen, Lydia had told everyone Stella liked women—not that there was anything wrong with that, except Stella's boyfriend at the time figured that was why she wasn't putting out and dropped Stella for Lydia. Even though she'd gotten exactly what she'd wanted, Lydia had enjoyed being a thorn in a variety of sides. Gripping the steering wheel tighter, Stella turned left at the light and headed toward the freeway.

She'd cleared her morning for the meeting at the bank, only to be turned down. *And looked down on.* If Mr. Henry, who'd worked at the bank since the beginning of time and had been great friends with her father, had been there, she might still have been turned down. But he would have done it without the little hint of glee dancing in the corner of his eyes.

She smacked her steering wheel. The tension in her body was enough to fuel her damn vehicle. Between the late vet student, the case of mistaken identity, and her physical reaction to Zach Mason, Stella's mood couldn't get much worse.

"Partners," she scoffed under her breath, grateful no one knew how much she talked to herself. At least she wasn't talking to her dad without realizing it anymore. For the first couple of months after he'd died, she had talked to him like he was still there. God, it hurt so much sometimes, she felt like her chest might cave in. Sometimes she wished it would, just to stop the ache. Even being riled up and mad felt better than the emptiness that all but echoed inside of her.

Zach had known him. There'd been a gentleness in the way he spoke of her dad, in the way he looked when he mentioned him. That, more than his offer of partnering or the way his smoky gaze bore into her like he could see her soul, had made her want to get closer to him. She wanted to know him, listen to him talk.

"To ask him about Dad," she reminded herself, hitting the freeway and feeling the tension seep from her shoulders. She was glad she'd set her farm visits for today, to coincide with the bank. It gave her an excuse to drive off her irritation without wasting time. Of having what she'd considered her plan B stripped away from her. There was no plan C for keeping the clinic—and her home—afloat.

Time was something else she was losing these days. There just wasn't enough of it. How her dad had done this and not drowned under the weight of responsibility, she had no clue. *We were supposed to do it together. We didn't even get that.* She'd come home, dragging the pieces of her broken heart behind her, looking forward to being his partner and starting fresh. Now she'd never know that.

Switching the radio on, she watched the houses grow

farther apart, the ocean far off to her left. She lived on the outskirts of town and sometimes felt like she isolated herself in her own little world. It was easier that way. She didn't have to pretend everything didn't hurt. Pulling off the freeway about ten minutes after she got on, she wound her way up to the Mainer Farm. They were a dairy farm and just one of the local families she did herd health checkups for once a month. She'd booked her bank visit around today so she wouldn't have to cancel any clinic appointments. She needed all the money new clients could bring in, but these monthly visits were a big part of her income. Currently she only had three families, though, since two had looked elsewhere after her dad had died and Stella closed up shop for a couple of months. She'd had no choice. But the impact of doing so had been a hit to the bottom line.

Lydia's suggestion to get a co-signer curled her stomach like sour milk. She shouldn't need one. *Dad didn't exactly leave the clinic in the best shape financially.* But who could she ask? Her best friend was getting married and Stella knew Megan and her fiancé, Adam, would help her if she asked, but she wouldn't. Couldn't.

Pulling up to the sprawling farm house that looked like something out of *Architectural Digest*, she cut the engine. Taking a second, she breathed in and out slowly. She'd figure something out financially. What choice did she have? Her father had been good at what he did, but in recent years, his debt had piled up and though he'd left behind a small insurance policy, he'd also wrapped his home finances up in his clinic. *Stop. It'll work out. No sense dwelling.* Her heart clenched. How many times had her father said those words to her? Right before he'd put her to work to pull Stella out of whatever mood she might have been in.

A knock on her window startled her and she jumped, then laughed. It was Colin Mainer, the farmer's oldest boy.

Stella got out of the jeep.

"Hey, Colin. Sorry, I zoned out there."

"No worries. How are you doing, Ms. Stella?"

She smiled at the formal tone. The Mainer kids were a sweet bunch. Their family had been a part of Brockton as long as Stella's own. Everywhere she went, it was a reminder that it was just her now. For as long as she could remember, she'd known if she ever needed to, she could return home and her dad would be there. And now he wasn't. Instead, every nook and cranny—or farm—reminded her of that.

"I'm good. Heard there's a new filly in your family," Stella said, grabbing her medical bag out of the back. The Mainers had a few family horses, and it was Colin's dad who'd helped her find Chocolate Chip.

Colin walked in step beside her, toward the barn. "Yeah, rough birth on Esther. We almost called you, but it was the middle of the night and Dad said he didn't want you dragging yourself out of bed and heading out here all alone."

Stella stopped in her tracks. She forced herself to count to five in her head. "You guys should have called. You can always call. And you absolutely should. I'm the town vet now," she said. People counted on her father. They always had. Doc Lane had been a good man and an even better doctor. The people of Brockton Point accepted her as one of their own even though she'd been away, but they hadn't fully adjusted to the fact that she was now filling her father's shoes. Whether it was because she was a woman, or they saw her as his daughter, or just weren't used to her in that professional capacity yet, she didn't know.

They approached the barn as Mr. Mainer, strands of his thick gray hair fluttering in the gentle breeze, came out.

"Stella. Good to see you, dear. How are you?"

They shook hands, standing in front of the gorgeous red outbuilding that had been rebuilt from the ground up after a fire several years ago. "I'm good. Colin says Esther had some trouble with the birth. You know you can call me."

Mr. Mainer sent his son a glance but gave Stella a smile. "Nothing we couldn't handle. Plus, knew you'd be here to check the herd. Don't worry about the filly. You can see her for yourself. Your dad would have given me that look you're giving me right now, but we did okay."

She nodded, needing to push the issue for personal and professional reasons. "Yes, he would have. And if you would have called him the other night, you should have called me."

Their gazes locked, and he nodded slowly, understanding. These people who'd relied on her father still saw her as Doc Lane's little girl. That needed to stop. She was very capable and couldn't be paid in suckers. These people had to understand that.

"Next time I will," he said, respect shining in his eyes. *That's right—I'm Doc Lane now. Tell your friends. And for God's sake, encourage them to pay me in something other than casseroles.* She was going to gain fifty pounds just from those.

"Let's take a look."

Going into the barn, inhaling the scent of fresh hay and mud, Stella realized this was her element now. She'd trailed after her father as a young girl, wanting to be just like him, but never truly understanding what that meant. He had loved animals to his very core. He'd never told Stella she should follow in his footsteps, but it hadn't ever occurred to her to do anything else. With it being just the two of them after her mother's death, he'd buried himself in the clinic and made Stella his little helper. She'd loved everything about it. When she'd gotten older, he started sending her to her aunt's horse farm out of state. She'd loved that, but even as a teen, she knew she wanted to work side by side with her dad.

Walking up to Esther, she let the mare sniff her hand.

"Hey girl." The filly nuzzled her mom. "She's a beauty. You did good, girl. Yes, you did."

Colin handed her an apple, then went to muck out some of the stalls farther down. Esther practically inhaled the fruit, not even letting Stella offer a bit to the filly.

"No problem with your appetite, hmm?"

"Eleanor will have my hide if I don't give you a casserole before you go. Make sure you remind me. Colin, you got the list?"

Colin nodded and held it up. With a smile, he gestured to the exit. "We'll meet you over there. Looks like you want a minute. You always did love horses. How's yours doing?"

She beamed. What little girl—heck, what kid—didn't want their own horse growing up? Now she had hers, and it was every bit as awesome as she'd imagined. She just wished she had more time to give C.C.

"She's great. Settling in well. She's not eating too much, but I think she's still getting used to the place and to me." She didn't share her concerns because she didn't particularly want to tell clients that she couldn't figure out her own horse.

Nodding, he and Colin started off, but he hesitated, looking back at her. "If I'd really been worried, I would have called you, Stella. Trusted you, just like I did your dad. He'd be real proud of you," Mr. Mainer said.

Stella nodded, her throat tight. When he walked out of the barn, Stella let herself into the stall and got to work checking the vitals for both animals. It was easy to imagine getting lost in this. Animals didn't judge. The world could learn a lot from them, she figured. Laughing when the filly nuzzled her stomach, she pressed her forehead to the horse's.

"You're a happy one, aren't you?"

She stroked Esther's flank. "You did good, girl."

Feeling more settled, Stella grabbed her bag and headed to the cattle barns. While she checked the animals, Colin and Mr. Mainer would walk along the front of the cattle, giving her information and details she needed to know. It wasn't overly pleasant, but it was routine and one of the first memories she had with her father. She'd always come with him to the checkups, and the first time she'd seen him put his hand elbow deep inside a cow, she'd nearly lost her Scooby snacks. She smiled at the memory and got to work.

When she'd finished cleaning up, she went to the main house to say goodbye. Mr. Mainer was coming down his porch steps, casserole in hand. It wasn't until he held it out to her that she noticed the envelope on top.

"Eleanor says heat it up at three-fifty," he said.

Stella accepted it with a smile. Apparently, everything was heated at 350 degrees. "I'll do that. Thank you. What's this?"

Mr. Mainer stood straighter, looking down at her—which wasn't hard at her height—and gave her a look similar to the one he'd given Colin earlier. "That there is for your worry over the filly and checking her when you didn't have to, and the rest is what I owe on my account. Should have had it to you sooner. Your dad and I, we'd get to talking and shooting the shi—bull and I'd plain forget to square up. I need to remember not to do that with you. I'll make sure I settle up with you monthly."

For some ridiculous reason, she wanted to give the money back. *Because you feel like dad would have, but that's exactly why he was in debt.* Debt he never mentioned. And now she had to run things, and she couldn't do it with hope and a smile. She closed her hand around the envelope. "I appreciate that. I really do. I'll see you next month. Make sure you call me if you need anything before then."

"All right then. Good to see you, Stella."

"You too, sir."

Maybe things will be okay after all. She drove back down

the winding road that had taken her to the Mainer's farm holding on to that thought. If everyone settled up their long running accounts, it would certainly be a step in the right direction. She needed to put her big girl pants on and stop accepting food for animal care. Not that everyone was like that, but at one time, way back in her dad's day, favors had been the currency of Brockton Point. But life didn't run on favors, and Stella Lane was not a fan of asking them.

She felt the tug in her wheel before the jeep made any noise. One minute she was driving, and the next it felt like the vehicle was slipping over a rocky river bed. The truck thudded and jolted as she tightened her grasp on the wheel and eased it to the side. Pressing the brake, she stopped the jeep but not the Mach speed of her pulse.

"Because what I really need right now is a flat," she muttered, her voice sounding tired even to her own ears.

She got out, slamming the driver's door. The gentle breeze wasn't as soft this close to the ocean. Taking a moment to breathe in the salty air so she could solve yet another problem without losing her freaking mind, Stella closed her eyes and leaned against the back of the truck. The rear tire on the passenger's side was flat. A piece of thick, jagged glass sparkled from the tread. She had a spare. She could change a tire. But part of her wanted to just walk over the rocky terrain and head for the ocean to just sit a while and figure out how her life had become this busy, unpredictable mess of complications.

"Think while you work," she muttered. She opened the back, grabbed the spare and the jack, and set it down beside the wheel. A little over a year ago, she'd been thinking about how to get Steven, her fiancé, to agree to move to Brockton Point so she could work with her dad. Now, she was broken down on the side of the road, stranded and alone. It felt like her life had done a one-eighty and she'd landed flat on her face.

Tears burned her eyes. She'd been so busy getting through every moment, she hadn't given herself time to grieve any of the losses she'd suffered in the last year. "And on the side of the damn freeway is not the time to start."

She reached up to close the back of the Cherokee just as a truck whipped by and pulled onto the shoulder, right in front of her vehicle.

See? Not alone. In Brockton Point, even on the outskirts, people were never truly alone. Stella just needed to get her bearings back. Get her feet under her.

The truck looked familiar, but it wasn't until Zach unfolded all six foot something of himself from the driver's side that she realized why. Aviators covered those eyes that could drown her in an entirely different way if she was open to such things. *What the hell? He just happened to be out this way? Great. Now he'll think he can be your knight in shining armor.*

Well, news flash, mister, I got this.

He strolled toward her, his jeans a perfect fit on his long, muscled legs. His T-shirt hugged his biceps, and her eyes were drawn to the swirl of tattoos that went from his elbow up under the short sleeve.

"You got everything you need, Doc?"

She had to give him credit for not asking the ridiculously obvious question: car trouble? "I do. What are you doing way out here?" she asked as she closed up the back of her truck.

He came close enough she could smell his cologne mingling with the scent of the ocean. Heady combination, and one that made her want to take a dive. Nope. Not going there. Not with anyone ever again. The best way to protect her heart was not to give it. Though, the way Zach looked at her when he pushed those glasses to the top of his Army-buzzed hair, he wasn't after her heart.

Well, she thought, her movements jerky and strained, *he can't have* that, *either.*

Chapter Four

Well, damn. Zach hadn't expected his impromptu detour to take a look at his property would end with an even better view than the one he'd just spent thirty minutes staring at. Stella Lane was huffing out heavy breaths, but he honestly couldn't tell if it was from irritation or exertion. She was going to hurt her shoulders if she kept reefing on that crowbar. He watched, waiting, knowing she'd never ask him for help. Stubborn, amazing woman. He wondered if there was anything she couldn't do.

"Do you have to stand there?" she asked, blowing hair out of her face as she glanced up at him.

"Want me to stand in the middle of the road?" He grinned at her, and to his absolute fucking delight, she grinned back. It changed her face—moving her from beautiful into breathtaking. Literally. Like switching on an actual light, his skin felt warmer.

"Not enough traffic. No point."

He shook his head and crouched down. "I don't doubt there's anything you can't do, you put your mind to it, but

I'm guessing by how hard you're trying to turn that bolt, it's stripped." He paused, letting the word settle in his brain and on the tip of his tongue. Her eyes widened, and her nostrils flared slightly. *Damn.* Maybe he should rethink wanting to work with her so badly. He could be setting himself up for a lot of cold showers.

Changing the course of his thoughts, he leaned in just a little. "Let me help. I won't tell anyone."

Those sexy lips quirked. He wanted to know what it would take to make her laugh without restraint.

With obvious reluctance, she said, "Fine. But I can change the actual tire."

He nodded. "Whatever you say, Doc."

He could say, with absolute certainty, that this was the most unique fifteen minutes he'd ever spent with a woman. She let him take the bolts off—which were really damn tight—and he moved out of the way so she could swap the tires. It frustrated him to see her struggle with the weight of the flat one. He could probably bench press her, but she was so determined to do it on her own, he didn't even try to help her. He did, however, tighten the bolts when she was finished. She had a smudge of grease across her forehead and several spots on her hands. When they stood, he looked down at her and, for about a second and a half, saw a vulnerability in her eyes that made him want to open her up and figure out why she was so wary. So guarded and opposed to leaning on anyone. *You're trying to be her partner, not her shrink.*

He stared at the small grease stain she'd given herself and, without thinking, pulled up the hem of his T-shirt. Stella's sharp intake of breath made him pause for a second, and the way she checked out his chest and abs made him rethink his idea. Her lips parted, but he focused on using the soft material of his shirt to swipe at the spot on her forehead. With one hand, he held the back of her head still and the other, he pressed his cotton-covered fingers to her skin and gently removed it. Or lessened it anyway. Her hair trailed over his fingertips, making him clench his jaw to fight back the wave of attraction.

Her eyes closed, and she swayed forward, her hands almost coming into contact with his stomach, which had his muscles tightening. Stella snapped back, yanked herself away from him.

"I'm not five. I don't need someone wiping dirt off my forehead."

"You're welcome," he said, letting his shirt drop back down.

Looking chastised, her cheeks turning a soft shade of pink, she grimaced. "Sorry. And thank you. Really. I appreciate it. What are you doing out here, anyway?"

Zach hesitated, looked out at the water, then back at her. "I'll show you."

He'd been on his way to his mother's, but decided he needed to see the land he'd bought. Knowing he had his own chunk of Brockton to come home to, a piece that was *his*, had grounded him. Definitely worth giving up most of his savings for. The calm it had brought the second he'd set foot on it proved it was worth the risk. He'd sunk his money into three properties. His mother's, a rental, and this land that he planned to build a house on. He'd look out the windows every day and be able to breathe knowing he'd done it; he'd succeeded.

"Show me what?" She picked up the tools and put them in the back of her Cherokee as a car whipped by. First in the whole time she'd been there. She might have been stuck on this road for a while if he hadn't happened by. Coincidence or fate? Didn't matter. He was glad he was there, but he wondered if there was anyone she would have phoned. Boyfriend? Definitely no husband.

When she shut the jeep and came back to stand beside him, he pointed to the water. The gravel shoulder dipped down to a slight ditch and then went back up, leveling out into what looked like just a vast amount of land. He started down the slope and held a hand out to her. She stared at it, then surprisingly, slipped her hand into his and let him help her both down and up. When she pulled her hand back on the other side, he shoved his in his pocket so he wouldn't be tempted to reach for her again.

"You showing me the ocean? I've seen it a few times," she said.

"They sold this land off in large chunks a while back," he told her.

Stella looked around. "There was a real estate sign here forever. People worried it would be some huge box store that bought it. I'd heard it was broken up and sold in pieces. Still a shame, since whatever gets put here will likely block the view. But it's better than some chain coming in and desecrating most of it with a parking lot."

Zach stopped and stared at her. "Jaded much?"

She pointed to the view. "Maybe a little more than I should be, but this kind of beauty shouldn't be the view for shoppers too busy to appreciate it."

"No. It shouldn't. But how about homes? The land was sold with the intention of creating a new subdivision of Brockton Point." They walked closer to the water, where the scent of salty air was strong and brisk.

"Homes would be good. I hope they don't do condos, though, or at least not really high ones."

From this spot, they could see forest on the other side of the ocean with a few houses dotting the far coastline. He remembered a few of those homes being fishing lodges or summer homes and wondered if the same families owned them. When they came closer to the edge of the bluff, they stared down at the water breaking against the lower bank.

Zach pointed to the right where there was a gentle curve in the landscape. "I own one point two acres in that curve right there. I won't be the first to break ground because I'm not ready to build yet, but my home will be one of the ones along this stretch."

Her eyes showed surprise. "It's a good spot."

Hands still in his pockets, he stared out at the water. "Knowing this was here, waiting for me to come home to, kept me going a lot of nights. Even when I left town, I knew I wanted to come back here. Live the rest of my life here, looking at this."

Stella followed his gaze and sighed. "It's a gorgeous view."

"I'm looking forward to someday," he admitted. Glancing down at her, he waited until she tipped her chin up. "How about you, Doc? What are you working toward?"

She closed her eyes, and he watched her inhale and exhale with great care. When she opened her eyes, stared into his, his own breath caught with the intensity he saw. "Being able to breathe."

• • •

Anticipation hummed through his blood as he turned down the familiar street to his mother's home. It had been his home after his father died. Memories slapped at him when he pulled up to the rancher. He and his best friend had spent many afternoons in that house, right there in the living room he could see through the large picture window. Even before they'd been able to move into the house, though, Travis had stuck by him no matter what. Through the taunting from the other kids, the occasional ass kicking from both the other kids and his dad. As if Zach had any control over how much money his parents had or how his dad drank away every penny, leaving them with nothing. He'd given them more with his death than he ever had when he was alive. As he shut off his truck, grabbed his bag from the back, and got out of the vehicle, he looked around and frowned.

His mom had had him when she was twenty, which meant that she'd just hit her fifties. From conversations with her, he knew she kept active and was happy. But the state of her yard, the overgrown lawn, didn't mesh with his expectations. His mother liked things tidy, and even before the Army had sharpened that instinct in him, he'd kept things that way so she didn't hassle him.

Her car wasn't in the driveway and there was no garage, so she must not be home from work. That was fine. She knew he was coming, he just hadn't given her an exact time. He slipped the key out from under the mat, reminding himself to tell her to knock that shit off. He didn't care how small she thought Brockton Point was, safety came first. Letting himself in for the first time in a very long time, he stood in the entryway and breathed it all in. Images came to mind like an old school slide show, flipping through his brain. Most of them, after they'd rebuilt their lives, starting with this house, had been happy. Until Travis died and Zach had spiraled into a pit of loneliness and guilt he couldn't see through.

Taking off his shoes and leaving them by the door, he walked through the house; very little had changed. Flipping the light on in his old bedroom, which now looked more like a generic spare room, he frowned at the burned out bulb. He'd planned to attack the yard first, but maybe he'd do a little tour of the inside and see what other things his mom needed taken care of.

"Time to make up for not being around to help," he muttered, unloading his duffel into the set of drawers at the foot of the bed. Felt weird to be back at his mom's place, but until he figured out a more permanent solution, it would have to do.

Zach made himself at home, changing his Blundstone boots for runners and heading out to the shed in the back to start up the mower. The breeze he'd felt by the ocean had not reached this far inland, and by the time he moved to the front lawn, his T-shirt was soaked with sweat. The good kind. Not the kind that came from trying to keep his eyes peeled for mortal danger while he dragged a wounded animal to shelter, watching his own back at the same time.

Shake it off. Definitely easier to do during the day. It was the nighttime that was hard. It was then he couldn't stop his brain—and he'd tried—from diving head first down one of two fucking rabbit holes: the death of his best friend at eighteen and the things he'd seen overseas. He honest to God didn't know which one haunted him more.

That's over now. Both of those things. They made you who you are. Move on. Man up. "Hooah," he whispered under his breath. Gripping the electric mower's handle tighter, he focused on the rhythmic back and forth motions and the feel of energy vibrating up his arms. He'd just tucked the mower back in the shed when he heard his mom's car in the driveway.

He knew she saw his truck. Being a blue, quad cab, it was a little hard to miss. She stopped and looked at it, but when her head turned and caught his gaze as he came through the side gate, her mouth dropped open. She shook her head a little and her hand flew to her mouth. He kept walking until he was right in front of her and then he wrapped his arms around her and picked her up, hugging her as hard as he could without breaking her. She hugged him back with all her strength.

"I don't have to ask if you're eating," she said when he set her down. She sniffled and looked him up and down. "Might need to ask *what* you're eating. Looks like nothing but muscle."

He grinned. "You say that like it's a bad thing."

"You look good, Zachary. Healthy. Happy." She hitched her purse on her shoulder and then put both hands to his face, looking closer with a mother's speculative gaze.

"I'm both, Mom. And home."

"Not just a quick visit or a few days of leave. For good this time?" She whispered the words.

"I promise."

She exhaled hard and smiled all the way to her watery eyes. "I'm going to make you your favorite meal," she said, starting for the path to the house.

"Pizza from Pop's?"

"Number hasn't changed. Call them while I shower and then we'll visit and talk about you mowing my lawn."

He didn't know why she was using her "mom" tone on him, but he just smiled and hoped that at thirty-two, he wasn't about to get grounded.

While she showered, he changed the lightbulb in his room, adjusted the hinges on two of her cupboards, and unstuck the screen door. Jeez. She could have called a handyman or something. He sent her some money now and again even though she had a good job as a secretary for the mayor. Didn't make sense to him that she'd let things run down. *Maybe she doesn't know how to fix this stuff.* He laughed out loud. His mother knew how to do everything. In that regard, his mother and Stella had a lot in common.

"Something funny?" she asked as she walked in, dressed in cozy clothes that he couldn't tell if they were pajamas or just lounge gear. Her dark hair was wet and cut short. Her eyes were the same color as his.

He turned, twisting the cap off a bottle of water he'd grabbed from the fridge. "I was just thinking it's not like you to fall behind on maintenance." He took a long swallow, nearly downing the whole thing, then gestured to the screen and the cupboard doors. "I tightened up a few things for you. If you make me a list, I'll take care of anything else you need done."

Guilt tickled over the edges of his ribs. Lots of kids went away. Zach hadn't done anything millions of other teenage sons hadn't, but he still wished she hadn't been on her own all these years. *You're home now, so things will be different.* Her eyes went over his shoulder and then she moved, stepping around him to go to the fridge.

Zach watched his mom as she pulled out a can of soda and popped the tab. She was aging well and that made him happy. When he was young, when his father had been a fixture in their lives, she'd seemed so much older. And now Zach understood how life, how one situation, could age a person both physically and emotionally.

"Stella says you're running the show for Brockton Days," he said, leaning a hip against her counter.

She nodded, excitement sparking in her gaze. "I am. Mayor Cambridge wanted a few things to run differently and she really liked my ideas, so we're moving forward with some of them. Don't think you'll get out of helping me either. We're doing it up big this year. Carnival style."

"I told Stella you'd be roping me in."

She regarded him with narrowed eyes for a moment. "Stella, huh? Not even Doctor Lane. You already get what you were after?"

He pushed off the counter. "I'm working on it. Carnival style? So what…guessing weight and bearded ladies?"

His mother laughed loudly, the sound bringing him back to some of his happier memories. "Not quite. But I'm thinking plenty of women will pay top dollar at a kissing booth if you're in it."

Zach scowled at her. "You'd pimp your own son?"

With a slightly wicked smile, she nodded. "The money goes back into the community. It's for a good cause."

Feeling restless in the small kitchen, he looked out the window again, watching as two birds swooped into the large maple tree that needed a trim.

"I'd rather do some heavy lifting. Set up and that sort of thing, but I'll be there. That tree needs trimming, Mom. Some of those branches look like they're dead or dying. Last thing you need is them falling on the roof."

"You call for the pizza in between all your puttering?"

Turning, he saw that she was looking at her watch, avoiding his gaze. What had he said?

"I did. What's going on, Mom? Everything okay?"

Now she looked at him and her gaze shone with happiness. "Things are wonderful. I have my boy home for good. What could be better than that?"

She put her soda down and stepped into him, wrapping her arms around his waist and giving him a hug. *Mom tactic*. He was old enough, and wise enough, to recognize a distraction when it was smacking him on the back.

When she stepped away, he arched a brow. Twisting her fingers, she sighed. "I kind of haven't done a few things on purpose. I'm sort of seeing someone. He's a great man. You're going to love him. You actually have a lot in common. But he's not great with idle time, so sometimes I leave things undone so he has something to do."

"Excuse me?" Luckily he wasn't drinking because he might have choked. He didn't know which piece to tackle first.

She straightened her shoulders and gave him that look that used to—correction, could still—make parts of him shrivel.

"Don't you talk to me in that tone. Shane is a good man and I'm a healthy, vibrant woman," she started.

Zach covered his ears. Yup. Thirty-two years old, standing in his mother's kitchen covering his ears so he didn't get too much information. He stopped short of actually singing out "la-la-la." She slapped his arm and laughed.

When he lowered his hands, he did so cautiously. "So you have a boyfriend."

Her cheeks went pink. "I suppose you'd call it that. He's a good man, Zach. I really do think you'll like him. He's loving and kind and makes me laugh."

"Why didn't you tell me?"

She shrugged as if they'd done a Freaky Friday. "Wasn't sure how serious it was or if you'd actually get your butt back here."

Zach stared at her a moment, weighing his words. "I told you I'd be back. I wasn't off doing nothing, Mom. And you could have come to see me. I've only been a few hours away for the past couple of years."

"A few? Seven hours is more than a few. I'm not complaining about what you've done or where you've been. You know how proud I am of you. I just wasn't sure how to bring things up over the phone. We've been together for about nine months now."

He almost made a crack about that but winced for even letting the thought pop into his head. She grinned, and he knew she could still read him too well.

"I'm happy, honey."

His heart clenched. Damn he wanted that for her. "That's good, Mom. I'm glad you're happy. You definitely deserve it."

"So do you. And now you're back to find your own happy. What happens if Stella doesn't want to take you on as partner?" She picked up her pop and drank.

Zach leaned on the counter and crossed his arms over his chest. "That's where I'm at right now. She wasn't very receptive, even though it's easy to see she's got lots going on."

His mom nodded. "Stella wants to carry on what her dad left behind. She figures because he didn't have help, she shouldn't."

Running a hand over his chin, he considered that. "She tell you that?"

She laughed. "Honey, this is still a small enough town that people talk. A lot. It's pieced together with what I've heard and what she's said. She's an independent girl. Always was. Might take some convincing."

He'd already figured out that much. "Any suggestions?"

His mom's smile was sassy. "Just be you. Never seen you go after something and not get what you wanted."

That wasn't entirely true, but what were moms for if not to believe the absolute best in their kids?

The doorbell chimed, and she went to the door. Zach grabbed his own soda and the plates she'd taken out. He set them on the table and grabbed some napkins. His mom walked back in carrying a large double pepperoni pie from Pop's. He'd missed that place.

"Smells delicious. I'm starving. You probably should have ordered two," she said, bringing it to her small, round pine table.

He laughed, as she'd meant for him to do. Other than Travis, she'd been his only constant. Once his father died, it had been her and him against the world. The small insurance policy she'd received after her husband passed allowed his mom to purchase the home she still lived in, and even though things had still been tough, it had all seemed easier. Happier.

Zach reached out and covered her hand. "I've missed you, Mom."

She smiled, and her eyes went a little watery again. "Back at you."

They ate in companionable silence for a short while, but when she'd polished off her second slice and he was going for his fourth, she met his gaze.

"I should probably let you know..." she started, her eyes shifting over to the clock on the stove.

When the front door rattled, he dropped his pizza, his brain and body going from relaxed to ready in an instant. His mother stared at him a moment, concern etching lines into her forehead. Right. Not everything was a fight or flight situation. He'd been out of the army for two years now and wondered if it was just coming home that had him more on edge than he'd realized.

His mom stood up and it dawned on him. His brows rose. "He has a key?"

He watched her cheeks brighten, and she stared past him as if the wall behind him had suddenly gotten interesting.

Zach pointed at her. "You *live* with him?"

"Stop it," she whisper-yelled, heading for the living room.

"Do we need to have the talk?" Zach followed behind her as the door opened.

"Hi honey," his mom greeted, shooting Zach a warning glance.

Her boyfriend was about Zach's height and twice as wide. Looking at him, Zach finally understood the word *burly* and the contrast sort of made him smile. His mom was small next to him, and the guy's beard and mustache seemed gruff in comparison to his mother's softness.

"You must be Zach," the big guy said, stepping in and closing the door behind him. He put the keys on the little hook beside the door.

"He is. This is my Zach, and honey, this is Shane."

Zach held out his hand, unsure if he was happy or a little weirded out. "Nice to meet you."

"You, too, son. Your mother is very proud of you and very happy you're home."

It was a good shake—solid and genuine. His mother's

eyes were full of hope and he smiled at her to convey his approval.

"I'm glad to be home, and even happier I'm staying. I think I stole a few of your jobs around here, though."

Shane laughed and when his mother moved around Zach, Shane put his arm around her, pulling her close. "She thinks I need to be busy every minute. She's not completely wrong, but I'm not sorry you got to the grass before me."

"We just ordered pizza. Come and eat. I want you two to get to know each other."

Shane looked down at his mom—he was several inches taller than her and a few shorter than Zach. "I'm just going to wash up. Be right there."

His mom smiled and accepted the kiss Shane gave her. *Okay. This is awkward.* She deserved someone, but he didn't have to watch. Shane walked down the hall while he and his mom returned to the kitchen.

"I was going to tell you." She pulled out an extra plate.

Zach tried to make light of it even though thoughts of what it would be like to live with his mother and her still fairly new boyfriend jumped around in his head. "What? That you're shacking up?"

She set the plate down and gave him a total mom stare. "You have a home here—I don't want you to think you don't. That'll always be your bedroom. Nothing has to be weird."

Except her saying it. The third slice started to slide around in his stomach. "Mom." He cringed.

Before she could say something he really didn't want to hear, he put a slice of pizza on Shane's plate and spoke. "Don't worry about it. I'm only here for a couple of nights. I've made other arrangements."

As a general rule, he didn't lie. But he didn't want her to think he wouldn't stay because she had a boyfriend. He was happy for her, but he damn well did not want to be in the next room.

"Zach."

Looking her in the eyes with a smile, he shook his head. "Seriously, Mom. I didn't come back to cramp your style. And I need my own space, too."

That part wasn't a lie. He just didn't know where he'd find it.

Chapter Five

By the time Stella had finished her morning rounds, checking on the two dogs she'd had stay overnight, she was running a bit behind for her scheduled surgery. She liked to get any surgeries out of the way early so animals had time to recover throughout the day. Zippo, the Australian Husky who'd had a tumor removal the day before was cranky this morning, but doing well. He'd just required a little extra attention, which Stella was more than happy to give. Stella figured humans could learn from animals and their ability to appreciate affection, giving or receiving and not wanting anything in return.

It was a relief to see the room prepped. Dexter waved to her through the window that separated the surgical room from the prep room. After wash up and prep, she went into the room where Dexter had already brought the adorable Miss E, a one-year-old Shar Pei. Looking nervous, she thumped her tail and wiggle-walked over to Stella.

"Hey sweetie. How you doing? Let's get you ready okay?" She nodded at Dexter. "Thanks for getting the room prepped."

"My pleasure," he said, lifting Miss E up to the bed.

As she walked through the routine spaying, as she'd done several times before, she reminded herself to talk about what she was doing, why, and how. Dexter was here, working, for free; hopefully he would get something out of spending time with her. *Jeez. Confident much? You need to get your head on right. Your job is to teach him.* Stella loved being a vet, but right now, or lately, all the other things tugging for her attention were distracting her from the usual joy she found being with animals.

When they finished and Miss E was resting comfortably in one of the back hotel rooms, as she liked to call them, Stella went to phone the owners. Her friend Megan was bringing her a late lunch when she got out of school. Stella smiled, thinking about how happy her friend was to be teaching at Brockton Point Elementary.

When the bell over the door chimed as she was checking the desktop calendar, she looked up into eyes she'd been trying very hard to forget.

"Hey, Doc," Zach said, strolling in as if he owned the place. *Ha! He'd like to.* So would several others—at least in part—if the piles of mail she'd sorted through were any indication.

The same aviator glasses sat on his head and today his well-fitted T-shirt was a dark green and showed a picture of a turtle with a caption that read: *What the shell?* He carried a Manilla envelope and keys in his hand.

"Mr. Mason. How are you?" Nerves danced in her stomach, which pissed her off. Men didn't make her nervous. She wasn't in or on any market and was quite content to be alone. Being alone was...comfortable. And the way she felt when Zach was in a room, or near her, was the opposite of comfortable.

His mouth turned upward. "Mr. Mason? We're going there, are we?"

She straightened and started to ask him what the heck he was talking about when Dexter came out from the back.

"Hey Dex," Zach greeted. Stella gaped at him. How did he just insert himself like that? *Oh my God. Do not take that thought anywhere. Stop it; stop it right now.*

"You okay, Doc? You look a little...warm." His brows bobbed up once.

She glared at him, fighting the urge to laugh because Zach Mason did not need another bump to his confidence. Sending a smile to Dexter, she said, "Dexter, Mr. Mason was here the other day when you showed up. I mistook him for you."

Dexter grinned, his cheeks going a light shade of pink. "I can see why. We're practically twins."

Zach burst out laughing and the twenty-two-year-old student, with curly, wayward black hair, thick-rimmed glasses, who stood not much taller than Stella joined in.

Stella stopped fighting her smile. "It's not like your resume came with a picture. I didn't know. Let me just tell you though." She gave Zach a mock glare, then smoothed her expression for her intern. "I'm very glad you're the real Dexter."

He smiled. "Thanks Doctor Lane."

Zach stepped forward. "She doesn't want to tell you, but I'm a real doctor, too. I'm Zach. How are you enjoying it here?"

Dexter shook his hand and his smile widened. "I'm really enjoying it. It's busy. Way busier than I expected. Doctor Lane never takes a break. I don't know how she does so much in a day."

When they stepped back, Zach moved to the counter and leaned against it. He set the envelope there and Stella looked at it, wondering what was in it.

Zach glanced back and forth between Stella and Dexter. "I've heard she keeps herself running. Seems to me, she could use some help."

Stella nearly growled and came around the counter, pointing at Dexter. "I have help. As you can clearly see." Help that didn't make her wonder if he looked as good out of his shirt as he did in it.

Unfazed, Zach turned his attention to Dexter. "How long are you here?"

One of the dogs barked from the back of the clinic, and though Zach and Dexter looked in that direction, Stella recognized it as one of her own dog's barks. She'd left the back door open to get a breeze rolling through the place. Fresh air was cheaper than air conditioning.

"My practicum is three weeks, then I have a course, and I come back for six more weeks." He hooked a thumb over his shoulder. "I'm going to make sure everyone's happy."

Stella checked the time and then smiled at him. "Okay. My friend is bringing lunch. We've got about forty minutes before our next patient."

"Yes ma'am." He walked off and Stella wondered when she'd aged enough to be called ma'am.

"Weird when people not that much younger than you start addressing you as a superior, isn't it?" Zach still leaned on her tall counter. He'd crossed one foot over the other and let his eyes roam over her in a quick perusal. Stella's skin heated. From just a look. He had a presence twice his size. It wasn't just that he looked good or that he smelled delicious, it was his confidence. His ease. The way he seemed to fit everywhere despite the size of him.

"You're older than me, so you probably get it more," she said.

He grinned. "True. I just naturally command respect."

Knowing Megan would arrive any minute, and not wanting the questions that would come from her love-happy, about-to-be-married friend at the sight of Zach, Stella attempted to subtly scoot Zach toward the exit. "What are you doing here?" She walked toward the door, hoping he'd follow.

He grabbed the envelope and pocketed his keys before doing so. They stepped out into the sunshine and Stella was grateful that there was a breeze. It had been unseasonably hot for almost the end of September.

Zach took up his leaning position on the porch railing. Stella had always loved that the clinic resembled the home she'd grown up in, right down to the front and back porches.

"Couple of reasons, really. When I was here, I noticed it looks like there's a setup in the barn for a hired hand."

The breeze would have ruffled his hair if it wasn't cropped so short on the sides and barely there on the top. His angular cheek bones and strong jaw, with just a hint of sexy scruff, suited the style. Not every guy could pull it off.

"You went from wanting to be a second vet to wanting to be a ranch hand?"

She knew it was more than that but didn't want to take him seriously, because she felt like accepting anything he had to offer could set off an avalanche of need in all areas of her life.

"Not quite. Was it once quarters for one?"

Stella smiled, remembering the stories her father and grandparents had told her. "It was. My great-grandfather raised cattle. They had several ranch hands."

His smile mirrored hers. "Which means it's at least habitable?"

"I already told you I'm not looking to hire anyone," she said. Though the exhaustion creeping into her bones and the bills piling up were definite hammers banging against her skull.

Any traces of humor fled from his expression, and she had an image of him, hardnosed and talking to his regiment or whatever the term was for the guys he would have overseen. Some people owned their air of command like a second skin. "And I told you, I'm not a school kid. But one thing at a time. I was wondering if I could rent the space from you."

She sank down into one of the Adirondack chairs, trying not to sigh at the ecstasy of getting off her aching feet. "What?"

"No one is using the space. Never met anyone who didn't need some extra cash, so I figured if I pay you rent, it's a win-win."

Stella stared up at him. The sun was a halo around his head. "You want to live in my barn?"

She had a twenty-five hundred square foot house she'd practically shut down because of costs that she could share with him. *You don't want to work with him, but you'll live with him?* But the rent idea was an interesting one. Gears turned in her overloaded brain. The farm house was huge, but too much upkeep for one person who worked twenty-four-seven. She'd moved her bedroom down to her father's old den and didn't even go up the stairs anymore.

"Why not? It's available. I wouldn't be in the way." He shoved a hand over his head and gave a frustrated sigh, like he was wrestling with something. "My mom has a boyfriend."

Stella blinked and tried to process that. "Uh, okay."

He stood taller and stared at her until more than just her feet felt achy. "My mom, who took great joy in telling me what a vibrant, *young* woman she still is, has a boyfriend. Who pretty much lives there. Sharing her bedroom. Which, you should know is *right* next to my old room."

Stella bit her lip. She could see, quite plainly, that he didn't see the humor in the situation. "Your mom has a boyfriend.

She boot you out so they could hook up?"

Zach didn't almost growl. He did. "Never mind." He started down the steps.

Stella laughed and, without thinking about it, jumped up out of the chair and followed him. "Wait. I'm sorry. It's not funny." Except that it was. Stella hoped she was still as *young and vibrant* as Sheila in twenty years.

He turned to look down at her, his gaze skeptical. She had to bite the inside of her cheek to keep from chuckling. "Why don't you just rent a place in town?"

Those mesmerizing eyes shuttered a second after they went impossibly dark. He held up a finger. "One, I don't want to live in town or spend weeks finding a place there." He held up a second finger. "Two, I want to be close to work, and eventually I'm going to prove to you that I'd be a good fit here." He lifted a third finger. "And three," he said, pausing and looking around. "This place is peaceful. I like it here."

Peace. That's what Stella craved as well and part of the reason she was reluctant to let go or give in to the vultures hovering over her many acres. It was her serenity along with her legacy.

"I don't think the barn is as equipped for a renter as you seem to think. Plus, winter is on its way, regardless of this deceptive weather."

Zach grinned and stepped into her personal space. She should have stepped back to make her feelings on that loud and clear. Except that, her feelings on it were that if she just stepped *closer,* they'd be touching, front to front. That she'd be close enough to put her hands against his chest or abs and feel the indentation of muscles that lay beneath his shirt.

"If I get too cold, maybe you'd bring me into the main house to warm up." That sexy grin made her insides get squishy.

Not good. No squishy stomach feelings. Stella *really*

missed the feel of a man's hands on her body. A man's breath on her skin as he trailed kisses along every inch. Her eyes locked on Zach's lips. He had a great mouth. *Bad idea.* Hooking up with him wouldn't be wise but getting paid for space she didn't use was. "Do you have references?"

Zach laughed. "To live in your barn?"

She crossed her arms over her chest and he scowled.

He handed her the envelope. "I didn't think to put references in there, but I'm certain my former Staff Sergeant with the United States Army would vouch for me. Or perhaps the American Humane Society or one of the clinics I worked at or ran overseas. I was at Pet Central for the last couple of years. They might say a nice thing or two about me. Maybe even my mother. I'll get you a list."

The tension left her body. Those were some pretty good references. Pet Central. Why did that sound familiar? *They offered to buy out dad.*

"Why did you leave a huge company like Pet Central? Personality conflicts?"

Zach laughed. Dammit. He had a great laugh, too.

"I wanted to come home. Being there was a necessary step financially, but it was never my long-term plan. You know how Netflix is better than being in a crowded movie theatre because you can be in your own space and relax?"

Her brows furrowed. "I guess." She hadn't been to a movie in longer than she could remember.

"That's how I felt about the big practice versus this one. I remembered what it was like to be here with your dad, the way he knew everyone, and they respected him. Trusted him."

Stella's heart pinched painfully, like a clip had been attached to one corner. "The barn hasn't been lived in for years."

Stella heard the car before it pulled into view. Zach glanced at it and then back at Stella.

"I could make a few adjustments," he suggested.

Which would cost money. "I can't afford that right now." She said the words before she could stop herself. "I'm sorry." And part of her was.

"If I cover the costs of getting it livable, you wouldn't have to worry about it."

Stella bit the inside of her cheek. It wasn't a horrible option. But it wasn't ideal either. She really didn't think he *could* make the old building livable. Not in a healthy, viable way.

He shrugged, pulling her from her thoughts. "That's fine. Just thought I'd see if you were interested."

He started to walk away, and she didn't know why she was pushing away a great opportunity. *You're hesitating because this idea is insane. But so are the freaking expectations of the creditors and the cost to run a small clinic...*

"I'm not using the upstairs of my home. I think if we work out a schedule for the kitchen, it could work. I live downstairs. There's a second washroom upstairs so you wouldn't need anything other than the kitchen to be shared. Well, and the laundry, but that's in the kitchen."

The car door slammed, and Stella had already seen it was Megan's vehicle, so she didn't break eye contact with him.

Walking closer, his size shielding the glare of the sun, he stopped directly in front of her and looked down at her with so much intensity, she *did* take a step back. But mostly, so she didn't sway into him.

"You asking me to move in with you, Doc?"

She held the envelope he'd given her up like a shield against her chest.

Before she could reply, Megan, her closest friend, chimed in. "Wait...what?"

Both of their heads swung in her direction. The dogs joined them, dancing around Megan, who bent immediately, giving them rubs, but kept staring back and forth between Stella and Zach.

"Meg, this is Zach Mason. Zach, this is my good friend, Megan Carter, soon to be Klein."

Zach stepped forward as Megan rose. They shook hands and the smile on her friend's face kicked Stella's nerves into high gear. She had two close friends in town and both would slay dragons if it meant getting Stella on a date. Or more.

"Very nice to meet you, Megan."

"You, too, Zach. Are you from around here?"

The dogs looked for love from Zach when Megan stopped rubbing. He held both hands down, rubbing their heads while he spoke. "Grew up here actually. Left when I was eighteen to enlist in the army. Now I'm home. I'm a licensed veterinarian and was hoping to convince your friend to give me a chance."

He made it sound so simple, but Stella sensed there was a lot more to each of those things than he gave away. He didn't carry the weight of war in any visible scars, but she knew that the worst scarring in life could happen on the inside.

Megan looked at Stella. "A chance?"

Stella swallowed, nearly choking on her own spit. "To work with me. That's all."

Megan's grin should have come with a warning. It would read: about to embarrass best friend. "And to live with you?"

Zach chuckled. "I like her."

The glare she gave him had no impact. "Zach's mom has a boyfriend and doesn't want him underfoot. He asked to live in my barn."

Megan shook her head, and Stella realized they were treating her like a ball in a Ping-Pong game, each volleying back and forth with information.

"Maybe I should explain while we eat. Did you bring sandwiches?"

Megan nodded and started to follow Stella back into

the clinic when an older Ford rumbled up the driveway and parked. Mrs. Carmichael. She hopped out of the truck with the energy of a twenty-year-old, despite being a senior.

Stella shielded her eyes. "Hey, Mrs. Carmichael," she called. As the woman cajoled her chihuahua out of the truck, Stella spoke in a quiet voice to Megan. "I might have to rain check lunch. She isn't even on the schedule today."

Zach hovered behind them as the elderly woman ambled over. "Sorry to just drop in like this, Doctor Lane, but Magnolia won't eat, and I'm worried with this weather she's dehydrated." She stopped in front of the three of them and looked at Zach. "Hello, Megan. And who is this?"

Great. Even the elderly weren't immune to Zach's aura of charm.

"Doctor Zachary Mason, ma'am. I'm a veterinarian looking to join forces with your beloved Doctor Lane, here," he said.

Stella's mouth dropped open and she could only stare. Megan, she noticed, bit back a laugh.

"Is that so?" Mrs. Carmichael looked at Stella for confirmation.

The envelope crinkled in her hand from scrunching it in her fist. "He's trying. That part is true. But his attempts aren't working."

Zach held her gaze, but Mrs. Carmichael interrupted their staring contest by leaning in and saying in a loud aside, "Is he all looks, dear? No substance?"

Megan laughed and put a hand on the woman's shoulder. Her dog was curled up in her arms, looking unamused and uninterested in what was going on.

"I'm sure Zach is an excellent vet, Mrs. C. You know our Stella, though, she has a hard time letting anyone in," Megan said.

This time, Stella's jaw dropped in response to her friend's

words. "Hey!"

Megan shrugged. "I'm going to grab the sandwiches, so you can eat even if it's not now." She walked away toward her car.

"Let's take Magnolia inside," Stella said, giving Zach another hard glare, which seemed to only make him smile wider.

"I knew your daddy well. Took care of my family's pets for longer than you've been alive. Also knew the few quacks who tried to open shop and steal his patients over the years. You let me be a trial run. I'll give it to you straight. You know I will."

Stella's fingers rubbed over her temple, trying to ward off the headache brewing. "I'm sorry, what?"

Mrs. Carmichael wagged a finger at Zach. "I'm not swayed by good looks, boy. I'll be honest and tell her if you're any good. You look at my Maggie for me. We'll know if you've got what it takes."

Stella expected him to say no. She couldn't even believe this conversation was taking place around her like she was trapped behind soundproof glass.

"Yes, ma'am," Zach said. He looked at Stella, a challenge in his twinkling gray eyes. "Unless Doctor Lane has an issue with this?"

"Why would she? Let's go," Mrs. Carmichael said. They walked up the stairs and into *her* clinic as Megan came to her side and watched them go.

"Guess we have some catching up to do. And how did that just happen?"

Stella's brain felt fuzzy. "I actually have no idea. But you know what? It's fine. I'm starving and I have"—she stopped and checked her phone—"twenty minutes until my next scheduled patient. Let's go eat."

As they went into the building, Megan gestured to the

envelope. "What is that?"

"Again, no idea." Stella's control felt like a loose thread being tugged.

Dexter was behind the counter when they went in, looking a little flustered. "Uh, Doctor Mason said he was just going to take a look at a drop-in patient?"

"No worries, Dexter. It's fine. This is my best friend, Megan. Meg, this is Dexter Braun. He's here from University of Maine and already doing a great job."

Megan shook his hand. "Nice to meet you. I have an extra sandwich, if you'd like?"

"Oh. Thank you, but I already ate my lunch. I was going to go clean up the stock cupboard, Doctor Lane, unless there's something else you'd like me to do?"

She came behind the counter and smiled reassuringly. "That's perfect. Thanks Dex."

When he left, she took a deep breath and let it out. Boosting herself on the counter, she thanked Megan when she passed her a sandwich and sat beside her.

"That dog in there is tiny. Tell me everything fast."

So much for lunch. She gave Megan a quick rundown of how Zach had shown up only a couple of days ago and bulldozed his sexy way into her life.

Megan grinned around her sandwich, looking ridiculous and adorable at the same time. While her mouth was full, Stella took the opportunity to talk.

"Don't even say it. One, I don't need a partner. Two, if I did partner with him, I can't sleep with him."

Megan choked. Stella was concerned for about five seconds until the cough turned into a laugh. "You're going to sleep with him?"

"Shh! No. But if he's around all the time, I'm not blind or dead. And, you know, it's been a while."

"Way too long," Megan agreed.

Stella wished Megan was less immune to her glare. "It's not nice to gloat. Speaking of getting some, how's your fiancé?"

Megan's eyes glassed over with love. Stella wondered if she'd ever feel that way for anyone again. Or if she ever really had.

"He's great. So is Charlie. Wait until you see Charlie in a suit. It's so cute it should be illegal."

Stella might not believe in happily ever after for herself—her own fairy tale had taken a lousy detour—but it suited Megan down to the ground.

"I can't wait. Speaking of wedding clothes, are we ever getting you a dress?"

Megan's gaze darted away. She picked at her sandwich. "Actually, that's what I wanted to talk to you about."

Stella's stomach tightened. She didn't like bad news. Especially when it concerned people she loved. That circle was growing smaller all the time and knowing that made it hard to breathe.

"What's wrong?" Stella wrapped the remainder of her ham and cheese sandwich.

"Nothing. Don't worry. It's just—"

The exam room door opened, and Mrs. Carmichael came through laughing loudly. "Can't believe you're Sheila's boy. You've definitely grown up. It's good to see you back."

She stopped at the counter and both Megan and Stella slid off it. Megan went over to the other side of the small reception area while Stella typed Mrs. C's name into the computer.

"Well, Stella. I can tell you, this man knows what he's doing. My Magnolia doesn't like just anyone, as you know."

Most chihuahuas didn't, but Stella bit her tongue.

"I didn't bribe her to say that," Zach said.

"I'm glad you're satisfied, Mrs. Carmichael. Everything

okay with Magnolia?"

"All of her vitals are good. She's not dehydrated, just a bit lethargic. Likely from all the sun they both got this morning," Zach said.

Stella wasn't quite sure what to make of the fact that Zach had nestled his way into her space so easily. What she did know was it felt good to have food in her belly and know she hadn't turned down a patient. Especially one handing over her charge card.

While Stella took care of Mrs. Carmichael's payment, Zach wandered over to talk to Megan. From across the room, Stella couldn't hear them. She hurried through saying goodbye so Zach wouldn't have time to work his magic on anyone else. Megan would be all too happy to jump on a hot guy's bandwagon if it meant the possibility of seeing her friend as happy as she was. Stella had tried to tell her that kind of forever wasn't in the cards for her, but Megan refused to believe it.

Stella joined them as Zach was talking. "I went to school with Adam Klein. Serious guy," he said.

Sounded right. Though, since Megan and Adam had become a thing, Megan's former employer had loosened up considerably. Stella hadn't been at all sure they were a good match, but what did she know about love?

"He still is, but not when he's with Charlie. That's his son," Megan said. She glanced up as Stella joined them.

"I have about four minutes before the patients start arriving again. Nice job with Mrs. Carmichael," Stella said. She could give him that. After all, he'd given her a few moments with her best friend and time for lunch.

"No problem. My pleasure. I hate being idle."

"You have that in common, too," Megan said, her grin growing.

Stella sent her a please-shut-up look that Megan ignored.

"Before you get busy again, I have a huge favor," her friend said, looking back and forth between Stella and Zach in a way that sent a bolt of unease through her. "I know you work Saturdays, but is there any way you can come into Lincoln with me tomorrow? They're having a huge sale on wedding dresses. Adam has been great about the costs, but I'd love to show him I can be fancy *and* save money. This is a forty-eight-hour sale that started already, and I really, really, really want to go try some on."

Stella sighed. "Really?"

Her friend laughed and looked at Zach. "I'm having a hard time finding *the* dress. But almost everything else is ready."

"I've heard it's a big decision. The dress I mean. Not marriage. You find the right one, you jump all over that," Zach said, his voice and smile genuine.

Stella stared, a little surprised. Did everyone believe in jumping in with both feet and eyes shut? *They haven't been engaged, deserted, and lied to. Cut yourself some slack.*

Again, she thought of invisible scars. Sometimes so much worse than the ones people could see.

"Stella is my maid of honor." Megan looked at her with a pleading gaze.

Guilt nestled at the base of Stella's spine. The wedding was coming soon, but she'd already taken a day off this week. She needed to talk to Taylor about organizing a wedding shower and a bachelorette party. Did people still do that? She hadn't been to a wedding since her teens and the one she was supposed to have hadn't exactly been traditional. "I can't cancel on my clients this late, Meg."

Megan bit her lip, and Stella's heart squeezed.

"I could help, you know."

If Megan were a cartoon, her eyes would have popped out of her head. "Stell, he could totally cover you. Please?"

She tried to breathe through her nose and keep her voice even. "Megan, I only met Zach four days ago. I'm hardly ready to hand over my practice to him."

Megan pointed at him. "You're letting him move in! And by the way, we're totally coming back to that."

Zach grinned, crossing his muscled arms over his chest. "She's got you there."

Stella wanted to throw her hands up and scream. This man was steamrolling his way into her life, personally and professionally. As if he could read her feelings—not that she was great at hiding them—Zach's smile faded and he stepped closer to her, charging the air around them. Megan picked up her purse and made herself busy by looking at her phone.

"I know I'm coming on strong, Stella. I'm not trying to bully you into anything, I swear. You have to admit, the timing is sort of perfect. You could consider it a trial, the job piece. Let me cover you. Go with your friend."

Looking over at Megan, Stella frowned. "What's in the envelope?"

Zach shoved his hands into his pockets. "My financials. Should have added references. But I'll get them for you."

Stella's chest tightened right down the center as if she was literally being pulled in two directions. *Your very good friend wants to go shopping for her wedding with you. And you have the chance to make that happen when all you usually say is no.* Not by choice, but necessity. Her schedule hadn't allowed a lot of time to plan with Megan. The wedding was just a couple months away. They'd chosen December thirty-first so they could start the new year as a married couple.

"It's just a couple of hours," Megan said, her voice quiet. "But I totally understand if you can't or don't want to."

She'd moved closer so that her words were for Stella only. Megan squeezed Stella's hand, and from the corner of her eye, she noticed Zach busying himself with the dogs, who'd followed them into the clinic, giving them privacy.

"Stell, it's fine. I totally sprung it on you."

Would it be so bad to accept a little help, especially if it wasn't technically even for her? It wasn't like he wouldn't get something in return. She was giving him a place to live. *For rent.* But she could have said no. *Which would be silly. He's trustworthy, you know his mother, and he's offering you cold, hard cash.* But covering her patients, even for a few hours, was different. She couldn't afford to pay him for his time, but she didn't want to owe him either. What would her clients say if she had a stand in? Probably, "About time." Especially if the man covering was one of their own.

"Your brain is going to shut down, you keep making it work so hard. It's a simple offer, Doc. I get that you don't want to loosen the reins, but I think, in your gut, you know I can handle your office for a few hours. Go shopping with your friend. Take a breather."

He straightened, and Nacho and Soda roamed toward the back of the clinic. Her judgment wasn't always great. Particularly not in men. "What's in it for you?"

He shook his head, like he was a little disappointed she'd ask. "I get to work, which I miss like crazy. I get to help a woman who doesn't seem to think she should ever accept such a thing, and I'm pretty sure you just agreed to let me move into your house, so I think I still owe you."

"I want the list of references, you know." It was the smart thing to do.

He nodded seriously and that loosened the heavy tightness in her chest. "Smart. I like smart. I'll have them for you by the end of the day. You got a price for rent?"

"Well, I need a new water heater, the fence on the west side of the barn needs repair, and we're running low on some stock at the clinic, so I was thinking about twenty grand?"

Megan covered her hand with her mouth, holding in her

laugh.

Zach didn't. His laugh rumbled from his chest and Stella's body lit up with desire. "Maybe we could negotiate a bit."

What was it about a man's laugh? Particularly a sexy, charming, too-comfortable-in-his-own-skin man who had been nothing but kind to her. "I think you got the all clear for shopping tomorrow."

Megan clapped her hands together, looking so hopefully, Stella couldn't believe she'd considered saying no when there was a chance not to. "You sure?"

Stella nodded. "Yeah. A couple of hours in the morning should be fine. I'll just have to make sure the clients scheduled are okay with that."

Right on cue, the next client walked through the door, her pot-bellied pig leading the way.

"Hi, Tawny," Stella greeted. "Hey Pork Chop."

"Hey Doc."

"Aw, I love pigs!" Megan hurried over to the pig, then came back and gave Stella a hard hug. "I'm so excited and we're so talking about this the entire ride there."

Stella laughed. "Don't make me change my mind."

"Okay, I'm leaving." Megan held her hands up as if surrendering.

"Let me walk you out," Zach said.

Megan's eyes danced. "Please do."

Stella shook her head. Her friend was a hopeless romantic. "Megan," she said in a warning tone.

"What? I just want to get to know your roommate a bit."

"Want us to wait out here, Doc?" Tawny, who wasn't much older than Stella and owned three of the gas stations in town, asked.

Zach rested a hand on Stella's shoulder. "I'll wait to bring some stuff over until tomorrow night?"

She nodded. Because what else could she do? Dexter

joined them in the reception area and Stella realized she hadn't even answered Tawny.

"Tawny, this is Dexter, my newest intern. He'll get you settled in an exam room."

People were used to seeing different faces in the clinic. Before her, her father had always had students—both from the universities and ones like Zach—who helped and trained. They'd be fine with Zach helping. She saw Megan was still trying not to break out in a happy dance and realized that the only one who didn't think she should accept help was her. *Well now you have. Let's just hope it doesn't backfire like so many of your other ideas do.*

Chapter Six

When Zach showed up the next morning, he expected Stella to tell him she'd changed her mind. He could imagine her wrestling between the need to not let her friend down and to let someone step in and help her and wasn't sure which choice would come out on top. As he parked, grabbed the coffees he'd picked up, and headed into the clinic, he was surprised by how busy it was at only eight in the morning. She hadn't been kidding when she said it was usually nonstop.

Three people were waiting with pets—a cat in a carrier, a bird in a carrier, and a German Shepherd whose attention locked on Zach the second he came through the door. A woman he hadn't seen before was behind the counter. She smiled at him and pointed to the headset, signaling one minute with her finger. Zach set the coffee tray down on the counter and smiled at the people in the waiting room. There wasn't even an attempt to hide their curiosity. The thing about Brockton Point, was its size was deceptive. There was no way to know everyone, yet people knew when an outsider was in their presence. *You're not an outsider.* That wasn't entirely true, but it would feel that way for a while yet. Being part of Stella's world would pull him into a fold he'd always felt removed from. Zach waved to the elderly woman with the cat carrier.

"You look a bit familiar. Are you the boy helping our Stella out?" she asked.

The shepherd whined, and his gray-bearded owner rubbed him, shushing him with a gentleness that didn't match his gruff exterior. *Looks can be deceiving.* God, he knew that so well. When he was younger, and his father had drunk away money for clothes or shoes, Zach had been painted with pity or derision. People saw what they wanted to see, and he'd worked hard to reinvent himself, starting with the outside.

Now that the woman had said something, Zach realized she looked familiar, too. "I'm Zach Mason. I've been away a while, but I'm home now."

The woman's eyes brightened even as the cat hissed, getting the shepherd's attention. "Sheila's boy. She said you were coming home. Glad to see you did safe and sound. You courting our Stella, or just helping her out today?"

Zach nearly choked. Could *anyone* court Stella without losing a body part? He chuckled. "Just helping out. She's a friend." *What? It could be true one day.*

"Can I help you?" The woman behind the counter asked, pressing a couple buttons on the computer.

He turned and looked over the counter. "Hi there. We haven't met. I'm Doctor Zachary Mason."

The woman stood, adjusting her silver-framed glasses. She held out a hand and he heard the woman behind him whisper, loudly, "He's a handsome one."

One of the two other people, he wasn't sure which since both were male and so was the voice, responded, "Leave him be, Margie."

The receptionist bit her lip, clearly fighting a laugh. She

shook his hand. "Jaz. I work on Saturday mornings since it's Doctor Lane's busiest day. She said you were coming in."

So she did have some help. Good to know. Stella came out of one of the exam rooms at that moment, her attention focused on the man holding a tiny piece of fluff that Zach was pretty sure was an adorable kitten.

"She's going to be thrilled, Danny. Just make sure you don't leave the ring on his collar too long."

The man, a tall blond who was probably ten years younger than Zach, beamed at Stella. "You don't think it's super cheesy?"

The woman with the cat—Margie—spoke up. "Ring? You proposing to Carrie, Daniel?"

Stella's gaze landed on Zach and a jolt of awareness flashed through his body, tightening his chest. Her shoulders went tense, her lips tight.

"Don't go spillin' secrets, Margie," the bearded man said.

"I'm proposing this morning," Danny admitted, his skin going a deep shade of red. Zach laughed, mentally wishing the guy luck. Hopefully he'd get through the proposal without looking like a tomato. *Own it, man. You love her, own it.* Advice he planned on taking one day, when he found the right one.

Stella cleared her throat. "Okay, who's next?"

Danny shuffled to the counter with the kitten, who yawned in his hands. Zach moved out of the way as Margie claimed she was next. Zach gestured to the coffees when he caught Stella's wary eye again.

"You can take them into the back room. I'll be there shortly," she said. No *hello, so glad you're here*. Nerves, he suspected. Letting someone in and letting someone help at the same time. He didn't know her, but he could read people, and Stella wasn't a person who did either of those things lightly. Which meant she must really need the rent money.

He wondered what it would take to get her to lean on him. Then he wondered why he wanted her to.

From across the waiting room, he heard the woman speak before Stella closed the exam room door. "That's Sheila Mason's boy there. Sure has changed. He'd look good next to you."

Zach chuckled as he walked down the hallway, imagining Stella's response to that.

While he waited, he looked around, a few memories creeping in of hanging out here with Stella's dad when he had nowhere else to be. Doc Lane had been a champion of underdogs, and as Zach stood there, staring at the wall of aging thank-you cards, his gut cramped at the reminder that someone who'd been so kind to him was gone. Zach didn't let himself dwell on loss. If he did, he'd drown in the endless swirl of hurt that came along with remembering the people who'd mattered to him who were no longer alive. Starting with Travis.

He shook his head, cleared his thoughts, and poked around more. The back room she'd sent him to was a perfect square with three doors off of it. One led out to the back porch, another to a bathroom, and a third to a supply room. Along the free wall, there was a counter, cupboards, and an apartment-sized fridge. A rickety table sat under a window, next to the door that led outside. If she had a staff, or ever took a rest, this was the break room.

Wandering back down the hallway he'd come through, he saw the surgery room and prep areas. Everything was clean and well kept, but he could see, just from looking through the window between them, that her equipment was dated.

Zach returned to the break room and stepped out onto the back porch. The air was crisp—the way September mornings should be on the coast—but he knew the sun was expected to scorch them again today. He breathed in, inhaling nothing but nature and peace. Hearing Chocolate Chip whinny in the distance, he started to step off the porch, but Stella spoke behind him.

"Sorry about that," she said.

He turned back to her as she was retying her gorgeous hair into a messy bun at the back of her head.

"You always this busy on Saturdays?"

She nodded, joining him on the porch. "Lately, it's any day that ends in 'y.' What are you doing out here?"

He glanced at her, staring at her profile as she looked out at her land. A little crease denting her forehead told him she was thinking too hard again.

"I think I have a crush on your horse, if I'm being honest."

The crease disappeared, and she turned to him, giving him a smile that kicked him right in the gut. Fuck. He'd have to remember, if he was able to make her face shine like that, that he wanted to be her business partner and nothing more. Zach figured Stella was the type to frown on mixing business and pleasure, and since he planned on sticking around, he could only have one. *Not that she's offering either.* Best to remind himself of that.

"That's cute. She's a good horse."

"She eating better?"

The crease reappeared. "No. I'm thinking of having someone else take a look at her. There's a vet a couple hours away in Mulberry."

It was his turn to frown. "There's a vet standing right next to you."

"I wasn't trying to offend you. It's just you have nothing more than my own equipment to look at her. I'd welcome your professional opinion, but"—she gestured to the clinic behind her—"you'd have the same resources I do."

He nodded, shoving his hands into his pockets. "Good point. Noticed you don't have an ultrasound machine." It was one thing that would make checking C.C.'s stomach a lot easier.

Stella gave him a half grin. "I don't have a million dollars, either, but I'd like both."

It was good she could laugh about it, but Zach wanted to know more. "I'm good with problem solving. You're running a busy ship here."

Letting out a huff of air and checking her watch, he barely heard her when she mumbled, "Feels like a sinking ship." Then she looked up, like she realized she'd said it out loud. "Never mind. I have to go meet Megan. Are you sure about this?"

He stepped closer, and she tipped her chin up. The desire to lean down and press his mouth to hers hit him without warning, so he stepped back, and she arched her brow.

"I'm positive."

"We have to review the roommate rules tonight."

He laughed. "Okay, Sheldon Cooper."

Stella's lips turned up in such an unguarded way, satisfaction filled him. He got the sense that not a lot of people could take credit for making her smile.

"What time is your last patient?" he asked, following her when she went back into the break room.

"Five, but I'll be back before then."

He heard the panic in her voice, like a mom away from her child for the first time. He needed to show her that she could trust him, rely on him. He'd missed working with animals. Hell, he missed being busy in general. Idle time wasn't his thing on a good day and now, being back in his hometown with memories attached to every corner, he did not need space for his thoughts to consume him.

"How about I make dinner tonight? To thank you for giving me a place, literally, to rest my head. When you get home, I'll head out, grab my stuff, and stop at the store. I can be back here by seven."

She turned slowly, and he couldn't read the expression on her face. "Okay. That sounds good. I'll see you in a few hours. I saw you met Jaz. Dexter isn't in today. I left my cell number behind the desk, but Jaz has it, too. There are back-to-back appointments booked, but you'll likely get some walk-ins as well. And a *lot* of questions about your intentions toward me personally and professionally. Try to ignore those."

He laughed. She was really going to let him do this. Zach rubbed his hands together, itching to get started. "I'm ready. Go; shop. Have fun. I hope she doesn't make you get one of those bright pink dresses. You'd look good in pink, but it needs to be soft."

He let his eyes move over her, and when they came back to her face, her mouth opened just a little. Blinking rapidly, like she'd lost herself in thought, she answered, "Megan loves me too much to choose bright pink. If she doesn't, it might be a deal breaker."

She gave him reminders, updates, anecdotes on patients, and altogether too much information as they moved through the clinic to the front.

Stella smiled at the waiting patients. "As I told you guys on the phone last night, Doctor Mason is going to help me out for a few hours today so I can go dress shopping with Megan."

"Oh, there's a wedding that should have happened years ago. They have a son," said Margie.

The bearded guy rolled his eyes. "Charlie's mom moved away, Margie. Megan was his nanny. You sure you should be driving, woman?"

Margie bristled. "What? Because I forget a few things? I'm fine."

Zach and Stella watched the back and forth and when he caught her eye, she just shrugged as if to say, *Small towns, what are you going to do?*

Zach waved, feeling as awkward as he did when he was a kid having to stand up in the front of the class. He wanted—*needed*—these people to accept him. He had a feeling that if they did, it'd be easier for Stella to do the same. Maybe he could talk her into letting him help her out part time like this until she was ready to admit she could benefit from him signing on.

Eager to start and to prove himself, he walked behind the counter to talk with Jaz.

"Who's first?"

She gave him a kind smile and stood up. "Mr. Darcaz, you can bring Blip this way."

Blip turned out to be a hamster and as Stella gave him a worried look from across the room, Zach led the way into an exam room and took a deep breath. He was back in his element. Everything else could fade away.

• • •

Zach slapped a folder down on the countertop with more force than he'd meant to. Jaz looked up with a smile. The one he gave her in returned probably looked a little pained. He wiped his forehead with the back of his hand. He was actually sweating.

"Sorry it's so warm in here. Stella doesn't want to use the air conditioning in the front of the house. She saves it for the hotel," Jaz said.

Zach looked at her, his forehead scrunched. "Hotel?"

"It's what she calls the room with the overnight animals. A/C is expensive, so she cuts costs where she can," Jaz said, her tone a bit defensive on behalf of her employer.

He liked the loyalty. Stella damn well deserved it. She deserved a fucking medal.

"It's animal comfort that matters," Zach said, accepting

the next set of files from her. There was no one in the waiting room at the moment, but he didn't trust it to stay like that. In just over an hour, he'd seen nine people and their pets. These people counted on Stella for everything from trimming nails to surgery for their animals. There had to be a way of streamlining the process without taking away the at-home feel. When he'd worked at Pet Central, there'd been several departments, including grooming and training, which meant, as a vet, he'd only seen animals who needed medical assistance.

The little bell over the door jingled with another arrival, and he looked up to see his mom walking in, carrying a cup so large her hand barely fit around it.

"Brought you some cold caffeine," she said to Zach. "Hey, Jaz. How are you?"

"Really good, Mrs. Mason. You have a very nice son," Jaz said, shooting Zach a smile. She was probably Dexter's age but looked younger with her dark hair in two braids.

Zach accepted the cola from his mom and took a long sip. Never too early. "You didn't have to do this, but thank you."

She beamed at him, making him laugh. "Just wanted to stop by and say hi. I'm glad you got Stella to agree to some help. It's about time, wouldn't you say, Jaz?"

Jaz turned in her chair and nodded. "Stella does keep herself busy. I'm glad she's getting to go out with Megan. The wedding is so soon."

"Weddings are wonderful," his mom said wistfully. She stared at Zach and he fought the urge to shuffle his feet.

"I don't know why you're looking at me like that, but stop," Zach said, taking another drink before setting the cup behind the high countertop, out of the way.

"Like what? Like a mother who just realized that now that you're home, it's more likely you'll meet a nice girl from here and give me grandbabies?"

A few moments ago, he'd been grateful for the breather, but now he wondered when the next patient was due.

"Maybe *you* should get married," Zach suggested, mostly joking.

His mom smiled, contentment shining in her eyes. "When he asks, I will. Now, are you really moving in with Stella or are you just being stubborn about living with me and Shane?"

The door chimed again and a man with two cocker spaniels straining against their leashes as they hopped came into the clinic.

"Turns out Stella needed a renter, so it's worked out for the best. Everything is fine, Mom. I gotta go," he said, leaning in for a kiss.

"Okay. I've got to get going anyway. I'll talk to you soon about that kissing booth for the fair," she said.

Jaz snickered and the man waiting just nodded a hello.

"Bye, Mom."

"Bye, dear. See you soon, Jaz."

Zach went back to work, intending to make Stella's patients so happy, she'd be begging him to come back.

Chapter Seven

Stella tapped her foot nervously, refusing to check her phone again. She had the volume maxed and it was on vibrate so there was no way she'd miss it if Jaz texted or phoned with concerns.

"You can't be this nervous about seeing her in the dresses," Taylor, the second of her close friends, said. She'd known Taylor longer than Megan as they'd gone to school together, but like Stella, she'd gone away for a while. Stella was glad they'd not only reconnected, but Megan was friends with both of them, too.

"She's nervous about Sergeant Hottie," Megan called from behind the fancy white door of the dressing room. The top of it had scalloped molding and glitter. Stella wasn't a huge fan of glitter or, if she was honest only with herself, bridal shops. Being in them made her heart feel like it didn't fit inside her rib cage. *Hey, that's sort of how Zach makes you feel.*

She groaned.

Taylor laughed. "Is she right? Tell me about him. I asked

Mom and she said that Zach's family lived sort of on the edge of town through most of his life."

Stella arched a brow and, hoping to get out of talking about Zach, called to Megan, "Do you need any help in there?"

"I've got her," the bridal boutique attendant said from inside the same stall.

Taylor nudged her leg. She'd tied her long blond hair back in a cool braid, and with her pretty floral skirt and flowing top, she looked like a modern-day Laura Ingalls.

"Quit stalling," she said.

"There's nothing to tell. In fact, you probably know more about him than I do if you asked your mom about him."

"True." Taylor nodded and turned her head to stare at Megan's dressing room door.

Stella stared at her friend, waiting. Her mouth dropped open to ask and then she realized Taylor had done that on purpose. Stella crossed her arms over her chest and Taylor laughed.

"You are so stubborn," Taylor said. "Fine. Since you're clearly so curious, Mom said his family didn't have anything growing up. Mostly on account of his father drinking it all away. They were poorer than poor and usually stayed on the outskirts of town. People tried to help, but, sort of like you, Sheila Mason wasn't a woman who accepted it easily."

"Hey," Stella said, dropping her arms. Her heart ached for what Zach must have gone through as a boy and then soared when she realized he'd not only pulled himself out of that life, he'd exceeded limits some people never even reached for.

"Adam said the same. About him being poor, I mean," Megan said. The lock on the changing room door slid open, and Taylor grabbed Stella's hand, squeezing it as Megan stepped out.

Stella gasped and covered her mouth with her free hand.

She wasn't a mushy, touchy-feely sort of girl. Even as a kid, she'd been raised by a man who knew a lot of things, but not how to coddle, play dress up, or paint nails. She'd learned from a young age that people and animals died. Life didn't work out how you planned, and the only option was to pick up and move on. She'd never loved sad movies or romance novels, and she wasn't particularly fond of country music. But looking at her best friend, glowing in what *had* to be her wedding gown, Stella wanted to believe in every fairy tale she remembered and even those she didn't.

"Oh, Meg," Taylor breathed.

Stella's eyes watered. "You look like a princess."

The upper half of the dress molded perfectly to Megan's body, outlining every graceful curve. The bodice narrowed at the waist before the skirt widened in a grand and elegant way. Megan turned slowly and they both gasped again when they saw the way the dress cut down her back, leaving enough skin to have Adam drooling. Silk, corset-like ties cinched the dress in a crisscross pattern on her lower back.

Megan looked over her shoulder, her eyes seeking theirs. "You like it?"

Taylor and Stella both jumped up from their seats and rushed closer, not touching, but nodded fiercely.

"It's incredible," Taylor said.

"Adam is going to swallow his tongue," Stella said, surprised that her voice cracked.

Megan gave a watery laugh. "Hopefully not before he says, 'I do.'"

The three women laughed together, and the bridal attendant was gracious enough to step back and give them their moment. *Their moment.* Stella couldn't believe she'd considered missing out on this. Her thoughts jumped to Zach and for the first time all morning, she didn't feel the curl of worry in her gut. She just felt…happy that she didn't have to miss this.

"Tell me you know this is the one," Stella said.

Megan's eyes filled with tears. "It is. This is the dress I'm going to marry Adam in. This is the dress I'm going to wear when I get my happily ever after."

Not liking the intense pressure in her lungs, Stella laughed, hoping to ease the inexplicable ache. "And the dress he's going to peel off of you to give you your real happily ever after."

Taylor snorted and nudged Stella with her hip. "Classy."

Megan laughed and they stood there, grinning like idiots, staring into the mirrors surrounding them. Three friends. So incredibly different in so many ways. *And it doesn't even matter.* Stella sometimes felt like she had no one because her parents had both died, her aunt and uncle lived out of state, and she only had a couple of close friendships. But in this moment, she realized she was luckier than most. *Family is what you make it.*

Megan looped her arms through each of the other women's. "Now it's your turn. I'm thinking a pale tangerine. You know, to make it Christmassy?"

Stella stared, her words stuck in her throat. *Best friend. Best friend. Best friend.* She met Taylor's gaze and was happy to see it was as appalled as her own. Megan looked back and forth between them in the mirror, a frown tipping her lips down.

"Like Christmas oranges. You don't think that'd be pretty?"

"Uh," Taylor murmured.

Stella bit her lip, digging deep for a smile.

Megan burst out laughing. "You two are too easy. As if. Christmas oranges. Give me some credit."

Deep breaths *whooshed* out of both Taylor and Stella.

"That's just mean," Stella said.

Megan arched her brows. "Almost as mean as moving in with a hot guy and not telling your best friends about it."

Taylor turned to look at Stella and crossed her arms over her chest. "Yeah. That's pretty mean, too."

Both of her friends were grinning, their eyes shining with anticipation. Stella backed up, raising her hands. "I only have a little bit of time. We'd better find our dresses."

They groaned and let it go. For the moment. Stella knew there was no actual escaping their inquisition. Even if she managed to do so at the store, they had a whole car ride home to trap her into the details.

Chapter Eight

It was close to eight by the time Zach grabbed all his things—not that there was much, seeing as he'd traveled light for several years now—and shopped for dinner.

It felt weird, standing on Stella's front step, huge duffel bag in one hand, sack of groceries in the other. When the heavy, farm door swung open, his heart squeezed tight. God, she was stunning—kick-in-the-ribs gorgeous. Even in lounge pants and a T-shirt. Her hair was up in another messy bun and she wore nothing on her face or her feet. He smiled at her, his body warming from the inside out, just from the sight of her. He wasn't sure if it was just base-level attraction or the fact that this wary, somewhat closed off woman had let him in—literally and figuratively, even if she didn't know it. That tugged at pieces of Zach's heart he hadn't thought much about in his quest to achieve his dreams.

"Hi." She stepped back so he could enter.

"Hey roomie."

"Ha." She shut the door behind him and led him to the kitchen. He'd seen her dogs out back and they'd run to greet him but taken off while he waited for her to answer.

"I had a key made for you while I was out. I figured you could use this door," she told him, pointing to the door beside the stove. The kitchen was dated, but clean, like the rest of what he'd seen so far.

"Thanks. I have my references, steaks, and potatoes."

She turned to take the bag of groceries from him. "That seems like a good trade."

It was her blinking and the way she kept glancing away from him that alerted him to her nerves. He set his duffel down a minute.

"You still sure about this?"

Stella held his gaze. "Seems silly for me to have all this space when you need somewhere to live, and I could use the income from your rent."

"It's a lot, I guess, picking up where your dad left off. Everything being on your shoulders must be heavy."

Her eyes darted down to his bag. "Grab that. I'll take you upstairs."

He didn't let his mind play around with those words. Upstairs was simple. Standard farm house with three bedrooms, a bathroom with an old claw-style tub, and a storage room with an angled roof. Probably a great place for a kid to play. The fresh air wafted through windows she opened, and she led him into what she'd called the master bedroom.

"It won't bother you, me being in here?" he asked as he set his bag on the four-poster bed. It was a masculine room with beige walls, a nondescript carpet and wide, double-paned windows.

"Why would it?" She stared up at him.

He kept his voice gentle. "This was your father's room?"

Stella nodded and gave him a small smile, different from the sad ones she'd shared other times Zach had mentioned her dad. "It was. But to be honest, he spent more time in the clinic than he did in this house. My memories are mostly there. This room...it's just a room."

Pointing to a door on the other side of the space, she walked forward. "There's a small en suite here. There are two more bedrooms. You can have the whole floor. Like I said, it's pretty much like having your own apartment, but we'll have to share the kitchen and laundry."

"I can live with that."

"You want to unpack?" Stella fidgeted with her hands, and Zach squelched the urge to take them both in his. To soothe her. This woman needed someone to give her a hard hug, and he was surprised by how much he wanted that someone to be him. *Not a good idea. She'd probably punch you.*

He grinned at the thought. Stella Lane was feisty and independent, and he looked forward to convincing her that he could be a huge asset in her life. Professionally. "I'll do it later. I promised you food."

"You did. I have a few things to do. Some paperwork, but if you need anything in the kitchen, make yourself at home. We can go over rules and boundaries while we eat."

As he followed her back down the stairs, he didn't keep the sarcasm from his voice. "Sounds fun. You take a look in the envelope?"

She glanced back up at him, and the worry and concern he'd noted had all but disappeared. "You asked for it. Thanks again for watching the clinic. Jaz said everyone acted like you'd always been there. And yes, I looked at the papers. You've amassed quite the nest egg."

They stepped into the kitchen and he heard the dogs at the door. "Watching the clinic was my pleasure. Honestly. I've missed working. I'd be more than happy to help you out any time." He beat her to the door and let her pets in, giving them some love. When he turned, rose from his crouched position, Stella was staring at him.

"What?"

She shook her head. "Nothing. They just…they treat you like you belong here."

Moving slowly, he crossed to where she was standing, leaning on the counter. "Ever think maybe I do? Sometimes things happen for a reason. Maybe I came back at just the right time, for both of us."

Attraction and a heavy dose of lust stirred in his blood as she stared at him. *Dammit. You need to keep your focus.* A workplace romance, especially with a woman like Stella, would wreck the plans he wanted to put into action. Her father had made Zach feel like he'd *belonged.* He wanted to. Very badly. Hearing her say the words stirred more than lust in him. It made him want things he'd never had.

She frowned. "You sound like Megan." Her voice was low, unintentionally seductive.

Turning her back, she went to the classic farm-style table and tidied the papers covering it. He unloaded the bag, setting the potatoes, salad fixings, and steaks on the counter.

"I can make the salad," she said, stacking everything into a pile.

"Thanks. Mind if I root through the cupboards, find the stuff I need?"

She shook her head, but her expression suggested she wasn't entirely comfortable. It took time to adjust to living with someone. *Like you'd know about living with a woman.* He'd never done it before, but he'd lived with several men in cramped quarters.

"I'm pretty good at being invisible," he told her, finding a pan under the stove and setting it on top.

The noise she made was somewhere between a scoff and a choke. "Yeah. Guy who looks like you, seems like he'd be totally unnoticeable."

Zach liked that she wasn't immune to his looks. Just like he wasn't to hers, but they could both keep boundaries in place if she agreed to take him on at the clinic. Hadn't she just said she had a list of boundaries? That could be one of them. No acting on the attraction.

"I've learned to be stealthy," he said, his tone teasing. He'd also been treated much like a ghost. When he wasn't, he was teased for all the things he didn't have. When he wasn't being labeled the poor kid, the one who had to have lunches shared with him and snuck shoes from the lost and found bin, he was being pushed around for his father's idiocy. But that was then.

Stella grabbed a bowl out of the cupboard near the stove, and when she stood, he realized they were in each other's space. She stared up at him, and he wondered if she was breathing. Her mouth was open, her lips bare, and he watched as she wet them quickly with her tongue. His stomach tightened.

"Breathe, Doc. You'll get used to me," he said.

Moving past him, she went to the other side of the counter and pulled a cutting board out of a drawer while Zach busied himself adding salt and pepper to the steak.

"I'm sure we won't get in each other's way. I spend most of my evenings at the clinic anyway. Most nights I grab a bowl of cereal or peanut butter and jam sandwich."

Opening the fridge, he wondered if that was all she ate, ever. There was some milk, a few slices of cheese, some apples and oranges, and a six pack of diet soda.

"Jesus, Doc. Who feeds you?"

"I just told you what I usually eat," she said.

He shook his head, grabbed the butter. "No wonder you're so tiny."

Narrowing her eyes, she grabbed a knife and started

chopping the lettuce. "Right, because if I ate more, I'd be taller."

Zach chuckled and took care of washing the potatoes before popping them into the microwave. They worked in companionable silence, but curiosity pressed hard.

"So, no boyfriend?"

She glanced up from her chopping. "No. Nothing even resembling one since I moved home."

"No time?"

She arched her brow. "Or inclination. I like things simple. There's nothing simple about dating in a small town."

"You went away for a while, right?"

She nodded, and he wanted to push, feeling like there was something there. His mother had mentioned a fiancé in Boston. Would Stella open up and tell him? More likely, she'd cut him off at the knees if he asked about her past. Slow and steady. That was a motto he'd learned to live by.

"Speaking of dating, it'd be nice if there weren't women in and out of here like a parade."

Zach laughed. "I appreciate your confidence in my prowess. I'll try to keep the parades to a minimum."

Her lips twitched. "I'd appreciate it."

He set the oven on broil to crisp up the potatoes. When she brought the salad to the table, he gestured to the pile of papers she'd set aside.

"That's quite the stack."

Stella sighed, and Zach's heart twisted in his chest. For a minute, he wanted nothing more than to lift the burdens that caused that sigh from her shoulders. Not because he wanted to work with her, but because no one should feel that much weight on their own.

"My dad left things a little…messy."

It surprised him she'd admit that much, but it was the "in" he needed. "I'm good at problem solving if you want to talk."

Moving to the cupboards, she pulled out plates, then grabbed cutlery from a drawer. "Unless you know how to make money grow on trees, I'd say there's no solving this one."

"Are things that tight?"

The look she gave him said more than she ever would. "I'm going to have a glass of wine. You want one?"

"Sure. You have red? It'll go nice with the steak."

She nodded and went to the pantry-like cupboard.

"You know, I have some ideas that would help you. Other than me working with you, I mean."

"Oh yeah?" Her voice leaned more toward exhausted than interested, but he was willing to take any opening he could at this point. Working today had left him wanting more. A lot more.

"First, I shared my financials for a reason. I'm serious."

She glanced up at him through heavy-lidded eyes. Probably tired, but she looked sexy as fuck. "Serious about what? You want a piece of a sinking ship, Zach?"

Damn right he did. "Yup."

She rolled her eyes. "Tell me your ideas. The ones that don't involve your money first."

Every tiny step forward with her felt like crossing a marathon finish line. "You have no online presence."

Stella's brows scrunched together. "Me, or the clinic? I'm on Facebook," she said, almost defensively.

He chuckled. Not exactly what he was talking about, but it wouldn't hurt. "I know. I sent you a friend request," Zach said, his lips quirking. "But I meant the clinic. You need a website more than anything, and a Facebook page would help. Just because you're the only vet in town and people are used to your presence doesn't mean you shouldn't do some advertising. Brockton Point is growing, new people are moving in all the time. You need to be part of the community, maybe organize some events to raise money for animal-related causes."

"That just sounds like more work, not ideas for lessening the load."

He finished up the final prep for dinner and when they'd sat down, he dove into both the food and what he'd been thinking since he showed up less than a week earlier. "I have an idea for C.C."

Stella paused, her bite of steak halfway to her mouth. "What does Chocolate Chip have to do with anything?"

She said she didn't want help, but curiosity shone from her eyes. He could see the soft spot for her horse shimmering in her gaze. They had that in common, too. Good thing he wasn't making a list of ways he and Stella were compatible. He had a feeling it would get lengthy.

Zach grinned. "I think she's lonely. That's my best guess and seeing if I'm right by adding a few more horses to the stable is a hell of a lot less invasive than checking for an ulcer."

Chewing her bite of steak, her brows drew together. "I don't exactly have the money to buy a few horses. That's care, grooming, cost of feeding them. And that's just to start. Plus, time I don't have."

He hadn't been sure, until this moment, if she was just being stubborn about the land and what she had around her or she truly didn't know how to utilize it.

"You won't need it. You rent out the stables. You hire a part timer to clean the stalls and do the grooming. Plus, you have Dexter. Rent out a few stables, C.C. has friends, and you're making money."

She sat forward. Her mouth opened and closed and Zach bit down on a bite of potato so he didn't grin like an idiot. Oh yeah, she needed his help.

"That is a really good idea. I honestly don't know why I haven't thought about it." She picked up another bite of steak and pointed her fork at him. "This is delicious, by the way."

Zach took a sip of the red she'd poured them. "Thanks. And I'd say you haven't had time to think about much more than getting through each day."

He knew those feelings all too well. One foot in front of the other until he got where he wanted to go.

"You'd be right." She ate in silence for a few minutes and Zach tried not to stare at her, but he couldn't help it. From the moment he'd met her, she'd been on the go and full of stress. Right now, in the quiet of her kitchen, sharing a meal with her dogs snoring by the back door, she looked almost settled. Nearly relaxed. And there was something inside of him, a longing that he'd buried deep, that ached to be the reason for that shift.

"What else? Since you've clearly given this some thought, what other ideas do you have?"

Cutting another piece of his steak, he asked, "What's it going to take, Doc? How do I get you to realize that taking a chance on me will be worth it?"

She sighed. "I'm not great at taking chances. I tend to end up on the losing end."

Zach gestured to the pile of papers. "That's only getting bigger, isn't it? At this point, what do you have to lose?"

She set her fork down. Stella stared down at the papers for so long he wasn't sure she'd answer him. Then her gaze lifted and with a sadness that turned his stomach, she said, "At this point? Everything."

Chapter Nine

What the hell was she doing? The food she'd truly enjoyed swirled around in her stomach. She'd already said too much, opened up enough for him to wedge his way in, and he didn't even know it. Getting a reprieve today, shopping with girlfriends like a normal freaking person, and sitting down to a real meal with good wine was tearing at all her seams. God, she was tired of fighting through every minute. Since her father's death—hell, before then—she'd been trying to get through, keep up, and not fall apart. And here was this man, this gorgeous, funny, solid man offering her so much and she couldn't even figure out why.

She knew better than to trust the desire to lean on him, take what he was offering. She'd let herself lean on Steven, let herself believe he wanted to marry her because she'd paid attention to words, not actions. In truth, he'd only asked her because he wanted her to stay in Boston and help run the clinic he was part of. He'd never intended to marry her, but she'd trusted him. Given him her heart. *This isn't your heart. It's your business and you are hovering only inches above rock bottom.* Stella didn't know if she could take another blow like she had. If she could reach for another faulty life line and survive the fall.

Zach was easy to talk to, maybe because he didn't know much about her, or maybe because his outside perspective wasn't based on what he thought he knew about her. Hell, maybe because she'd had a glass of wine before he arrived. Whatever the case, she was at the point that she really was going to lose everything if she didn't try something new. His rent would give her a little break, but it hardly covered everything. The bank had turned her down flat and she'd rather borrow from a stranger than grovel to Lydia. So, she dove. Head first and hoped like hell she didn't land on concrete. He wanted to know? *Fine. The only place to go after rock bottom is up.*

"I need to come up with a balloon payment for a loan my father took against the house."

There. Just saying it lightened her shoulders. She hated the anger that simmered below the surface that her father had let things get so bad and not reached out. *Just like you've been doing.*

"Shit. He really left you with a lot."

She nodded, staring at her fingers on the table so she could avoid Zach's gaze. Why the hell was she embarrassed? It wasn't her fault she'd inherited debt. Stella lifted her head, held her chin high, and met his gaze. Standing, she gathered their plates and took them to the sink. Had she truly thought he'd have an answer? There were no answers. Though his idea for Chocolate Chip was a great one. She should have considered it before.

Turning, she pulled in a sharp gasp. He was right there, standing in front of her, looking at her like he cared. Like he wanted to help and whether it was the wine, the company, or just sheer exhaustion, she had to fight the urge to physically lean on him.

"I can help cover the balloon payment."

Her gaze shot up. "What?"

"Let me in, Stella. You don't have to do this alone."

"Why? Why do you want this so badly?" Her heart raced, and she gripped the counter behind her, feeling like it was safer to lean on that rather than him.

His expression changed, and she knew—she could see—that he understood his answer mattered. Zach held her gaze, making it feel like, with just a look, he was drawing her into a hug. He looked at her like he was someone she could rely on—as though he wanted to be there for her. She didn't want to like the feeling. Other than Megan, she hadn't leaned on anyone in a long time and even then, she didn't unload even a tenth of the stress she so often felt. Keeping it to herself, relying on herself, was part of her self-preservation.

"I came in one time after...well, let's just say I'd been messed up a little by some jerks I went to school with. Instead of heading home, I came to see if your dad needed any help with chores. I'd followed a stray dog a long while before that, through the woods at the edge of your land. I met your dad and he said I could drop by anytime. Sometimes I came with my best friend, Travis. Lots of times, I just came here when I needed somewhere to be." Zach paused.

The edges of Stella's brain shadowed with memory. *Hmm.* Her dad had a good amount of high school kids who'd drop in and do chores for extra cash. Back when he'd had some, obviously, because he hadn't left her enough to farm out any of the little jobs needing to be done. She didn't remember Travis exactly, but she could see that he meant a great deal to Zach. And clearly, so had Stella's father.

Zach huffed out a breath, moved across the kitchen to the back door, and stared out the window beside it.

"He took one look at me and knew not to ask any

questions. Instead, he cleaned me up, put me to work stocking supplies. When I finished that, he got me to change all the cages, giving them fresh water and blankets straight out of the dryer."

The tight set of his shoulders was new. He always seemed so confident and relaxed. At ease. This side of Zach, the one lost in thought, tugged at something inside of Stella. It made her want to do more than accept comfort; she wanted to give it. She could see her dad giving Zach work to busy himself. That had always been his own way of coping. Plus, he'd never stand for a kid being hurt. Anything or anyone, really. He was the ultimate champion of underdogs.

"Did you...get hurt often?"

Zach glanced her way, then looked down at his hands. "Not really. Most of the time it was just verbal."

"Was it always the same kids?"

He looked up. "Not really the point here, Doc. The point is, when I needed a place to be, he gave me one."

She imagined it was never easy for him to seek refuge and knew her father would have made that easier on a young, powerless boy. She also recognized from his tone that he didn't want to discuss that part of his life. *Which is good because you two don't need each other's life stories.*

Zach took another deep breath, like he needed to steady himself. "We sat on the back steps of the clinic at the end of the day, and he told me strength wasn't about how hard a man could punch or the words he could throw, but whether or not he got back up once he'd been kicked down."

Stella's eyes burned. "How old were you?"

Giving a short, humorless laugh, he replied, "Fourteen. Too young to realize he was right."

A sad smile tilted her lips. "He did have an annoying habit of being right about a lot of things. I would have been ten. I don't remember you. At least, I don't think I do."

He set that heated, somewhat gloomy gaze on her again and Stella felt like she'd been prodded with electricity. "I'd seen you around. Playing with the dogs or with dolls on the porch."

Faded memories had her smiling. "I only play with the dogs now."

It seemed like he leaned in closer, but he hadn't even moved. The air left her lungs and the room at the same time when his gaze wandered over her body before moving back to her face.

"You're definitely all grown up. He'd be proud as hell of you."

Deep down, she knew that. But on the surface, the part of her that was barely treading water, the piece of her sinking under, she felt like a failure. She'd wanted to do this *together*. *We were supposed to do it together, Dad.* She'd wasted months of her life trying to convince her fiancé to come home with her so they could start their lives together. Where she'd grown up. Where her dad lived.

"He was a good man."

Needing the space, she went back to the table and grabbed her wine. The dogs whimpered, and Zach opened the door for them. He gestured to the porch with his chin and she brought his wine outside, too, handing it to him.

The cool breeze of the evening wafted around her and made it easier to breathe. Crickets chirped in the twilight while the dogs gave happy yips and chased each other around. Stella leaned against the door jamb, wondering what kind of changes Zach was thinking. Looking up at the sky, her heart pinched again, thinking about how many changes she'd already endured. Stella had never been one to fight progress or shy away from shaking things up. But so much at once—

"He wouldn't want you to feel buried like this." Zach's voice was soft, like a caress.

Tears threatened, making her feel weak. "Then he shouldn't have left everything such a goddamn mess."

Zach moved to stand in front of her and took the wine from her hand. He set both his and hers on the little table she had there.

"I've been wanting to do this since I met you," he said.

Stella's breath caught, and she looked up at him, the heat in his eyes so intense, she couldn't force the air out of her lungs. Surprise and disappointment warred with each other when he yanked her against him and wrapped his arms—those large, strong, gorgeously tattooed arms—around her and held tight.

When her breath finally expelled, it felt more like a sob, and though she'd regret it later—most likely—she leaned on him, into him, and wrapped her arms around his waist. She nearly lost the battle against tears when his hand came to the back of her head and stroked over her hair in a move so sweet and so gentle it both broke and healed something inside of her.

They stood there, him holding her, and her letting him, for longer than she should have allowed. When he finally pulled back, looking down at her with a tenderness that made her heart swell, she tried to laugh it off.

"Totally not what I expected you to do," she whispered.

Zach stepped back, but the heat hadn't left his gaze. "You needed that more than being kissed senseless. Besides, that's not what I'm after. That's not why I came here or why I keep coming back. I'm not looking for a lover, Stella, especially not one that I want to enter a business relationship with. I want to work with you. I want to be part of what your father built, part of what you're trying to keep going. And I could help. It doesn't make you weak to accept help."

She sighed, hating that she felt the loss of his body heat—of his body—surrounding her own. Giving herself a minute to gather her thoughts and catch her breath, she was thankful for the little bit of physical space.

"I can't pay you. Whatever money I get goes back into the clinic. At the moment, I'm barely staying afloat, so you should know, right off, if you truly want in, you're asking permission to board a sinking ship."

Zach's eyes lit fire, making Stella's belly do the same. "I'm a great swimmer. And I guarantee you that I can help plug the leak. Give me the chance."

"If I give you some of my patients in exchange for help with the...balloon payment...and you take on all new patients, with me taking a commission, it might work."

She was thinking off the top of her head now. She'd agreed to open her house to him, but this...giving up a piece of what her father had worked so hard to build, felt harder. *If you want any chance of saving his legacy and making this work, you need to do something. Zach is offering you several somethings.* She thought of Megan and how she believed things worked out as they were meant to. If Stella let herself believe in signs or fate or karma for just a second, she could admit that Zach's timing in her life couldn't be better.

She didn't need to tell him that some of those clients paid in casseroles, since she planned on him putting a stop to that. He looked like he had *way* more backbone than she did.

Zach kept staring at her, and even though she felt nerves tickling her spine, she didn't avert her gaze. Nerves were preferable to attraction. Because he was right—if they worked together, even if she was entertaining the notion for the short term—it wasn't smart.

"Buy in makes me a partner," he said, picking up his wine.

Her heart spasmed just from the word. She *hated* that word. It suggested she rely on someone else...for good. "No. You'd be a...colleague. A second doctor at my practice.

Something like a shareholder. Like…I own the salon and you rent a chair from me," she replied.

Zach's brow arched, and his lips quirked up in a sexy smirk. "We're not hairdressers."

She thought it was a good analogy. They worked together but she was the boss. "Of course not, but it's a similar idea."

See what happens when you let someone in? He wants a bigger piece of…of what, Stella? Of the debt? He's offering you a hand to pull you out of the goddamn quicksand you're slipping into. Let him. You get the better end of this deal.

Zach closed the space between them, leaving her just enough room that she could breathe. "I give you enough to make a dent in the balloon payment, we do a trial basis, then you make me partner. I want a say in helping you turn this place around. And I want it on paper that I get a say. During that trial, you let me explore the options I think will improve things financially."

She started to balk, and he raised a hand. "With your approval."

Trial basis sounded more doable than partner. Only one of those words shot fear into her heart. Only one of those opened her up to being hurt or left behind.

"If this doesn't work, any of it, you walk away without issue or reimbursement."

He stared at her, and for a second she wondered if he could see her heart trying to beat out of her body through several different pulse points.

"No."

Her mouth dropped open. "What?"

Now he did invade her personal space, and only part of her felt annoyed by it. The other part of her felt…the opposite of annoyed, especially with the memory of how it felt to have his arms around her, his hand in her hair.

"I'm not promising to walk away from you without

issue, Doc. I think that's part of your problem. You assume people will. I won't. I came home to stay. My word means something and when I say I want in, I want all the way in. Things go sideways, we'll figure it out, readjust and reevaluate, but I won't just walk away from you. Any man who would is a fucking idiot."

Stella leaned against the door jamb so she didn't sway. Was she that easy to see through? That transparent? *This is business, not personal.*

"Sometimes, you jump in without a safety net, Doc."

"I'm in charge," she said, needing him to at least acknowledge that.

"It's your show."

She glared at him. "Until you get your cut."

Zach's grin made her stomach dance. "If we get there, through the trial, and things are moving in a way that I can take a cut, I'd say we'll both be doing pretty well. At this point, do you have any other options?"

She hated that he was right. More, just the thought of bringing him on—which panicked her less than it had a week ago—now seemed soothing. A way out. A light in a constant shroud of darkness. Maybe because all her other options had been taken away.

Stella held out her hand, done with indecision and questioning. She was tired of living in the dark. "I guess this makes us part—co-workers."

Zach grinned. "You won't be sorry."

But as he shook her hand and sparks fired over her skin making her feel alive, she wasn't so sure.

Chapter Ten

Zach was no stranger to hard work and long hours, but he was exhausted and his day was far from over. He took the exit off the freeway that brought him into Portland, with what felt like nerves swirling in his gut. He'd told Stella he'd have the money for her within two weeks, thinking it wouldn't be that hard to take a loan against his property. His investments were tied up and he couldn't access them without a huge penalty. Which he wasn't concerned about because he thought borrowing on one of the two places he owned would be an easy fix.

The manager of the Brockton Point bank, Lydia-something-or-other, had snootily explained to him that he didn't qualify. He'd had a flashback to high school, the way she'd looked down her nose at him. She'd even *tsked*, as if she was sorry to be the bearer of bad news. Oh, she'd given some reasons, but he'd stopped listening after she said no because his priority was getting the money so Stella wouldn't shut him out.

Whether she was willing to admit it or not, they were a

damn good team. Zach didn't want to give her any reason to change her mind. After one week in the clinic, and her house, he had a good handle on how things operated. And how much needed to change so they could see a profit. Zach followed the directions his phone gave him through the blue tooth and stopped at a traffic light. It had been a while since he'd been in a town with an actual strip mall of box stores. He should text Stella and see if she needed him to pick up anything.

Like you're a couple? He laughed out loud, shook his head at the thought, and pressed the gas when the light changed. If she was reluctant to be partners in the clinic, she was hell-bent on them ignoring the attraction that simmered just below the surface any time they were within five feet of each other. Best to ignore it. *She has the right idea there.* Why make things complicated? He didn't want or plan to, especially when her walls were up. But then she'd join him on a consult or he'd see her with the animals or Dexter or Jaz and her softness undid him. It was in those moments he was sure he saw the real her—the one who was unafraid to be open.

Stop worrying about getting her to open up and think about the list of ideas you want to run past her. There were a surprising number of opportunities without a lot of effort on their part, but he could totally see how she'd overlooked them. Stella Lane was a machine. He wasn't sure how she'd managed so much on her own without crashing. Her work ethic and attitude were just two of the things he admired about her, and she didn't stop once the clock did. She had several drop-in patients a day, phone consultations, and home visits. There could be another intern, another vet, and a full-time assistant and still be enough work to keep everyone busy.

Pulling up to Pet Central, he hoped his friend and mentor,

Doctor Andrew Clark, hadn't forgotten he was coming today. As one of the original investors and owners of the large chain store, his friend's schedule only got crazier as he tried to fit it all in. He recruited vets for his business, gave talks and lectures at universities, contributed to programs overseas—which was where Zach had met him—and still saw a regular rotation of patients at his Portland location. Zach didn't miss working here. It had a completely different vibe—certainly less personal than what Stella's clinic offered.

Grabbing his wallet and cell phone from the seat next to him, he got out of the truck and headed for the automatic doors of the megastore Andrew had tried to convince him to join more than once.

Pet Central was a colossal building with high ceilings, tall windows, friendly staff, and just about every pet accessory, food, and gadget possible. Including top of the line veterinarians. Zach had learned a lot from Andrew when he'd come to work with his unit in Peru. When he'd graduated, Zach had carefully considered the offer his mentor had made—his own location overseas—but decided all he really wanted was to go home. To start his life there. Of course, the money he'd made taking a stateside position for a couple of years before heading back to Brockton was what had given him the money he'd wanted—needed—to accrue. Not that it did him a damn bit of good right now. Being so close to having what he wanted meant he had to swallow his pride and secure financing to help Stella.

He approached the reception counter and smiled at the woman whose nameplate read Celeste.

"Hi there," she greeted, putting her clipboard down on the high counter to give Zach her full attention.

"Hi. I have an appointment with Andrew. Is he around?"

A woman with hair so high Zach wondered how she held it up approached the counter with a basket full of cat toys and treats. In an instant, another Pet Central employee was at the counter.

"Did you find everything you were looking for?" she asked the woman.

"I'll see if Mr. Clark is available," Celeste said, pulling Zach's attention back before she disappeared through a swinging door. The white walls with the bright yellow letters shouting PET CENTRAL were almost blinding. Zach thought of the quiet, calm interior of Stella's clinic. It could use a fresh coat of paint, but basically, it was like walking into a cozy home. It made people feel comfortable. Big chain stores like this one were more about looks than individual patient quality. The doctors were top of the line, but appointments were booked in small blocks of time and, like a high-end restaurant, turnover was expedient. There wasn't time for chatting about how someone's granddaughter was feeling after a bout of the flu and there definitely wasn't time to throw in a nail trim just because it was hard for the owner to do.

The woman beside him dug through the basket. "Do you think I need anything else for a kitten?"

Zach's brows rose. Christ. She had enough for ten kittens. He looked at the items she loaded onto the counter.

"I think you're set," the employee, whose name Zach couldn't see because of her long hair covering it, said.

"You already have kitty litter and a box?" Zach asked.

The women looked his way. The customer widened her eyes, giving him a sultry smile.

"Would you believe I *did not* grab those things?" Her voice lowered as she looked him over. She stepped closer, making it hard not to inhale the heavy scent of her perfume. Without meaning to, he mentally compared it to the berry scent of Stella's shampoo. Since he'd started at the clinic with her, he'd craved berries more than he ever had in his life.

The woman was still eyeing him up in a blatant way. It took Zach a second to realize that the sultry look and smoky voice did not do one thing for him. Sure, she was attractive, but there was no spark in his blood, no zap of electricity that usually came with a good-looking woman expressing interest—even just visually.

"Can't stay out of it even if it's not your place, can you?" Andrew's booming voice asked as he came through a door to Zach's left, behind the counter.

Zach turned away from the woman and greeted his friend and former mentor. Andrew came around the counter and Zach met him halfway before the two exchanged a handshake and a slap-on-the-back hug.

"How are you?" Andrew asked. His wavy hair was liberally streaked with white strands and a few more lines had settled around his eyes.

"I'm good, thanks." It was true. Not everything was settled, but he was really good. Stella was a huge part of that.

"I'm glad you reached out. I have an envelope for you, right here." He patted the pocket of his white coat, but didn't slip his hand in. His eyes twinkled, reminding Zach of the first time he'd met him. Not that he'd typically notice a twinkle in any guy's eyes, but they'd been dead tired and feeling low when Andrew visited their unit. The upbeat attitude had revived them. Excited them.

"You sure this is what you want? Still time to say yes and come back. I'll give you a spot at this clinic so you're close to your beloved hometown."

They moved away from the counter and Zach headed in the direction of the large, circular waiting room. Opaque squares of glass made the rounded wall seem huge. Wooden benches attached to the wall went all the way around, offering plenty of seating. Nothing but the best. And the most. The biggest and the best were two of Andrew's favorite words.

"I'm happy where I am."

"So, you got in. Interesting," Andrew said.

Zach didn't know what was so interesting about that. He'd told Andrew his plan when they'd spoken a few months back, even mentioning his hometown by name.

"I did. She's not ready to call me partner or anything yet, but I'm getting there, and it's where I want to be."

Andrew nodded, still staring at Zach, as if he was assessing the truth of his words. Pulling an envelope out of his pocket, his mentor passed it over. Zach took it and looked down at it. His name was on the front.

Zach gave an embarrassed laugh, stopping short of shuffling his feet. Fuck. This felt awkward. "I figured there'd be paperwork to sign. You said you'd talk to your lawyers about drawing something up."

Before replying, Andrew looked around, probably making sure he wasn't talking business in front of customers. Zach had assumed they'd at least head back to his office.

"Saw something in you the first time we met, Zach. I told you that then and I'm telling you now. This is a personal loan."

Zach's jaw dropped. Accepting a business loan was one thing, but he didn't expect Andrew to dip into his personal accounts to bail him out.

"Andrew, I appreciate it, man. So much. More than I can tell you. But—"

His friend held up his hand. "I know what I'm doing, son. Not my first time. You need an investor, I'm happy to invest. I do it through the company, you'll need four other people to sign off on it. Take the money, Zach. I know you're good for it. We'll talk repayment when you're ready."

It was too much. Too good. And just like Andrew Clark to go over and above.

Andrew clapped him on the shoulder, squeezed his arm,

and Zach's throat tightened. He firmed his lips and nodded briskly. "You won't regret this. I'm going to help her turn her clinic around and I'll have this back to you, with interest, before you know it."

"I trust you. Wish like hell you worked here with us. That place—that woman—must be something special."

There was no missing the curiosity in Andrew's voice or gaze. Zach wasn't up to giving away details because truthfully, Stella was this hard-to-describe enigma who worked her way under his skin in less time than he'd known was possible. The kicker was, she had no idea, and if she did, she wouldn't want to be there. He didn't want her to be.

"You have no idea," Zach said.

"I'll come out and check for myself one day soon."

"Mr. Clark? Phone call for you," Celeste said quietly from beside them. Both men turned to look at her, and Andrew gave her a wide smile, then looked back at Zach.

"We'll be in touch."

He watched his friend walk away, barely registering the fact that Celeste was still looking at him, a tentative smile on her face. Zach waved and left the building, getting back in the truck, feeling like he was in a daze. Just like that, he'd secured his piece of the pie. Smiling as he backed up out of the lot, Zach imagined telling Stella tonight; about handing her the money. She'd accept it a little warily because she knew this money brought them one step closer to her least favorite word: partners.

Pulling his truck into a spot behind On Dec, a small bar he hoped had good beer on tap, he realized he was starving. His mouth watered at the thought of pub-style wings. He wondered if he should text Stella and ask her to meet him. She still hadn't responded to his earlier text asking if she needed anything. *Maybe you should make some actual buddies, so you think about something other than her.*

Pulling open the door, Zach was greeted with what he figured was the Friday after work crowd of Brockton Point. The place was more like a neighborhood pub than a bar, though maybe things kicked up a few notches at night. Brockton had never really been a party town—or if it was, he'd never been in that circle. Now that he could be in any circle he wanted, he just didn't care anymore. Weird how life worked.

"Hey there, handsome. You can sit anywhere, and I'll be right with you," a waitress with very thick bangs said.

"Thanks."

She probably meant at the tables, but Zach headed for a stool at the bar. The lighting was dim, but brighter than he'd expected. Music pumped in the background—classic rock, thank God. He'd learned to enjoy the simple things in life and there wasn't much a good beer and equally good music couldn't cure.

The bartender was a tattooed giant with a wide grin. It was second nature for Zach to check out the surrounding areas, assess the people in his field of vision, and places where people could hide out of his line of sight. He'd gone into the army with that particular skill, but it had been honed to a… well, a lethal degree. It was as automatic as breathing for Zach to assess a person's physical strengths and scan for weakness in case he needed to use that to his advantage.

"How's it going? You new around here?"

Now that he was closer, Zach vaguely recognized the guy. Likely, they'd gone to high school together, but since he spent a good portion of his time keeping his head down, Zach couldn't be sure. He'd had other things to worry about besides making friends.

The guy put a small, square napkin in front of him as Zach answered. "Technically, I'm from here, but I've been gone a long time."

"Welcome back then. Declan James. I own the place," he said, putting out a hand.

Zach shook it, more certain now that they'd gone to school together. Like every other kid, he knew which kids were popular, which were stoners, which ones to steer clear of. If memory served him correctly, Declan was a quarterback and ladies' man.

"Zach Mason."

The guy's brows drew together. "Mason. And you're from here? Is Sheila your mom?"

"Uh, yeah." Zach wasn't sure he wanted to know why the bartender knew his mother.

Declan laughed. "She's a hoot on karaoke night."

Groaning out loud, Zach shook his head but shared in the laughter. "I bet. What night is that? I want to make sure I stay away."

"Every Tuesday. Come on. You could do a mother-son duet," he said, still chuckling.

Not in this lifetime or any other. "Not even for large sums of money would I consider that." It was weird to think of his mother having a social life. Having a boyfriend. Maybe she came here with him.

"I hear you. Can I get you a beer?"

Zach nodded, pleased to see his favorite craft beer on tap. "Absolutely."

Declan grabbed a pint glass from below the counter. As he poured, he glanced back at Zach. "We must have gone to school together. Something about you seems familiar."

Zach crossed his arms on the bar, feeling looser and more relaxed than he had in a really long time. "I was just thinking the same thing. Brockton High class of...?"

"2004," Declan answered.

"Long time ago now," Zach said. In some ways, not long enough. In others, it was like only seconds had passed.

Sliding another napkin under the glass, Declan nodded, but then his eyes widened slightly, like he'd just remembered something. "You were friends with Travis. The kid who died senior year."

Zach's stomach spasmed hard. Fuck. Why did it still hurt all these years later? He pressed his hands flat on the bar. "Yeah. We were best friends."

Declan stepped closer. "I'm sorry, man. You left town shortly after, right?"

Zach's throat went dry. He'd grieved. He'd dealt with this. As part of his return from combat, he'd had mandatory counseling. Yet it still hurt to push the word from his lips, "Yes."

"That was sad. Really fucking sad, man. It was the first time I realized that we weren't invincible, you know? When you're in high school, you think you'll live forever and it's only going to get better. It was a hell of a way to realize life doesn't last forever. I'm really sorry for your loss."

Zach could only nod as he blew out a breath. Declan tapped the top of the bar, his lips in a tight line before he wandered off to fill a couple of orders. Zach turned on his stool, breathing through his nose like the shrink had taught him. The conversation was a reminder that he needed to go visit Trav's family. Particularly his mother. It had always been part of the plan, but the piece he kept pushing to the bottom of his list. Because as hard as it had been to talk about Travis just now, seeing his mother, or any of his family, was going to be worse.

Not today. Zach rolled his shoulders trying to release the tension. It had been a good day. He'd hang on to that for now. Have a beer, go home, see Stella, and give her the money. *A good day.*

The smack of billiard balls caught his attention. There were pool tables around a wall that didn't completely close off the room he was in from the other. It was an interesting focal point—a divider of sorts, and the rusty-red brick added warmth to the large space. An empty stage lined the far wall with a small dance space right in front. It wasn't fancy, but it was homey. Inviting. He'd definitely stop in again. Sipping his beer, he watched what he could see of the pool game. The end of the table came just past the faux brick wall, so he only saw someone when they walked to that end to take a shot.

The blond playing looked like she knew what she was doing. He wouldn't mind a game. When he'd been on the base, they set up all sorts of makeshift games to occupy their minds when they weren't actively working to keep themselves and others alive. Might be nice to play on a real table.

Zach sipped his beer and wondered if he could coax Stella into a game one Friday after work. *Shit. You don't even mean to think of her and you do.* She didn't strike him as the type to hit the bar, though.

Finishing off his beer, Zach stood, intent on the pool table. He was pulling his wallet out of his back pocket when the hair on the back of his neck prickled. Like he was fourteen again, his breath halted. Standing at the end of the pool table, ready to take a shot, was Rick Growski, the once upon a time high school all-star, smug-ass dickhead who'd taunted Zach about all the things he had no control over. Being poor, having an alcoholic father, needing school-provided lunches, his mother working as a maid for Rick's family. *Fuck.* He'd worked his ass off to come home feeling good about himself and for the most part, it wasn't even those awful memories making his gut churn. It was knowing that his best friend's last night on earth had been spent at a party Rick threw. A party Travis had been invited to and begged Zach to come to. Zach had refused. Travis had died. Logically, one didn't cause the other but fuck if he could make his heart settle or his mind remember that. Rick started wandering to the bar, the blond tugging at his belt loop and leaning into him. When the guy turned and headed in Zach's direction, he waited to feel more of the same—guilt, anger, powerless. Instead, he felt nothing. Rick's eye caught his and stuck. They stared at each other for a moment before a waitress stepped in front of Rick's path.

"Get you something, honey?"

Rick's eyes roamed over her before he answered. "Couple more beers."

"You got it."

When she turned to walk to the bar, Rick's gaze came back to Zach's. His chin jutted out sort of like his paunchy stomach. "I know you?"

A smile tugged at Zach's lips. He crossed his arms over his chest with deliberate slowness and leaned against the bar. "You don't know shit."

Rick scowled, looked like he wanted to say something. He even took a step forward before swatting his hand in the air at nothing and turning away.

Restlessness consumed him. Time to go. He finished off his beer and tossed five bucks on the bar.

"You out of here?" Declan said, coming back. He pushed the money toward Zach. "First one is a welcome back drink."

"Thanks, man."

"No problem. I'd buy you drinks all day long if you want to put Growski in his place like that again. Guy is a dick. Always was. You'd think growing up, he'd change." Declan shook his head like he was disgusted. Zach could relate.

He was surprised when Declan leaned forward, rested his forearms on the bar. "I kinda remember you now. You kept your head down a lot. Lived on the outside of town, right? Rick the dick used to give you a hard time. I'd put it away with all the other high school memories, you know? There was a group of us that tried to put him in his place, but it never did any good. Some things never change. I kick him out about once a week for being a drunken ass."

Zach met the bartender's serious stare, wondering how he could serve such a prick. But then what he'd said sunk in. "You tried to stop him?"

Frustration washed over Declan's face. "It didn't take, clearly."

Zach laughed, happy he could. "It'd take a hell of a lot more than an ass kicking to make that guy likable."

The fact that, despite keeping his head down, he wasn't so invisible all those years ago was salve on a cut. "Thanks for trying."

Declan nodded, glancing over when the waitress called his name.

"Thanks for the beer." Zach was almost to the door when Declan called his name.

"Me and a couple of friends play poker once a month. If you're interested, we'll be playing next Saturday, here. Just go around the back."

"Big group?" He didn't really have money to be throwing away if it was a huge buy in.

"Nah. Just me, my buddy Adam, if he doesn't bail, and his soon to be brother-in-law and partner. They're good guys."

"Sounds good. Thanks for the invite."

Declan flashed a smile that Zach would bet money made panties drop. "You might not be thanking me after I take your money, but you're welcome."

Once he got to his truck, Zach gave himself a minute to absorb what had just happened. It washed over him and he felt...okay. He was okay. Rationally, he knew Rick wasn't directly responsible for Travis's death. No one was. But like everything else in life, there were moments leading up to the ones that stuck with a person that could have changed the outcome. Zach left town thinking he was to blame for Travis's death. That going with his friend could have somehow prevented the accident. It was a hell of a thing to sit there now and realize that he wasn't the only person he'd blamed. But the hell of it was, it didn't matter who got blamed. Travis was gone.

"And you're here. So, move on," he said to himself, putting the truck in drive.

Since he hadn't ordered wings, he swung through a drive-thru, ordering enough for him and Stella, in case she was hungry. It surprised him, as he drove toward the farm, how much he hoped she was home. There was something about her that soothed him. She was a live wire at the clinic, but when she stopped, when she was in the comfort of her home, she was quiet and peaceful. Still. He wasn't sure what it would be like—living with her, whether they'd pass each other in the kitchen, watch television together like real roommates or avoid each other. They'd settled into a routine surprisingly fast and she was becoming a fixture in his day from the time he woke up and made breakfast. Everything about her pulled him in, but they were both keeping a strong cage around the attraction that simmered. They were in a good place. He wanted to keep them there.

Her car was there when he pulled up, and the dogs, used to him now, barked out a greeting from the porch. He glanced over at the clinic, saw she'd left the lights on, and wondered if he should go turn them off. Food first.

"Hey guys," he said, once he'd grabbed the food and headed to the front door.

He gave them a couple of pets each before going in. He'd expected Stella to be watching Netflix or going through paperwork.

"Stella?" He walked through the foyer, down the hall, past the living room and into the kitchen. Setting the bags down, he went to check her bedroom. The door was ajar and she wasn't in there either. *Where the hell is she?*

Worry stirred in his gut. He didn't ignore his instincts. Heading back out the front door, he hurried down the steps and ran the distance to the clinic.

Using the key she'd given him, he let himself in through the front entrance. The last of the day's light came through the windows, but otherwise, it was dark. Except, when he stepped all the way in, for the light shining from the office behind the reception desk. Stella had basically deemed the room off-limits during her initial tour. She used one of the exam rooms as a makeshift office, which was something he planned to talk to her about—it was a waste of space.

"Stella?"

He heard shuffling and a thud. Zach was around the desk and standing in the doorway when Stella muttered, "Shit."

When he peeked in, she had one hand to her head and the other at her side. Zach came all the way in and didn't think twice about stepping into her personal space. Her fingers were pressed to her forehead, but he saw traces of red and his stomach tightened.

"You hurt yourself," he said, frowning.

"Solid diagnosis, Doctor Mason," she stared up at him, her scowl slightly crooked.

It was only after he moved her hand that he noticed the slightly dazed look in her eyes. Leaning closer, he caught a hint of whiskey. If he was to guess, really good whiskey.

Doing a quick assessment, he saw it was only a scratch on her head. He moved to what he assumed was a desk, despite the fact that he could not see the surface of it for all the paper on it. He grabbed a tissue and brought it back to Stella, who'd remained in the exact same spot.

Bending his knees, he met her gaze as he brushed the tissue against her cut. She closed her eyes and breathed out a long sigh as she swayed toward him.

When she inhaled, her hand came to his chest. "You always smell so good. It drives me nuts."

Stella licked her lips, her eyes locked on his and she brushed against him. Zach put his hand on her hip to steady her. Right. To steady her. The air stilled between them and their combined breathing all but echoed in that silence. She stared at his lips and he nearly groaned at the desire he saw there. When she looked back up at him, the pressure in his chest became painful. Her fingers walked up his chest slowly and he wasn't even sure if she meant to be seductive, but it was, and he couldn't breathe. He could only wait.

With the tip of her index finger, she traced his lips, watching the movement, and Zach fought the urge to part his lips and suck her finger into his mouth. Instead, he let out the breath he was holding and felt the shiver that traveled through Stella. She inched closer. He stood still, like granite. Moving her hand to his jaw, she stroked the skin there and his body felt like she'd lit it on fire.

They'd both fought this for a good reason and as she inched closer, it took everything in him to remember why. He wasn't sure he'd ever wanted to kiss a woman the way he wanted to kiss Stella right now. He was ready to push all his sensibility and control aside when she went up on tiptoe, bringing her mouth within touching distance. Then she wobbled unsteadily, and it cleared his brain. Reminded him that he had long-term goals and wanted this woman's respect, trust, and confidence more than he wanted her in bed.

Which was saying a hell of a lot.

Chapter Eleven

Stella was the perfect amount of tipsy. Enough to give in to the temptation she buried daily and not chastise herself for it. But Zach took the choice away as he stepped back. The air grew cold and mortification washed over her, chasing away any traces of her buzz. Rejection was sobering. He held her gaze and she knew—she *knew*—he'd done the right thing and still, she wanted to storm out of the room and hug him in equal measure.

She turned toward the desk where she'd been trying to sort through the piles of paper. In just over a week, Zach Mason had made her life…breathable. She couldn't muddle that by sleeping with him. *Whoa. I was just taking a little taste. Just a kiss. No one said anything about sleeping.* She snorted. If she ever got Zach in bed, she would *not* waste her time sleeping. But they weren't going there. Because he was in the middle of pulling her business—which was her life— out of the quicksand.

"Why are you in here all alone, Doc?" She appreciated that he kept his distance and didn't ask her to turn around.

"I need to clean this out. We need the space." The fact that he'd slid into her practice with so much ease and made things smoother was tough to swallow. When her dad died, she'd promised herself she'd make him proud. Like she'd planned on doing when he was alive. Instead, he'd died, and she felt like she was the one buried.

"Why tonight? Why now? And where'd you get the whiskey?" His tone went soft and the room no longer felt cold.

She pointed to the shelf where she'd left it while going through her father's textbooks. She'd never seen him open one, but they'd sat on those same shelves for as long as she could remember.

The sound of his feet shuffled across the room and then he was standing beside her, knees bent to see her face, whiskey in hand. "How much did you drink?"

She shrugged, her thoughts a little blurry. "Not enough. How'd you know it was whiskey?"

The smile he gave her made her insides feel just like the first shot of the aged malt. Warm and tingly. *God. You must still be buzzed if you're using the word tingly.*

"A man goes without the finer things in life long enough, he learns to recognize them pretty easily."

Her body was starting to feel heavy, and she was regretting her effort to sort through the mess her father had left behind. This one was literal, not financial. The man was a damn hoarder.

Zach screwed the cap onto the bottle and placed it on the desk. He surveyed the room, and Stella watched him. It was no hardship.

"You were gone a while," she said.

Glancing at her, he nodded. "I have your money. Stopped by On Dec on the way home. Shit. I brought you food. Let's go eat."

He'd brought her food? For some unfathomable reason—probably the single malt whiskey—the fact that he'd thought of her, just that simple gesture, made her want to cry. She wouldn't, but she'd hold on to that the way others would a kind word or embrace.

"We should have another shot first. Then it'll be like I wasn't drinking alone," she said.

Zach lifted the bottle. "You don't have a glass."

She laughed, and heat zipped up her spine making her forget that she knew all about how workplace romances ended. Maybe they didn't always crash and burn with a guy proposing just to avoid losing a good doctor, but still. It wasn't wise. *And you are? Yup. Older and wiser.* "You too delicate to drink it out of the bottle?"

The lust she'd felt had been reflected tenfold in his gaze earlier, but now he just looked amused. It settled the temporary awkwardness she'd felt. Unscrewing the cap he'd just replaced, he took a quick swig. Stella watched his Adam's apple as he swallowed. She had the urge to move in, go up on tiptoes, and press her mouth to the column of his neck. He lowered the bottle and passed it to her.

Looking up, swallowing down tears so she could choke down the whiskey, she whispered, "Happy birthday, Dad," before taking a drink.

"It's his birthday?" Zach asked, taking the bottle from her.

Stella nodded, staring at his chest. Setting the bottle beside her on the desk, he moved in, and without warning, yanked her into a hard hug.

"Shit. I'm sorry."

All she could do was nod. Being sorry was as useless as tears. But that didn't change the fact that she felt both.

Zach's arms created more warmth than the alcohol. She gave herself one more minute of just letting it all go, and when it was up, she pushed back, away.

"You said you brought food?"

Shoving his hands into his pockets, he smiled. "And money."

"Then you are definitely my favorite person today." They shut the lights off and locked up, walking over the gravel, up to her farmhouse. It sat like a sentinel, watching over the land. White washed with nearly wraparound porches, it looked sturdier than it was. *Kind of like you.* There were repairs and renovations needed. Maybe, if things kept moving forward, she could take care of some of them.

The dogs greeted them with the enthusiasm of long lost friends. Zach laughed when Nacho jumped up, planting his paws right on his chest. It didn't even cause him to step back.

"Down, Nacho. That would have knocked me over completely." Stella laughed, even as the dog wagged his tail and dropped to all fours.

"I'm a little bigger than you," he commented, walking toward the kitchen. Stella followed behind, enjoying the view. He was definitely bigger than her; he was bigger than a lot of people. But he moved with a gentleness that surprised her, like he knew his size alone could intimidate and wouldn't want that.

Still feeling the brave that came with several shots, Stella poked him in the side. "Size isn't everything."

Zach turned—almost in slow motion—and looked down at her with more fire in his eyes than there was whiskey in her belly. When he stroked a hand down her hair, she nearly purred and leaned into it. Sometimes she was so damn tired of looking out for herself. It would be so easy to let him take over...just for tonight as he seemed to want to. But, she knew better than most that it wouldn't last. Nothing did. And she wasn't getting caught up in a whirlwind of emotion and sensation—no matter how great those sensations might be—

just to have the proverbial rug ripped out from under her feet. No thanks. She was better off alone. *Like you have a lot of choice there.*

"You have more heart, despite your size, than most people I've met. If heart counts for size, you have me beat."

Tears filled her eyes and she sniffled. It was strange, how he didn't know her at all, but he knew exactly what to say to make her feel like herself again. Feeling that tug in her belly, the desire to be closer to him, she was about to give in, make another attempt at crossing a line she shouldn't when he dropped his hand and stepped back.

"All right, food, water, and Tylenol, then you need to get some sleep."

She opened one of the takeout bags and snagged a fry. "Pretty sure I don't need a babysitter." Taking the sleeve of fries out, she took the plate he handed her and went to the table.

"You do remember what tomorrow is, right?"

Sitting in one of her ladder-back chairs, she pulled her knee up to her chest and picked at the fries. She wasn't all that hungry, but she appreciated his gesture, so she kept eating.

"Saturday." It was usually one of their busiest days. Zach joined her at the table, his plate loaded with a couple of burgers and fries. He handed her a burger, but she shook her head.

"Brockton Days?"

Stella's shoulders sagged. Shit. How had she forgotten about that? *Because you have eight dozen other things on your plate.*

"It'll be fun. I'm excited."

Rolling her eyes, she finished another fry. "Everyone and their dog, pig, or cat will be there. It's a chaotic free for all."

Taking a large bite of his burger, he grinned around it. "Come on. It's a great opportunity to mingle with the locals and the businesses. Plus, there's games and fried food. How bad can it be? I'll win a big teddy bear for you. And this year, you won't be alone at your booth."

No. She wouldn't be alone this year. *And what about the next?* Best not to think about that, since she still had this one to get through. She thought of a bright spot and grinned back at him.

"You'll meet Charlie and Adam. That's Megan's fiancé and his son. He loves horses as much as you and I do. Charlie, not Adam." She remembered the look of fear on Adam's face the first time he'd climbed onto Chocolate Chip in an effort to show Megan how much he loved her. Would a man ever climb on a horse for her? Her brain was hitting that muddled point between loopy and maudlin.

"I look forward to it. I have to help my mom out as well. She signed me up for a couple of hours at different booths, but I'll still be there to do animal checks with you."

"Which booths?" She didn't get a chance to wander the fair last year as she'd been busy helping her dad. It was a happy memory and made her smile.

Zach dragged a couple of fries through ketchup. "Dunk tank is one, but I'm hoping she was joking about the other."

Stella simply stared and waited.

"I don't remember there being a kissing booth," he said, his voice rather grumbly.

Stella's smile widened. "Oh, there most definitely is." Just because she hadn't wandered the fair didn't mean she didn't hear chatter. "Last year, Jeb Stanson punched Curtis Holden in the nose for kissing Sonja Winston."

Zach leaned back in his chair. "Well, I doubt it'll be that exciting this year."

Zach had left immediately out of high school, and though Stella didn't know what he'd looked like then, she was certain he'd changed, matured, and filled out. He might not think the booth would be exciting, but the women of Brockton Point—particularly the single ones—were going to double their contributions once they got a look at Doctor Zach Mason. Stella pushed her fries away, hoping it was the blend of alcohol on the heels of an emotional day causing her mixed feelings about Zach kissing someone.

"You look done, Doc. You should get to bed."

You really should. Before you do something stupid and ask him not to make you go alone.

· · ·

The Saturday sun greeted Stella several hours before she was ready. Dragging herself out of bed, into a shower, and cursing the invention of alcohol and sexy men who were also sweet, she dressed and went into the clinic. Zach, the show-off, was already there, looking way too happy for the hour and the pounding in her head.

"Morning," he said, looking up from a file he had in his hands.

Stella mumbled something unintelligible and walked to the back room to gather the equipment they'd need for the day. They had two overnight guests. Mr. Wimbly, a gray tabby, and Prickles, a hedgehog. Their respective owners would be there shortly to pick them up. Stella opened Mr. Wimbly's cage, and he yawned through a long meow.

"I feel you, buddy. Did you and Prickles have too much to drink, too?" He arched his back as she stroked his fur. When he lay down, batting at her fingers, she checked the incision site visually and was pleased to see he looked good and wasn't licking.

When she turned, Zach was leaning on the wall watching her with a soft expression she couldn't quite decipher. Her eyes went to the coffee in his hand and she considered tackling him. Her desperation must have shown because he laughed, pushed off the wall, and handed it over.

She appreciated that he didn't try to make conversation before she was ready. They loaded her Cherokee with supplies: pamphlets, treats, training mats, toothbrushes, and signage her father had made years ago that could definitely use some updating. The fairgrounds at the north end of Brockton Point, overlooking the water, not far from where Zach owned property, had held the festival for over twenty years. It was as much a part of the town as the rocky landscape.

Local vendors, food trucks, artists, and anyone with wares to peddle was there, setting up their booths. She drove her Cherokee to the spot she'd been assigned, and she and Zach worked in tandem. A table was provided for them to set up their display items and without a word, they agreed on placement and product choices.

Zach adjusted the signs he'd attached to the table. Stella was thinking about the day she'd spent with her dad last year. He'd been trying to get her to open up about her breakup while she'd dodged most of the questions.

"Hey, you okay?"

Stella glanced over, her head feeling clearer than it had earlier. "I'm good. Thanks for the fries and burgers last night. I don't think I said that."

"You're welcome. I'll have the money in your account by midweek, so while I'm kissing strangers, you should think about us making things more permanent," he said, his lips tipped up in a quirky smile.

"No wonder you're single," his mom said, coming up behind him. She had a clipboard in one hand and a ball cap on her head, along with an official looking badge that read: STAFF.

Stella was positive Sheila would have cuffed his head if she could reach it. Just her tone made Stella smile.

"Hey, Mom," Zach said in a monotone voice that just made Stella's grin bigger.

"Hi." She arched her neck so he could kiss her cheek and the warmth filling Stella's chest had nothing to do with whiskey or the aftereffects of it.

Sheila patted his arm and then came to Stella, arms open. "You're not just Chuck's vet anymore," she said, referring to her dog and pulling Stella into a hug. Apparently, the Masons were huggers.

When Stella pulled back, she looked at Zach. "I never even thought for your mom's to be one of the files I passed over to you, but I will."

Zach's grin was quick and cheeky. "No way. She'll make me work for free."

Laughing, she waved to one of the vendors across the way. "Pretty sure that's what I'm paying you, too."

"Okay," Sheila said, consulting her clipboard. "I have you on the kissing booth at two. Traffic tends to be heaviest around then. You can go from there to the dunk tank." Sheila smiled at her son and then looked at Stella. "I'm sure Zach could cover you if you want to take part in another booth. Maybe the kissing booth? It might be our moneymaker this year."

She started to laugh and say no, but Zach cut her off with a sound that was a cross between a grumble and a growl.

"That is *not* a good idea."

Both women stared at him, and though she had no intention of letting Brockton's selection of grumpy old men donate a dollar a kiss, she arched her brows and crossed her arms over her chest.

"And why is that?"

His mouth opened and closed. Then he looked at his mother and communicated his dislike of the idea with just his eyes. Stella was partially amused. And a little...pleased.

So he didn't want her to kiss someone? Interesting. Maybe she wasn't the only one who felt something last night. She didn't think she was, but most men would have given in to the moment and kissed her. Not Zach. So maybe the thought of her kissing someone else got under his skin. *You don't need to be anywhere near his skin! What do you care if he cares? He's your part— Oh my God, no he's not. He's your colleague. Nothing more. Nothing less.* He just happened to be the one who held her when she felt like she might fall apart, the one who brought her dinner because he was thinking of her, the one who called her on her attitude and made her laugh.

"I'm going to grab some donuts and coffee before people show up." Zach stalked off toward Food Row.

Sheila turned her body and regarded Stella with a curious gaze. "I'm happy enough he's home to stay. Understand that. There's nothing like being thousands of miles away from your child. It sucks in ways you can't possibly imagine. Knowing he was that far away, originally, because he was hurting after the loss of his friend only made it worse. So having him home is a dream come true. Literally. But now you've given him roots when he's been floating around trying to figure out where to land. That's icing on the cake. But the way he's looking at you? The respect I have for you and had for your father? That would be an entire tub of whip cream on top of what is already the most delicious dessert a mother could ask for."

Stella rounded the table, touched and concerned. "Sheila, Zach and I are colleagues. I don't know what you saw, but we're just…friends. I'm grateful to him and I think…" She stopped, staring in the direction Zach had gone. She hadn't admitted this to him yet, but she looked at his mom and shared her thoughts. "I think it's going to be a really good long-term match." Which meant anything other than friendship and a working relationship was out of the question.

Zach's mom gave her a look that Stella couldn't quite

decipher, but she thought it held a bit of amusement. Shaking her head, she squeezed her arm and tapped her clipboard. "I'll catch up with you later, sweetie. Hope your day goes well."

Stella busied herself with moving things around the table, only to put them back where they'd started. Sinking into the metal folding chair, she looked around at the other people rushing around. Laughter rang out, along with some hammering and the hum of many voices. She'd almost given this up. Even without her father, it felt right to be part of this age-old event. But there'd been a moment, when she thought she'd found her forever, that she'd considered not coming home. The idea never sat right, and when she'd pushed her fiancé to see her point of view, he'd shared his own.

He'd shattered her heart and her confidence, telling her that he had never wanted to marry her. That he thought they were a good match, good *partners,* and he liked sleeping with her. Who the hell said that? He *liked* sleeping with her? She'd nearly smacked him for that one, and then it registered that they'd never wanted the same things, and she'd almost given up all she'd worked for and thrown it away on a once-respected mentor turned crush turned so much more. She knew the rumor around town was that she had been left standing at the altar, but like most small-town gossip, it was only partially rooted in truth. There'd been no altar. Just a broken engagement and stone wall built around Stella's heart.

She'd gotten in her car that afternoon and while driving, she realized not only was she not that person for *him,* she might never be that for anyone. Learning that mixing business and pleasure meant when one ended, so did the other had been a lousy side effect.

"You're thinking way too hard, Doc," Zach said, setting coffee and a large honey crueler in front of her. As if on cue, her stomach growled.

"Thanks," she said, not looking up. He had this weird ability to see too much and she wasn't sure what her gaze would reveal just now.

"So, was it busy last year?" Zach took the chair beside her and they settled into an easy conversation that chased away the bad memories and useless regrets. When people started showing up, coming by with their pets to get free advice and samples, everything else fell away. They worked well, side by side, agreeing on many of the same tips and suggestions. When it was time for Zach to head to the kissing booth, Stella almost asked him not to go. Instead, she pulled her bag out from under the table and unzipped it.

"You're not even going to wish me luck?" Zach's grumpy look matched how Stella was feeling, but she just shook out the T-shirt she pulled from her bag and grinned.

"Aw. You want me to feel sorry for you because a gaggle of women are going to be throwing money down to kiss you? No way. But, since you'll be the center of attention, we should advertise."

She held up the shirt that read: LANE VETERINARY CLINIC. Zach's scowl deepened, and he grabbed the shirt, tugging it out of her hand.

"Is gaggle even a word?"

She bit her lip, trying not to smile. "Pretty sure it is, but I could be wrong. It might be you'll have a horde of women."

"Is that more than a gaggle?" He yanked off his T-shirt, revealing washboard abs—the kind she'd only read about—and rendered her speechless. She stared at the sculpted flesh, imagined running her fingers up over the curves and lines.

Her lips parted, and her breathing slowed. Not her heart though. It revved up like she'd pulled a string and set it free. She'd obviously seen a six pack before, and she knew he had great arms, but good God, he should have given her a warning. Given everyone a warning. Just a heads up or a *hey,*

I'm about to make you salivate. He tugged the other shirt over his head and she immediately missed the sight of those cut abs and defined pecs. He had a light dusting of chest hair, the same color as his head, but not nearly as thick and she wondered if it was soft.

"You don't close your mouth, something might fly in," Zach said. He walked over to the table, tossing his shirt on the chair where he'd been sitting. When he leaned down, into Stella's breathing space, she slammed her lips together.

"There you go. You okay, Doc?"

She nodded, her eyes narrowing because there was no way—humble or not—that he didn't know how mouthwateringly good he looked. Unless he'd never seen a mirror. Or looked down. Jesus.

"You going to come by and pay for a kiss?" His words were teasing and husky and snapped her out of her ab-induced trance.

Stepping back, she laughed too loud to sound natural. "You wish."

His eyes heated, going darker. "If you change your mind, I'll give you a good deal."

He was out of her line of vision by the time her pulse returned to normal. *Normal. Ha!* She wasn't even sure what that looked like anymore.

Chapter Twelve

I'm hungry. That's it. I've been sitting here for twenty minutes by myself. I'm allowed to take a break, wander the fair, say hello to people. Excuses. Everything Stella said to herself was an excuse. She wanted to see who was paying to have Zach's lips on theirs. Leaving a sign that said "back soon," she detoured to grab some food first. *That's right. Stick to your story.*

With a hot dog in one hand and a large cola in the other, she made her way through the crowd. Her eyes were drawn to the table of bracelets and other trinkets handmade by a local artist she loved. The pottery called to her and she thought about picking up the vibrant blue bowl that would look amazing in her kitchen. But she kept walking, saying and nodding hello.

Laughter trickled through the crowd like a waterfall coming at her from all sides, and she forced herself to roll her shoulders, loosen the knots there. It was past time she not only start attending these events but enjoying them. For so long now, she felt like she'd been ghosting through the moments in her life. There in body but not in spirit. Now, with Zach, she could take a deep enough breath to start living again. To some degree.

She saw the lineup for the kissing booth and stopped in her tracks. *Holy hell. The line was never this long for Curtis Holden.* Of course, he was nearing sixty, balding, and had a beard like Santa Claus.

"Stella!" Charlie's voice called out through a part in the crowd and he came running.

Bracing for impact, she was ready for him when his arms wrapped around her waist. Megan and Adam followed behind, hand in hand. Stella grinned and lifted her cola as a greeting.

"How you doing?" she asked Charlie, kissing the top of his wavy brown hair. She inhaled the scent of his soap and smiled wider. She knew how much he balked at taking a shower or a bath.

At nearly nine, he was almost as tall as her. He craned his neck back and smiled a gap-toothed grin. "I'm good. Meg said we could come out and see Chocolate Chip soon and she said there's another doctor working with you."

He stepped back, eyeing her hot dog. She wasn't actually hungry, so she handed it over and greeted Adam and Megan when they came closer.

"I see you're all caught up on the news," she said, ruffling his hair. She looked at her friend and fiancé. "You guys been here long?"

Megan smiled and glanced over her shoulder. "Nope. But, apparently, we came at the right time. Looks like the kissing booth is quite the attraction."

Adam's brow furrowed, and he looked down at Megan, making her laugh and go up on tiptoes to kiss his cheek. "Not for me. Just for the other women of Brockton Point."

"Nice save," Adam said, pulling her back to kiss her lips.

Charlie hooked his thumb at them and leaned into Stella. "They're always kissing. No one even pays them to."

All three adults laughed, but Stella's eyes wandered to the lineup. There were several grandmotherly types, but there was a good portion of women her age. *Good. Maybe one of them will take him off the market and then I won't be so tempted.*

"You paying for a kiss?" Megan asked as they walked around the back of the lineup.

Stella's stomach twirled, and she made an exaggerated scoffing sound that she knew was a dead giveaway. Megan arched her brows, a knowing smile tipped her lips up.

Stella stiffened her shoulders and tried to appear unaffected. "Of course not. Even if he wasn't an employee, I wouldn't. Who wants to kiss a guy after he gets through with a horde of women?" She gestured to the line and something tickled the back of her mind, a memory from last night.

Adam glanced over. "Looks like there's a lot of people who would want to."

She scowled but he was as unfazed as Megan. They were enjoying this. Unable to look away when they got closer to the front of the booth—not from standing in line, but from moving up to the table beside the kissing booth that was selling books. Zach caught her eye from where he stood laughing heartily at whatever Mrs. Portinni was saying. The heavy-set woman was old when Stella was a girl and even though she must be nearing eighty, she acted and looked like she was in her fifties. She tapped her cheek and Zach pressed his lips there, laughing when she tried to shove a dollar bill toward him.

"You already paid," he said. He winked at Stella.

She was about to...what? She didn't know what she was about to do, but everything stopped for a moment when Lydia Rae Simpson waltzed up to the booth, her pouty lips more than ready for the press of Zach's. Stella's stomach turned, and it wasn't amusing anymore.

"Meg, look, it's a copy of Origami Yoda," Charlie said behind her.

Megan was standing beside Stella, a solid presence who understood just how much she disliked this woman.

"Do you have that one, bud?" Adam asked behind them. It felt like she was in a circle where she could see out, but no one could see in. No one could see the way her heart kicked her in the ribs as Lydia teasingly flashed a twenty-dollar bill.

"I think he needs to make this one worth it, don't you guys?" Lydia turned her body and waved the crisp bill. The lineup hooted and hollered, some of them laughing, a few of them chanting "make it worth it."

"You okay?" Megan whispered into her ear, breaking Stella's trance.

Zach's eyes trapped hers like a vice—maybe even the same one that squeezed her heart painfully. *Your heart has no rights here.*

Stella shook her head and looked at her friend. "I need to get back to the pet booth. Come see me when you guys are done, okay?"

She didn't wait for an answer, but instead pushed through the crowd, making sure she didn't have to watch Lydia's bitchy lips touch any part of Zach.

Nearly back to her table, Stella ran into a brick wall, or what felt like one. Strong hands gripped her shoulders, and when she tipped her head back, she was staring up at Declan James's handsome face.

"Hey, Stell. How's it going?"

Pasting a smile so wide it hurt her face, she said, "Great. Good. I should have figured you'd be here, too."

Dropping his hands, but not moving back, he looked out at the crowd. "It's about the easiest day of advertising

ever. I sit back and drink beer with people. Can't beat that."
He looked around, not picking up on her mood thankfully.
Maybe she had an ounce of professionalism left in her blood
despite all the jealousy zipping through it.

Looking back at her, he asked, "You getting lots of
drop-ins? There's a lot of new faces in the crowd," Declan
said. He wore a T-shirt and jeans, his hair the kind of messy
that always looked good. Unfortunately, the thought of him
kissing someone—and if rumors were true, he did a lot of that
and more—didn't bug her at all.

"It's been steady. I was just grabbing a drink," she said,
holding up her cola as proof.

"You should drop by for a beer later. On the house."

A beer sounded good. A lot better than whiskey. She
didn't get to tell him, though, because Zach walked up beside
her and looked at Declan. They were about the same height
and similarly built. Looking back and forth between them,
she wondered if the two of them behind the kissing booth
might cause heart attacks or swoon overload in the women of
Brockton Point.

"You keep giving your beer away, you're going to lose
money," Zach said. His tone sounded friendly enough, but he
sidled up to Stella so their arms were touching.

Declan, unbothered even if he did notice Zach's territorial
stance, stuck out his hand. "Hey, man. Good to see you."

Zach shook his hand and Stella avoided looking at him as
she asked, "You two know each other?"

"Zach came into the bar last night. Haven't seen you
there in a while. Not since Meg's graduation. All work and no
play kinda sucks."

The heat coming off Zach's body took the chill out of her
own. "Been a little busy."

People milled around them, and she realized they were
standing in the middle of what was supposed to be an aisle.

All she really wanted to do was get back to the table, away from Zach and Declan and the tumble of feelings assaulting her heart. *Again, with the heart.*

"You need to get some help, Stella. You can't keep running on empty." Declan's voice went all big brothery, but Zach must not have recognized the tone because he put a hand on the small of her back and moved even closer.

"She has it. I'm working with her now. She won't have to push herself so hard anymore."

Declan's surprise was evident. "You're a vet?"

Word was going to travel anyway. Might as well help it along. "Yes. He is." She stopped, thought for a second. "He's actually an Army vet as well as an animal doctor. He's working with me temporarily. Speaking of which, I need to get back to my table. Nice to see you, Dec." Finally, she looked up at Zach. The usual smile and casual expression he wore was nowhere to be found. "You should get back to the booth. Wouldn't want to disappoint all of those women."

Slipping past both of them, she hurried back to the table and was beyond grateful that there was a woman browsing through her pamphlets. The black-and-white shih-zhu she held on a leash danced at the sight of Stella.

"Doctor Lane, there you are. Mitsy and I were wondering when you'd be back."

Stella flipped over the sign she'd left, grateful she had a distraction. "How are you, Mrs. Hardy?" Kneeling, she clicked her tongue, then smiled at the dog. "Hey, girl. How are you?"

"She's doing so well. Those dental chews you recommended have been working wonders on her teeth."

Pushing up the dog's lips to check for herself, Stella nodded with approval. "Very little plaque. How about a treat?"

Grabbing one from the bowl on the table, she made Mitsy

sit and then gave her the treat along with encouragement and rubs.

Stella brushed off her jeans when she stood up. "Sorry I don't have cookies to offer the humans."

She felt Zach's presence before he rounded the table. Mrs. Hardy straightened and gave Zach a smile. He, in turn, crouched down to greet the dog.

"Who is this handsome man?" No one spent a lot of time beating around bushes in their town.

Once he'd greeted the pup, Zach stood, glancing at Stella before extending his hand. "Doctor Zach Mason. I'm working with Doctor Lane now."

Mrs. Hardy beamed. "That's wonderful. I always wondered why your father didn't bring on anyone else. Some people thought he just liked being on his own," she said, shaking Zach's hand.

They chatted back and forth for a few minutes, but Stella lost the thread of the conversation. When Mrs. Hardy walked off with Mitsy, she busied herself rearranging the pamphlets.

"Temporary?" Zach bit out the word.

She grabbed the dog treats and filled up the bowl. "We haven't made anything official."

He stepped into her path. "I'd say my money transferring into your account shores things up a little. What the hell was that?"

Looking up at him now, she was surprised by the frustrated set of his brows and his mouth. No calm there now. "What are you talking about?"

He leaned closer. "You know exactly what I'm talking about. The snooty bank woman started flashing her money around making sure everyone was watching. The only person I'm looking at is you and your face looks like I just punched you right in the stomach."

Dammit. He was entirely too observant. She tried to

step around him as she avoided his gaze. "I don't know what you're talking about. You're free to kiss whomever you want. And I don't care what you charge them."

Way to go. You even sound like you mean it. Zach put his hands on her arms and unlike when Declan had done the same, her heart tripled its pace.

"Good to know, Doc. Just so we're clear, there's no charge for this," he said.

Before she could even process the words, he'd tipped her chin up and his mouth was on hers in a hard, demanding kiss that stole her breath. His lips were soft, and after the initial touch, he gentled, his hands smoothing up her arms and finding their way into her hair, tangling there and anchoring her to him. Stella put her hands on his wrists. They didn't even wrap all the way around. She was losing herself, finding herself, in the feel of his lips moving against her own. She sighed and would have sunk into him, given up fighting the attraction she'd felt from the second she'd laid eyes on him, if a little voice hadn't interrupted.

"Ew. Now they're doing it. I thought there was only one kissing booth," Charlie said.

Zach pulled back slowly, and his eyes burned so bright she was surprised her skin wasn't on fire. Flustered and turned on, she stepped back, short of breath. Megan and Adam stared with amused grins and Charlie looked like he'd just eaten a bouquet of lemons.

Yes. Word would travel quickly, she thought. And now, they'd given the gossips something to say. With her lips still tingling—yes, actually tingling—from the heat of his, she couldn't bring herself to regret it just yet.

But she was almost positive she would.

Chapter Thirteen

Zach wasn't a risk taker by nature. Even after enlisting, he'd done what he had his whole life—measured the odds and outcomes and made choices using his gut. There was a difference between that and laying things on the line...taking a chance. As he pulled away from Stella, her taste still on his lips and his tongue, he wondered if, this time, the reward was worth the risk. Jesus. He'd never felt that much over a simple kiss in his life. Not that it had been simple. No. Because, one, it was Stella and there was nothing fucking simple about this woman. Two, because they had an avid audience, and three, because this town traded gossip like currency and he knew she wouldn't want to be part of that. *And four, you work for her, you idiot. This was the exact thing you were supposed to avoid. If you could avoid it last night while she was looking at you with those gorgeous fucking eyes and delectable fucking lips, you should have been able to walk away this time.*

But he didn't regret it. Couldn't when the fire was still burning in his gut and her gaze. Definitely not when sealing his mouth against hers had felt like he was finally where he was meant to be. He wasn't some dreamy-eyed sap who attached meaning to every little thing, but there was no way he could write that kiss off as nothing. Even though he had a feeling she would. And that they both should.

"Is that your boyfriend, Stella?" the little kid standing in front of the table asked. Zach presumed this was the infamous Charlie. He turned, giving both him and Stella the physical space they needed. Holding out his hand, he shook the little guy's hand first.

"You must be Charlie. I'm Zach. I work with Stella." Charlie beamed a cute grin at him, easing some of the tension out of his body. He held out a hand to the man standing beside Megan.

"Zach Mason."

Eyes a little cool, definitely assessing, he offered his hand. "Adam Klein."

"The fiancé," Zach said.

Adam looked down at Megan, who looked as adorable today as she had the other day when she'd shown up at the clinic, and ran a hand down her hair with so much affection that Zach's stomach tightened. He wanted that. He wanted the familiarity, the closeness, the certainty that there was a person made for him. Preferably, one who could rock his world with just a kiss. *Not Stella. Not Stella. Not Stella. That's right. Keep telling yourself that.*

Glancing over at her, he wondered what she was thinking. Had he embarrassed her in front of her friends? He'd booked it out of the kissing booth when he saw her face go paler than vanilla ice cream, and when he'd found her, she'd been standing too damn close to a guy he thought he could be friends with. But seeing Declan so close to Stella hadn't made him feel friendly. Instead, it made him feel possessive as fuck and he didn't like the feeling. Apparently, it made him lose his mind and kiss the woman he was trying to build a long-term business relationship with. *Stupid, stupid, stupid. She was already looking for any excuse to throw her walls up.*

"Adam, you and Zach went to school at the same time. He's old, like you," Megan said, grinning up at her guy.

He tapped her nose with his index finger and muttered, "Good thing you're cute." He looked at Zach. "You went to Brockton High?"

Not wanting to talk about his school days or his past, Zach nodded and looked at the time. He cut off any further conversation by announcing, "I have to go do an hour in the dunk tank. Remind me to say no next year."

Stella looked at him, her gaze unreadable. "I'm sure it wasn't all that bad."

Shoving his hands into his pockets so he didn't reach out and pull her close, he shook his head. On his way around the table, he leaned down to speak to Charlie.

"I hear you like horses."

The perma-grin the kid wore widened. "I love them. My dad doesn't, but he's getting better around them now."

Zach grinned up at Adam, then back at his kid. "We're going to be getting a couple more at the farm."

"Really?" This was said in unison by Adam, Megan, and Charlie.

"We're looking into the possibility. I think you're going to be late," Stella said.

"We'll be looking for someone to help us brush them and feed them if you know anyone," he said to Charlie.

As expected, the kid's eyes went huge. "I could do that. I help with C.C. when I'm there. Right, Stella? I help a lot."

Stella's frown finally faded, and she gave Charlie a warm smile. "You do, bud. You're a great help. We'll talk about it more after we get the other horses, okay?"

Zach was happy to leave on a better note than he'd shown up on. The last two days had been a freaking see-saw where

Stella was concerned, and he knew it was going to be even harder to keep his distance. She got to him on every level without even trying. Maybe getting dunked in a bucket of cold water was exactly what he needed.

• • •

He didn't want tension simmering between them like a boiling pot. Stella had given him the keys at the end of the day, after they'd loaded the Cherokee, and crawled into the passenger side. The wordless gesture got to him nearly as much as the kiss. She wasn't a woman who gave up control or asked for anything. She was tired, possibly hung over, and he wasn't even sure that they weren't both mad at each other. If they were, he wasn't entirely sure why. He knew why he was mad at himself. So much for discipline and long-term planning. It had been more than a little while since he'd gotten close to a woman. He'd dated in the last couple of years, but nothing more than casual hook ups and having a good time. Neither of those involved reading into every little thing. *You're going to drive yourself nuts.* But, she'd needed something—even if it was only something as small as a reprieve from driving home—and she'd counted on him. She'd *asked* him for help. Sort of. *You're kind of making a big deal of her tossing her keys at you.* But since she had, he was taking charge.

She didn't notice until he passed the exit for her place.

"Where are we going?" She sat up straighter and turned her head to look at him. He glanced over. God, he liked the way she looked at him. Always a little on guard, like there was never a simple answer. He wanted to break down that guard and be the one who made her sure.

"Home." He smiled and looked back at the road. Only a few cars shared the space with them and she stayed quiet until he took the next exit, rounding the corner that would lead them back to Stella's.

She poked him in the shoulder with her index finger. "You forget to take the exit, Rookie?"

He laughed, happy she was relaxed. He took the road he knew would lead to an area of her property that had untapped potential. The sky was growing dark with the stars beginning to peek out. He'd missed that when he lived in the city. Today had been a long day, but there was enough light for them to get where they were going.

"You think I'm lost?" His chest tightened, a quick, hard spasm as he thought he hadn't felt more at home—more *found*— anywhere than he did beside this woman when he'd chipped away at that hard, gorgeous outer shell.

"You took the wrong exit," she said.

"On purpose, and this goes to your property."

She was quiet while he drove, the road getting bumpier as he turned down a path that wasn't used by anyone. Hopefully, he wouldn't get them stuck. He'd come out this far on one of her ATVs the other night while she'd been pouring over bills. Zach hated seeing the worry that furrowed her brow every time she did that activity.

"This is the edge of your land," he said, pulling to a stop in the middle of nowhere. Trees surrounded them, the path barely wide enough for her jeep.

"I know." There was no hiding the curiosity in her tone.

Zach turned off the vehicle and got out. He planned on opening her door, but she was out before he could. He stood at the front of her Jeep and crooked his finger. "Come here."

She narrowed her eyes at him and stood her ground, making him smile.

Taking a deep breath, he saw that crease in her forehead that meant she was overthinking things. "Zach. What happened earlier can't happen again," she said. Her voice was clear and calm, like crystal in the quiet of the forest.

He knew that. They worked together and though he didn't know her story, he knew enough about life to know mixing business and pleasure, especially a very tiny business where they'd be glued at the hip, had the potential to end poorly. He tried to joke his way out of having a conversation he didn't want to have. "You mean you getting jealous of my kissing another woman?"

Her mouth dropped open like she couldn't believe he'd said that. Then she rolled her eyes and huffed out a half laugh, half breath. "The kissing in general."

Zach nodded. She was right. Didn't mean he had to like it.

"I know. I get it. I didn't mean for it to happen today. I'd like to think I'm not the only one who's been fighting whatever this is between us. But I also know that we want different things. My main priority is making you see what we could have together. Professionally."

She continued to stare at him, and he wasn't sure what to make of her expression. Would she admit that she was pushing down her own feelings?

"What are we doing here, Zach?"

Of course not. Stella Lane, admit weakness? "I'll tell you if you come here and trust me for five seconds." He didn't want to be pissed that the only thing she had to say about the kiss that had rocked his world, was "never again." He didn't think either of them believed it, but he'd leave it alone for now. *This is what you want. Stop being a jackass. You don't want this complication.*

Stella walked to the front of her vehicle like she was on a plank over an alligator-filled body of water.

When she was in front of him, he reached for her and paused. "I'm going to lift you onto the hood of the jeep. Then I'll climb up beside you. Don't argue."

She started to, but he did as he said, putting his hands

on her hips, loving the feel of them, and boosted her up. Her hands came to his shoulders, gripped there, and then she was on the hood. He jumped up beside her so they were sitting side by side.

"We going to stare at the stars? I'm not making out with you."

He pushed back, leaned on the windshield, and grinned. "Again. You mean you're not making out with me *again*."

She looked up at the sky. "I'm pretending you didn't say that."

"Mature," he said, liking the way her lips curved up as he stared at her profile. "We could look at the stars if we wait for it to get darker. You ever sit still long enough to do something so peaceful?"

He wouldn't admit, not out loud, that she was the kind of woman who made a man want to look at the stars. Maybe even wish on them.

She was perpetual motion in human form. Part of him wondered if that was because standing still, *stopping,* hurt. He knew the feeling. After Travis had died, he couldn't stop to breathe or it crushed him. So, he'd packed up, run off, and put every angry, hurt feeling away in a box and focused on the future. On moving forward. Over time, he'd had to unpack those feelings, sort through them, and give himself time to fall apart.

He looked over at Stella where she sat, breathing in the fresh air, her hair loose around her shoulders. Had she ever given herself the luxury of falling apart? It hadn't been that long since her father died. Those kinds of cracks in someone's heart didn't fade quickly, if ever.

"How you feeling, Doc?"

Stella turned her head to look at him. "Tired."

He feigned shock. "I thought superheroes didn't get tired."

She turned her head and those gorgeous lips tipped up. The smile felt almost as intimate as their kiss. Fuck. He was in big trouble if a couple stars, a gorgeous woman, and the tilt of her mouth were turning him inside out and making him forget the reason he was here.

"I'm hardly a superhero. That would be you, Mr. Army Sergeant, Defender of Animals everywhere."

She looked away, staring out at her property, but Zach couldn't take his eyes off her.

"Your dad was mine," he said quietly.

Her quiet intake of breath was not lost on him. It nearly echoed in the silence. Turning her head slowly, she whispered, "Really?"

Zach nodded. His throat tight. "Him and the guy that used to be mayor when I was a kid. That's probably dumb."

Stella bit her lip and he looked down at her hand, resting on the hood of her Cherokee. He wanted to reach out and take it, entwine their fingers.

"It's not dumb. Why?"

"Hmm?" He looked up at her again.

"Why were they your heroes?"

You really do not know how to get to the point. How do you get on these tangents? Focus! But he couldn't not answer her. "They saw the good in people even when it was buried so deep you'd need an excavator to get it out. Your dad made me feel like I mattered at a time when I wasn't sure I did."

Tears filled her eyes, and he forgot to keep his distance. He caught the first one on his thumb as he cupped her cheek. "I didn't mean to make you cry."

She sniffled and smiled through watery eyes. "It's the good kind. He'd have been happy to know that."

"I thought I'd come back and maybe convince him to let me work at his side. I never expected you," Zach admitted.

Stella's breath caught. He heard the snag and he wanted,

with every molecule in his being, to lean over and take her mouth in a kiss that would drown them both.

The air pulsed between them. Or maybe his heart was just working its way out of his chest. He looked at her lips, then back up to her eyes. Seeing the turmoil in her gaze had him dropping his hand. He'd never cause her pain. He might not have kept his hands off her like he'd told himself to, but he promised himself, right this second, that he wouldn't be responsible for the uncertainty on her face.

"What are we doing, Zach?"

"We're sitting on your Jeep on your land, under a sky that'll soon be filled with stars. We're being grateful."

"Okay. For something in particular, or life in general?"

He wanted to take her hand, but he knew they had to redraw the line. He wanted to be her partner, and she wasn't the type to be okay with gray areas. Not without a lot of resistance. He figured there was a reason, but before she'd ever tell him, he had to show her that he was someone she could count on. That together, they'd turn things around and maybe she could take a break from staring at the pile of obligations that was dropped on her shoulders along with the weight of her father's death.

"That, sure. But, also, I'm grateful you're giving me a chance. That you've let me in. Not just to your home and your practice, but maybe even your life. At least a little bit."

She was quiet a moment and then she pulled her knees up to her chest, wrapped her arms around them. "I'm grateful, Zach. I didn't want to need anyone. Still don't. But in a very short period of time, you've made my life easier. I'm not always receptive to help. You bulldozed over that, and I'm the one who is benefiting from it."

Curling his fingers into fists so he didn't reach out, didn't touch her, he sat up. "We're both going to benefit. This land? You never use it. It's here, but untouched."

She frowned, and her shoulders stiffened. "Those bills I pour through constantly? There's a way to make them all go away. My father had multiple offers to buy pieces of his land. To sell it off chunk by chunk until it was a very lucrative puzzle full of pieces that no longer belonged to him. He didn't do it. And I won't, either, Zach. No outside sources. I let you in. You clearly caught me at the right time, and I don't have so much pride that I can't admit that I'm lucky you did. We'll turn things around, but I won't sell off parts of this place so that some big shot investor can throw some condos or box stores down."

So she had received offers. Not surprising. "I wouldn't ask you to. That's not why we're here."

She put her head on her knees, turned so she could look at him. It was hard for him not to want to pull her closer, wrap his arms around her.

"Why then?"

Zach pointed to the trees. "You don't have to sell the land, but if we clear some of it, sell the lumber, we'd bring in some serious coin."

Sitting up, she looked around. "What?"

He couldn't hide his smile. "You don't have to let it all go to get something out of it. I've looked into buyers, and I figure if we clear even five acres, we can bring in some money. Every little bit counts, right? Plus, moving forward, if you have this land cleared, we can consider—and don't shut me down here—renting some of it."

He'd spent a lot of nights thinking about this. Stella looked around at the trees, like she was seeing them for the first time.

"Who wants to rent this?"

"There are several farms around here busting at the seams. We have options, Stella. *You* have options. I know you don't want big business in here, I get that. I did the big business thing for a while with Pet Central. It was great for the time being, but really, it let me save up for what I really wanted."

"The property by the water?"

He smiled. "Definitely that. Sometimes, thinking about the house I'd build on that piece of land was all that kept me going. I have a rental property as well, but that land is the thing I consider mine. My tie to this town. I grew up wishing I had a stake in this place, literally and figuratively. Like your father did. Like you do."

She waited so he continued.

"I had an opportunity to stay with Pet Central. I came to you because it's not what I want either. But we've got options if you're willing to explore them."

Her demeanor visibly changed, like the little bit of hope he'd given her filled her with a tangible energy. *Perpetual energy*, he thought again. She smiled at him.

"All this because my dad was nice to you?"

"It was more than that. My family didn't have a lot of money. I don't want to rehash the past, but let's just say it can be hard on a kid when they're judged for something they can't change. I always felt like I was on the outside, and in a town like this, that's the same as not existing. I had my mom, but until my dad died, she had her hands full and I never wanted to be a burden to her. I had your dad. He made me feel like I was part of something. Like Travis did. But then Trav died." His jaw clenched, and he stopped talking. If he wanted her trust, he had to go all in. As much as he could, anyway. "My best friend died, and I felt like it was my fault. I couldn't stand it, so I left. But even when I ran, I knew I'd be back. My mom is here. My home is here. Your father was important to me and more than that, he made me feel like I mattered. One day, Brockton is going to be big enough there'll be other vets in town. Hell, we might even get a Costco. But right now, in this moment, you have the monopoly on taking care of animals. If I want to be here and I want to be a vet, I need you to want me. To need me. I'm trying to find a way to make you need me so I can stay and be part of what your father built. Of what you're trying to keep going."

He pushed off the hood because he couldn't be beside her, baring his soul, *and* sit still.

Stella pushed to the edge of the hood, her feet dangling, and he turned, stared at her, sitting there in the almost moonlight. He never thought about karma or kismet, like he'd suggested the other night, but he knew, in his gut and his heart, that he was meant to be right here, by her side. Maybe he didn't know all the reasons yet, but he trusted his gut. They were going to build something together. And it was going to be fucking magnificent.

"I didn't want to let anyone in. That's hard for me because people leave. I don't want to rehash the past, either, but let's just say I don't have a whole lot of faith in long term. Or forever. Or things working out in some predestined way. But I like that you have a connection to my father because I'm scared I didn't have enough of one. I thought there was plenty of time. I could go away to school, come back, and grow old learning from him. Maybe even teach him a thing or two. But then he died without warning and I realized how alone I am. Trying to keep this place going, that's the only connection to him I can focus on now. I feel like he'd be happy you're here. So if you want it on paper, I'll do that. We'll negotiate, and I'll obviously take the bigger share, because by now you've figured out I need the control. But I don't need it all. Not if you're serious."

He stepped closer, stopping short of moving between her knees. "I've never been more serious. This isn't some passing whim. I want this, Stella. With you."

Her breath hitched, and he moved in just a little more.

"This business. You want the business."

Zach could only nod as her eyes messed with the cadence of his heart. Fuck. He wanted more than that. Really wanted it. But he'd take what he could get.

"Yes," he said, his throat suddenly raw.

"Just you and me. No one else, Zach. My dad didn't bring in others, so we don't either. I like the ideas you've come up with. They're good. They're tangible, but the best part of them is that we don't have to rely on anyone other than us."

He thought of Andrew's check, which he'd already cashed and transferred. Worry gnawed at his gut. That was different. Even her father had taken a loan. He hadn't sold out, but he'd taken that stupid balloon mortgage that was half the reason she was so far in debt.

"Just us," he promised. He took her hand in his, squeezed. "Just us, Stella."

He liked the sound of that too much, even knowing she'd only let it be business. He could imagine what they'd be, on every level, if she dropped those shields. *One step at a time.*

"Okay, then."

She inched a little closer, her lips hitching up in a smile. "Partner," she whispered.

Chapter Fourteen

The following Sunday, Stella was awoken by two things simultaneously: her phone ringing, and the sound of her ride-on lawn mower. Blinking herself awake, she startled when she saw the clock said it was after nine. She never slept in. She didn't even set an alarm because her busy brain always woke her by dawn.

Her phone kept ringing and she sat up, grabbing it off the charger beside her bed. It was Parker, Megan's brother.

"Hey, Parker," Stella said, her voice still rough and sleepy.

"Hey. You sleeping?" The surprise in his voice matched her own.

"Just woke up. How's it going?" Stella threw back the covers and got out of bed. Walking to the window, she saw Zach on her mower, zigzagging around her overgrown yard. Nacho and Soda chased after him, and she smiled at their enthusiasm.

"Good. I wondered if you'd grabbed the steaks because I'm at the store and there's a wicked sale," he said.

Stella flipped through her memory and cringed.

"Dammit. I didn't. I forgot." She hoped he thought she meant the steaks, but the truth was, it had slipped her mind that she'd invited Parker, his husband Garrett, Meg, Adam, and Charlie over for a BBQ.

"No worries. I'll grab them. Six of us?"

Stella watched as Zach did circles on the lawn mower. She laughed when the dogs followed his path. "Seven, actually."

"Oh yeah? I heard you've got a man in your life," Parker said, his tone somewhere between teasing and big-brotherish.

"I hired someone to help out with my practice," she replied, moving away from the window to grab some clothes.

"Uh-huh. I heard he's pretty easy to look at."

Stella rolled her eyes, wondering if it was Megan who'd told him. "He's an excellent vet."

"Okay. So, seven?"

She paused, thinking about Zach and the fact that he was outside mowing her lawn. And enjoying it. *You slept in for the first time in years.* Though she wasn't normally impulsive, Stella went with her gut.

"Can we make it eleven?"

"How many men do you have there?"

Stella laughed. "I'm going to invite Zach's mom and her boyfriend, and I figured we should invite Dec and Taylor, too."

"We could make it an engagement party," Parker suggested.

"Aw. You're the sweetest big brother."

"I consider myself yours, too, sweetheart, so you can fully expect me to grill more than the steaks tonight."

"I'll take care of the side dishes. See you later, Parks."

"I mean it."

Her heart smiled. "I know you do."

Stella pushed down the emotions swamping her and texted Declan and Taylor before phoning Sheila and asking if she'd like to join them all for dinner. By the time she showered and made her way outside, two travel mugs of coffee in hand, Zach had finished half the lawn.

When he saw her, he cut the engine. "Morning, Doc."

A zap of awareness traveled up her spine at the sound of his voice. *Don't complicate everything.* When she got closer, she handed him a mug. "Morning. You've been busy."

Nacho and Soda bounded over to give her some love. She set her coffee on the mower and bent to rub them. "Good morning to you guys, too." When she straightened, Zach was staring at her. Despite the breeze whispering around her, heat suffused her body and she reminded herself, *again,* that she was finally able to breathe. She didn't need to cut off her own supply of oxygen by blurring the lines she and Zach had drawn.

"What?" She tucked a lock of hair behind her ear but refused to look away.

Zach continued to stare a moment. "Nothing. You're just softer around the animals. It's nice."

Meaning what? She was hard at other times? *Not hard. Guarded. Cautious. And rightfully so.* Too many times, the proverbial rug had been ripped from under her feet, and she didn't want to be left flat on her ass ever again.

"So, we're kind of having an impromptu get together tonight. Well, I'd already invited people, but forgotten, and then Megan's brother, Parker, called to ask me about steak and I remembered. I thought, since we're already having people over, the more the merrier." Was she rambling? She might have been. He was staring at her with a strange expression. "I invited Declan and my friend Taylor—you haven't met her yet. And I invited your mom and Shane. Because I thought it would be nice. I hope I didn't overstep. Also, it's kind of an engagement party now. That was Parker's suggestion." What the hell was wrong with her?

Zach's brows rose, his mouth lifting in a restrained smile, like he was trying not to laugh.

"Hopefully you don't have plans." She hadn't thought of that. Shit.

Zach climbed off the mower, handing Stella her coffee before sipping his own. "Mm. Nothing better than coffee you don't have to make yourself."

Stella's heartbeat was doing something funny. Jumping jacks or something, and she wondered if maybe she was having some sort of arrythmia. He watched her over his travel mug.

"Say something," she blurted. Nacho barked excitedly.

"Anything I can do to help?"

That was it? Did he roll with everything so easily? "You don't mind that I invited your mom?"

"I like my mom."

Because she was feeling oddly like a school girl who had no idea how to talk to a man, Stella poked at him. "And her boyfriend?"

He scowled. "If he makes her happy, I'm sure I'll like him, too. Thanks for inviting them."

"Thanks for doing the lawn."

They continued to stare at each other. She should offer to take over the mowing, but she knew he'd refuse. Besides that, he was clearly enjoying it.

"You're welcome. Is there anything else you need done for company?"

Stella looked around the yard. They probably wouldn't get too many more days of this late summer. "Why don't we set up some lawn games? Charlie will love that. I'll run into town later and get stuff for salads, and Taylor said she'd take care of bringing a cake. Dec will bring beer and wine."

Zach set his cup on the mower and picked up a stick, tossing it for the dogs who gave chase. "You and Dec ever date?"

Stella frowned. "Uh, no. Why?"

Zach shrugged but didn't look at her. "Just curious."

Neither of them needed to be curious. If she let herself indulge in the memory, Stella could still taste his lips on hers. She could still feel his fingers digging into her skin as he kissed her senseless. So, she didn't indulge. Because they both knew there was something more important at stake here.

"I don't exactly have a lot of time to date. Free time hasn't really been in huge supply."

The dogs came back, Soda carrying the stick. Zach took it and threw it long again. Stella did her best not to stare at his arms and the way his muscles bunched as he whipped the stick ten times farther than she ever could.

"You've got more time now," he said.

She smiled. "You're right. I do. Thanks to you, I have some space in my schedule. Which means I can make time for things I enjoy."

Zach turned, and his gaze burned into hers. "Awesome."

Why she wanted to mess with him was beyond her. Except that she was feeling lighter and happier than she had in a long while. Stepping closer, she looked up at him. God, he was tall and built and smelled so good she wanted to bury her face in his neck. Which was exactly why she *should* find a date. Find someone to distract her from the feelings Zach brought out. Feelings she didn't want. There might be time in her schedule for a fling, but there was no room in her heart for anything more.

"You know what I haven't had in forever?"

Zach looked at her lips, licked his own. Stella's belly tightened. His voice came out rough when he asked, "What?"

She breathed in, deep and slow. "A good, long, hard ride."

His jaw dropped, and his eyes darkened to an almost feral shade. "Is that so?"

Stella nodded. "It is. Would you mind?"

His hands went to his hair and he tunneled his fingers through it. So he didn't touch her? "Doc," he said, his voice low and needy.

She bit her lip. "I'll only be about a half hour once I get Chocolate Chip saddled up. When I get back, I'll take care of setting up some of the lawn games. I think I have bocce and ladder ball."

Zach scowled, realizing she'd been messing with him. He leaned down so they were eye to eye. "You're a bit evil." He tried to fight the amused quiver of his lips but lost.

She poked him in the belly. Which was rock hard. "You're a big boy. You can handle it."

"Payback is a bitch, Doc."

She took her coffee and turned, shooting him a sassy smirk back at him over her shoulder. "I'm a big girl. I can handle it."

With a smile on her face and some free time on her hands, Stella headed for the barn.

· · ·

With the evening growing dark, the lights Zach had hung around the back porch resembled stars close enough to touch. Stella tossed the two balls held together by a thin rope toward the ladder. When it looped around the rung she wanted, Charlie jumped up and down then came to give her a high five.

"We win," he said.

Stella high-fived him. "Yeah we did."

"Because Stella cheats," Declan said, glaring at her.

"You're just a poor sport," Stella returned.

"This does not count as a sport," Declan said.

Taylor laughed, going to retrieve the bolas. "I think

you're both lousy winners and losers," she said.

Declan pointed at her. "See? That attitude there is why we lost."

Taylor laughed harder and shook her head. "No way. We lost because you missed three shots entirely."

From the wide, refinished porch, Megan, Adam, Sheila, and Garrett watched, amused expressions on all their faces. Parks was manning the BBQ, and Zach had gone to show Shane around the clinic and property. Stella's heart felt oddly full as she laughed along with her friends.

"She's got you there, Dec," Garrett said, saluting him with his beer before taking a long pull.

"Steaks will be done soon. You want to grab the salads, Stell?" Parker asked.

"Rematch after dinner," Declan said.

Taylor handed him the bolas. "Maybe you should practice while we eat," she said.

Charlie laughed, and Declan zeroed in on him. "You think that's funny, squirt?" He picked him up, making Charlie squeal in delight. "Next time, it's you and me against the girls."

Still laughing upside down, Charlie looked at Stella. "Okay. I don't mind losing to girls."

Shane and Zach were on their way back when Stella took the steps up to the porch. She was still laughing as she walked toward the back door. Sheila followed behind her.

"Let me help you with the salads, hon," she said.

In the kitchen, Stella couldn't keep the smile off her face. She pulled out the potato and pasta salads from the fridge.

"These look delicious. Thank you for inviting us to join you," Sheila said.

"My pleasure. I'm glad you guys could come."

Sheila grabbed the green salad while Stella pulled a few bags of chips out of the pantry.

"It's good to see my boy so happy," Sheila said as Stella grabbed napkins and paper plates.

She looked up and saw Zach's mom was watching her. "He's been a huge help. I didn't want to admit I needed it, but he kept pushing and I'm glad he did."

"Your dad would be so proud of you, Stella."

Tears pushed against the happiness bursting inside of her chest. "I hope so. I'd like to think he'd approve of Zach being here. That maybe he'd have done the same thing."

Sheila nodded. "Until he left for the army, Zach didn't have a lot of great male role models. I know your dad mattered to him. Thank you for letting him be part of this."

Stella knew she should be the one thanking him. "I know he's happy to be home. I'm glad the timing worked out so well."

"There's nothing a parent wants more than to see their child happy."

Nodding, Stella ignored the tightness in her chest. Her dad had seen her happy. He'd seen her get her degree, her license, and he'd helped her through her broken engagement. It didn't feel like enough, and she knew she'd never stop being angry he'd been taken too soon, but she found comfort in Sheila's words. If nothing else, he'd known she was home and happy.

"I'll take these out," Sheila said, stacking one salad on top of the other and heading for the door.

Stella took a deep breath and let it out. He'd be happy with the choices she made.

"You okay, Doc?" Zach asked from behind her. He was too quiet for such a big man.

Sniffling just a little, she turned. "I am." And though Stella believed in the second shoe dropping more than glass slippers, she really was.

Chapter Fifteen

Zach didn't mean to sneak up on her and he expected her to brush off her obvious emotion. She was more than a little sensitive about showing weakness. Instead, she gave him a luminous smile after he asked her if she was okay.

"I just came in to see if you needed anything else brought out," he said, coming over to take the napkins and plates.

"That was thoughtful," she said. He watched her visibly collect herself and didn't mind. He knew a thing or two about wanting to control how people saw him. But he hoped, in time, around him, she'd feel like she didn't have to put on a mask.

"My mother told me I wasn't being a good host," he said, making her smile.

He liked seeing her with her friends—people he knew she considered family. It was like seeing her with the animals.

"I like your mom." She loaded up a tray with dressings, salt, pepper, and chips.

"The feeling is mutual."

As they moved toward the door, she stopped and tipped

her head up, looking at him. Fuck. He lived with her, saw her every day and *still,* every now and again, her beauty grabbed him by the throat.

"Shane seems nice," Stella said.

"He is. He was in the army as well and loves animals and my mom, so it was pretty easy to make conversation with him."

She continued to stare in that assessing way she had. "Easier than you thought it would be?"

He nodded. "Yeah."

She laughed, and he opened the door, gesturing for her to go first. They were an eclectic bunch, he thought, as they sat around a huge picnic-style table that was made from a long, refinished door.

"This table is incredible," his mom said, beaming at Stella.

"Thanks. Taylor made it. She's incredibly talented. She refinished the dresser in my bedroom as well," Stella said.

Taylor blushed visibly. Her pale skin made it easy to see that compliments overwhelmed her. "It's just a hobby."

"Damn well shouldn't be," Dec said, dishing up a huge scoop of potato salad.

They passed the bowls around as Garrett and Parker put a steak on each plate.

"You know, someone with more manners might say something like, 'it's a shame to waste your talent, Taylor.' Something a little less caveman-ish," Adam said, grinning at his buddy.

Zach had spent enough time listening to the two rib each other while losing fifty bucks to them at their poker game to know that it was good-natured.

"Not all of us have your finesse with numbers and words, Klein," Declan said.

Parker snorted out a laugh. "I'm sorry. Was that out

loud?"

Garrett chuckled and leaned in to kiss his husband's neck. "I'd be careful before you start teasing Adam about his finesse with words given that your proposal included the words 'come on man, we totally should.'"

The group laughed, and Zach took a seat next to Stella, his thigh accidentally brushing hers. He ignored the electricity. Getting to this place with her where he was sharing her business, her home, and her friends—well, he'd been on the outside looking in for so long, he didn't want to risk the feelings overwhelming *him* right now.

Declan turned to Taylor. "I apologize, Tay. Your work is exquisite, and I think your talent should be showcased to the masses."

Megan bit her lip and stared at Adam, but the others laughed.

"You're a jackass," Adam said.

"Aw, there's that finesse you speak of, Gar," Stella said.

"Speaking of furniture, I'd love to replace a couple of things at our place," Megan said.

"Like what?" Adam glanced at her as he cut into his steak.

"Nothing major. I was just thinking it would be nice for me to have my own desk. You know, for marking and stuff," Megan said, taking a bite. She sighed in pleasure and looked at Parker. "You're a genius with meat."

The guys burst out laughing and Garrett slapped Parker on the back. "I tell him that *all* the time."

"I like your chicken better, Uncle Parks," Charlie said.

"Oh my," Zach's mom said, but her eyes were dancing, and Shane put a hand on her back and whispered something in her ear that made her chuckle.

They chatted over salads and steaks, sipping on the excellent craft beer Declan had brought. Charlie and Declan chatted about comic books while Taylor and Megan filled his mom in on the wedding and their recent shopping trip.

Stella, like Zach, ate quietly, taking it all in. The sky grew darker and the lanterns she had set up around the patio, along with the bulbs strung along the rail, lit the place up. The stars made their presence known, shining alongside the moon, and Zach held onto the moment. He'd landed exactly where he wanted. Looking around the table, his chest filled with satisfaction. With more than he'd expected. He didn't want to mess this up. Stella nudged him with her knee.

"You okay?"

He looked down at her. "I'm good, Doc. Really good."

Her gaze held his and for the first time since he'd met her, he noted that her eyes had lost the layer of exhaustion and worry. Damn if he didn't feel a deep swell of pride for being part of that. And damn if he didn't want to keep being the reason for the sated smile on her lips.

Chapter Sixteen

Zach did his best to pretend the owner of the collie he was currently checking out wasn't standing too close. Every time he moved, he brushed the woman's arm, which he was pretty sure she intended. His mouth tightened when the wrinkled woman with spry eyes and a streak of blue in her silver hair inched closer.

"You can sit down, Mrs. Vondri," he suggested again.

Her dog panted heavily as Zach pushed on his stomach and rotated his legs to ensure there was fluid movement.

"I don't recognize you. Stella says you lived here before. Why don't I recognize you?"

Shifting so he could move to the other side of the exam table—and put it between them—he shrugged. Telling her it was because she was forty years older than him probably wouldn't go over well.

"Not sure. I've been gone a long time." He checked the collie's ears. The dog just sat there, accommodating as could be. A far sight better than the poodle who'd bit him first thing this morning.

"So you weren't always an eye treat?" Mrs. Vondri finally sat in one of the chairs.

Zach coughed and looked over at the woman. She beamed. "I'm sorry?"

"You know…a treat for the eyes. Like eye sugar."

Jesus. Someone save me.

She snapped her fingers and pointed at him. "Candy. You're candy for the eyes."

He tried to ignore her and the nauseating taste in his mouth. "Looks like Snowball is doing well. He could stand to lose some weight though. I'm going to recommend a different brand of dog food, okay?"

The dog, who had very little white on his black coat, wagged his tongue like he understood the word food.

"None of that expensive crap though. I love him, but if I'm eating cheap, so is he."

Lifting the dog down, Zach reattached his collar. "It's not more expensive than what you already use."

"You're a nice boy," she said, standing to take the leash.

Zach went to the sink to wash up. "Thanks. Dexter will help you settle up at the front desk."

"Sure, sure. Everything has a price these days." She continued muttering as she shuffled out of the room, the dog leading the way.

He heard Stella's voice in the hallway greeting her before she popped her head into his exam room. "How'd that go?" Her voice was hushed.

He didn't particularly like the way his heart quickened at the sight of her, but he knew she'd like it even less. It was one thing to be attracted to someone, but sharing close quarters with her for hours every day, then going home with her at night, made it difficult to deny his feelings.

"I think I need a shower. I feel dirty."

Stella laughed as he dried his hands. He liked the sound.

"Better you than Dexter. Are you busy after work?"

Walking to the door, he stopped in front of her. He liked the way she tipped her head back and held his gaze. "You asking me out?"

She made a half-scoffing, half-snort noise. "Uh, no. Unlike Mrs. Vondri, I do not need a treat for my eyes."

Heat burned his skin. "These walls are too thin," he growled.

Stella snickered. "Yup. We need to go over some applications for the assistant position."

He was pleased she agreed that hiring a part timer was worth the expenditure even though they hadn't rented out the stables yet. They'd had four acres of land cleared and already sold the timber. They'd chosen two other plots of land to do the same.

"Sounds good."

They walked side by side to the reception counter where Dexter was accepting payment from Mrs. Vondri. She waved goodbye to Zach and Stella. As she pushed on the door, it opened all the way and a tall, dark-haired man let Mrs. Vondri pass before coming in with a very large tabby cat in his arms.

Zach was looking for visible injuries on the animal—they didn't have any tabbies on the books today. Stella had a habit of letting anyone walk in off the street and get care. Could be great financially, but it was hell on her schedule. Other than emergencies, Zach suggested they insist people schedule appointments.

When he raised his eyes to the owner's face, his stomach clenched.

Colton Dean. All-star ass clown. Best friend to Rick Growski. Smooth and slick, like he'd always been, the former football player had aged decently, except for thinning hair and a small paunch. His suit fit perfectly, and he held himself with the air of a man who liked getting his own way. *Or confidence. Now that you have some, you ought to recognize it.*

Colton looked at Stella. "Hey, uh, I haven't been in before, but my cat keeps throwing up. I wondered if you could take a look at her."

Stella glanced at Zach. "New client. All yours."

Looking down at Stella, he kept his voice low and tried to unclench his jaw. "We talked about this. People make appointments. No more walk-ins."

It was stupid, completely stupid to be bothered by this guy's presence. What the hell was wrong with him?

Stella smiled, her eyes darting to Dexter and Colton watching them. "Okay. But maybe we say that next time? We can't let the animal suffer because of new policies. And this could be defined as an emergency."

Shit. She was right on that one. The animal shouldn't suffer, but he didn't want to either. Travis had spent his last moments with people like Colton and Rick. Zach had expected to struggle with memories of Trav once he got home, but he didn't expect these guys to be triggers. Fuck. He hated that word. *Triggers.* He hated this feeling. Clenching his hands into fists, he counted in his head like the shrink had taught him. He would *not* lose his shit over seeing some dickhead from high school. *You can't bring Travis back.* He knew that. He accepted that. What he couldn't accept was the fact that maybe, just maybe, if he'd gone to the fucking party *with* Trav, he'd have been able to stop him from giving in to the stupidity that Growski's parties were known for.

"Doctor Mason is our newest vet and can fit you in, but in the future, unless it's an emergency, you'll need to make an appointment."

Colton looked back and forth between Stella and him. When he locked eyes with Zach, there may have been recognition, but Zach didn't wait long enough to find out. His heart was going to beat out of his damn chest. Sweat dotted the back of his neck. Fuck. He hadn't suffered a panic attack for months. He'd all but stopped having nightmares of being overseas. Why now? Air *whooshed* out of his lungs and he shook his head, trying to clear it.

His stomach pitched, and he felt like once again, he was back in high school, helpless. Or worse, stuck in a fucking deep, dark trench with no plan of escape. "Actually, Doctor Lane will have to help you. I have an offsite patient."

Stella stared at him, her jaw dropping. She knew he was full of it, but thankfully didn't call him on it. *You're a professional. What the hell is wrong with you?*

Looking at Colton, then Stella, he muttered, "Sorry."

He couldn't…he just couldn't close himself into a room with this man. Cat or no cat.

Again, Colton looked at him, and Zach could see the subtle signs of recognition—like he couldn't quite place him.

Then the guy pointed at him, shaking his finger as he struggled to place Zach. His face showed the "aha" moment and he went back to petting the cat. "We went to high school together." The cat let out a rumbling purr, looking quite content.

"We did."

More recognition dawned. Zach watched it shadow the man's eyes like a shade being pulled down. "You were best friends with Travis."

Anger burned in his chest. He stepped forward, pointed. "Don't you say his name."

"Zach!" Stella stood in front of him, like at five foot nothing she could be a shield or a barrier between the two men. Yeah right. He could fucking bench press her in his sleep.

Forcing air in and out of his lungs, Zach dropped his

hands and stepped back.

"What's going on?" she whispered.

His heartbeat slowed, settling into a normal pace. It was a good question. What was going on? *Nothing. It was just a moment. It doesn't define you.*

Colton stared at Zach, understanding clear in his eyes. While Stella stammered awkward apologies, the guy just nodded. At least he had the decency to look uncomfortable. The cat made a low mewling sound and Zach's attention sharpened on it.

"I...uh, that was a long time ago. I was kind of a dick back then. I'm really sorry about your friend," Colton said.

He wanted to stay mad. He wanted to punch the guy. But Colton looked sincere. He looked genuinely sorry. Zach had been so caught on thinking about how Travis's death had changed him, he hadn't given any thought to how it had changed the lives of others. Colton continued to stare at him, and the anger in his chest dissipated until it was more regret than fury. Colton shifted, his eyes dropping to his cat and then moving to Stella. "I guess I'll make an appointment. With you, Dr. Lane, if that's alright?"

Stella stepped forward, but continued to look at Zach, confusion and irritation creasing her forehead. "No, please. Come in. I have a few moments right now. Dexter, why don't you and Doctor Mason go check on C.C. before his *off-sight* appointment?"

It was phrased as a question, but Zach heard the steel in her tone. Turning abruptly, he walked through the back hallway and straight out the door, letting it smack against the frame. A moment later, the screen door creaked, and Dexter followed him.

"Sorry about that. Not my most professional moment," Zach said. He was man enough to know he should set a better example.

"No worries. I hated high school, too. Couldn't wait to get out. Thought everything would be different when I did. Sometimes things don't change."

Zach shoved his hands into his pockets and tried to think of the right thing to say to the young man looking at him. This was the same spot where he'd received advice from Stella's dad. At the time, he thought life would never get better. It did, but only because Zach had made the decision to turn the tides in his direction.

"They can. Change, I mean. You just have to decide what it is you want to be different and make it happen," Zach said quietly.

Dexter leaned on the door frame, pulling his glasses off to clean them on a cloth he pulled from the pocket of his white, three-quarter-length coat. "Sure. That sounds easy."

He waited until Dexter put his glasses back on. "No. I didn't say it was easy. But change doesn't happen unless you want it."

Mouth twitching, his lips moving side to side, and then Dexter sighed. "Just because you change doesn't mean the people around you will."

Zach couldn't argue that point. He untucked his hands and stood taller. "No. But the way they affect you will. You're in charge of that." *Like you were just now?*

Dexter nodded slowly, and Zach realized he'd given up that control in front of Colton. He'd let the mere presence of a former jock knock out years of training, forgiving, and moving forward. The worst part was Colton hadn't been a jerk just now. Zach was. And what the hell did that say about him?

Not wanting to think about it right now—or examine his feelings too closely—Zach gave Dexter a pat on the back and went down the porch steps.

"Let's go say hi to the horse." He'd be apologizing to

Stella later, no doubt.

He wasn't looking forward to the lecture he was sure to get from her on proper patient etiquette, but even that would be better than facing the fact that he hadn't moved on nearly as much as he'd hoped. Saying and doing were two different things, and clearly, he had some work left to do.

Chapter Seventeen

Zach left before Stella could talk to him about his behavior. For someone with so much confidence, it was unsettling to see him frozen in the moment. Uncertain. It didn't fit with the impression she had of him. *Of how he's let you see him.* Like her, she knew he harbored some issues that he wasn't overly eager to share, but this was the first time he'd worn that. She'd been irritated with her own response. Instead of being focused only on presenting a professional front, she'd been...worried. She'd wanted to know why he looked upset and more than that, she'd wanted to soothe him. *Men like Zach don't want to be soothed.* Part of her wanted to tell Colton to leave if he made Zach that uncomfortable. The other part of her—the one who had spent the last year proving to this town she could fill her dad's shoes—couldn't tolerate unprofessionalism. Their names were linked now and whether they were the only vet in town or not, word of mouth mattered.

Switching off the light in the exam room, she headed toward the back of the clinic to check on the animals one more time. The operating room was small and efficient, but today, as she'd been stitching up a bunny who'd hopped onto broken glass, she'd felt more aware of the room's shortcomings. She stopped outside the sterile room and looked in.

The lighting over the operating table needed to be replaced and an ultrasound machine really would be nice. *It's worked just fine for a long time.* Her father had been old school, not caring for new technology, regardless of how much easier it could make his job. *Or, he couldn't afford it and didn't want to tell you.* Shaking her head, she reminded herself that she was clearing the avalanche of debt one small payment at a time. There were nights she went to bed without worrying at all. When she reached the back room, Dexter was petting the rabbit inside one of the cages.

"Hey. You're still here. I thought you'd gone," Stella said, coming over to look at the grey fluff ball. "Hey. How you doing, pal?"

"He's still quite lethargic," Dexter said, stepping to the side so Stella could pet the rabbit.

"It's normal after surgery. You did well in there. The stitches look good."

"I was grateful my hands didn't shake," he said. He had a quiet voice and personality, which the animals responded to.

Stella glanced at him, remembering that when she'd been his age, she'd fallen for her mentor. God, what an idiot she'd been. *How about what an ass Steven was?* A fantastic vet, he gave her special attention, and she'd been easily wowed and all too grateful. *Stop. The past is the past. It brought you here. And where is that exactly?*

"You get in the zone, focused on doing whatever needs to be done." She shut the cage and locked it. The bunny was their only guest this evening.

"Reading about it and doing it are completely different."

Stella laughed, and they walked out into the mini break

area. "That's true of most things. Listen, about today, with Zach—"

"I think he felt really bad," Dexter interrupted, then realized he'd cut her off and looked down at the floor. "Sorry."

She waited until he looked up again, curious that the young man had so easily sided with Zach. *Why? He's got people skills in spades and Dexter looks at him the way you did Steven.* Still, even professionals made mistakes and acknowledging them was the only way to address them.

"I'm sure he did. He let emotion get in the way of professionalism." *And then he hightailed it out of here before facing the music.* That was another interesting reaction. Colton had obviously brought up memories Zach didn't want coming back.

"It has to remain about the patient. And only the patient," Dexter said, like he was quoting a textbook. A little piece of her wondered how she'd feel if Lydia walked into the clinic, but she told herself she'd do exactly what needed to be done, with the detachment necessary. *And want to claw her eyes out the entire time.* But Dexter didn't need to know that.

"That's right. Anyway, it's been a long day. You should head home. Are you getting a chance to see any of Brockton?"

Dexter grabbed his light jacket and backpack off a chair, putting them on. "My uncle took me to The Yacht for dinner last night. The food was awesome. I had lobster bisque and had to stop myself from licking the bowl clean."

Stella laughed. "That's understandable. That place is one of the best in the Point. My friend's brother is the head chef there. He often has dinner parties to try out his new dishes. He actually cooked for us last night."

The student's jaw dropped. "That must be horrible."

Pleased with the way he'd lost some of his shyness, she nodded. "Yup. Terrible. All that delicious food he makes us try. His husband is a chef, too, works at The Vista on the other side of town. Different style of food and ambiance, but definitely worth checking out."

"Are they both huge?"

Stella's brows snapped together, and she thought about both men—tall and equally good looking, one with dark hair and a Clark Gable sort of vibe and the other with fairer hair and bright blue eyes that matched Megan's. "Not at all. Why?"

"If I could cook that well and someone else in my house did, too, all I'd do is eat."

Laughing, she followed him out of the break room, down the hall, and to the reception area. "No. They stay in good shape and give the rest of us reason to work out."

She walked him out, locking up behind them. As he got on his bike, Stella stood on the walkway, the sound of banging ringing faintly in her ears. She waved when Dexter did, glad that he was working out so well. Worry over sharing her space, *her dad's space,* and giving up control, even temporarily, had stopped her from realizing how helpful so many extra hands would be to her own schedule. The buzz of adrenaline she rode most days, trying to get from one thing to another, had dulled and left a calmness in its place.

Stella frowned when the banging continued. The closest neighbor was a good two miles away. Turning, she took the gravel path that led around the clinic. She spotted Zach's truck in the driveway. At least he was home. Her heart dipped like an elevator dropping. *This is not his home. It's temporary.* The living situation, at least, was supposed to be.

Carrying on down the walkway, she spotted him near the barn, wielding a hammer with a toolbelt wrapped around his middle. She stopped in her tracks. *Huh. Apparently, I find toolbelts sexy.* To be fair to her neglected libido, Zach Mason could make anything look sexy. She didn't have to act on anything to admit that. There hadn't been a night since their kiss that she didn't relive it, whether she wanted to or not.

She made her way over and was beside him before he noticed her. Sweat dampened small patches of his shirt and her skin tingled, thinking about other ways to get sweaty. *Stop it. Think about something else.*

"Doc." His tone was clipped, snapping Stella out of her inappropriate daydreaming.

Was he mad at her? He pulled a nail from the pocket of the belt and set it against the fencing, angling it so it went into the post when he hit it.

"What are you doing?" she asked.

He paused, mid swing. "Guess I don't have to ask why you haven't fixed this, if you don't know. The fence is falling apart. If we're going to offer boarding to other horses, who may or may not be as tame as C.C., we might want to ensure we don't lose them."

She frowned at him. "I know what you're doing. I meant, *why* are you doing it? And why right now? Why did you leave earlier without saying anything?"

He sighed, resumed hammering the nail, pounding it in, before he set the hammer down and turned to her. "I'm fixing the fence because it needs to be done. Now because I had the time and sometimes it feels good to pound the hell out of something. I didn't realize we were checking in and out with each other."

Wherever he'd gone, it hadn't helped him shake his mood off. "What did Colton do to you?"

His body went rigid, like it had earlier today. He picked up the hammer. "Nothing. I'm sorry about that. I let personal shit get in the way, and I know that can't happen."

Interesting. The tough vet with the great smile, the confidence of ten politicians, and a swagger that would make Chris Pine swoon, didn't want to share his secrets. Yet, he'd made it clear he'd be all too happy to know hers. Since he'd arrived, he steadily chipped away at her shields and now, looking at him, the tension so clear in his body, she wanted to do the same. She didn't want him to be so upset. So alone.

Stella reached out, put her hand on his arm. He froze but didn't look at her. "Zach."

Still nothing. She stepped closer, heard C.C. neigh in the stables. "Look at me."

He set the hammer down again and did as she asked. "It's water under the bridge, Doc. I overreacted. It was a minute. It won't happen again. Let it go."

Not thinking, she took another step. He had no visible marks—no external injuries—but she saw the hurt written all over him. "I'm sorry he hurt you."

Zach's mouth flatlined, his jaw going tight. She thought of what she'd want—what she'd craved so many nights as she stared out of the same windows her father had and acted without regret. She already knew Zach well enough to know he'd do the same for her. Stepping right into him, she wrapped her arms around his middle and held hard. It took a second, but his arms came around her and he hugged her back. The crickets sang as Stella closed her eyes and breathed in the scent of Zach's warmth. It seeped into her bones where a chill had set in—long ago—and thawed some of the brittleness inside her body and heart.

He pulled back too soon. "Thanks for the hug, Doc. But I'm fine."

She groaned in frustration. "You're stubborn as hell."

Arching a brow, he picked up the hammer and moved down the fence. He put his hand on the next post and moved it back and forth. "These need to be reinforced more than I'm doing now. You get a heavy wind and they'll be down. But for now, get over here and hold this."

Doing as he asked, since it benefited her, she pushed her hands against the post while he secured it with another long nail.

He glanced up. "You want to trade secrets, you go first."

She flashed him a quick grin. "I have no secrets."

"Right." He pounded the nail, the vibration going right through her.

They moved down to the next post. She should grab those planters she'd been thinking about. This had been her home growing up, but since she'd returned, it hadn't felt like it. Until Zach.

"I miss my dad. I was thinking of planting some flowers, grabbing some big planters like Taylor has at her inn. But part of me feels like if I do that, if I put my own mark on this place, it's like saying he's gone." The words came out rough and unexpected. Somehow, saying this to him was easier than she'd thought. Maybe because they were still strangers in so many respects. He wouldn't coddle the way Megan would and it wouldn't take away from more important things the way it would if she'd confided in Taylor.

Zach stopped and did her a favor by not looking as if he felt sorry for her. Instead, he nodded and held her gaze. "He is gone, Doc. Making this place a home honors him. It doesn't erase him."

Stella bit her lip, the tears ready to fall. When he put it like that, it seemed silly she hadn't tried to do that already. She did not want to cry. She was happy. For the first time in so long, she was happy. *Doesn't mean you can't cry or have, as Zach would call it, a moment. It doesn't mean you have to be okay every damn time.* When he put the hammer down, she started to back away, but he caught her wrist.

"Nuh-uh, don't back away. Come here. You hugged me when I acted human. Your turn."

She sniffled through a half laugh and let him pull her in, trying to ignore how good it felt. *We could be friends. Friends hug.*

He rubbed her back, nearly obliterating her walls. "Colton and another kid waited for me once, down on Main Street. I delivered newspapers and did odd jobs because sometimes it was the difference between eating and not. They taunted me, took all the newspapers and trashed them. I egged them on, hoping they'd settle for beating the shit out of me instead of taking away money I needed. But they knew what they were doing. They shredded everything. I had to pay for them out of my paycheck."

Stella's head whipped up, hissing like he'd poured scalding water on her bare skin. "That's horrible."

He looked past her. "At least I didn't get fired."

Now she vibrated with frustration for him. "Well screw him. He can take his animals to the next county."

Zach smiled and picked up the hammer. "Thanks. That means a lot, but like I said, it was a moment. It wasn't really even Colton as much as his asshole friend, Rick Growski."

Stella all but stomped after him to the next post. "That doesn't make it okay."

"No. It doesn't, but that's not the point, Doc."

She crossed her arms over her chest. "You don't have to bury this and pretend to be all macho."

Zach snorted and tugged on a lock of her hair. "I'm not pretending anything. And this shit *is* buried. Or I thought it was. I waited to come home until I was sure I could deal. I don't know what happened earlier, but I didn't deal. I forgot for a second that I'm not some powerless kid. I'm a trained professional, I was in the army. I own two properties and work for the hottest vet in Brockton Point. But I slipped today."

Stella smirked at him over the hot vet comment and couldn't help but think that he was the one deserving of that label. "Have you had counseling?"

"More than you'd think. Today shouldn't have happened. It shouldn't have bugged me."

Stella poked her finger into his chest and ignored him when his lips tilted up. "Like hell it shouldn't have. You go after everything with such single-minded determination. I thought it was just because my dad made an impact on you, but there's more there and if you don't deal with it, it'll keep coming back when you don't want it to."

Zach's laugh told her he considered the conversation over, which was fine. Because if she pushed too hard, he could do the same.

"You're cute when you're mad. When it's not directed at me, that is." His eyes moved past her again as the sound of a car rumbled up the drive.

She turned to see a vehicle she didn't recognize. "Who's that?"

"The future."

He tossed the hammer on the ground and started walking. Once again, she was forced to follow. She huffed out a breath, realizing she'd chased after him more than once today. She did not chase after men anymore. *Not even one who dropped his guard in order to comfort you?*

"Who is that?" she asked again.

A man got out of the four-door car and leaned in, pulling out a large black bag. He waved when he saw Zach, who waved back.

They were getting closer, and Stella was grateful she'd worn her runners that morning. She always chose comfort over glamour.

"Kurt, thanks for coming," Zach greeted, putting his hand forward.

Kurt shook it and glanced at Stella. "No problem, happy to. This is a gorgeous place."

He looked familiar, but Stella couldn't place him. "Zach," she said, her voice low.

Zach turned and gestured to her. "Kurt, this is Stella

Lane. She owns the place."

Kurt stepped forward, hand ready. "We've actually met, but it's nice to see you again, Ms. Lane."

Photographer. Stella's brain flipped back through memories and placed him as the guy who'd tried to take photos for a real estate magazine when she'd first returned. Everyone had been certain she'd sell and flee.

She shook his hand but released it as quickly as possible. "I remember you now."

Zach looked between them. "You know each other?"

Before the guy could respond, Stella spoke. "He works for a real estate firm outside of town who had their eye on my dad's land. He came to take pictures."

Shoving his hand into his pockets, her *partner* had the decency to look abashed. "Uh, didn't know that."

"I actually work on contract, not *for* Best Bet Realty, Ms. Lane. And truthfully, I've been wanting to photograph your property for a long time. It's gorgeous. Like raw, untouched beauty."

Swallowing down her anger and the feelings of betrayal battering her senses, she shook her head. "Well, you can't."

Zach's head whipped her way. "What? Yes, he can. Kurt, why don't you walk around and take a look, give me a minute with my *partner*." The last word was said through gritted teeth.

Kurt hitched his bag on his shoulder and walked away. Stella watched him go and whirled on Zach.

"What do you think you're doing and better yet, *who the hell do you think you are?*"

Zach erased the space between them and bent his knees so they were closer to eye level. God, what she wouldn't give to be taller than someone and look down on *them*.

"I'm your partner and I'm doing us a favor. That guy is taking pictures for the website and one of the signage boards

I rented on the freeway. To promote the practice. He's doing it *for free* because he thinks this place is beautiful and worth sharing. He's going to help us spread the word in exchange for putting his name on the photographs and advertising."

Her lungs deflated like a balloon and her breath *whooshed* out. *Oh.* She hated that his ideas were so good. But she wasn't entirely in the wrong.

Giving him back the same attitude he shared with her, she straightened her shoulders and glared at him in a way that hopefully made him feel like the short one. "No matter how good your ideas are, do *not* blindside me with anything. Or we won't have a partnership. This is still my place, Zach. Even when we draw up a contract, I'll own the bigger share. Don't make decisions about the practice or this farm without talking to me. That's nonnegotiable. Don't ever go behind my back again."

His breath didn't whoosh out, but his shoulders lost their stiffness. "Fair enough."

"That's it?"

He shrugged. "What else is there? We were both wrong. End of story. We move forward."

"Fine."

They stared at each other, neither one moving. Zach's lips quirked, and she held her breath.

"You're drawing up a contract?"

Rolling her eyes, she did her best not to laugh. "You're impossible, you know that?"

He poked her shoulder and any residual worry or anger she had melted.

"Admit it, Doc. I'm growing on you."

She wouldn't admit it. Not to him or herself.

Kurt cleared his throat behind them, and they turned in unison.

"Uh, should I come back?"

"No," Zach said, shooting Stella a glance.

She'd lectured him on professionalism. Best to follow her own words.

"No. It's not necessary. We appreciate you coming out. I have to feed my own animals, so I'll let Zach show you around to get the photographs you need. Thank you for doing this for us."

"My pleasure. You remind me of your dad," Kurt said.

The words stole her breath. "You knew him?"

When was she going to stop being surprised by the amount of people who did?

Kurt nodded. "I came out once to ask if I could photograph the bluff at the far end and he...well, he told me it was private property and to...um...put my camera in an awkward place."

Stella laughed. "That sounds exactly like him."

Zach caught her eye and smiled.

"And for the record, I was told the real estate company had spoken to you first. I'm sorry about last year, about showing up without permission. It was foolish not to make sure first that you'd actually given it."

The past was the past. That's what Zach said. He might drive her a little nuts, but he was making her realize that embracing the future didn't erase the past; it just meant you'd learned from it. Accepted it so you could carry on.

"Thank you. I look forward to seeing your photographs." She looked at Zach and swallowed the rest of her pride. "I'll see you later. And thanks."

His grin messed with her balance. "For what?"

With a smile and a lighter heart, she gestured to the fence. "For fixing the fence."

Zach's laughter followed her into the house, and for the first time in too long, she didn't feel as alone in the big, rambling space, as she usually did.

Chapter Eighteen

For the second time in a month, Stella was able to leave work early. The last patient of the day wasn't hers, so she left to pay bills and grab a few groceries. Since she had time, she'd texted Megan to ask if it was okay to drop by. Excited to have a little free time to visit some of her favorite people, Stella turned the jeep down a tree-lined drive. Similar style homes dotted both sides of the street—a picturesque example of American suburbia at its finest.

At one time, Stella had thought she'd live on one of these streets. She'd wanted to work with her father, but she hadn't expected her husband to want to *live* with her father. *Maybe there is something to Megan's whole theory about things working out as they should.* Because, truthfully, she didn't want to live anywhere else. Being at the farm made her feel closer to her parents. It made her feel more herself.

Here and now. Which, compared to even a month ago, was a much better place to be than she'd have thought. The practice was doing well. She received less casseroles every week. Smiling at that, she turned in to Megan's driveway and grabbed her purse. When Megan hollered to come in, Stella did.

Megan was in the kitchen when Stella let herself into the quaint little house where the family of three lived.

"Hey," Megan said, finishing off what looked like a peanut butter sandwich.

"Hey back. How's it going?" Stella hung her purse on the back of a chair and went to the countertop island and slid onto a barstool.

"It's great. I had a really good day." Megan was beaming, and it made Stella smile.

Her friend had wanted to be a teacher for so long. They'd only known each other for the last year, but there were some people who just clicked into place like a missing Tetris piece.

"No weird things up noses or climbing the walls?"

Megan put her plate in the dishwasher. Laughing, she shook her head. "Not today."

Megan grabbed a couple of cans of soda before sitting beside her at the counter. "You want something to eat?"

"Nah. Thanks though." She opened the soda Meg passed over and took a sip.

"How's the hot-shot vet? Any more kisses?"

Way too hot. Stella choked a little on some soda that went down the wrong way. "No. That was a one-time thing. We talked about it, and *both* of us agreed that we want the business piece to work. He's really good, Meg. He's excellent with animals and really knows his stuff. He has a unique perspective—I guess from army training or working overseas, but it's almost like he scans the situation first, does some sort of mental checklist, and then gets started on what needs to be done."

Megan arched her brows. "Sounds very thorough. Probably the type of man who would be just as... comprehensive in any job he undertakes."

Stella stared at her a moment. "I *think* the innuendo there is that you're saying he'd be good in bed, but does that make me the job he'd be undertaking?"

Megan laughed. "Over, under…however you'd prefer."

Stella laughed but did not want those images to enter her head. If the kiss was impossible to forget, she couldn't even imagine how she could stir herself up with a little daydreaming.

"While any of those sound appealing, it's the after I'd be worried about."

"Maybe you shouldn't worry so much. Things worked out for me and Adam."

She smiled at her friend, pleased with the happiness that overtook Megan's eyes at the mention of him, No one had ever looked at her like that. Maybe if someone had, she'd be more willing to leap.

"Yes, they did. But that doesn't mean it would work for everyone else. Certainly not for Zach and me. I mean, can you imagine if you had to stay and work with Adam if you hadn't gotten together in the end?"

Megan frowned, which didn't suit her. "It almost didn't work out for a minute there. And it was horrible. But again, how do you know where things will end if you don't let them start?"

Stella shook her head. "I'm finally able to breathe. That's enough for me. I'm happy. I'm not looking for sunshine and flowers."

Megan bumped her shoulder with her own. "A little sunshine is good for you."

Stella slipped off the chair. Her friend was a relentless romantic. "Then I'll spend more time outdoors. He's on my off-limits list. No dating employees."

Realizing what she'd said, just as Adam walked into the room, Stella wished she had the ability to vanish into thin air. It would seem her true special talent was being able to fit her whole foot into her mouth. Megan had worked for Adam for five years, caring for Charlie. When Megan had finished her teaching certificate, she'd planned to move out and move on. Instead of asking her to help him find a new nanny, he'd asked for help finding a wife. When it all went down, Stella had wanted to tell Adam what an idiot he was not to see what was right in front of him. She wasn't the only one either. He'd almost lost her, but eventually, he'd smartened up and got the girl. A little piece of Stella had worried that he wouldn't be all Meg deserved but watching them now, she knew, if there was a meant to be, it was them.

Adam gave Megan a sweet smile and winked at her. Uptight, rarely chatty, almost-always-in-dress-pants Adam, winked at her friend. And Megan giggled. Good God. It was almost nauseating, but mostly adorable.

"Normally, I'd agree. But every now and again…there's a loop hole," Adam said. He walked to Megan and kissed her cheek, whispering something in her ear that led to a breathy sigh.

"I'm going to shower, then I'll head over and pick Charlie up at his friend's. Bye, Stella." He lifted an arm in the air as he walked out of sight down the hallway.

Stella closed her eyes and breathed through her nose before facing her friend. "Oh my God. I'm sorry, Meg. You know what I mean. I love that things are great for you two, but my own frame of reference didn't end quite the same."

Megan waved off her concern and got off her stool. "Don't worry about it. You know I would normally agree, too. But sometimes, life does what it wants, and you just go along for the ride. Want to sit outside?"

"Sure. And I think you mean *hormones* do what they want, and you go for the ride," Stella said.

Megan led the way through the patio doors onto the

small concrete pad that was set up with a bistro set and BBQ. Sitting with their drinks, they caught up on some of the local gossip. Who was seen leaving Declan's bar with whom. What hair dye color Letty Steiner bought this month—the orange had been a nightmare on the eighty-five-year-old woman, but she was switching to light blue.

"One of the teachers at Brockton Point Elementary is pregnant," Megan said.

She heard the touch of wistfulness in her friend's tone. "Nice." She didn't ask who. Their town was small enough that Stella knew some of the long-term locals or the more colorful characters around, but the population had been increasing steadily for years. While it was still typical to run into someone she knew when she was out, it seemed there were new faces all the time.

Stella set her can down. "Is that making you think about being pregnant? Oh my God—*are* you?"

Megan's face scrunched up and she laughed. "No. I'm not. And maybe. I like the idea that we're a family, the three of us, but I want more. I'm just not sure if it's too soon, or if I should work for a few years first."

Stella couldn't really speak to that. "Have you talked to Adam?"

Megan took a sip of her pop. "Not yet. We've got the wedding. I don't want to send him into a panic. Best to go one step at a time. Actually, he probably has a spreadsheet somewhere with a timeline."

Laughing, even though it could be true, Stella tried to imagine having her life that perfectly laid out. No spreadsheet could account for the kinks life threw without warning.

Megan leaned over with a smile. "Tell me more about Zach."

She sighed. It surprised her to realize there was a lot she could tell. They'd become friends somewhere along the way.

"He's charming, but not arrogant, which I misunderstood at first. I thought he was just overly confident, but he can back himself up whether it's with animal care or marketing. His ideas for the clinic don't have me cowering, but they're making a big impact."

Megan scrunched her brows. "Can he back up his confidence in his kissing skills?"

Stella stared at her, doing her best to keep her lips from tipping up into a smile. "Aren't you getting some on the regular? If you are, then shouldn't you be able to focus on something else? If not, Adam *did* say he was jumping in the shower."

Megan's eyes glazed over a little at that and Stella belly laughed. The sensation was almost forgotten. Funny how different the world looked and felt when she didn't feel like it was sitting on top of her.

Because she knew Megan wouldn't give up and because she'd want the same details, she gave in. "His kissing skills are phenomenal. I almost wish he'd been bad at it. Then maybe I could forget and move on rather than reminding myself that we're keeping things professional and platonic."

Megan started to speak but Stella pointed at her. "No more. Platonic and professional."

Her friend's lips turned up in a stubborn smile. "Boring and boring."

Boring was safe. She liked safe. Especially where her heart was concerned. "He's got his own things going on. He doesn't need complications any more than I do."

Megan leaned in, more serious now. "Everything okay?"

She nodded, not wanting to over confide or break Zach's trust. "He came back with the intention of working with my father. He's got this attitude that makes you think nothing gets to him, but I don't think that's true. Little things do. Things that suggest to me that maybe he's not as *over* the past as he says he is." She thought again of his reaction to Colton.

"Adam said his family didn't have much growing up. Said their fathers shared a lot of traits."

Stella frowned, knowing Adam's own childhood had been extremely hard thanks to being abandoned by his mother and left with his abusive, alcoholic father. She hated the thought that Zach had gone through anything similar.

"I don't think he was treated all that well. Plus, his friend died right before he left town and when he talks about it, there's just something...dark in his gaze."

Megan nodded again. "Adam mentioned that, too. He didn't know much more than his friend died because of guys being guys at a party. Some weird, freak accident."

"So sad," Stella said. She wanted to change the topic. If Zach wanted her to know more, he'd tell her. She wouldn't think about how much she wanted him to share his secrets. With her. *Can't take what you aren't willing to give.* Needing to change the topic, she smiled at Megan.

"So. Less than twelve weeks. Any rules or restrictions for the bachelorette party?"

Just like that, the conversation brightened and didn't make Stella's heart feel so heavy. Or needy.

Chapter Nineteen

As she drove back into town, she contemplated stopping for groceries. But instead of being the responsible adult she knew she should be, she swung her car into the back parking lot of Declan's bar. Dec offered an all-day breakfast special. She'd get some delicious scrambled eggs with a great view. Why couldn't she feel about Zach the way she did about Declan? Like he was a friend. A *hot* friend, but not one she wanted to cross a line with. How come the guy that ended up inspiring all sorts of wicked fantasies had to be the one in her house and her clinic?

Her Converse slapped against the concrete and she marveled at how nice it felt not to have so much weight on her shoulders. There was paperwork to do, and she needed to clean out the barn; she had a couple loads of laundry and really did need food. But she could take this extra half hour and show her face, remind people that Stella Lane did, indeed, exist outside of her clinic walls.

Declan was behind the bar when she stepped inside. He was a known player with a heart of gold, a love of all things super hero, and a strong business sense. *Might be the perfect candidate for getting this restlessness out of your system. A hell of a better choice than someone you'd have to see day in and day out. That's how the term "friends with benefits" came into existence. There must be something to the theory.*

"Hey there, Stell," Declan greeted, looking up from cutting limes.

"Hey, yourself. How's it going?" She boosted herself onto one of the stools at the far end of the bar. Bruce Springsteen played over the speakers, telling the dozen or so patrons about Thunder Road.

"I'm good. How's saving the animal kingdom going?" He slipped the limes into a small bowl and cleaned the cutting board.

"It's…really good actually. Zach is making things a lot easier. Plus, I have a practicum student who is doing really well. I'll be sorry to see him go. How about ordering me your all-day breakfast special?"

Declan wiped his hands and came over, setting a napkin in front of her. "You got it. How do you want your eggs and what kind of toast?"

Her mouth watered. "Scrambled and whole wheat."

"Want a drink?"

"Orange juice."

"Sounds good. I like Zach, for what it's worth. And not just because I got to take his money at my poker game." Declan punched in her order and poured her an orange juice.

Stella bit down on her lip to hide her grin. "I heard about that. The other night was fun. We don't do that often enough."

"It was fun. We know some good people."

Declan came back over, folded his arms over his chest, and though they were pleasant to look at, with all the ink trailing up and over in a series of patterns and designs, Stella's stomach didn't stir or dance.

"Speaking of two of those good people, Taylor and I were wondering if maybe we should throw a joint shower for Adam and Meg."

Declan's brows slammed together. "Unless we're talking the slippery wet kind of shower, I'm pretty sure Adam would not want a piece of that."

"Oh, come on."

"No way," Declan said, grinning. "Bachelor party. That's what dudes want."

She laughed at his indignation. "Adam isn't exactly your typical *dude*."

Dec nodded. "True. He'd probably like it less than most guys."

Stella gave up and took a sip of her orange juice.

Leaning on the bar, Declan grinned again. "All this wedding shit make you dreamy eyed?"

Stella leaned in as well. "About as much as it makes you that way."

His bark of laughter was the reaction she'd hoped for. "No thank you. I like my life the way it is."

Stella started to say "me too," but realized that feeling that way was fairly recent. She *did* like things the way they were now.

"Having a guy around the house full time isn't giving you any ideas?"

Giving him a saucy grin, she just stared and he laughed again.

"Well, I'm glad he's making life easier on you. He seems like a good guy. You deserve that. Maybe he'll be the one to change your mind."

When she looked up at him, his grin was far too wide. "Says the lifelong player."

His smile didn't fade. "You play while it's fun. You stop when it isn't. If I met someone who made me feel like Meg makes Adam feel or someone who took the weight off my shoulders as visibly as Zach's removed it from yours, maybe I'd reconsider eternal bachelorhood."

She didn't want to talk about how Zach made her life better. Worse, she didn't want to rely on it, even though she knew she already was. "You went to school with him, right?"

"I did. Didn't know him, really. He was always on the edge of the social groupings. There, but not really part of anything."

Uncertainty made her pause, but she needed to know. "How did his friend die?"

Declan looked around to make sure his staff didn't need anything. There were less than a dozen people in the bar currently. He leaned on the counter, his usually happy eyes very somber.

"Growski and a bunch of other kids had a big party at the end of the school year. Do you remember that unused barn at the back of the Bakerfield property? No one in that family had stepped on the land in years?"

Stella thought about it and recalled the barely standing structure. Her father used to take her along when he did home visits and they'd pass it on the route through town.

"I've never actually been on the property, but I remember the building. It was torched years ago, wasn't it?"

Something flashed in Declan's features that warned Stella of what was to come. Her body tensed, ready to receive a blow.

"It was. That year. Growski and some others had conned a bunch of the quote unquote social outcasts into believing they were invited—that it was a graduation truce. I'm not sure what happened when they got there, but I know it wasn't pretty. Something similar to college hazing, and in the end, Travis Mackleby died. No charges were pressed because it was ruled an accident and there'd been a lot of drinking. But it was pretty traumatic. I remember counselors coming in, talking to a lot of the kids."

Learning that made Stella's stomach feel as if she'd swallowed a lemon, rind and all. A fierce…what? Loyalty? Protectiveness? A sadness that she, or someone, couldn't have saved Zach and Travis's family from that pain.

A cook tapped the bell, and Declan went to get Stella's breakfast. Before he came back, someone slid onto the stool beside her. She already knew it was Zach by the time she turned her head. It was like his scent had imprinted on her senses. Dammit. She didn't want to look at him while she was feeling so much *for him*.

"Why so glum, Doc? We should be celebrating," Zach said, his smile making her heart bounce again. Her heart was such an idiot.

Declan placed her food in front of her with a napkin rolled around utensils. "Hey Zach. How's it going?"

"Not bad. When's the next poker game?" he asked.

Declan grinned. "Not next Saturday, but the one after."

"I'll be there."

"Glad I didn't scare you away."

Zach nodded. "I was just lulling you into a false sense of security," he said, making Declan laugh while he stole a piece of bacon from Stella's plate.

"Seriously? That's mine," she said.

Zach grinned and put half of it in his mouth, leaving half sticking out as he leaned his face forward, taunting her. Declan arched his brows and winked.

"You're a dork," Stella groused. She itched to snatch the half piece back. *With your fingers!* She picked up her fork and scooped up a bite of eggs.

"How about I order you one?" Declan said to Zach.

"Sounds good. Extra bacon. And I'll take a Coke, please, when you have a minute."

"I happen to have a few of them right now. It'll be slow for another hour yet." Declan wandered off to do as he'd said, leaving Stella almost thigh to thigh with Zach.

"Look at us spending our time off together." Zach nudged her with his shoulder.

"Stop it. We both ended up at the same place. It's a little different." She liked bantering with him, but she couldn't stop thinking about Declan's words. The urge to hug him was irrational, but that didn't make it go away.

"Yeah, but I'm going to talk you into a game of pool and when I beat you, you're going to concede that the website and the photographer were both great ideas."

Stella laughed around a bite full of eggs. "What makes you think you can beat me? Or that you have to do so in order for me to agree?"

Declan put a Coke in front of Zach and walked away to help a customer.

"You can be a stubborn woman, Doc."

She started to argue, then quirked her lips and offered him another piece of bacon. Funny how, with the right tone, he could make the word "Doc" sound like a caress.

He widened his eyes in a teasingly mocking way. "What? Sharing without making me beg?"

Instant images of making him beg flashed in her brain, sending way-too-pleasant tingles across her skin.

"Remember that when I kick your ass at pool."

His deep laugh turned Declan's head and he looked over, a question in his gaze right before he gave her a smile that made most women melt. Why couldn't *that* make her shiver?

Because life is never that simple.

Chapter Twenty

Zach couldn't remember the last time a woman challenged him, turned him on, and completely delighted him all at the same time. Probably never. He'd spent his teen years too wrapped up in real-world problems to get close to girls. He stayed under the radar, and he'd never met any girls there.

Once he was in the army, a couple of buddies had found out he was a virgin and promptly helped him address the issue. It didn't take him long to feel more at ease with women and he found he liked the way they talked; the way they thought. So even when he wasn't looking to score, he enjoyed just spending time with women. He didn't get much opportunity though. There'd been a brief relationship while he was in Mexico and a handful of flings since then.

Stella Lane was unlike any woman he'd ever met. Such a combination of stubborn pride and soft kindness. Not to mention drop-to-his-knees fucking gorgeous. She was the kind of woman a man didn't get over. Or at least, he wouldn't.

"You going to keep staring at me, or are we going to play some pool?" Stella rubbed the end of the stick with the blue chalk, her eyes dancing in a way he hadn't seen before. Should have known she'd be competitive.

"I like staring at you. It's a good view," he said, racking up the balls.

"An off-limits view," she reminded, coming around to break.

"Remind me why that is again."

She'd started to lean over the table but stopped. "Why what is again?"

He didn't know why he was stirring up a conversation like this when he agreed whole-heartedly with her views. But other parts of his body strongly disagreed.

"I kind of get the whole we-work-together thing, so we shouldn't, but I get the impression you keep yourself off-limits in general. Haven't seen any suitors showing up at our door. Who broke your heart, Doc?"

A flash of pain widened her eyes and was gone before he could be sure he saw it. But it was as if his heart recognized it. He knew she'd been hurt. But *seeing* it in her face made him want to smack heads together.

"Tell you what; since I have a few questions of my own, why don't we say every time one of us makes a shot, the other has to answer a question. Honestly."

He stepped into her space and brushed a lock of hair off her cheek. "I'm always honest."

Stepping back, she smiled and set herself up to break. She looked over her shoulder at him, caught him checking out her ass, and smirked. "Do we have a deal?"

He was a good shot, so he nodded. He wanted to know more about her, whatever it took.

She sent the white ball blazing across the felt and the rest of the balls scattered. A striped one went into the corner pocket.

"First shot doesn't count," he said.

Stella glared at him and walked around the table. "Don't cheat. I'm stripes, and you owe me an answer."

"Fine. But you know what they say about payback."

Stella paused, looking at the table before deciding where to shoot. "That's the second time you've said that with no follow-through. I'm not scared. Where was your first time?"

He smirked. Cute. But, in his opinion, she'd wasted a question. "Texas. I was nineteen."

Stretching, she set the cue so she could hit a bank shot, but missed. Unfazed, she walked over to him.

"Why didn't you come back to Brockton sooner?"

Zach's throat went dry. Because he'd associated "making it" with a dollar amount. Once he'd been able to sink his money into a tangible future in the place he loved, he'd set his plans in motion. "You didn't sink your last shot. My turn."

He went to the end of the table and lined up a shot, then sank it. He wanted real answers. "Why'd your last relationship end?"

Even as he moved to line up his next shot, he saw her face go pale. His stomach cramped—he wanted her to open up, but he didn't want her to be uncomfortable.

Stella's fingers tightened around her cue. "He asked me to marry him. I said yes. When I tried to make plans to move forward, he kept stalling. Then I asked him about coming back here to live, and he told me he'd never wanted to marry me in the first place. I was convenient and a really good vet."

As if ice water had been dumped down his jeans, Zach froze. "What the actual fuck? Are you serious? Who was he?" Zach didn't resort to violence unless he had to, but he'd be fine with kicking that guy's ass all over town and back.

"That's a lot of questions, Mr. One Shot." Color splashed over her perfect cheeks again, but he could see she was still shaken. He was a little shocked she'd given him so much.

He sank a second shot. "What's your favorite color?"

Stella's eyes widened, then narrowed. Zach laughed and lined up his next shot, hoping she didn't say pink.

"Yellow."

He could live with that. Lining up the white ball, he angled the cue and pulled his arm back, enjoyed the sound of one ball cracking off another and the sight of the red ball sinking.

"Crap," Stella muttered.

Zach moved around the table and reached out, tilting her chin up. "I know you said we can't go back there, but do you think about it? The kiss?"

Maybe he could live with not kissing her again if he knew he wasn't the only one affected. With his fingers resting just under her chin, he felt the increase in her pulse. It made his blood rush. He dropped his hand.

"Yes. But I was serious about us not going there, Zach. Ask me where I met him."

He didn't think he wanted the answer. Mostly, because he could predict it. "He was your boss?"

She nodded. "My mentor actually. It'd be like me taking advantage of Dexter. In hindsight, it never should have happened. I feel like he should have known that, the way I do as an adult and a professional."

"I'm not Dexter, and you're not the ass clown who didn't know how lucky he was to have you. This is different."

He hadn't intended to try and convince her that they'd be good together. They both had a lot to lose if things went sideways. But he'd never been great at denying the truth, and the *truth* was that Stella Lane was under his skin in a way no other woman had ever been.

"I'm getting so I kind of like having you at the clinic with me. Let's not do anything to wreck that."

He held her gaze and swallowed down the want consuming him. "We can be friends though. Give me that, at least," he said.

Stella smiled and the strain he'd seen earlier vanished. "Surprisingly, you already have it. Now take your damn shot."

Zach hoped his grin hid the disappointment he felt over not having the right to pull her against his body and wrap his arms around her. He'd never wanted to fucking cuddle a woman as much as he did this one. Maybe because it was so out of character for her to lean on someone that when he got to be that someone, nothing else mattered. "Blue ball... hmm, how appropriate is that? Corner pocket." He shot and missed.

Stella's smile ate up her whole face. "Can't win 'em all."

Lining up a shot, she got it in with little effort. "What if I hadn't caved and let you join the clinic?"

"I tried not to give it a lot of thought because I've always felt like if you have a goal you should bulldoze your way toward it, and thinking of ways it might not work out just fucks you up. *But.* I had a backup plan of opening a clinic closer to Bristol. Close enough to still live here, but they don't have anyone local." He was glad it hadn't come to that. "It's your shot."

She sank the next one but said nothing, lined up her next shot, and sank that one, too. When she missed the third, she came to stand in front of him.

"What did you miss about Brockton?"

"That's a good question. Other than my mom, I guess, not a lot. Things weren't easy growing up, but I had some good memories here. When Travis died, I needed space from them, but now, I can drive by places we used to hang out, like Pops or the arcade, and it doesn't bring shit up. I never felt like I belonged when I was younger, and now that I'm older, I've realized I'm the only one who gets to decide where I land. Besides, you know your dad mattered to me."

That stupid puppy dog look crossed her face again.

"That's sweet."

"Yeah. I'm like cotton candy. Ask your next question."

Stella snorted a laugh and patted his chest. "I know you can't build right now, but you knew you were coming home so why didn't you vacate your rental property?"

"Tired of living with me?"

She blanched. "What? No. I just wondered."

Zach shrugged. "Honestly, I thought I'd bunk at my mom's for a bit. Hadn't counted on her shacking up with Shane."

"Your turn to answer," he said, sinking a shot. He grinned and leaned on the table.

With her hand, she gestured for him to get on with it. He had so many things he wanted to ask her but knew to keep it light. They were getting to a good place and he planned on staying there.

"When's the last time someone did something for you for no reason other than the fact that you deserve it?"

Those dark eyebrows drew closer to each other, like he'd stumped her. In that moment, he decided he wanted to be the answer to the question. He wanted to be the one who took the weight off her shoulders and put the smile on her face. She had a list of reasons why they couldn't and shouldn't, but he could wait. He could show her that, just like he'd been right about them being good professional partners, they could have more. A whole hell of a lot more. Zach knew how to fight for what he wanted and right now, he couldn't think of one thing he'd ever wanted more than Stella Lane.

Chapter Twenty-One

Finishing up the paperwork on the last couple of patients he'd seen that day, he filed them and stretched long and hard. He liked the quiet of the clinic. Things were good.

Checking the clock on the wall, he decided there was plenty of daylight left to do some of the things that needed to be done. Stella wouldn't be back for a bit and he had a surprise he hoped she'd like. He'd offered to do the farm visits for her, but she seemed to like them, which worked in his favor as he liked the clinic.

Zach smiled as he headed for the house to change. He knew she'd mind him taking charge—the woman was too stubborn to ask for anything and took offense when someone did something for her.

"Easier to ask for forgiveness," he muttered.

He made a quick stop to visit C.C. before gathering his supplies and getting started. Opening the doors to the clinic to let the air in, he spread the tarp and began painting the walls. He wasn't sure how long he had, but he figured the farm visits often took a big chunk of time. She'd left midafternoon, and he'd boxed up everything in the office in between patients with Dexter's help. His gut clenched when he heard tires on gravel. Leaving the roller in the tray, he went out to the porch of the clinic.

A newer model, red Toyota parked, and Zach hoped like hell he didn't have a drop-in patient. Things had been getting better in that regard, but people still treated Stella's clinic like a twenty-four hour drop-in center. A blond woman—attractive and probably about his age—got out of her car. Long legs and high hair, she was the kind of woman who knew she was attractive but pretended she didn't. She didn't have an animal with her that he could see.

"Help you?" Zach asked.

She eyed him up-and-down before landing on his face. Before Stella, that kind of look would have at least stirred his blood. Now? Nothing. He could appreciate her looks and that was it. *Shit. Your life is going to be split down the middle between "before Stella" and after.* He sincerely hoped the *after* didn't wreck him.

He came down the steps as she approached and introduced herself. "Hi. I'm Cindy Harmen. I'm looking for Doctor Lane or Doctor Mason."

"I'm Zach Mason," he said, reaching out a hand, belatedly realizing it had paint on it. He pulled the rag from the back pocket of his jeans and wiped his hand. She smiled and shook it without reservation.

"Nice to meet you. I saw on your website that you've got space to rent for horses."

"We do." He did a mental victory pump. He'd told Stella the website would help them.

"I'm not happy with the place I'm boarding Clover, and I've just moved to Brockton so even if I was, I was hoping to bring her closer. No sense having a horse if you need to drive an hour to ride her, right?"

He glanced back at the clinic. "I agree. Uh, I can show you the space. Why don't you come check it out? You can meet Chocolate Chip. That's Doc Lane's horse. We have two other horses coming on Saturday."

"What a cute name. Are you sure? It seems like I caught you at a bad time."

Zach smiled. There was no bad time to improve cash flow. "Just let me shut the door, and I'll walk you down."

He didn't want Stella coming home and going into the clinic. Since the workday was technically over, he hoped she'd just head to the house. But not if she saw the door wide open. Joining Cindy, he gestured to the path that led to the barn.

She grinned. "Are you new to the area?"

The gravel crunched under their feet. Cindy's shoes were better suited to a shopping mall than rugged terrain, but they went well with the short shorts and sleek tank top.

"I'm not actually. I grew up here. I joined the army right after high school, and I've been gone for a while."

When they reached the barn, she paused and looked up at him. "You don't look familiar."

He needed a shirt that said it for him. "I've changed I guess." Or maybe he just wasn't on the outside looking in anymore. No more hiding in the shadows.

She inched a bit closer. "Change can be good."

Zach stepped back and gestured for her to go ahead of him. She nearly tiptoed her way over the ground, which made him wonder how much time she actually spent in barns. But her reaction to the horse was genuine, and even if he couldn't see it, the horse would have been able to tell.

"Oh, you're gorgeous. Hello, Chocolate Chip. I'm Cindy. You're a beauty."

Chocolate Chip nuzzled her hand while Zach moved around to the other side of them. "Tell me about your horse," Zach said. Putting one foot on the slatted fence, he watched the interaction of horse and human. Animals could tell things people couldn't.

"She's just like this girl. American Quarter horse, but her coloring is different. My Clover is honey colored. Gorgeous mane. Oh, yours is pretty, too," she assured C.C., earning a nuzzle.

"She friendly? C.C.'s been lonely and could use a pal."

Cindy leaned on the rail and looked over at Zach. "She's a sweetheart. I always think animals need company as badly as we humans do."

"I agree." And like animals, Zach trusted his instincts. "We'd be happy to board Clover here for you if you like the facility. I'm working on the stalls now, but the barn is in good shape. And Stella or I are around, so you know she'll have easy access to a vet. Stella mentioned opening up her back fields some, making more room to ride."

"That sounds perfect," Cindy said, beaming at him.

"Let's head up to the clinic. We've got some paperwork there."

The sun was slipping behind the mountains when they walked back to the clinic. He pulled his keys from his pocket as they chatted.

"Are you happy to be home?" Cindy asked.

"Very. It's nice to be back. Feels different, that's for sure," Zach said, letting them into the clinic.

"All your old friends have grown up?" She said it in a teasing tone.

Zach went behind the counter to grab the paperwork he'd made up himself. The door to Stella's dad's office stood open so he closed it. He'd all but finished by the time Cindy showed, but he still needed to put away the supplies. Hopefully the open window in the office would keep most of the paint scent from invading the reception area. It wasn't too bad right now. Zach refocused, realizing she'd asked him a question.

"Not so much. I didn't have many friends growing up so in some ways, Brockton is new to me, too. Adult perspective and all that."

"Being a teenager sucks," Cindy said. She followed the statement with a loud laugh.

Zach couldn't disagree, so he just smiled and grabbed a pen.

"Well, since you're an old kind of new here and I'm brand new here, maybe you'd like to join me for this work thing I have to attend in a couple of weeks?" Cindy leaned both arms on the countertop as Zach slid the contract over to her.

Maybe he needed help getting his mind off Stella. Either way, he didn't want to be rude, so he asked, "What sort of work do you do? And what sort of thing?"

"I'm a legal secretary for Maxwell and Hawk. I guess they do a big event in the fall to raise money for charity. A lot of the local businesses take part. There's a dinner and silent auction at Weaver Hall. I'm pretty sure there's dancing, too, but I won't ask that much of you," she said.

Stella hadn't mentioned anything, but then, she hadn't done a great job of aligning herself with other businesses. She'd been too busy. That's where he came in.

Mingling and meeting with other local business owners? That could only work in favor of the clinic. Stella liked keeping a low profile, but he'd done that for most of his youth and had no reason, not anymore, to hide in the shadows. The clinic could use some cross promotion. "You know, that sounds great. Is it too late to contribute to the silent auction? Stella and I can both offer a first check up and we can put together a gift basket as well."

She'd started filling out the paperwork, and when she glanced up at him, her eyes slightly hooded, she held his gaze. The sultry look had the opposite effect of what he knew she was going for, and he wondered how to tell her it was less of a date and more of an opportunity. *Because that doesn't sound rude, you jackass?* He cleared his throat. "Stella and I have been looking for ways to further promote the clinic and our services."

She continued to smile as if he hadn't just spelled it out for her. Hadn't he? "My bosses would love that. I've kind of walked right into having to finish off the organization of that part," she said.

He stepped back and crossed his arms over his chest, hoping he still looked friendly enough. The way she eyed his arms, she didn't take that the right way either. "Okay, I'll put something together and drop it by next week?"

"Sure. It's two Saturdays from now." She hesitated. "But we could always get together before that."

The clinic door opened, saving Zach from answering. Stella looked from Zach to Cindy and back again. She was dressed casually, her hair soft around her face, her purse slung over her chest, drawing his eye to the way the strap intersected her breasts. Dammit. Insta-spark. Every single time. He'd waited ten years to come home and make a place for himself. Patience was definitely one of his virtues. And the woman looking at him was worth every damn drop of energy he possessed.

"Hey. Late appointment?" Stella asked, smiling at both of them as she walked to the counter.

"Actually, Cindy here is filling out the paperwork to board her quarter horse, Clover, with us."

Stella's eyes lit up and Zach's stupid heart tripped like an overexcited puppy. "That's fantastic. Have you met Chocolate Chip? Oh. I'm sorry. I'm Stella Lane."

Cindy shook Stella's extended hand. "Yes. She's beautiful. So is your property."

"Thanks. It's been in my family since always. What's your last name?"

"Harmen. I'm new to Brockton."

Stella walked behind the counter and the scent of her hair wrapped around him. His muscles tensed. Pulling her purse off and setting it on the counter, she took the paperwork and looked over it. Lifting her head, her brows scrunched, and she looked around. Zach's heart hammered, and he hoped like hell she didn't go into the office right this second. He did not want to do this with an audience. Stella looked back at the papers, and he released a pent-up breath.

"You have transport arranged?" Stella asked. Zach couldn't take his eyes off her and, like she sensed him, her eyes darted his way. She looked…out of sorts.

"I do. Zach said the others are coming Saturday?" Cindy asked.

Stella kept her focus on the other woman, ignoring Zach. Did she know he could read her? Even from a simple glance?

"They are. Well, this is a nice surprise to my evening. Chocolate Chip is lonely, and Zach is certain this is the cure," Stella said, picking up her purse again.

"I'm glad Clover won't be alone."

Stella walked around the counter. "It was nice to meet you. I'll let you two finish up."

"I'll be home in just a bit," Zach said. He knew how it sounded and didn't even know why he'd said it in just that way, but he needed Stella to know he could be trusted. Even if she didn't want him like that, he wouldn't just jump on the next opportunity. She held his gaze, quietly assessing him. When he broke eye contact to look at Cindy, she looked confused and he felt like a bastard.

Stella surprised him by smoothing the awkward tension pressing in on them. "Zach rents the upstairs of my home." Was she giving him an out? He didn't want it. Cindy seemed appeased. She pressed a hand to her chest. "Oh, okay. Not what I thought you meant." She looked at Zach. "I don't need to start my social life in a new town by asking out another woman's man."

Fuck. He watched Stella's shields go up. Stella's brows rose. "You're in luck. Zach is definitely not mine."

Staring at her, he wanted to shout, "I want to be," but knew she'd just close up more. "We're colleagues," Stella added.

Her words were true, but they rubbed against his skin like sandpaper. Why did she expect everyone—*him*—to let her down? "As your colleague, I accepted an invitation on our behalf to a charity event a couple of weeks from now."

Cindy's eyes volleyed back and forth between them and he grimaced. This wasn't fair to her. He smiled in her direction. "I'll talk to Stella about the gift basket."

Silence smothered him. He almost laughed, thinking that in high school, he'd never had this sort of problem. He and Trav used to lament the fact that they spent most weekend nights on their gaming systems. Away from the fray. If Travis could see him now, trying to placate two women, his friend would laugh his ass off. God, he missed him. Blinking, Zach tried to wrap things up.

"Anyway, let's get this finished," he said to Cindy, hoping his voice was still smooth and friendly.

Stella put a hand on the door. "Nice to meet you."

"You, too," Cindy said, but her smile wasn't even close to what she'd started with. Zach felt like a complete dick. Cindy's hand scrawled across the paperwork and the only sound in the room was their breathing and the pen scratching.

"I didn't mean to put you on the spot with the invite. I'm not usually so forward," Cindy said, not looking at him.

"You didn't. I'm sorry, I was accepting on behalf of the business. I didn't actually realize you were asking me on a date." *Awkward.*

She glanced up. "And if you'd realized?"

He hated the words he knew he had to say, but they were kinder than the truth. "We're kind of burning the candle at both ends trying to revamp the clinic. Things are more than hectic, so dating hasn't really been on my agenda." Not since his eyes had latched onto Stella that first day.

Cindy nodded. "Fair enough. Sorry for the mix-up. But, you're still welcome to come with me. For the clinic."

He smiled. "I'd really like that. Thank you."

She finished up in silence and Zach didn't try to strike up any further conversation. This wasn't his forte. While dating hadn't been on his agenda, neither had falling for anyone, and he had the uncomfortable feeling that his heart had already accepted what his brain wouldn't. Stella Lane was the woman he wanted. When Cindy left, he stood on the gravel drive, waving and then looked back at the farmhouse. Was she pissed? Did she think he was going out with Cindy because he was attracted? Did she care or was she relieved? *Now you sound like a chick.* Because he didn't want to face her while his thoughts were so unsteady, Zach decided to finish up in the office and hope for the best. Warmth suffused him when he realized he could give them both space, but at the end of the day, he'd still be going to bed under the same roof. She'd let him into her life, and now he needed her in his. He just needed to show her that the past didn't have to predict the future. As soon as he cleaned up a bit.

Chapter Twenty-Two

Stella paced the living room then stopped when she realized what she was doing. Soda whined from her spot by the fireplace and she kneeled to pet her.

"Sorry, girl. Everything is fine." And it was. She'd wrapped up the farm visits and had been looking forward to coming home, putting on some cozy clothes, and maybe watching something on Netflix. Maybe seeing if Zach wanted to join her. Nerves skittered up her skin and she rose, almost letting herself pace again. She didn't want to date Zach, so what did she care if someone else did?

"You don't." But the air in the clinic had felt ripe with tension. It wasn't hard to see that Cindy was eyeing Zach in a way that shouted she was interested. She couldn't get a read on Zach though. He'd seemed almost nervous and then when Cindy had made the comment about him being Stella's man, he'd stiffened at Stella's response.

She left the dogs and went to the kitchen, pulling open the fridge even though her stomach was spinning in circles and she didn't want to eat. Shutting the fridge with a thud, she went to the window and peeked through. The light was still on in the clinic, but Cindy's car was gone.

"He was generating business. And if it was more, good for him." But still, the thought of him going out with Cindy, or anyone, made her want to dig her nails into something. She *hated* feeling jealous, but she refused to lie to herself and knew that was the feeling leading the way right now. It was stupid. She had no claim on Zach. When her phone buzzed in her pocket, she almost dropped it in her effort to distract herself with something else.

Megan had texted asking if she wanted to come to a cake testing on the weekend. Stella smiled and typed back a response.

Do I want to try multiple flavors of cake? Yes please.

Forcing herself to stare at the screen and not out the window, she waited for a reply. She'd thought being part of the wedding and the planning would be hard; maybe bring up bad memories of what wasn't meant to be. But the more time she had to help Megan plan her day, the more excited she was for her friend. *And that time has been freed up, thanks to Zach.* She groaned and looked out the window again.

When her text beeped, she looked back at the screen.

Megan: *Speaking of yummy desserts, how's Dr. Hottie?*

Stella: *Stop it.*

Megan: *Start it.*

Stella laughed and replied: We're partners. It was hard enough letting him into my practice. I'm not starting a romantic relationship with him.

Megan: *Who said relationship? You're both adults, why not hook up? You know you want to.*

The idea had merit, but she worried once wouldn't be enough, and it wasn't like she could sleep with him and walk away. He lived in the same house. Worked in the same place. Even if they agreed to a short-term thing, there was no way to keep it from getting awkward.

Stella: *Wanting something doesn't always mean getting it. It's too complicated.*

Megan: *Do you ever turn your brain off? Just go with what you feel?*

Easy for her to say. She had Adam. Though it hadn't been an easy journey for her friend either, things had worked out well. But Stella didn't want the same things Megan did. Not anymore. Letting someone into her heart meant getting it knocked around again. And she couldn't do that. It was too bruised to survive another assault.

Stella: *I feel like you have better things to do than worry about my sex life.*

Megan: *Want me to find you a hook up?*

Stella snorted with laughter. When Adam had tried to get Megan's help in finding him a wife, she'd started several online dating profiles for her boss and from the stories Stella had heard, none of them ended well. Maybe because they were meant to be together and they'd both been fighting it, but still. Stella did not need Megan's assistance finding a date or anything else.

Stella: *I'm good.*

Megan: *Okay. I'll talk to you tomorrow.*

Stella: *Night.*

Stella continued to stare at the phone. She could find her own damn date. But when she looked up, stared out the window toward her clinic, she knew she didn't want to date. She didn't want to let herself be vulnerable again. And if she were willing, she wasn't sure how any guy could compare to Zach. She *hated* that he'd gotten under her skin and dangerously close to her heart with his kind, steadfast nature. His hot body and wicked smile didn't hurt, but lots of guys were good-looking. That didn't make them all *good*. More than anything else, that was the piece pulling her under; Zach's innate *goodness*. He was the kind of guy that wouldn't mess around with a woman's heart. Maybe because he'd suffered loss or been on the outside looking in, but there was something about him that said when he was in, he was *all* in. And the thought of going all in with *anyone* again, scared the hell out of her.

Tossing her phone on the table, she gave up trying to distract herself and went to see why Zach was still at the clinic.

As she walked through the door, she almost walked into him. His hands went to her shoulders, bracing both of them so they didn't collide. A simple touch shouldn't make her feel so much. She'd spent too long trying to feel nothing.

"Hey." He stared at her, his forehead creasing.

Looking at him messed with her brain and her heart. Averting her gaze to his chest, she noted the yellow splotch near his collar bone. She touched her hand to it and, arching a brow, she asked, "Finger painting?"

He dropped his hands and ran both through his hair. "Uh, not really. See, the thing is, I wanted to talk to you about before."

Stella's heart bounced around in her chest like it was made of rubber. *Ha. If only.* She didn't want to do this. Keeping this line drawn was getting harder, the reasons getting weaker, the want getting...deeper. She inhaled sharply, stepped closer to him. He smelled like outdoors and man and...paint?

"Zach?"

"I...uh, wanted to do something for you. At the time, it seemed like a good idea, but now you're here, and I'm wondering if I've crossed a line. Fortunately, you can't really fire me, but I'd like you not to hate me either. So just know, I had the best of intentions." His voice was low and rough. Turning, he walked toward her father's office. She didn't want to be in there. She avoided it when possible. Unlike the house, which just made her comfortable, being in his office, knowing he'd never be in it again, made her feel alone. Like a person who woke up every morning forgetting what it was they were supposed to be sad about. Then she walked in there and the pain hit her like a fresh slap in the face.

Stella followed because she didn't know what else to do. Zach pushed the door open and stepped aside so she could go through first.

She felt Zach behind her as she made her way forward, slowly, like she was treading along a path of honey. Nearly robotic steps carried her over the threshold. Inside, the walls had been painted a soft, buttercream yellow. *What's your favorite color?* The fresh evening air pushing through the screen of the open window had dulled the scent. Turning, she took it all in, her heart doing a thunderous dance. The color was beautiful; soft, fresh, *new*. Tears pricked her eyes. Dueling emotions warred. *He stripped the room of memories.* Memories that hurt. *He gave you a fresh start.* She looked at him, watching her from the doorway, his gaze intent, careful, and, if she wasn't mistaken, loaded with emotion. She pulled in a shuddery breath.

Zach pulled in his own breath. "I've moved everything into one of the upstairs rooms in the house. I didn't throw out anything."

Stella touched the clean desktop. Zach had obviously wiped it down along with the empty shelves.

"I'd come home from school and he'd be going through paperwork here. If I wanted to tell him about my day, I'd sit right there," she said, pointing to the rickety old chair that had heard as many stories as the rest of this room. "Sometimes, I'd just follow him around the clinic. But I knew, when we were in here, I could unload anything I was feeling."

A thick, uncomfortable ball of loss lodged in her throat. Zach closed the space between them. He didn't touch her, but she could *feel* him. His natural scent washed over her, and she thought she could recognize it, *him,* anywhere. He'd done this for her, and she didn't know if she was mad, sad, lost, or turned on. Like this room, Zach brought all her emotions to the surface. She turned to face him and saw the lines of worry creasing his watchful eyes.

Her feelings were gale force winds and she was the unsteady vessel, not ready to face the elements.

"Stella, breathe. I'm sorry. I thought it'd be okay. I overstepped. I can fix it. It's just paint," he whispered.

He looked ready to scoop her up and crush her against him, or maybe she was projecting her needs. God, she was tired of pushing forward without moving anywhere. Zach had barged into her life and demanded she live it; forcing her to recognize it was her father who'd died, not her. That she was in charge of her future, and she couldn't have one standing still. She looked around the room again, biting the inside of her cheek hard enough to make herself wince.

"I kept it as it was because it kept him here, but I couldn't come in. Not if I wanted to breathe," she said. The lump in her throat grew. "Now he's gone."

She whispered the words without emotion and realized she'd been pretending otherwise. Keep moving forward, one foot in front of another, and she'd stay ahead of the pain.

Standing still, Zach facing her, *there for her,* she was tired of trying to outrun it. "He's gone," she whispered again, her voice breaking.

Zach put his hand to her face, cupping it, his thumb brushing gently over her cheek. When she bit her lip, still trying to fight back the feelings, he used that same thumb to pull her lip free.

"Baby," he whispered, his voice guttural. "He wasn't in this room." He moved his hand down, trailed it along her neck, over her shoulder, and let his palm rest just above her heart in a gesture that was more sweet than sexual, but still added pressure to her rib cage. "He's right here. Always."

The tears fell and before she could wipe them away, he yanked her against him, wrapping his arms around her so tight she shouldn't have been able to breathe. But she could. The pressure inside of her loosened as she hung onto him, her arms crossing over one another around his neck. His hands stroked up, down, back up, and she knew he meant to soothe, but something inside of her broke free along with the grief. The reminder that she was still alive, and it was time she let herself remember that. Pulling just her head back so she could see him, she stared into his vivid blue eyes. She saw the sheen in them and knew they were both done running. They'd both felt loss and come out on the other side.

"I miss him," she whispered.

Zach lowered his head until their foreheads touched. "I know. I'm so sorry."

She shook her head. She didn't even know what he was apologizing for; the paint? The loss of her dad?

"I can change it back," he told her, his voice steady. Solid. Like him.

Stella's fingers toyed with the hair at the nape of his neck and because she was plastered against him, she felt the shiver wrack his body. Sensation traveled over her skin like tiny revelations awakening her.

"Doc?"

She smiled at the nickname. He used it to put a bit of space between them, emotionally, but she knew it was too late. Trying to live a life that wouldn't leave her wallowing in a pile of regret had meant not really living at all.

"Thank you," she whispered.

He sucked in a breath like she'd slipped off her clothes and she knew why. Stella had fought him every step of the way. Moving forward also meant saying goodbye. And she hadn't been ready. *It's time.*

They stared at each other, their eyes locked as tightly as their bodies. Pulling one hand from his neck, she ran it along his shoulder, felt the coiled strength there. Traveling up, she brushed her fingers over his smooth, clean shaven jaw. She touched her fingers to his lips, he sucked in another breath, and then made her do the same when he kissed the delicate skin of the tips. She licked her lips and a different kind of pressure filled her chest, while dizzy butterflies filled her stomach.

Zach's eyes searched hers, silently asking her if she was sure. His hand pressed her closer, the feel of his palm on her lower back flaming the fire burning inside her chest. No, she wasn't sure. But she was tired of wondering. Lifting up to her tiptoes, she pressed her mouth to his in a kiss that left no room for anything except the visceral emotions he'd stirred in her from day one. As he tilted his head, slanting his mouth over hers and took control of the kiss, she was happy to let go, to give in. To surrender.

Chapter Twenty-Three

Cupping both of her cheeks in his palms, Zach's heart actually ached with the need to be closer to this woman. She turned him inside out in a way he'd never known. Instead of just making him feel like *part* of something—a feeling he'd craved his whole life—Stella made him feel like *he* was something. His hands stroked over her body once, then found their way into her hair. The scent of it teased him, made him want to bury his face in her neck. Pulling back enough that he could see her heavy-lidded gaze, Zach forced himself to slow down. She had to be sure. He was preparing to ask her if she was when she stepped back and took his hand. Without a word, she pulled him through the door and their hurried steps over the gravel toward the main house covered the sound of his heavy breaths. Fuck. There'd be no walking away from this. Stella Lane was going to ruin him for any other woman. He hadn't even gotten her naked yet and he felt like he was shaking.

The dogs didn't even raise their heads when Stella and Zach moved through the living room toward her bedroom. At the door, she turned and looked up at him with so much affection, his heart did one of those double beat things. He'd had enough sex to know when it was more. Everything about Stella Lane was more. And he wanted her to be his. *Slow down. Don't go there. Live in the moment.* But he'd spent so much of the last ten years working toward his goals, trying to get back to the place he started that he hadn't even considered the place he'd end up belonging, was not a place at all.

"Zach?" That one whispered syllable asked so much. Was he sure? Hell yes. Did he want this? More than anything. Would it change things between them? Damn right it would. But they could deal with that later.

Stroking a finger along her jaw, he pressed his lips there, trailing his mouth along the delicate skin there. He smiled against her when her breath caught. The tension in her stance, in her ragged breath, told him she wanted this as much as he did. He kissed a path to her ear, nipped at her lobe, and whispered, "Breathe, Stella. Let go. I've got you."

With his hands on her waist, he backed her into the bedroom. The evening light slipped through the part in the feminine curtains. Lifting his head to take in his surroundings, he smiled. She was so tough on the outside, but in here, and inside of her, there was a softness. In her room, it came through with pretty pillows, a light, flower-patterned quilt on solid, four-poster bed, and a trio of fat, short candles on the sturdy wood dresser. Outside of this room, her gentle center shone through in the way she treated her friends, her animals. Other people's animals. The way she gave people everything they needed, even when it meant leaving nothing for herself.

When he looked back at her, he saw she was fidgeting, her fingers clasped together over her stomach. Unwilling to let her retreat or pull away, he took one hand, ran his thumb over her palm.

"Your bedroom is sexy. Feminine. Bold. Like you," he said.

One side of her mouth tipped up. "Thank you. I'm glad

you like it."

Feeling too far from her, he pulled her back against him so their bodies were perfectly aligned. "I like *you*."

Pressing her hips forward as she wrapped her arms around his neck, she smiled. "I can tell."

His laugh turned into a harsh groan when she kissed him, anchoring her hands in his hair and taking what she wanted. As long as what she wanted was him, he was more than okay. Running both hands down her back, cupping them over her jean-clad bottom, he boosted her up and stepped forward at the same time. He fell with her onto the bed and braced himself on his forearms so he didn't squash her. Her small physical stature made it easy to forget that she was one of the strongest people he'd ever met.

Zach brushed her hair behind her ears with his fingers, letting them linger on the outer shell of her ear. Stella turned her face into his hand and exposed the sexy column of her neck. Pressing kisses there, he reveled in the feel of her underneath him, restless, wanting. She was caught up in what had sparked between them from the beginning. Letting his hands roam, he swallowed every sigh, every gasp, and marveled at the feel of her hands on his skin. She pulled at his shirt, wrestling it up between them when neither of them wanted to part. Taking a quick second to remove it, he lowered himself into her waiting arms. When she pulled him closer, it did what nothing else could, what he'd already fooled himself into believing he'd attained; she made him feel like he was finally home.

• • •

Yup. Definitely ruined for any other woman. Stella curled into the crook of Zach's arm, her nose brushing against his skin, sending mini aftershocks through him. His heart continued to race as fast as his thoughts. He shouldn't even be capable of thought, but his mind was spinning. He'd made it thirty-two years without having his heart broken by a woman. Sure, it had been jostled around by a couple of women. It had been flattened when Travis died. But, so far, it had never been in jeopardy of being mangled. *Until Stella.*

It was too easy to imagine waking up wrapped around this woman, and wasn't that a landmine waiting to be stomped on? Stella shifted in his arms, and Zach rolled to his side so he was facing her. He brushed a lock of hair off her face, tucking it behind her ear.

"You okay?" He needed water. He felt like he'd spent a month in a desert.

"*Okay* is probably too mild a description for how I feel. Boneless might be closer," she said, a smile tugging at those gorgeous lips.

"That's not a bad thing." He leaned in, kissed her softly, thinking how much he'd like to just stay in this bed with her all night.

He'd worried she'd close up once they'd had sex. *Face it man, you were worried she'd regret it.* All the reasons not to still hung between them, and he'd been certain those were the thoughts that would pull her out of her lust-filled haze and break the mood between them. So when she sat up, he braced himself, held his breath.

"I'm hungry," she said.

A laugh burst free and he tugged her back down over him. She pressed her nose into his neck and inhaled, turning him on again. Basically, all she had to do was breathe and he was there, ready. But the fact that he'd been worrying while she was thinking about her stomach was damn funny.

"I'm glad I amuse you," she said against his skin.

He ran his hand up the length of her back, over her spine, and enjoyed the tremor that wracked her body.

"You do that and a whole lot more," he admitted.

Stella lifted her head and folded her arms across his chest, staring at him. When he didn't expand, she asked, "Such as?"

Zach tapped her nose with his index finger. How could someone be cute and jaw droppingly sexy at once? "You amuse me. Confuse me. You inspire, motivate, and frustrate me."

Her lips pressed into a pout, and he kissed her, quick and fun before flipping her so he was looking down.

"You also turn me on, drive me crazy, make me think about things I didn't know I wanted."

Her eyes widened. "Zach."

Too much, too soon. Rein it in. He kissed one cheek. "You make me want to be more, Stella." He kissed the other cheek. "You're an amazing woman."

When he looked at her again, he saw the worry still clouded her gaze. Hoping to distract her, lighten the mood, and loosen up the knots forming in his chest, he ran his hand down her side. "You also have an incredible body."

She smiled. "As do you."

He was happy she thought so, but he still needed to get them back to the light, easy place they'd been a moment ago. Running his hand over her stomach, his heartbeat ramped up at the way she sucked in air, so sensitive and aware of his touch. Stella tunneled her fingers into his hair, trying to pull him back for a kiss. Instead, he pulled back and smiled at her look of surprise.

"Thought you were hungry," he said.

Scowling, she yanked the sheet up over her and he laughed again. Having her cover her body was a definite punishment.

"I could wait to eat," she said. Her brow arched in challenge. One he was definitely up for.

"I don't want to wear you out."

"As if you could," she said.

"I could try," he whispered.

She nodded. "Do that."

Fuck, she was adorable. He leaned down, pulled the sheet from her curled fingers, he pressed a featherlight kiss to her neck as his hand traveled back down. "Hmm," he murmured against her. "I changed my mind. I think I'm hungry, too. Your skin tastes like strawberries and honey." His fingers squeezed on her hip as he nipped at her shoulder, soothed the spot with his lips.

Stella tilted her head to the side, encouraging him to take his fill. "It's my body soap."

"It's my new favorite."

Stella smiled up at him and ran her hand over his jaw. "Probably won't smell the same on you, but you're welcome to try it later when we shower."

"You're pretty funny, Doc."

Her leg brushed along his and then wrapped around his thigh, pulling him tighter against her. He groaned and lowered his head to kiss her.

"I have my moments. Though right now doesn't feel like one of them."

"No? How do you feel right now?" He was almost scared to hear her answer.

She stroked her hands up his back and met his gaze, her own unguarded. "Happy," she whispered.

He vowed then and there to be the reason for that happiness as often as he could. As often as she'd let him. For as long as she'd allow. Hopefully, by the time she realized she'd let him all the way in, she'd be as far gone as he was and wouldn't be able to untangle herself without a fight. Zach didn't want to think that way, but if she tried to put her shields back in place, he was confident in his own ability to fight for what he wanted. If he wasn't capable, he wouldn't be here now. And there was absolutely nowhere else on the planet he wanted to be.

Chapter Twenty-Four

Stella eased away from Zach, squinting when she turned her head in the direction of the window. The sun was already shining through her useless excuse for curtains. She'd known when she bought them she shouldn't choose pretty over practical, but she'd given in, arguing with herself, that she'd be less likely to press the snooze button with the light coming in.

Moving with quiet ease, she stepped into underwear and pulled on a pair of lounge pants before grabbing a tank top from her drawer. Her eyes wandered to Zach. He looked so peaceful and sexy. How could someone be sexy in their sleep? The sheet bunched around his waist, dipping low on his rippled stomach muscles, one leg bent over the sheet, the other tucked underneath it. The pale cream color seemed lighter against his tanned skin. His chest had a sparse dusting of hair that tapered into a narrow line, which led under the sheet. Memories of last night made her want to crawl back into bed and forget the real world was waiting.

Like every other area of her life, Zach looked like he

belonged in her bed, in her room. *In your heart?* Nope. She was almost thirty years old and knew better than to wrap everything up in a pretty bow. It was sex. They were both single, consenting adults who enjoyed each other's company. She rolled her eyes and yanked on her tank top. Glancing at him again, she sighed. But wow. He was a drool-worthy present deserving of a big-ass bow. An almost-smile touched his lips and those dark lashes created a crescent shape on his cheeks. He could be on the cover of a magazine with his rugged, yet somehow smooth good looks. He was tall, and every muscle looked like it had been chiseled for viewer satisfaction.

Forcing herself out of the room, she went to the kitchen and opened the door for the dogs. Little worries popped into her brain as she made coffee. *It's fine. Just good sex between friends. Colleagues. Partners.* She groaned, spilling water on the counter as she poured it into the machine. She was making too much of this. Zach probably had sex with loads of women. She frowned at the thought. But he was a guy. Guys didn't attach loads of meaning to sexual encounters. They'd needed each other last night. *Or, you needed him.* She thought of the office and the pretty color he'd chosen for the walls. He was thoughtful. In bed and out of it. But that didn't mean she couldn't redraw her lines. Which was what she should want. But part of her didn't. A big part of her, and that was scary.

Their lives, professionally and personally, were intricately wound together. If things went south…

Would you just stop thinking for five seconds? At least until after coffee! Can you just enjoy the morning after?

"Mmm. That coffee smells almost as good as you do," Zach said, startling her.

She spun around, smacking herself against the counter. She rubbed her hip, swallowing down curse words.

"Good morning," she said. Did she sound squeaky? How

the heck could someone look so good in the morning?

Zach stared at her as she rubbed her hip and he came closer, making her heartbeat speed up.

"You okay?" He placed his hand over hers, pushing it out of the way and using the other one to pull her shirt up a bit, checking the spot she'd slammed into the edge. His fingertips ran over the bare skin, making her shiver, even though she felt nothing close to cold.

Shooing his hands away, she slipped out from between him and the counter to grab cups. "I'm fine. You just startled me."

She pulled two cups out and kept her back to him, needing the moment to school her features. Good thing he didn't have x-ray vision, or he'd see her heart making a crazy attempt to jump out of her rib cage just to be closer to him. *Play it cool.* No big deal. They'd slept together and now they'd just carry on as they were, working together and growing the business. Until it wasn't working for one of them and then he'd be the one to go.

A cup clattered against the countertop. *He's not leaving. Stop making things awkward. You didn't even want him here six weeks ago and now you're worrying he'll go?*

Stella's breath caught when Zach stepped behind her, aligning his front against her back, pulling her against him with his hands on her shoulders. He kissed the top of her head and the gesture was so sweet she nearly turned into him to bury her face against his chest. She breathed through the moment, hoping the longing would pass.

"Why don't you go sit on the porch? I'll bring out the coffees in a minute."

See? He can be normal. How about you try it. "I've got it," she said, her voice reasonably steady. She didn't need him to take care of her or act like her boyfriend. They'd just see how things shook out.

He nuzzled her neck, making it difficult to keep her emotions in check. When he pulled back, his hands replaced his lips and he rubbed at the knots making her back ache.

"I would have thought you'd be a lot more relaxed this morning," he teased.

"Ha," she said way too loud. "I'm totally relaxed."

"Let me get the coffee, babe," he said, his lips brushing her temple.

Oh God. She was such an idiot. She could fall for him. She could totally fall head over heels for this man. Had she learned nothing from the past? *Zach isn't your ex. He's here because he wants to be.* He wanted to be part of the clinic. The intimate connection between them hadn't been part of his plan. Had it? Her stomach tumbled.

"Jesus, Stella, it's just coffee."

She eased away from him and avoided his gaze. Just coffee. Just sex. Just a guy standing in her kitchen stealing her breath. "I said I've got it."

His frustrated sigh was hard to miss, but she didn't look up when he stalked out of the room. Stella set the cups down and lowered her head, trying to catch her breath. In her defense, it had been a very long time since she'd had a morning after with anyone. But still, she was really botching it up. Huffing out a breath, she poured the coffee. *Act normal. Think you can handle that?* She'd apologize, and they'd head off to work and everything would be fine. Happy with that plan, she leaned on the counter, sipping her coffee despite the sting of heat it left on her lips.

Looking to the stairs, she wondered if she should go up and apologize to Zach. The dogs whined at the door and Stella decided to wait on Zach. *Because you're a chicken and don't want to face him yet.* Letting the dogs in, she poured kibble in each of their bowls. She was trying to decide what to make for breakfast when Zach joined her again. He'd put on a shirt and a pair of athletic shorts. Stella missed the view of his chest and the little trail of hair that led from his belly button to—

"Seems you've always had a stubborn, independent streak," he said.

It was then she noticed he had something in his hand. He smirked, knowing he'd caught her interest. He picked up his coffee and blew on it before sipping, still holding some sort of oversize notebook that looked vaguely familiar.

Lowering his cup and setting it on the counter, he shook his head. "You really won't ask?"

She held his gaze, refusing to give in to the curiosity of seeing what he held. "None of my business." But curiosity clawed, making her fingers itch to touch the book. *Better than itching to touch him.*

He gave a shrug and leaned against the counter. "Fair enough. Why don't I just share some anyway?"

Feigning indifference wasn't easy, but as he flipped through whatever it was he was holding, she pulled some eggs out of the fridge.

Zach cleared his throat dramatically behind her. "When I get older, I want to run my own farm. Like my dad, but different. I'll have one hundred horses and kids from all over will come to ride them because they'll be the best horses in the world. And I'll have the prettiest farm. All by myself."

Stella nearly dropped the egg she was taking out of the carton when she whirled around. "What is that?"

Zach's smile grew, eating up his handsome face. "Just a little something I found while I was transferring a few of your dad's things to a different box. The first one broke."

He flipped another page and continued. "My best friends in third grade are Taylor Jones and Mona Warner. We like to play survivor in the woods behind my house."

Setting the egg down carefully, she stomped over to

Zach. He must have realized her intent because he held the book up, extending his hand as high as he could. She swatted his stomach.

A low growl left her throat. "What are you reading?"

He grinned, and despite the embarrassment creeping over her, she had to fight back a laugh. He glanced up at the cover, which she could now see. "All about me, grade one through three," he chanted.

Laughing when she attempted to jump and pull his arm down, he put his other hand on her hip, spreading his fingers wide to hold her back.

"Here I was wondering all about the gorgeous, mysterious, stubborn vet and all your secrets were tucked away in a primary scrapbook."

His deep belly laughs at her feeble attempts to climb him spurred her on. She continued to poke him in the stomach as he evaded her, holding her off and teasing her. She didn't even remember grade three, never mind writing that. When she tickled him, he laughed and squirmed away, but just switched arms and moved into the living room.

The dogs barked with happy enthusiasm. Stella still fought her grin. "Give it back. You're being a jerk."

"Now, now. That's not nice. Say something nice, Doc."

She bit her lip to keep from laughing. Always a deal with him. "I don't hate you." She put her hands on her hips and smiled.

Zach chuckled and shook his head. "Nope. Not good enough. Let's see...my favorite band is No Doubt and if I could meet anyone, it'd be Amelia Earhart because I did a report on her this year—"

She launched herself at his middle, sending him stumbling back a few steps. He laughed, even as he tried to right himself, but he tripped over one of the small round footstools she kept by the couch. When he landed partially on it, she joined him quite by accident. The good news was that his surprise fall had loosened his grasp and from her position on top of him, she was able to scoot up and grab it. Making a break for it, intending to run, she screamed, then laughed when Zach grabbed her around the waist, capturing her against his body.

"You did not just do that," he said, his breath warm in her ear. She could hear the combination of smile and disbelief in his tone.

She stopped fighting his hold and looked down her nose at him. "The evidence suggests I did."

He took the book from her hand, but instead of trying to hang onto it, he set it on the coffee table with no effort. Stupid, long-armed tall guy.

"You think you're so tough," he whispered, his tone teasing and sweet. The sweet nearly undid her. *See, he's not running. He's not leaving. Trust him. Trust yourself for once.* But she'd done both before—trusted herself and others and it had gotten her nowhere.

She lifted her chin. "I knocked you over, didn't I?"

He laughed and brushed the tip of his nose along hers. "That was luck."

She winced, pretending to feel bad for him. "Was it? Or are you just a little unsteady on your big clown feet?"

Zach only laughed harder and Stella squirmed to free herself. He shifted, stilling her movements and her breath. Every part of him was lined up perfectly with every part of her.

"Clown feet?" He chuckled again, nuzzling her neck.

Whatever. So she needed to work on her trash talk. "No one's ever told you?"

He lifted his head. "You are the most stubborn woman on the planet."

She shrugged. "At least I have normal-sized feet." Zach growled and pressed tiny, breath-stealing kisses beneath her ear lobe. "You know what they say about big feet."

Tamping down on the giggle that wanted to burst free, she sighed like he wasn't affecting her at all. "That the owner needs big shoes?"

He shook his head. "It was just coffee, Stella," he whispered.

Stella stilled. "I know. I'm sorry."

Lifting his head, Zach stared at her and all amusement fled. He looked so serious. "Don't close up on me."

"I don't know what that means," she said, knowing it was, at best, a lie.

So did he. "Yes, you do. Don't shut me out."

If she didn't, she'd lose herself again. And she wasn't sure she could survive the impact. But he'd already given her so much. It was her turn to give a little. And if she landed flat on her face, she'd get up and dust herself off. What choice did she have? Walk away now, or enjoy their time together and do her best not to fall? Of the two, only one allowed her the right to reach up and pull him down so his mouth was hovering just above her own.

"I'll try not to," she whispered, arching up so she could kiss him and forget everything else.

• • •

By midafternoon, Stella had seen a half-dozen patients, spoken to one of the two horse owners to confirm their Saturday arrival—Clover had come early—spoken to a contractor about repairing the fence around the outskirts of her property so Zach didn't have to, and managed to go a whole five minutes without thinking about sleeping with her partner. God. How did she have a partner? Whose body and laughter turned her on in equal measure? *Oh, you're in so much trouble.*

Despite the fact that her first appointment had included giving a skittish Great Dane antibiotics, the not thinking about Zach proved to be the most difficult task. By the time she heard Megan's voice, followed by Charlie's, in the waiting room, she was ready for a break. Signing her name to the bottom of the paperwork, she pushed back from her desk. She hadn't moved anything into the newly painted office yet, but somehow, it didn't feel as wrong as it once did. *Funny how a night, and morning, of amazing sex makes everything seem just a little brighter.* She knew it was more than that. She knew it was because of the person she'd been with, but she didn't want to focus too much on that right now.

Opening the door to see Charlie staring up at Zach made her heart zip around in circles. Megan was leaning on the counter, and Zach was staring intently at the little boy, who put his hands on his hips. What a sight. Something in her chest tangled up, making breathing close to impossible.

"Well, if you do become a vet, you're obviously going to come work here with me and Stella, right?" Zach was asking.

Charlie nodded seriously, then knelt to play with Nacho, who often came down to the clinic to hang out. They were the first to notice Stella standing in the doorway. Both of them—dog and boy—filled with delight the way a balloon did air. *Hmm. Perhaps that's why I like animals and children so much—they're honest in their reactions and always happy to see me.* And, if she were being truthful only in the recesses of her brain, the idea of caring for them didn't terrify the hell out of her. They were safe. Animals and children, by nature, didn't manipulate. They didn't leave.

"Stella!" Charlie rushed her and wrapped his arms around her middle. She gave a slight "oof" when his head smacked against her chest.

Leaning back, she looked down at him. "It's only been a few days. You miss me that much?"

Charlie's laugh warmed her heart and that warmth traveled all the way through her. "You, and maybe C.C. a little."

She ruffled his hair. "I figured. Wait until you meet Chocolate Chip's new friends. We've got one down there now, and two more will be here this weekend."

"Zach said I could help brush them, but I don't want C.C. to get jealous," Charlie said, looking back at Zach for confirmation.

Zach nodded, but his eyes latched onto Stella and awareness zipped through Stella's system. She thought of the blonde from the other day and felt a stab of jealousy at the thought of Zach giving his attention to another woman. Now that she knew what his hands and his mouth felt like, knew how he whispered sweet and sexy things in the dark, and held onto her like a vice during the night, she knew she didn't want him sharing any of it with another woman. As though he sensed her thought, he looked at her, his gaze drinking her in as if he hadn't had a drink in ten lifetimes. She nearly fanned herself when thoughts of this morning popped back into her head.

Zach took a step toward Stella. "It'll be fine. They'll all get plenty of attention. Why don't we head down there now? Did Stella tell you about the big fund-raising event this weekend? We're doing a pet wash."

"Like a car wash?"

Zach laughed, putting a hand on Charlie's shoulder. "Yup. But with pets. Think you could give us a hand?"

Charlie looked at Megan. "Can we, Meg?"

"Your dad and I have a couple of appointments, but I'm sure we can drop you off and then join you when we're finished. If Stella doesn't mind."

Megan looked at her and Stella saw the curiousness in her friend's eyes. Yeah, yeah, they needed to talk. Seeing as she'd forgotten all about the stupid fund-raiser, she didn't mind at all. Zach came up with all these ideas and it seemed like she barely agreed before he was putting them into action. The idea of relying on others so heavily was hard for her, but Zach thought nothing of asking the town to pitch in, donate, support their local businesses. It was easier for him, maybe, because he had no legacy involved. No shoes to fill.

Zach cleared his throat, and she realized she hadn't answered. "Oh yeah. Of course. The more the merrier."

"We'll meet you girls down in the barn," Zach said, winking at her. The door had barely shut when Megan whirled on her, stalking so close, Stella nearly backed up.

Megan pointed between Stella and the back of the clinic. "You did it! With him!"

Every part of her skin flamed, starting with her cheeks. She pushed past her friend, taking the files she needed to put away to the cabinet. "What are we, fifteen?"

Megan followed, not put off by Stella's snappiness. "Nope. Not fifteen. We are full-grown adults and we share all the juicy details."

Stella yanked open the top drawer and shifted through the files, slamming the first one between two others. "Uh, no, I don't think you're a full-grown adult at all."

Undeterred as only a close friend would be, she invaded Stella's space while she filed the next two patients.

"And is Zach?"

Stella turned her head. Megan's grin was infectious, making it hard not to laugh. "Is Zach what?"

Megan's eyebrows bobbed up and down comically. "A full…grown…adult?"

Stella belly laughed. "You're such a dork. Did I do this to you with Adam?"

She slammed the drawer and grabbed her keys from the counter, gesturing for Megan to get out from behind the reception area.

Megan picked up her purse and waited at the door. "Nope. But you did tell me and him that you'd do terrifying things to his boy parts if he hurt me."

That was true. The thought of Megan's tender heart being hurt by Adam had worried Stella immensely in the beginning. But this was different. Stella didn't need anyone watching out for her or her heart. Because this was just a fling. Two friends following through on mutual attraction.

Megan continued to stare.

"I did do that. But Zach doesn't need a warning. We hooked up. No big deal. I'm not you."

Megan froze. "What's that mean?"

Realizing how harsh the words had been, she rubbed Megan's shoulder. "Nothing bad. I just don't want to make a big deal of it. Zach and I aren't you and Adam. It's just sex, not a prelude to happily ever after."

"Because the thought of wanting that again terrifies you?" Megan asked softly.

Stella's hand froze on her friend's shoulder. How did people keep turning things around on her? First Zach this morning, and now Megan. Dropping her hand, she tried for indifference.

"I'm not scared. I needed sex. I got it. End of story."

Megan arched one brow and crossed her arms. "Is that so?"

Stella shrugged, averting her gaze. "It is absolutely so."

"Maybe Taylor and Zach would hit it off. They got along well the other night, but if you're not interested in anything more with him—"

Stella's jaw dropped when her friend's sentence trailed off. "When did you get an evil streak?"

Megan didn't look sorry. "When did you start lying to your best friend?"

Guilt swamped her. "I'm not lying. Fine. Last night was amazing, and I wouldn't mind a repeat performance. Or three. But, that's it. I'm not scared. I'm just not worried about mapping out a future with him. The practice is finally turning around and that's been my sole focus. Having him here has allowed for small pockets of more, but I don't want the full-meal deal. I'm more of a…piece-meal girl."

Megan's burst of laughter startled her. "You're so full of it. You just need the right man in those pockets and trust me, you'll find more room."

Stella shook her head. "Says the hopelessly in love romantic."

She chose to ignore Megan's muttered, "You'll see."

Though the sky was bright and blue, the breeze was a good indicator that fall had arrived. Stella was glad she'd pulled on a warm sweater that morning. After she and Zach had showered, and he'd done as he promised, using her strawberry-scented soap on her body. She shivered, and Megan obviously noticed.

"I love this weather. It's sunny but not too hot. I hope it doesn't snow for the wedding."

The trees surrounding the land waved back and forth, blowing both of their hair around. Stella pulled hers up into a ponytail as they walked. "Even if it does, it'll be perfect. I hope it doesn't get much colder before the weekend though. Washing dogs in low temperatures doesn't sound fun."

Looking around, she decided that Zach may have come up with the fund-raiser, but she could still put her stamp on things. They'd set up behind the clinic. People could park in the lot, bring their dogs around back, and that way the water would roll off the slight incline. Plus, there was a hose out back, a covered cement pad area, and easy access to the clinic if they needed anything.

Megan stopped walking beside her just before they

approached the barn. The whinny coming from the stalls made Stella smile. She could hear Zach laughing, but couldn't see him from where they stood. Her heart, though, it beat heavy in recognition.

"Meg! Come meet Clover," Charlie hollered from the opening of the barn.

"You okay?" Megan asked, bending her knees to look directly into Stella's eyes.

Startling, trying to breathe through the pressure pushing against her rib cage, she nodded. "Yeah. For sure." Why did she feel like she was lying? She *was* okay. It was the worry over staying that way—okay—that unsettled her.

Smiling brightly and setting her negative thoughts aside, she linked arms with her best friend. "Come on. C.C. has perked up some since we got her a roommate."

Zach was saddling up Chocolate Chip while Charlie was petting Clover's flank. Another thing Zach had been right about. She wasn't entirely convinced that an ultrasound wouldn't be needed for C.C., but she'd been eating more and certainly showed more signs of being happy. *No one, not even animals, likes to be alone.*

Stella focused on helping Charlie mount C.C. He'd gotten quite good at maneuvering the horse and had a gentle hand with the sweet animal. Pressing her own forehead to Chocolate Chip's, she breathed in. Charlie bounced gently in the saddle, eager to ride.

"You're a good girl, aren't you, C.C.? You ready to trot?"

She let Charlie signal the horse's release and gripped the rope to lead the way. Charlie held himself upright, speaking encouragingly to the horse while Stella gave them a wider and wider berth, maneuvering them in a circle.

"Go faster, Stella. I can do it." Charlie beamed.

From the corner of her eye, she saw Zach was smiling at her, too, but in an altogether different way. She wasn't sure what he was thinking, but she felt the heat of his stare the way she had his caresses that morning. What would it be like if she gave in, let herself just fall? Let herself *feel?* She knew he wasn't going anywhere. *Because of the practice.* Stella hated the fact that she didn't entirely trust her own judgement. Not where her heart was concerned.

The practice was her focus and that was something she couldn't forget. Zach was the kind of man who could make a woman forget. *Not you. You aren't the kind of woman who forgets what it feels like to have your heart used as scrap paper.* So there was nothing to worry about. Nothing at all.

Then why do you feel like you're already half gone?

Chapter Twenty-Five

Zach rolled over in Stella's bed, the delicious scent of her hair teasing him awake. He took the moment of quiet to look at her, curled on her side, all peaceful and serene. Something she rarely was while awake. Her hair fanned out on the pillow, lips parted slightly. He didn't know how, now that he knew her taste, he'd ever be able to look at her without needing to kiss her. Touch her. Want her.

She was gorgeous, and it wasn't just the sexy shape of her body or the inviting shade of her eyes. As one of the hardest working people he'd ever met, it was easy to admire her. Easy to see why others respected her. He'd thought—for sure—that she'd shut him out after they slept together. Instead, she'd surprised, and thrilled, the hell out of him by embracing whatever it was going on between them. They hadn't discussed it, but they had both stopped pretending it wasn't there. And he was so fucking happy he felt like he could burst.

They'd worked side by side or crossing paths all day and still, by the time they'd gone down to the barn to work with the horses, he knew it was pointless to try and get her off his mind. And truthfully, he liked thinking about her. He liked talking to her and being with her.

Now if he could just get her to drop her guard all the way, he could tell her he didn't foresee a time when he wouldn't want to be by her side. He smiled at the thought, his eyes wandering around her room, charmed by the subtle sexiness of it. Stella was more skittish than any horse he'd worked with, and he knew a gentle approach was necessary. He didn't mind. Like the other things in his life he'd wanted, she would be worth the wait.

He was looking at her when her eyes fluttered open.

"It's creepy if you stare longer than ten seconds," she said, her voice rough and sexy as hell.

"I think fifteen is the cut off for creepy." He kissed her.

She reached up, running her fingers through his short hair, her nails along his scalp, and a shiver raced over him.

Stella sighed against his lips and then turned on her side, snuggling back into the pillow. Zach shared the space and put his arm around her waist, loving the feel of her body melding with his. In sync.

"I can't believe I let you talk me into an afternoon of washing dogs." She rolled her eyes at him, but her words held no venom. It would be fun. Stella could use some fun. Before he'd come along, work had been her only outlet.

His phone buzzed on the nightstand. Craning his neck, he saw Andrew's contact pop up. Zach turned back to Stella, knowing his friend would understand if he called him back later. It was too early for a phone call anyway.

"You'll love it. More than that, the people who show up will love it. They'll tell their friends about these two gorgeous vets who are raising money to help families in need pay their vet bills."

She scrunched her brows together. "That is a pretty good

cause. And I do like how you streamlined it so now if people can't pay their vet bill, they have to apply for this help. You're very clever, Doctor Mason."

He grinned, his hand sliding up-and-down her skin, pushing the thin tank top she'd slept in up over her sexy stomach. "You forgot gorgeous."

"And egotistical?"

His bark of laughter turned into a groan when she let her nails slide down his back, leaving a trail of heat. Hard not to have some ego when a smart, funny, gorgeous woman was wrapping herself around him like she couldn't get enough. When she pulled back with a happy sigh, he pressed a kiss to her forehead. As much as he'd like to stay exactly where they were, they had things to do.

"I have to run that gift basket over to Cindy at the law firm today. I'll be back in plenty of time, though, and Dexter is helping with the setup this morning."

The easy, happy light that lit her eyes only seconds ago dimmed. He'd seen her school her features before. She had a switch that turned off her expressions and left a person feeling shut out. Zach hated it. More so now that they'd been intimate.

"Oh. Right. I forgot about that." She started to roll away from him, and he stayed her with a hand on her hip.

"That still okay?"

She shrugged, avoided eye contact. Zach trailed his hand along her jaw while he waited for her to answer verbally.

"Whatever. I'm not sure what a few free checkups and some top of the line dog food will raise for charity, but better than nothing, I guess."

"I think it'll be appreciated," he said. He'd been clear with Cindy when she stopped by that day, and Stella had been right there when he'd told the woman they *lived* together for Christ sake, so Zach didn't buy that she could be jealous.

When Stella said nothing, he filled the silence that hung between them.

"Contributing to the community has a direct, positive impact on our business. One of us should be there next Saturday and I know this part of networking isn't your favorite. You get invited to a significant number of events as a local business owner and I'm happy to go on our behalf."

Stella kept her gaze on the ceiling. "I've been a little busy. And quite honestly, until you came along, I didn't actually want to bring on more work. I couldn't handle it, but it makes more sense now. So, you're still going out with Cindy next weekend then?"

The sharp edge in her tone sliced through him. He sat up and looked down at her, waiting for her to do the same.

Finally her eyes came to his, but her jaw stayed locked, her lips pressed into a hard, flat line.

He took her hand, needing to touch her, needing her to understand. "I'm not *going out* with Cindy. I accepted the invitation on our behalf and made it clear that my schedule didn't allow room for dating."

Stella tried to pull her hand free, but Zach held tight. "Right. Your busy schedule. Definitely no time for dating."

Zach wasn't sure what to say. The nuances of relationships—ones where his heart was as invested as the rest of him—were not his strong suit. "You know I said that because you're the only woman I want to be with, right?"

He hadn't planned to lay it out there like that, but the surprise in her eyes, followed by the softening of her gaze, made him glad he'd said it aloud. Leaning over her, he put his free hand on the other side of her so he was caging her in. Keeping her close.

"Jesus, Stella. How could you think I'd want someone after having you?"

Her eyes got suspiciously bright and his heart twisted

in his chest. He knew the how. Stella's own heart had been worked over by a jackass who hadn't known a good thing when it was right in front of him. Zach released her hand to cup her jaw.

"I didn't want to hurt Cindy's feelings, so I told her I was too busy. But the truth is, I only wanted you."

She breathed in and out quickly, like she was fortifying herself. "When I met Cindy I had no intention of sleeping with you so having me wasn't an option."

"I know. Doesn't mean I didn't want you. Or want you to want me back."

She almost smiled, and he brushed his thumb over her lips. "That's a lot of want," she said against the pad of his thumb.

"Tell me about it."

When she laughed, the tension seeped out of his bones. Then she turned serious again, and his stomach tightened. "I don't know what this is. I don't want to think too much about it, honestly. I've never embraced happiness, just letting things happen around me. I was always working toward something or working to get over something."

Zach nodded, feeling another link locking tight in the chains that connected them. "I get that. You know I do."

"I don't want to analyze this right now. Not yet. But while we're doing whatever it is we're doing, it's just me and you. No one else."

Zach arched his brows and tried to tease his way around the jolt of happiness firing through him. He let out an exaggerated sigh. "You want to wear my class ring or my letterman jacket, Doc? Both?"

She swatted him and tried to sit up. He leaned closer, kissing her neck because he knew she liked it. Her collarbone because he liked it. The little hollow in the center of her throat drove him nuts.

Working his way up to her lips, he paused. "No one else, Stella." He swallowed down the word that lingered in his brain and on the tip of his tongue. *Ever.* No one else, ever. He could feel it, but she wasn't ready to hear it. She wanted to stay in the moment and he could give her that much. Right now, she was his and for as long as she was, he'd take whatever he could get.

Chapter Twenty-Six

Stella ducked for cover but laughed loudly as the massive sheep dog shook off the water from the bath. She wasn't sure how much money they were raising, but Zach had been right about the fun. She loved having so many people enjoying the property, the animals, and each other.

"Come on, Columbo, out you get," Stella said.

She patted the ground beside her, encouraging the dog to jump out. Dexter grinned, his glasses slightly crooked on his narrow nose. He was enjoying himself as well and getting acquainted with far more of the town than Stella had expected to show. She'd been so worried about relying on anyone, not wanting to be let down, that she'd closed herself into a little box. Zach had made her open it, and the result was an outpouring of support. If she were the kind of woman to tear up, this would have flipped the switch.

"I'm not sure he trusts you now, Doc," Ed Holter, who owned the nursery in town, said. He chuckled and leaned forward, patting his knees. "Come on, boy. The good doctor made you smell better without me having to wreck my back."

Stella grinned when the dog jumped out, raced around his owner, then gave another water-launching shake. The heat of the sun beat down on all of them, even in the shade, and made drying the animals a lot easier. This summer-like fall was a blessing. Stella's property was busier than she'd ever seen it. Zach had invited Declan who brought a couple of BBQ's in the back of his pick up and was grilling hot dogs. She'd offered to pay for them, but he said it was a chance for him to socialize outside of the bar and he could talk up his business while he served.

It seemed she was one of the few who'd been too busy getting through her workload to think about what Zach termed networking. Across the yard, Zach was tossing a ball for Carrie Ableman's retriever, while her twin toddlers laughed and looked up at him. Looking at him was no hardship. Neither was being with him.

Trying to keep things light and casual, without attaching weight to every little thing, was proving difficult. *You want to wear my class ring or letterman jacket?* She grinned at the memory of him teasing but having them both acknowledge exclusivity had mattered. More than she'd let on.

"Sigh. He's so dreamy," Taylor said in a sing-song voice when she appeared at Stella's side.

Stella smacked her friend playfully. "Shut up."

Stella wiped a strand of hair off her forehead with the back of her hand. A couple of kids raced across the yard, dogs chasing after them, much to their delight. A strange happiness surged through her. She saw people every single day, but she was only now realizing the difference between that and actually socializing. If Taylor and Megan weren't already well-established friends, they probably would have written her off.

"I'm only sort of joking," Taylor said.

Stella turned her head to see Taylor's wide grin. "He's

off-limits. For now, anyway."

It seemed impossible for her friend's smile to get bigger, but it did. "Look at you committing to *for now*. When did you learn to jump in with both feet?"

Stella knew her friends loved her so the teasing didn't bug her, but it made her wonder how others viewed her. Was she that standoffish? Did she give a back-off vibe even to those close to her?

"I'm trying not to muck up all the lines between personal and professional, and since I've already overlapped them, I'm just trying not to let history repeat itself."

Taylor hooked her arm through Stella's and squeezed. "Mistakes help us get it right the next time."

"You're as bad as Megan. I'm trying to enjoy the ride," Stella said.

Taylor burst out laughing and Stella realized how the words had come out. "Honey, there isn't a woman in Brockton Point that wouldn't enjoy that ride."

Stella pulled her arm away, heat rushing her face. "Have I suggested you shut up yet?" She couldn't fight the grin, though, as Taylor continued to laugh.

When was the last time she'd stood around gossiping over a guy? Her teens? She *wasn't* in high school anymore. But the butterflies zipping around inside of her suggested something more than a crush. Something dangerous and deep. Something she did *not* want to think about right now.

Behind her, Dexter was chatting with Charlie and mentioned going down to see Chocolate Chip and the other horses. Stella hooked a thumb over her shoulder.

"I need to get back to work."

"It's nice, seeing you like this," Taylor said.

Tilting her head, trying not to be insulted that people kept saying things like that, she asked, "Like what?"

Taylor smiled. "Happy. Light. Without the weight of the

world on your shoulders. Shields lowered."

"I don't have shields."

Again, Taylor laughed. "Right. You don't have shields, Thor doesn't have a hammer, and Iron Man isn't hot. Glad we cleared that up."

Stella started to reply but came up empty. Iron Man *was* hot. Dexter called her name so she turned, grateful for the distraction.

"I told Charlie and a couple of the kids I'd take them down to the stable, but Mrs. Ritter wants her poodle washed. She asked if we know how to do bows in her hair."

He looked terrified at the thought, making Stella laugh. She waved him off. "I can't do bows, but I'll take care of the wash. No riding today, okay Charlie?"

His bottom lip came up, but he nodded. He was such a good kid. If she ever had a little boy—*you did not just go there.* Stella took a deep breath. But some thoughts tumbled into a person's head without warning or the ability to stop them, and her brain wondered about a little boy with Zach's crooked smile and gorgeous eyes. Her heart felt like Captain America was squeezing it in his fist. Stella breathed through it and pasted on a smile.

Charlie tugged on her hand. "Meg said we could maybe come over on Saturday. Can I ride her then?"

Saturday. Zach would be out with Cindy. *It's business.* And Zach wasn't a jerk. He was a good man. He kept his word, not secrets. She could trust him. Hadn't he proved that time and time again? Stella could entertain friends and not worry about whether or not business was turning into pleasure if he wasn't with her.

"Sure."

"Cool." Charlie raced to catch up with Dex and the kids.

Stella turned back to Taylor. "He's such a sweetie."

Taylor looked in the direction they'd gone. "He really is.

Megan got her fairy tale there."

Her heart pounded, like it was doubling in size, creating an intense pressure in her chest. "She did. I'm really happy for her and Adam and Charlie."

Leaning in, Taylor caught her eye. "Me, too. Everyone deserves a fairy tale."

Stella sighed. "Life doesn't work like that, and not everyone wants one."

Shaking her head, Taylor took a step back. "Not true. Not everyone wants the *same* one. But we all deserve to be happy. However that looks for us, Stell. I'm going to get a hot dog and flirt with Dec."

Stella laughed. Watching her friend walk toward the BBQ, she tried not to think about happily ever afters. She really was okay right this minute. More than okay, and happier than she'd been in a long time. She looked over at Zach who was walking toward her. Knowing he was the reason worried her, but not enough to put an end to whatever this was between them. She'd avoided it because of her previous experience, but being with Steven was absolutely nothing like being with Zach.

"You look pretty serious, Doc," Zach said.

Tired of everyone discussing her shields and seriousness, she ignored the butterflies hopping around in her stomach and stepped into him. Surprise registered in his gaze just before it was covered with heat.

His hands went to her hips and she pressed a light kiss to his mouth. She was tired of worrying about every single, little thing.

"What's that for?" he whispered, his forehead touching her own.

"No reason. Is that okay?"

He grinned. "Completely okay."

People were looking. She knew it. This town loved gossip

and tended to add their own details to every story. Well, let them talk. Because Taylor was right. Zach *was* dreamy and if it didn't last, she'd deal. But for however long they worked, she planned to enjoy herself.

Still, she didn't need to overdo the public affection. She stepped back. "This is a great turn out. People are donating even if they aren't getting their dogs bathed."

Looking around the property, she spotted Taylor flirting with Declan who flirted right back. Megan was up to her elbows in a tub full of pot belly pig. Norman Kent had raised pigs as long as Stella had known him. He was nearing his seventies and treated them like a cross between children and dogs.

"We should make it an annual thing," Zach suggested, following her gaze.

Her heart rate doubled, and she didn't even know why. "Hmm. Maybe."

She felt Zach's eyes on her and couldn't avoid meeting them. "What?"

"Too long term for you, Doc?"

Surprisingly, it wasn't. She could picture them doing this again next year. There was something about Zach that made her believe he wasn't going anywhere. Or maybe she just wanted to believe it. But in this moment, it felt true.

"I didn't say that. I just think we should see what kind of money we bring in before we offer to bathe the town's animals every year from here on out."

Zach reached out and played with a lock of her hair. He frowned and reached into his pocket, pulling out his phone, which must have vibrated. Stella glanced down and saw the screen said Andrew.

"You need to take that?"

He shook his head, slipped the phone back into his pocket, and returned his hand to her hair. There were people everywhere, but the action isolated them, pushed them into an intimate bubble where all she could see was him.

His head lowered, but before he could kiss her, someone behind him said his name. Zach turned with a small groan, the smile still hovering on his lips. Then his face paled, his eyes widening.

"Mrs. Mackleby."

Stella didn't recognize the woman, reminding her that Brockton Point was no longer as small as it had once been.

"It's good to see you, dear. Your mother told me you were back, and when she mentioned you were doing a fund-raiser today, I thought I'd come say hello."

Zach stared at the woman like he didn't know how to respond. Gone was the charismatic, flirtatious, but genuine charmer he'd been from the beginning. He was so still and quiet, the moment felt suspended.

Stella put her hand on his arm. "Zach?"

The woman turned to face Stella. "Oh, forgive me. I'm Kimberly Mackleby. I knew your father. He was a wonderful man. I've never been a pet owner myself, but many of my friends have sung his praises and yours."

Hearing about her dad was a double-edged sword that made her both happy and a little melancholy. Stella extended her hand. "Thank you. I appreciate that." Zach continued to stand there as if he'd lost the ability to speak. "How do you know Zach?"

Eyes darting between Zach and Stella, she replied in a shaky voice. "Oh, Zachary and my Travis were the best of friends."

Zach snapped out of whatever trance he was in and gave a tight smile. "That we were. You look great, Mrs. Mackleby." He leaned in and kissed the woman's cheek. Though he'd recovered himself, Stella could still see he was shaken.

"Travis would be so proud of you," she said.

With his smile in place, Stella would have thought he was fine except she felt him stiffen beside her.

"You're doing alright? I really meant to come and visit. I've been buried in work since I got back and...that's just an excuse. I should have made time. I'm sorry," he said.

Mrs. Mackleby patted his arm. "No need to be sorry. You come visit any time you like. It's good to see you. I should go. I've left a donation." She turned to face Stella. "The people of Brockton Point are very lucky to have you, Doctor Lane."

When she turned to go, Zach breathed in deeply and slowly let it out. Stella stared at him. For someone who'd worried about her dealing with her father's death, it didn't seem he'd dealt with all his own demons.

"Zach," she said softly, putting her hand to his arm.

Unlike his usual response, he stayed stiff. Closed off. "We should get back to it."

"Stella, we need more towels," Jaz said, coming to her side. "Sorry to interrupt, but there are none left. I thought maybe I'd throw a load on, but then we're short a pair of hands."

Zach gave her a tight, phony smile and nodded. "I'll see you in a bit."

Watching him go, unease clawed its way into her belly. They'd slept together. They hadn't promised to love, honor, and cherish. Maybe she could handle this newfound living in the moment thing, but she could not, no matter how much she'd matured, handle secrets. Not if they could affect her. And seeing Zach shut down in a way he never had—even when he'd run into the jerk from his past—affected her more than she wanted to admit.

*

The rest of the afternoon faded into evening, and by the time the stars danced in the sky and she finally had a glass of wine in her hand, Stella was exhausted. Zach had kept himself busy for the rest of the day, like she had. He'd been in the shower when she came into the house, so she grabbed some wine and cozied up in one of her porch chairs.

Taking a sip of the sweet liquid, she thought about how the simple changes had made everything so much easier. Perhaps there was something to everyone's conclusion that she was stubborn. But her father hadn't asked for help. When his wife had died, he'd raised Stella on his own. He'd helped her pay for school, run his practice, made home visits, participated in every community event imaginable, and still wore a smile at the end of every day. *I miss you, Dad.*

"You want company, or feel like being alone?" Zach leaned against the open door off the kitchen. He wore loose-fit sleep pants and a dark T-shirt, his feet bare and his hair still damp. He looked tired and a little rumpled, and her insides went all warm and fuzzy at the sight of him. *You're so screwed.* Stella never ran from her problems, even when they scared her, so she shifted over, making room for him.

He sat down and put his arm around her, pulling her into an embrace that felt more like comfort than a sexual advance. It was then she realized he was comforting himself. Her heart rate whipped itself into a frenzy. But a piece of her liked the fact that, even if he had shut her out a bit today, he found solace with her near.

"I think you hurt Travis's mom today," she said quietly, her head on his chest.

He took the glass of wine from her hand and took a long swallow. "I know. It wasn't my intention. I saw her, and I felt like no time had passed, yet everything has changed."

Stella took a deep breath. "That's what happens when time passes—things change."

He looked down at her as he gave her back her glass. "Thanks Confucius."

Laughing, she leaned farther into him. "It's okay to miss him still."

Zach didn't respond. Instead, he stared out at the inky sky and Stella stared at his profile. She realized she wanted him to open up to her. Whether it was because she'd done the same with him, when she hadn't meant to, or simply because she could see he was hurting, she didn't know.

"I guess it doesn't matter how long someone has been gone. I keep thinking the pain will disappear. Then someone says something about my dad and it brings it all back. Which is weird because it makes me so happy to hear about him. People tell me stories I don't know and it's like getting another piece of him. But it makes me sad. It makes me miss him all over again."

Zach nodded, and Stella gripped the stem of her wineglass, digging for patience. She wouldn't push.

"I thought Travis and I would grow old in this town. We were friends from kindergarten. He shared his lunch with me almost every day because I never had one. He didn't care that my clothes were torn or old."

When he paused, Stella breathed a sigh of relief that he was talking. She set her wine down on the little table beside her and tilted her head onto his shoulder.

"As we got older, I used to wish his family was mine. I used to wish my mom would leave him. Now I get that she was scared, but when you're a kid, you don't get it."

Letting her hand settle on his thigh, she wished she could carry the sadness she heard in his tone.

"When my dad died, I thought there was something wrong with me. I wasn't even sad. That sounds terrible, but with him gone, we weren't always wondering if he'd come home drunk or come home at all. He had a small life insurance policy and that's how my mom got her house," he said.

Stella looked up. "That's a lot of baggage for a kid."

Zach gave a humorless laugh. "When we moved into town, rather than living on the outskirts, some kids were a little more receptive to me. But by then, I didn't care. I had Travis and my mom. I didn't need anyone else. But Trav...he needed more, I guess. And after he gave me everything he had, I should have been there for him."

Stella turned her body so she could see him. With a hand to his jaw, she turned his face toward hers so she could press a kiss to his lips. "If you were even one-tenth as loyal back then as you are now, I'm sure you were there for him whenever he needed you."

Zach covered her hand with his and leaned into her touch. "Not the night he died. I wasn't there. Maybe if I had been..."

Stella waited for him to continue, but he didn't. Instead of pushing him, wanting to be what Zach *needed* in this moment, she drew her knees up and curled closer, nuzzling her face in his neck to breathe him in.

If he didn't want to tell her, that was fine. But the small part of her that hated secrets and not knowing wondered why he felt like he could have stopped his friend's death. She was about to suggest they head inside when he spoke again.

"A bunch of the guys who'd been dicks to us growing up— Rick, Colton, that whole group, they started being friendly to us. I wanted nothing to do with them. Travis and I were a unit. A team. It'd been that way so long, I never considered it could go another way. Rick was having this huge party and Travis wanted to go. It was the only fight we ever got in. He was pissed I wouldn't go. Said we always did whatever I wanted, and he was tired of living in social isolation with me. That sure, maybe some of the guys were assholes, but people changed. Maybe it was time for me to change, too. I told him to go without me. Said he was welcome to make new friends and do all the changing he wanted, but I was fine with the status quo. I was fine, with or without him."

Stella's heart squeezed when his voice cracked. "You were kids."

Taking a deep breath, he moved her hands from around him and stood up. He walked to the railing and gripped it with both hands, staring out at the sky. Stella wrapped her arms around her knees, her heart hurting for the kid he'd been and the man who'd carried this all these years.

"We were practically men, Stella. He went to the party. If I'd gone, if I'd sucked it up and tagged along, I would have stopped him from drinking so much. I sure as fuck would have stopped him from doing anything as stupid as jumping off a goddamn roof into a pool."

Stella gasped, and Zach's shoulders hunched. She wanted to go to him but didn't know if she should.

Zach hung his head for a moment, then turned around to face her. He didn't leave the railing, but his gaze burned into Stella's.

"They said it was an accident. It *was* an accident. He went to jump, slipped, smashed his head on the way down and landed on the concrete."

Stella's throat tightened so fast and hard she wheezed. Zach closed his eyes, rubbing the heels of his hands against them. Working on steadying her breath, Stella lowered her legs as Zach did his hands.

"I should have been there."

Unable to stop herself, Stella stood and launched herself at him. "You were a kid! You were both kids, Zach. It *was* an accident. It is not your fault."

His arms came around her, but his tone was distant. "Says you and the army shrinks. But the bottom line is, if I had been there, it wouldn't have happened."

She reared back, clenching her fists in his shirt. "You don't know that. You *can't* know that. The very same thing could have happened if you two had gone together. Maybe you'd have gotten caught up and done the same. You can't know. Would you have blamed yourself if it had been Rick or Colton?"

Zach practically snarled. "Fuck, no."

Putting both hands on his cheeks, she tilted his head down. "It is not your fault."

"He was my best friend."

"Friends fight. They make mistakes. If he'd been hit by a drunk driver, would it be your fault?"

Zach's brows pushed together, and she could feel his pain radiating against her and she wished she could absorb it. Take it from him.

"One decision and everything went sideways."

Threading her hands through his hair, she went up on tiptoe. "That's how it works. Sad as it is to say, life is full of a series of choices that lead us one place or another and we can't go back. We can't change what's happened. But that doesn't mean the results of whatever choice you *didn't* make are your fault. If he'd gotten laid by the hottest girl on the planet that night at the party, would you have taken the credit?"

As he laughed, Zach's fingers dug into her waist and Stella relished the sensation. They were both here. The past couldn't be undone, but they had a say in the future through the choices they made. And at that moment, Stella chose Zach.

"Were you at the party?" He pulled her tighter against him.

"What?" The flowery scent of the night air, the emotion, and the moon shining down on them intoxicated her, swirling around them, making her want to push the world away.

"You said the hottest girl on the planet. From where I'm standing, that's you."

Smiling, she arched closer just as one of his hands roamed down and the other tunneled into her hair.

"I get it, you know," she told him, her heart fluttering.

He continued to stare, and she wondered if she could tell him the truth of what had been haunting her for too long. *He told you his truth.*

"Tell me," he whispered.

She nodded and took a deep breath. "My dad had a heart condition he didn't tell anyone about. The doctor must have thought I knew because, at the hospital, he mentioned it."

Zach smoothed her hair back from her face, and his eyes *told* her he understood how she felt, standing there, learning about it from a stranger.

"Baby, I'm sorry. But how is that the same?"

When his hands slid down to cup her face, she put hers on his wrists, gripping tight. "I keep thinking that if I'd come home in better shape, not shaken up from being dumped, if I'd kept in touch better, come home more often…anything. Maybe he'd have told me. Maybe I could have done something."

"Stella," he said, his voice a harsh, aching whisper that, oddly enough, soothed her like an embrace.

Forcing herself to let go of that demon, just as Zach was trying to do with his guilt over Travis, she took another fortifying breath. "We want to believe that, if we only knew, we could control the outcome. But we can't. We don't always know and we do the best we can in the moment."

When his mouth crashed against hers, she knew the conversation was over. Zach boosted her so she could wrap her legs around his waist and he headed for the house. His lips never left Stella's, and he hugged her so close only air could fit between them. She felt, quite literally, consumed. And she wanted nothing more than to give him everything he needed. Zach didn't put her down until they reached her bedroom. In the dark, with him over her, she could forget that they were both slightly damaged. In the quiet, with the only sounds being their combined breaths and the heavy beat of their hearts, Stella wondered if she'd been too quick to dismiss a second chance at forever. Zach had given her back her business. Her life. And quite possibly, her belief in happy endings.

Chapter Twenty-Seven

Zach phoned Andrew back and got his voicemail. For some reason, his friend had called a total of nine times in five days. Since the pet wash, they'd been running their asses off and Zach hadn't been able to talk. The moments he wasn't buried in work, he was immersed, completely fucking submerged, in all that was Stella. He wondered if it was possible to be addicted to a person. Just being around her made it feel easier to breathe, to smile, to laugh.

When he'd told her about Travis, he'd expected to feel some relief at getting it off his chest. He *hadn't* expected it to unleash a frenzy of feelings from both of them. Like they were drawn together by the things in their pasts that they couldn't change or forget; it entwined them. Stella's walls all but crumbled that night he made love to her, and he found himself wanting to do anything and everything to be what she needed.

Tossing his phone on the kitchen counter, he decided that if he couldn't get a hold of Andrew by tomorrow, he'd tell Stella he needed a day and go find him. Hopefully it wasn't anything health related. He'd even tried the clinic, but they kept saying he was unavailable. Stella was curled up on the couch with her laptop when he joined her in the living room.

She glanced up from the screen. "Hey."

"Hey." He was so fucked. She wore a pair of pajama bottoms and a tank top. There wasn't a drop of makeup on her face and her hair was up in some weird-ass bun thing on her head. And he practically drooled at the sight of her.

Dropping down beside her, she laughed when it jostled her into him. "Looking at porn?" He leaned in to see what she was doing.

Stella laughed. "Uh, no. Just checking the website actually. I was thinking we could start a newsletter. We could do it monthly, maybe include some coupons, some health advice?"

Zach grinned up at her. "That's a great idea."

She nudged him. "You don't have to sound quite so shocked."

"Our Facebook page is getting several hits, too, and people have commented that they really enjoyed the pet wash. Definitely needs to be a yearly thing."

Stella glanced down at him and their gazes held. She'd done that a few times in the last couple of days: stared at him like she wasn't quite sure she could believe he'd be sticking around. If he had it his way, he and Stella would only dig in deeper. He wanted to plant roots, and he wanted to do that with Stella Lane. In every way possible.

"I never check the Facebook page. Do you comment back?"

He gestured to the computer. "Check it. And yeah. Sometimes. It's easy enough to do from my phone." Stella clicked on the home button instead of typing Facebook into the address bar and when the page came up, Zach's stomach seized so sharply, he choked on his own breath.

"You okay?"

Stella was looking at him with concern, but Zach's eyes went back to the screen. *No fucking way.* His chest tightened, and he felt like he couldn't breathe.

"Zach?"

"Huh?"

She nudged him again. "What's wrong?"

He sat up. "Nothing. I just swallowed wrong. I need a drink."

Getting up, he left her there and hurried into the kitchen, his heart nearly beating out of his chest. He pulled his phone out of his pocket and brought up the internet. He went to the local news page and sure enough, there it was again. The headline read: CEO OF CHAIN STORE PET CENTRAL ACCUSED OF EMBEZZLING HUNDREDS OF THOUSANDS OF DOLLARS.

"No. No." His fingers clutched so tightly at his phone that the case cracked. "No."

Clicking on the story, he was reading it so intently that he didn't hear Stella come up behind him.

"Hey," she said, her hands smoothing over his back.

He whirled, unintentionally startling her. "Hey."

She stepped back and frowned. "What's going on?"

Fuck. What the hell did he say? "I, uh, it's just this news story. It surprised me is all. Sorry."

Coming to his side, she looked down at his phone. "Oh, Zach. I'm so sorry. That's your friend, right? Andrew Clark?" She touched his phone, scrolling upward to read the story. "That's horrible."

When she looked at him, her eyes were full of compassion and regret. "I'm sorry."

"Yeah." What else could he say? *Tell her. Tell her that you borrowed money from him.* Why the fuck did he borrow money from him? Because he'd *trusted* him. And Stella trusted Zach. Getting to that point was a victory, and the thought of stripping that away made him feel physically sick. *You can fix this. Call the bank. You've been here a couple months now. You have options.* Could he just give Andrew back the money and not be implicated in any way? If he was somehow linked to Andrew financially, would it implicate Stella? The clinic?

Zach shoved his phone into his pocket. Running his hands through his hair, it took effort not to yank it out. What the hell had he done?

Stella stepped into him and put her hands on her chest. "It's never easy to see your idols fall. We feel like the people we admire are untouchable. But they're human, and we're human, which means we can't blame ourselves for believing in them."

He stared at her, his hands still in his hair. Was she talking about herself or him? "I need some air."

Stepping back, she lowered her hands and he saw the touch of hurt in her gaze. Yeah. He was shutting her out and yes, he felt like a jackass for doing it, but he needed to figure out a way to fix this. To unentangle himself from Andrew. Without Stella knowing.

"Okay," she said, still regarding him carefully.

"I'm sorry. I just, I'm really surprised. I think I'll try and call him."

Understanding washed out the concern. "That's nice of you. I'm sure he could use some support. And it did say alleged, right?"

He nodded, his throat too dry to talk.

Stella came closer again and hugged him. With her head on his chest, she squeezed him tight. "I'm glad you're here. At the clinic. I'm sorry this is happening to your friend, but it could be worse."

When she lifted her head, he could only nod. Yes, it could be worse. She could find out that he hadn't told her the whole truth before he had a chance to fix it. He'd tell her everything. As soon as he got some answers.

. . .

Zach had driven all the way to Andrew's house to see if he was there. He wasn't. He'd called before wasting the two hours, but worried his calls were now getting dodged. Which made no sense since Andrew had been trying so hard to get a hold of him. He'd hung around for a bit, staring at the damn-near stately mansion his former friend owned. He felt like a damn fool and that wasn't even the worst of it. *No. The worst is that you inadvertently dragged Stella into this. And then you didn't fucking tell her what was up.* Because he was determined to fix it. Zach had spent the last ten years of his life aiming for one goal: to belong. He thought that meant living in Brockton, working there, and being an integral part of the community. But it didn't. Now, the only thing it meant to him was Stella loving him back because he knew he loved her, and everything he'd attained meant nothing if she didn't want him.

Because he wasn't quite ready to tell her everything, though he would tonight, he drove by his mother's house since it was on the way. Coming back into Brockton as the sun dipped into the sky should have been a solace. He should have told her before he left. He knew not telling her was the same as lying, but he wanted to have answers. She'd definitely have questions. And anger. And hurt. Zach slammed the steering wheel. He'd rather pull his limbs off than hurt her.

The urge to unload, give her the whole story and figure out how to deal with the situation *together* was suddenly consuming. And if his mother hadn't been playing with her dog on the front lawn while Shane used a weed trimmer around a couple of trees, he'd have kept going. Just to get rid of the ache in his chest.

Instead, he pulled into the driveway and got out of his car.

"This is a nice surprise," his mother said, dropping the ball she'd been using for Chuck when he bounded toward Zach.

"How's it going?" Shane asked, cutting the motor on the trimmer.

His mother stopped in front of him before he could lie and say he was fine.

"What's wrong?" His mom put her hand on his arm and Chuck, picking up on her tone, whimpered.

Shane set the trimmer against the tree and wandered over to them.

"You alright, son?" With a graying goatee and arms as wide as the tree trunk, his voice shouldn't have seemed so gentle. Zach looked back and forth between them and realized he was happy he came home, if for no other reason than to see his mom had finally gotten what she'd always deserved. Happiness. Someone to share her life with. Someone who appreciated her, protected her, welcomed her son into the fold as if it had never been a question. His own father had made it a fucking question. But not this guy. No, he was stable and solid and his mother was stronger because of it. Which was saying something since she was damn strong anyway. He wanted to be that rock for Stella, but chances were good, he'd already let things go too long to make that happen.

"Honey, you're scaring me," his mom said.

Zach shoved his hands through his hair. "I fucked up."

Shane folded his arms over his wide chest and kept quiet while Chuck went back to his ball. His mother was clearly waiting for him to say more, to say something. But what the hell could he say?

"What happened?" She kept her hand on his arm and

guided him to the stairs. Shane followed but stayed standing when they sat on the steps.

With as little detail or emotion as he could, Zach opened up. "I wanted in so bad, I didn't take the time to consider all of the possibilities. Or the outcomes. I had no reason not to trust Andrew. Hell, I was flattered he believed in me so strongly. That he'd want to invest in me."

"Why wouldn't he?" Shane asked.

His mom smiled but Zach just stared.

Shane shrugged. "It's no secret you work your ass off to do what needs doing. Anyone with eyes can see you're good at what you do. Regardless of what it is."

Not having had any semblance of a relationship with his father, Zach was caught off guard by the depth of emotion he felt from hearing the certainty in Shane's tone.

"Army teaches you to believe in yourself. You forget that?" Shane's brows furrowed as he narrowed his eyes at Zach.

Surprised he could laugh, Zach did just that. "No, sir."

Shane nodded. "I'm going to get a beer."

When he went inside, Chuck followed. His mom leaned her head on his shoulder and didn't press him.

"He's a good man," Zach said, breaking the quiet.

"So are you."

"I screwed up, Mom. I should have told her before she cashed the check that it was a loan. I have the money, but it's tied up. I didn't give her all the facts and she's going to hate that."

His mom nodded against his shoulder. "She is. Just like you would. You know enough about half truths from your father to know they don't feel good."

Zach flinched. "I'm not him."

His mom straightened and turned her body to face him. "You listen to me, Zach. And you listen damn well. You are nothing like your father. *Nothing.* I never got a chance to tell you I was sorry about subjecting you to the life he offered us, but I wasn't entirely sorry for choosing him."

Anger still burned in the pit of his stomach. "How could you not be? And why would you be sorry? It wasn't your fault he was a useless asshole."

One side of her lips tipped up. "Watch your mouth. And no, it's not my fault he was, but I chose him. And I stayed. I should have done better for both of us."

He thought of Stella busting her ass to make things work at the clinic, in her house, in her life. She hadn't complained even though he was almost positive she'd been waist deep into drowning when he'd showed up. But she'd kept going. Kept fighting. Like his mother.

"Why aren't you sorry then?" Zach looked back at the screen door, then met his mom's gaze. "You could have had someone like Shane for a lifetime."

His mom grinned. "I've still got a lifetime in me. And if I didn't choose your father, I wouldn't have you. People make mistakes, honey. You pick yourself up and carry on. I didn't know how to leave, so I stayed and did the best I could. But sometimes I feel like I let you down."

Reaching out to squeeze his mom's hand, he shook his head. "You didn't. I wanted to make you proud. I hated that people gave us food hampers at Christmas and you never got birthday presents. When I left, after Trav died, I promised myself I'd come back and you'd never go without again." He shook his head once more. "But while I was gone, you were making sure you were fine. I should have stayed. I should have helped you out *here* instead of running off."

She clucked her tongue at him. "You did what kids do. They grow up. I don't resent that, and I knew you'd be back. I don't need you to take care of me, honey. I just want to know you're okay. That you're happy. That's all I need."

Nodding, his throat tight, he couldn't help feeling like he'd wasted a lot of time worrying about getting everything just right. Coming back with enough money, becoming something through the army, getting his vet license. He'd wanted those things, but it was more than that—he thought he needed them to prove what kind of man he was. Having all those things hadn't stopped him from being less than the man Stella Lane needed at her side.

His mom patted his hand. "You made a mistake. How are you going to fix it?"

Inhaling deeply, he exhaled slowly. "I'm going to go home, tell her everything, and in the morning, I'm going to figure out a way to get Andrew his money back immediately. There's no record of it so I don't think Stella can be implicated in any way."

"I can help," she said, glancing at him from the side of her eye.

Zach smiled. "I'm not taking money from you, Mom."

"Stubborn."

He laughed. "It's a lot of money. If you've got that kind of nest egg, you use it for you and Shane. If I didn't have any options, it would be different. But I kept my options in check and took the easy route borrowing money from Andrew."

She stood and dusted off her pants. "You have, not once in your life, taken the easy path. You were a bit impatient to get on with your plan, but as always, your heart and intentions were in exactly the right place."

Zach rested his forearms on his knees. "I hope Stella can understand that."

When his mom said nothing, he looked up. Her brows were arched, and she crossed her arms over her chest.

"What?"

Giving him the full-on-mom look, she tilted her head. "Since when are you afraid to fight for what you want? It's what got you into this—charging full steam ahead."

He winced. "That was to work at the practice."

"You want Stella?"

Zach stood up, his heart jumping. "More than anything."

"Then do the right thing and if it pushes her away, fight for her."

He could do that. He could definitely do that. There was no other option because he didn't want a future that didn't include Stella. Kissing his mom on the cheek, Zach walked to his car, determined to show Stella what kind of man he really was. The kind who could own up and come clean and still be strong enough to fix things and make them right. Who he was had nothing to do with being able to buy into her clinic or own a house. Why the hell had it taken him so long to see that?

Doesn't matter. As long as you can make her see you're better together.

Chapter Twenty-Eight

Stella set the coffee down in front of Zach's friend. Whispers of unease bristled the hair on the back of her neck, but she tried to ignore the feeling. *Same way you ignored Steven's repeated protests that everything was okay.* Ignoring her gut had never worked out any better than following her heart. She hadn't heard from Zach in hours and though he'd said he was fine when he left, she knew he'd been less than honest about that. The worry in his eyes and the rigid set of his shoulders made her certain there was more to it than his concern for a friend.

"Thank you. I knew your father," Andrew said, picking up the ceramic mug and wrapping his hands around it.

Her heart muscles tightened, but it was more anticipation than sadness. She was growing to like other people's versions of her father. "How?"

"I'd asked more than once if he wanted to partner up. Perhaps do some cross-promotional events. Pet Central prides itself on innovative techniques and community partners."

He said the words like he had memorized them rather

than felt them. Since Andrew was acting like she hadn't learned of the news story—which she wouldn't have if not for Zach—Stella acted as if she didn't.

She thought back to the pile of "offers" she'd sorted through and shredded. Pet Central had been in that pile. She was glad she never gave in to the urge to take a quick fix way out of the mess. *And not just because of Zach or the current headlines.* She'd held strong and the clinic was bouncing back thanks to hard work. *Team work.* Best of all, it was hers. And Zach's. Theirs. *Ours.* The word sent a series of flutters through her body.

"You said you worked overseas with Zach?"

Andrew nodded. He stared into his mug, and Stella wondered how much longer Zach would be. "I did. He's an excellent vet. A good man."

"He is."

There was more, but he kept his eyes on his coffee. Nacho came up, sniffed at him. He set his drink down and rubbed the dog's head. Soda joined them, vying for her share of attention.

"Gorgeous animals. All I ever wanted to do was help animals. Make a difference. Working with pets is like working with children, you know? They can't speak up for themselves. They need advocates and caregivers."

Stella smiled, rubbed Soda's back the way he liked. "That's a good way to put it."

"I got lost. I'm sorry I brought Zach into that."

Her stomach clenched tightly, and Soda whined, nuzzled her palm, like she could read the tension that coated her from his words. The front door closed, and she heard his boot steps even as the dogs rushed the door.

"Stella?"

She knew his voice, his footsteps. Both were heavy and it made her stomach feel the same.

"Do you have company?" He stopped in the doorway of the kitchen, the dogs at his sides. Like they accepted his place here. "Andrew."

His friend stood, turned to Zach, who came to Stella's side. She watched as shock, anger, and worry collided in Zach's expression while he looked at Andrew. When his gaze turned to her, there was so much regret in it, her knees almost buckled.

"Sorry to drop in like this," Andrew said, a tight smile stretching his features.

"I've been calling you. I went to your house," Zach said.

Stella was surprised by the venom in his voice. She'd never heard that tone from him and was about to say something when Andrew stood.

"Zach."

The two men stared at each other, and Stella's pulse raced. This was more than eye contact between them. It was silent messages that flipped Stella's stomach upside down.

"Should I give you two some privacy?" She stood.

They weren't touching now, just standing side by side, but Stella felt Zach's tension as clearly as if his arms were wrapped around her body. Something was wrong. She breathed through her nose, forcing the worst-case scenarios to take a back seat.

"It might be best, Zach," Andrew said.

Zach reached for Stella's hand and linked their fingers. The pressure settled her stomach. "No. Stella and I are partners."

Turning his back on his friend, Zach bent his knees to look at her. She couldn't see Andrew through Zach's body, but even with the illusion of privacy, she sensed the other man's restlessness.

"What's going on?" she whispered.

"I let you down," he said clearly.

Her heart dropped into her stomach like a hammer coming down. "What?"

"I couldn't get access to my money right away. The bank wasn't able to let me borrow against my properties or cash out the investment."

Stella kept her breath steady. Okay. So he'd gotten a loan? She'd tried to do the same.

"I borrowed the money from Andrew."

She stepped back even as she opened her mouth to gasp. No sound came out, and she felt like she was choking on dry air. She pointed around him. "That Andrew? The one currently embroiled in a public scandal? You let me put *his* money into my father's clinic when you knew how much I didn't want outside help?"

"Stella," he said, the emotion in his voice cracking her heart. "I'm sorry. I'm going to fix it."

"How?" She stepped back farther. "How could you possibly fix it?" She pressed her hand against her chest, trying to press the ache back inside.

Zach turned to Andrew. "I'll have your money for you soon. Very soon. There's no record of anything which I'm guessing you thought was smart thinking on your part but wasn't. You can't prove any financial connection between us, and you sure as hell can't connect any dots to this clinic. I'll have the money wired to you, but I don't ever want to see you again."

Andrew's face paled, and even though her own anger bubbled like a pot about to boil over, she felt a twinge of sympathy for the man. He looked ten years older than when he'd walked into the house.

"Believe it or not, the money isn't why I was calling, or why I'm here. I need a favor."

Zach's harsh bark of laughter was as far from humorous as it could get. "You have got to be fucking kidding me. You want a favor? There was no way you didn't know when you lent me the money that this storm was brewing, that it was coming right at you. You let me think you believed in me and the truth was, you were just looking to store a little cash for a rainy day. Off the books."

Andrew let out a weary sigh, shoving both hands in his pockets. He didn't deny anything Zach said and now, despite her anger, Stella's sympathy tiptoed toward Zach. She knew what it was like to have someone special let her down. Use her. Walk away without a backward glance.

"I'm not proud of anything I did, but my faith in you was one hundred percent genuine. You are one of the best veterinarians I've ever worked with. You have more heart than anyone I've met. I wish I could say I was half the man you are, but I'm not. But I am sorry. Really damn sorry. And I hate asking you for anything, even my money back, but I need more than that. I need you to be a character witness and sign a document saying the money I gave you was not in connection with Pet Central. That it was a personal donation for a community project we're working on together."

Stella felt like she might throw up. She pressed her free hand to her stomach.

Zach put his hands to his hips and bent his head. When he lifted it, looked at Andrew, she could *feel* the anger vibrating off him.

"You want me to lie for you?"

"I need you to do me a favor, just as I did you one so you could be part of this..." Andrew stopped, gestured to the window in the direction of the clinic. "Part of this run-down practice you were desperate to join. It's not a big deal, and there's no reason to get all worked up. I just need a letter saying we're in a partnership, it's aboveboard and the money was donated from my own account. Then I'll be out of your life."

"Get out." Zach's voice shook, and Stella wrapped her

arms around herself, trying to fight the chill she felt.

"Zach," Andrew said, his tone pleading.

"Get the fuck out. I'll wire your money to you. You don't want me as a character witness, Andrew. Trust me on that. Because obviously, I never knew you at all."

Stella's heart clenched at the crestfallen look on Zach's face. Though he clearly meant it, he didn't feel good about it. And even now, while she worried the exact same thing was true of her—that she didn't know Zach at all—she ached for him. Because she knew what it was like to be let down by someone you loved. Even though she'd promised herself it would never happen again, that too had been a lie. Standing here now, looking at Zach, seeing his pain and feeling it as her own, she knew she loved him. Once again, she'd chosen wrong. And the only person she had to blame was herself. She'd known better, and she'd fallen anyway.

Chapter Twenty-Nine

Zach walked Andrew to the door, more to slam it behind him than anything else. He pressed his head to the cool wood for a second and then straightened up, turning toward the kitchen. Stella stood in the hall between the living room and the door. His hands reached out, and she stepped back. It was like she'd kicked him the heart.

"You should go." Her tone was eerily calm. It made his blood cool and his heart pound.

"Stella, please. We need to talk," he said, unable to keep his own voice steady.

"The time for talking would have been when you couldn't get the money. When you gave me the check. Before we'd slept together. *After* we'd slept together. Basically, any time before your friend showed up on my doorstep looking for you."

Her doorstep. Her home. Her business. He'd worked so fucking hard to work his way in, and he'd wrecked it all by doing the one thing he shouldn't have—withholding information.

"I should have. You're right. But I wanted to fix it."

She crossed her arms over her chest, and he saw her shiver. He wanted—needed—to pull her into his arms but he'd lost that right.

"It wasn't broken. Until you."

She turned her back on him and walked to the living room. The dogs were sleeping by the fireplace. They were so used to his presence, they'd didn't stir.

"That's not entirely true," he said. He didn't want her calm facade. He deserved to be yelled at. He deserved her anger. He'd expected it. The aloof shield was worse.

She didn't turn until she'd walked to the window. Putting distance between them, he'd bet. Physically, emotionally. She was right fucking there, and he already missed her.

Her gaze was quiet like the air between them. He hated it. Even when she had been adamant about not letting him in, there'd been a spark in her eyes. Now, they were empty. *You did that.*

"I was surviving. I would have figured it out."

"You were drowning."

She scowled, and his heart lurched. He'd take any show of emotion he could get from her right now.

"Maybe so, but I was doing it on my own terms."

He wasn't arguing semantics with her, especially since he knew he was dead wrong. Taking a couple steps toward her, he stopped in the center of the floor when she backed up so she was touching the wall. Breathing through his nose, he told himself she had the right to be hurt. To not want him close.

"I'm sorry, Stella. I was wrong, and I *will* fix this. The money isn't linked to you in any way. I won't have anything to do with Andrew again. I feel like an idiot for taking the money. Andrew has been like a dad to me. More than just a boss or a teacher. He was a mentor and someone I trusted. At the time, I was happy that he considered me worth the risk."

A flash of pain came and went in her gaze. "Funny, I thought you were, too."

He swallowed down the groan of pain her words caused. "Stella, I should have said something. I was wrong. People make mistakes. But we can get past this. Being here with you, not just in the clinic or in your home, but with *you,* is the best thing that's ever happened to me. I don't want to lose you. I'll do anything to make this right."

Her shoulders stiffened, and she pressed off the wall. "You can't. You can't make it right." She was back to that emotionless tone that felt like shards of glass raking over his skin. "You know how I feel about people keeping things from me. You knew how I felt about accepting help, big business, outsiders taking part in my father's legacy. You *knew* all of that. And you still held out. Even today, you could have come clean, but you didn't."

Panic ramped up his pulse like he was back in the army running drills. "I was scared you'd shut me out like you're doing right now. You're not exactly easy to get close to, Stella. Chipping away at your shell is one of the hardest things I've ever done. You're right, I should have told you. I knew it the whole time and especially today, but every single day I've been with you, all I could think was how much more I want with you. And I was terrified of ruining this, what we have."

Ignoring her obvious body language, he stepped closer and put his hands on her shoulders. "I was scared because I'm crazy about you."

Her lips quivered, and it broke his fucking heart. Because it was his fault. "At least Steven didn't know."

Like she'd given him a gut shot, he dropped his hands and curled his shoulders. "What?" His voice was thick.

"I never opened up to anyone the way I did to you. Not even Megan or Taylor, and they're my closest friends. I never told anyone else about my dad's heart condition. I didn't think I had anything left to give after Steven. I felt stupid and naïve. I planned to marry him and still, I never let him in the way I did you. I never let him know me the way you do. Did. The money doesn't matter anymore because, as you said, it'll be cleared up soon enough and our names aren't attached. Though, I wonder why, if you can suddenly get that money, you didn't just ask me for more time rather than give me someone else's money. I'll refund your investment. I want you to go."

"You can't afford to return the money, and I don't fucking want it. I want this, Stella. *Us*." He knew how to fight but he was losing. She was building up her wall, one metaphorical brick at a time right in front of him.

"There is no us."

He slammed his fingers into his hair and turned, paced the room. When he looked at her again, his stomach flipped. He'd waited his whole fucking life to feel like he belonged. And he'd found it. Not in a place, but in her. And he'd wrecked it.

"Don't throw things away like this. Fight for us, dammit. I know you care about me. Don't use this as an excuse to shut me out. I fucked up. We can get past it. Please."

She crossed her arms, gripping her elbows. Breath unsteady, she looked down. "Don't make this harder."

He stalked toward her, but she didn't lift her head. He wanted to shake her, hug her, kiss her. "Don't throw this away. I'm begging you."

When she looked up, tears shone in her eyes. "I can't trust you. At the end of the day, you made the decision that suited you best. I've already been in a relationship like that. It's not what I want. When you lo—care about someone, truly care, you put their wants and needs ahead of your own. You had the chance to do that more than once and you didn't."

His throat felt thick and he had to fight the urge to yank

her against him. "Stella."

"Go. I'm asking you to go. You can come for your things another time, but I can't...I can't be around you right now."

She turned, snapped her fingers which alerted the dogs, and they followed her into her bedroom. She shut the door. Zach stared after her, his heart in his throat. As he left the house—because what choice did he have—he realized there was something worse than never belonging anywhere. Worse than losing his friend to an *accident*. Accidents happened. Loss happened. People dealt with it every day. But to have it all, everything he'd wanted in his grasp, and have it stripped away by his own idiocy, by his own hand, was a pain he'd never known.

• • •

Zach hadn't felt this level of internal crazy since the day of Travis's funeral. That day, he'd moved and breathed and functioned by rote. Socks. Pants. Shirt. Tie. Get in the car. Attend the service. Breathe in. Breathe out. His mom hadn't asked questions when he'd shown up. She and Shane had been watching a movie. He'd said he needed a place to sleep and gone to bed. But he could hear them moving around the house.

And you're hiding in your old bedroom like a fucking wimp. No. He was pulling his thoughts together, trying to figure out how he was going to fix this. *I can't trust you.* Those words were etched into his brain and just thinking them made his fingers clench.

"I'm damn well going to prove you can," he whispered, pushing off the way-too-small-for-him twin bed.

Walking into the kitchen, he grunted hello and went for the coffee. He'd poured a mug and leaned against the counter before he looked at them.

"I take it things didn't go as planned?" His mother

asked as she glanced over from the table where she had the newspaper spread out in front of her.

Shane leaned back in his seat, one foot resting on his other knee. He said nothing, but Zach felt the quiet assessment.

"Nope."

His mother's face showed disappointment. Perfect. One more female he'd let down. Chuck wandered in, happily trotting over to Zach, who set his coffee down to give him a good rub.

It was stupid, but last night, when Nacho and Soda had immediately gone to Stella, it was one more kick in the teeth. Those dogs loved him. But when they'd had to choose… *Yeah, like you wouldn't have chosen her, too.* "You're a happy, boy." Chuck lay down and rolled so he was belly up.

"More than you," his mother muttered.

"Sheila," Shane said. The tone, the quiet warning, felt like he was taking Zach's back.

His mom bristled. "What? Half his problem is keeping everything in. Must be a guy thing. Stubborn, macho stupidity syndrome. I think you can die from that."

Shane cracked a smile and Zach couldn't help it; he laughed. "Not sure it's an actual thing, Mom."

She folded the paper together. "Oh, trust me, honey. It is. Life is too short to waste it harboring everything inside. Did you tell her how you feel?"

She didn't let him answer. "Of course you didn't. Probably didn't want to put yourself out there or whatever stupid phrase kids use these days. She can't read your damn mind." Rising from her seat, she shook her head at him, disappointment in her gaze, and walked past him.

He fucking hated disappointing her. Disappointing himself wasn't a whole lot of fun either. He couldn't even think of the way he'd let Stella down. Chuck followed after his mom. Damn dogs knew who to side with.

"We aren't talkers, that's all. Women don't get that," Shane said, picking up his coffee.

Zach didn't know what to say to that. He wasn't wrong since not talking to Stella was part of what got him into this mess.

"We're doers." Shane set his cup down and stood up. He was almost the same height as Zach, and though he had twenty years on him, in pretty damn good shape.

"That a thing?"

"It is. So, you fucked up. It happens. How are you going to fix it?"

Irritation prickled. If he knew exactly *how* to fix it, he wouldn't have slept in his teenage bed. Zach picked up his coffee, took a long swallow, and missed the specialty beans Stella ground. *Right. You miss her coffee.*

"I need money. I need to see if I can flip one of my properties and pay off a loan. Then I need to show Stella I'm not going anywhere."

Shane nodded. "Okay. See? Doers. So finish your damn coffee and get it done."

Zach smirked. "Uh, thanks?"

Shane clapped him on the arm. "No problem. Your mom is right about one thing. Life is short. Makes it seem shorter when you drag all that baggage with you. We all fuck up, kid. It's what you do about it that makes you the man you want to be."

He stared at this man he hardly knew and realized that he'd already been a better father figure in twenty minutes than his own had been all his life.

"What if I can't fix it?" He didn't mean to utter the words. The thought paralyzed him. What if he couldn't get her back?

The soft smile Shane gave him told him everything he needed to know about how the guy felt toward his mother. "What if you can?"

Zach nodded, finished his coffee, and said goodbye. He didn't want to talk. He needed to *do*.

Chapter Thirty

Stella stared at her ceiling, her eyes feeling like she'd rubbed them with sand. She hadn't slept all night. Hard to sleep with tears wracking her body. Once she'd started—the second she heard the door close behind Zach—she hadn't been able to stop. It was as if she'd unleashed an ocean of hurt and holding back had been impossible. The dogs had rallied around her on the bed, one at her front, one against her back, and absorbed the impact of her crying.

Rubbing the heels of her hands over her eyes, she startled when she heard a knock at the door. The dogs jumped off the bed and her heart leaped with them, her first thought being that it might be Zach. Stupid, stupid heart. She hadn't learned a damn thing. Weaving her way to the door like a drunk on a bender, she realized she was wrong. She had learned something. She'd learned that while she may have cared for Steven, and she'd certainly been infatuated with him, she hadn't truly loved him. She knew the difference now. *Since Zach.*

Sniffling, she pulled the door open and was greeted by

Meg. The ready smile on her friend's face slipped immediately.

"What's wrong?" Megan asked, coming into the house, her hands full of coffee and a bakery bag.

"Bad night," Stella said, her voice rough.

How on earth could she feel like crying? She had nothing left. She was probably dehydrated she'd cried so much, yet her throat thickened, wetness pricked at the corner of her eyes, and her heart squeezed painfully.

Shutting the door and following Megan into the kitchen, she breathed through her nose. *Just breathe. In. Out. You can do that. You just have to get through this minute. One minute at a time.* It felt like too much.

Megan put the coffee and bag on the counter, shrugged off her purse, and stepped into Stella's space without any warning. She wrapped her hands around her fiercely and squeezed the air out of Stella's lungs.

"What are you doing?" Stella whispered.

"Whatever you need. Tell me. What's wrong?" Megan spoke low and soothing in what Stella thought might be her classroom voice.

"Why are you here?"

"I thought I'd stop by and say hi on my way to work. You're always in the clinic at this time. When you weren't, I thought maybe I'd interrupt some morning fun and say hi to you and Zach."

The smile in her friend's voice proved her undoing. She bit her lip to hold back the sob, her body tensed, and her breath stuck in her lungs like a thorn.

"Stella. You're scaring me."

She was scaring herself because she didn't think she'd ever let anyone have this kind of power over her feelings. She couldn't control the merry-go-round of feelings spinning out of control inside of her.

"Zach isn't here," Stella whispered.

Megan pulled back, gripping her shoulders, then slipped one arm around her, nudging her toward the living room.

"What happened?"

I fell in love. Stella bit the inside of her cheek. God, she was such a fool. "He lied." She pushed the words out of her mouth and the rest of the story tumbled after them. Megan held her hand, squeezing it, patting it, listening without interruption.

When she finished, Stella felt like she'd completed a marathon. Her breath sawed in and out, her eyes were wet but gritty, and she had a stitch in her side.

"I'm sorry, Stell. What are you guys going to do?"

Stella flinched. "You guys? There is no 'you guys.' *I'm* going to take control of my clinic and refund Zach's money. I'm going to get up every day like I have been and care for animals. I'm going to figure out a way to carry on my dad's legacy without burying myself under a pile of debt." Which, she knew, might include selling off pieces of the land. Big pieces. She needed a serious cash flow if she wanted to pay Zach out.

"You're not going to give him a second chance?" The surprise in Megan's voice raised Stella's hackles.

"A second chance to what? He lied. Repeatedly. It wouldn't even be a second chance, Meg. He had many opportunities to tell me what he'd done. He chose not to."

Her friend bit her lip and stared at the brick mantle. Unease dislodged the thorn in her side.

"You think it's okay that he held back all of that information? That he invested *someone else's money* after I'd specifically steered clear of that path? You think—"

Megan put her hand up, cutting Stella off. "No. No. Of course I don't think that's okay. But it was a mistake."

"It was a choice," Stella said, her tone hard. She didn't want to take out her hurt on Megan, but she wasn't responsible for what Zach had done. Megan was supposed to have her back. Rising, she walked over to the fireplace, resisting the urge to pace.

The silence in the room was broken by Nacho and Soda's snoring. They hadn't slept much, either, and this morning, she knew they missed Zach's presence. His absence was like a huge crater. A sink hole getting wider. Swallowing her.

"I was afraid to ask you to be my maid of honor," Megan said, her voice so quiet Stella almost didn't hear.

Taking a seat in the easy chair opposite the couch, she tucked her legs up under her and stared at Megan, not understanding. "Afraid seems like a funny word."

Megan shrugged. "I love you, hon, but you can be intimidating." The words *whooshed* out of her friend like they'd slipped.

Stella's forehead scrunched. "Intimidating how?"

Gesturing to her with a wave of her hand, Megan scoffed. "How? You're all Miss Independent, I don't need anyone, romantically or otherwise. You're like Superwoman. You plow through everything without complaint. Someone has a problem? You fix it. Someone doesn't have money to pay, you eat the cost. You keep going like the energizer bunny and that's a little intimidating."

Stella didn't see it that way. She called it surviving. "That still doesn't explain why you'd be afraid."

Megan's eyes darted past her then, clearly bracing herself, she met her gaze. "It's scary to need someone, want someone in your life, that you aren't sure needs you back."

Mouth opened, Stella didn't know what to say.

Megan got up, came over to the chair, and knelt in front of it. She grabbed Stella's hands, her eyes wide and worried. "You're so great, Stell. You're kind and caring, but tough as steel. But you're so determined to make it on your own, you never ask for help or a shoulder to cry on."

Stella pulled her hands free. "So, because I can take care of myself, I should just let go of the fact that Zach so blatantly went against my very well-known wishes?"

Megan leaned back and sighed. "No. Of course not. But when you fall in love, you do stupid things. When you admire and respect and care for someone, you work so hard to make them see the best of you, that sometimes you hide the other stuff until you're sure."

"Sure of what?" Her friend wasn't making any sense.

"Sure they're hooked. Sure they won't walk away even when you screw up. Adam almost let me walk away because he was scared to be in love. With anyone. Maybe Zach didn't know how to tell you. Not in a way that wouldn't put your shields back in the lock-and-load position."

Stella nearly growled. "I'm so tired of hearing that I have some invisible shields. It's ridiculous."

Megan's face fell. "But it's true. You keep people at arm's length for a long time. You don't want them to see that you're human. That you might need a little help financially. Or physically. Garrett or Parks would have gladly helped you around here with fixing fences or painting. They didn't want to suggest it, though, because they didn't want to insult you. Adam and I could have helped you financially—or at least with a sounding board—if you'd opened up. But you don't. You take it all on yourself, so other people, people who love you, feel like they should be able to do the same."

Stella focused on breathing in and out while she absorbed her friend's words. "I'm thrilled to be your maid of honor," she finally said.

Megan smiled. "And I'm thrilled you agreed. But I was scared to ask because you always seem like you don't need the same thing as us mere mortals do. Love, affection, forgiveness."

Huffing out a breath at that ridiculous statement, Stella

tried to glare at her friend, but failed. "Just because I didn't need a fairy tale doesn't mean I don't want you to have one. You know that, right?"

"I do," Megan said softly. "But when I was missing Adam, when I was sure things wouldn't work out, I wished I was as strong as you. I wished I could just go about my life not needing anyone else. Not giving my heart away and feeling the pain of having it tossed back at me."

Stella didn't feel very strong right that minute. She felt dangerously close to crying. Again. "I've often wished I had your happy, positive outlook on things. So I guess we're even."

Shaking her head, Megan gave her an uneven smile. "No. We're *different*. You're more cautious with your feelings and you have good reason. A lot of the people you've given your heart to have let you down or left in some way. It's okay to be scared, Stell. And it's okay to screw up. Because if someone loves you, they don't walk away. Do you love him?"

Blinking back tears, Stella slowly nodded. Zach was mostly in the wrong, but she knew she wasn't easy to get close to. She'd made him work for every step forward they made, often fighting him on simple ideas with the clinic just because she feared giving up control. She'd been waiting for him to mess up. For any excuse to walk away because then she could be the one who did. And it didn't really matter who did the walking. Either way, she'd ended up exactly as she'd feared she would: alone.

. . .

When Megan left for work, Stella forced herself to shower. She got ready for her day and forced herself through it. She was busier than normal with Zach not there. He'd texted and said he'd be happy to come in and see his patients but understood if she didn't want him there. She hadn't responded because she didn't know what to say.

By the end of the day, seeing twice as many patients as she had in a while, she was exhausted. Churned up and restless, thinking about Megan's words and Zach's apologies, about the loneliness that had settled inside her like a plague, she went to the barn. A ride on C.C. would clear the cobwebs. *Won't fix a broken heart though.*

Dexter had already seen to the horses feeding and stall cleaning, but Stella took a moment to greet each of them before focusing on Chocolate Chip.

Stella grabbed the saddle pad, and she mumbled more to herself than the horses, but they took whatever attention they could get.

"Nothing wrong with being independent. Less pressure all the way around, right, girl?" She pulled the girth off the wall where Zach had made everything easy for her to reach.

Chocolate Chip snorted, like she was in complete agreement with Stella.

"At least someone is."

She hated the loneliness spearing her chest. "He was wrong. Not me." While that might be true, it didn't make her feel better. It didn't make her want him out of her life. When Steven had asked her to stay, she'd said yes. When she'd hedged and said she wanted to move home, he'd upped the ante to get what he wanted: a strong, young veterinarian in his clinic. She'd compared Zach to him, but in truth, all Zach had ever wanted, even though he hadn't gone about it the right way, was her. The clinic. To be part of what Stella also wanted: carrying on her father's legacy.

It took some of the edge off, getting the horse ready. By the time she was ready to boost herself into the saddle, she could breathe. Until she settled herself on the horse's back and Chocolate Chip shifted and became agitated.

"Hey." Stella leaned over, petting her mane and talking

softly. "What's wrong, girl?"

C.C. whinnied, but it wasn't the same conversational sound she'd made when Stella came in. She nudged her forward, thinking it had just been too long since she'd ridden her.

"Come on, C.C." She nudged her with her heels again, but C.C. just shifted restlessly. Stella felt the slight tremble in the horse's muscles through the saddle. She dismounted immediately.

Coming around to nuzzle C.C., she pressed her forehead to her nose. "What's wrong, sweetie?"

The horse shifted, nudging Stella with her nose, and tears clogged her throat. She took her time removing the tack, soothing her horse, and trying not to worry until she could do an actual exam.

As she went through with a checkup, starting with C.C.'s legs, Stella's fingers itched to pull out her phone and call Zach. She loved horses. But he was better with them. *You're better when he's here.* The thought lodged in her head the way the golf-ball-sized lump did in her throat. C.C. protested and shuffled back when Stella ran her hands along the area between the knee and hoof. It was slightly swollen. She checked the shoes, earning more of C.C.'s ire.

Short of transporting C.C. to a bigger city or having a vet come to her, Stella could only do so much with her assessment. Zach was right. They needed an ultrasound machine. More than one if they were going to have horses living here. Yes, they could get along without it, but for how long? How much of her own vision could she see through if she was unwilling to accept that whatever her father had wanted for this place, he wasn't here anymore. This was on her. She had to make some decisions, not just for her, but for her animals. For the animals she pledged to care for and look after. Zach might have withheld some information, but it had been with the same goal in mind.

As she nuzzled C.C. again, it hit her hard, right in the chest. She didn't want to do this alone anymore. She didn't want Andrew's money. It was wrong. But that didn't mean there weren't other ways. Zach had given her ideas on how to be creative. He'd maximized their time and funds by thinking outside the box. It was time for her to do the same. She'd put her heart and her life in carefully labeled boxes in hopes of controlling the outcomes. But she couldn't control death or loss or falling in love any more than she could be certain that if she'd known about her father's heart, she could have saved him. Both Megan and Zach accused her of hiding, of keeping her guard so tightly in place that people not only couldn't they get in, but she couldn't get out.

"Time to break out, girl."

The horse whinnied once more. Maybe it was animal speak for "It's about time."

Chapter Thirty-One

Stella dug her heels into Clover's flanks. The horse picked up the pace and Stella tried to clear her mind. Too many things were rattling around, needing to fall into place. *It's happening. Just breathe.* Unfortunately, she couldn't ride, breathe, and *think* at the same time. No matter how hard she tried to focus on fixing things, her thoughts wandered to Zach. To how much she missed him. It hadn't been easy keeping him at arm's length. *Or making Dexter keep him there, you coward.*

But she had to do this her way. She needed to show him that she'd been wrong, too. Even when she'd given in to letting him be part of the clinic, letting him into her heart, she'd kept her distance. And when he'd messed up, she'd turned him away. She'd asked this entire town to give her a chance to prove herself, to see that she could fill her father's shoes. But her father never would have turned someone away for making a mistake. Especially if it had been made with the best of intentions.

She'd moved from feeling betrayed by Zach to being

angry at herself. She still hated that he'd accepted money from a third party and felt relief that doing so hadn't dropped them headfirst into a scandal. Stella was so caught up in protecting what her father had built, she'd been running it into the ground. Without Zach, she would have. Maybe Dad wouldn't make the choices she was about to, but he wasn't here anymore. She pulled the reins, bringing Clover back to a trot.

She'd barely slept all week. After the first night, she'd switched to the couch because the scent of Zach lingered on her pillow. She'd been there ever since. At night, when she couldn't sleep and thinking about Zach hurt, she made plans. Those plans meant giving up more control, but it also meant having a life. Mr. Henley's truck came into view when Stella hit the top of the hilly field. She could melt down when everything was said and done. When she could breathe.

He was standing with his son, arms spread, as his son nodded along. Stella dismounted, leading Clover over and waving at them.

"Well, hi there. Gorgeous girl, she is," Mr. Henley said, coming close.

His son, Nick, smiled at her. "Hey, Stella. How's it going?"

They shook hands. She'd gone to school with him as well, but they hadn't been close. Nick never stuck around school or played sports. He was a farmer's son and had all the responsibilities that came along with it. Which, apparently, had paid off.

"You excited?" she asked, the hurt in her heart over selling this piece of land all but gone. Her dad would be happy. *She* was happy. This was a good decision personally and professionally.

"I am," Nick said, his grin growing. "Dad's giving me twenty dairy cows of my own."

It was a fresh start for both of them. A way to make it

on their own, with their fathers' blessings. Stella knew, in her heart, that her father would approve of this plan. He'd cared for the Henley's cows for years and now the next generation would benefit from the proximity to the clinic.

She chatted with them for a few more minutes, happy she'd dragged herself out of bed to take a ride. "I need to get back. I have a carpenter coming with my sign."

"That's great news, what you did there. My Mabel talked to Kimberly and she was just touched beyond belief. You're a good girl, Stella. Your daddy would be proud."

Stella smiled, swallowing down tears. For the first time, in maybe ever, she agreed.

When she got back to the house after getting Clover settled in the barn, Megan's car was in the driveway. She glanced at the clinic. The town was surviving with her shorter hours this week. She hated knowing that part of the reason everyone was so understanding was because they knew she and Zach had fought. That they'd broken up. Word traveled through some secret portal like fairy dust being sprinkled over the gossips.

Megan was sitting on the porch steps, Nacho on one side and Soda on the other.

"You're alive," she said, looking Stella over.

Stella offered a smile and hoped she didn't look as tired as she felt. "Looks that way." She took a seat beside Nacho, who nuzzled into her, then wrapped her arms around his shaggy neck.

"I came by to see if you were mad at me."

Staring at her friend, Stella waited, but when Meg didn't elaborate, she asked, "Why would I be mad at *you?*"

"I wasn't sure if maybe I overstepped. I know you have reasons for being cautious, Stella, and friends are supposed to be supportive. They're supposed to have your back and trash talk idiot guys who do idiotic things. Not suggest second chances. At least, not at first."

Stella laughed. "True." She gave the dogs a signal for them to go play and turned to look at Megan. "They're also supposed to tell you when you're making a mess of things. You should be able to tell me anything, Meg. And I know I don't overshare like you and Taylor do—not that I'm complaining—I love when you guys do it. I'm just not used to having a bunch of girlfriends. Honestly, I'm not used to having a lot of *people*. Growing up, I followed my dad around and hung out with the animals. I think you were right. I was scared. Still am. I'm scared of needing someone, whether it's you and Taylor or Zach. And I'm scared of not being enough. My dad was enough. When my mom died, he took care of everything. Me, this clinic, the house. I don't remember him having help. But I'm not him. And I don't want to do it alone anymore. Even though it scares me not to."

Megan's smile was as bright as the sun in the sky. She wrapped her arms around Stella. "It scares everyone. Needing others, loving them, makes us vulnerable. But it also makes our lives fuller. Better."

Stella nodded. She'd been thinking the same thing all week. Not having Zach around had been harder than trusting him. Harder than leaning on him. And maybe he wouldn't give her a second chance, maybe he would and they wouldn't work, but she wasn't living her life if she didn't try.

Megan stood up. "I just wanted to check on you, but Parks made me promise that we'd schedule another BBQ."

Stella had worried so much about being alone and she wasn't. She had a family. The one she'd made for herself. Megan squeezed her shoulder and with a serious look, pointed her index finger at her.

"You're loved, Stella. Unconditionally. Not everyone leaves."

Zach did. Megan's features softened, like she could read

Stella's thoughts.

"You asked him to go," Megan reminded her softly.

"And I did. Because you asked. But I never said anything about coming back. I'm always going to come back, Stella," Zach said as he rounded the corner of the house.

Stella and Megan both gasped at his sudden appearance. What was he doing here? She wasn't ready to see him. She'd made Dexter tell him she'd be in touch.

Megan stepped back. "I should go. You okay?"

She shook her head, then nodded. Undecided. But she would be. "Go. I'm fine."

Megan sent a tight smile Zach's way and walked to her car.

"I parked by the clinic. Dexter said you were out for a ride."

He looked so good it stole her breath. How did she begin? Was she ready to say all the things she needed to say? She hadn't even showered; the sign hadn't arrived. She wasn't *prepared*.

"Did you come for your things?" Looking at the ground, she cursed herself for starting there. But what if he had? What if he'd just come to remove all the physical evidence that he'd been in her life. That he'd made it better.

"Sort of."

She looked up and watched him walk closer. So much for him declaring his undying love and begging her to take him back. He hadn't come for her. Just his stuff.

Every part of her ached to fall into him and forget that they'd hurt each other. He'd given her so much. Maybe she didn't deserve to ask for more.

Stammering, trying to figure out a way to stall, she looked back at the house. "Oh. Okay. Uh, I'll get out of your way. We should probably book a time to talk about patients and stuff." *Stop it. What are you doing? This is your chance to tell him how you feel. To tell him you're sorry. That you forgive him. That you need him.* She was still acting scared. Curling her fingers into her palms, she tried to inhale some courage.

The scent of his cologne wafted around her and her knees all but buckled. *Just the wind. It's cool out. Right. Keep telling yourself that.* She needed him to step back, out of her space, but she couldn't form the words so she just stared at his chest, hoping he'd go around her, leave her there to figure out how to breathe again.

"Patients and *stuff*?" His voice was deep and rough.

She glanced up through lowered lashes. "Yes. I know I still have a contract to honor."

He stepped closer. "Screw the contract."

Her head snapped up. "What?"

"You're right, Doc, we need to sort some stuff out, and I thought I could do this in some mature, romantic way but I can't. Because looking at you and not touching you is fucking killing me."

Her heart beat out of control. She couldn't even talk over it. So she just soaked up the sight of him.

It's your turn to leap. "I'm sorry," she finally whispered.

"*You're sorry?* What the hell do you have to be sorry for?" His tone was husky, and it roamed over her skin like a welcome caress.

"For fighting you every step on making this place better. For trying to keep you out. For sending you away. For not giving you another chance."

She heard his breath hitch. He reached behind him and pulled some folded papers out of his pocket and handed them over.

"What is this?" She took them.

"You said second chance, Stell, and I'm having a hard time breathing, thinking maybe you'll give me one, but you need to know, either way, whether you can forgive me or you can't, *I'm* sorry. I messed up."

She unfolded the papers and saw that he'd signed over the deed to his land by the ocean. Stella looked up at him, studied his face. "Again, what is this?"

"I sold the property. I thought it would take some time, but there were developers salivating to get it. They actually had a bidding war. I sold it in twenty-four hours."

She shook her head, not understanding, her heart thrashing around, making her feel too many things at once. *He makes me off-balance. In the best way.* "Why? You love that land. It's what you came home for."

Zach stepped up to her, stroked one hand down her hair, and she sighed, leaned into his touch. She'd missed his touch.

"It's land. I thought it was significant. I thought it meant I had a place to belong. I was wrong. *You're* where I belong, Stella. We can sort shit with the clinic, we'll figure it out, swear to God, but none of it matters if I don't have you. I need to know what it'll take to get you to forgive me."

Stella bit her lip, unsure if she was dreaming. She hadn't been sleeping well so there was a chance she could be hallucinating. But she could smell his cologne and hear his uneven breaths. *This is real.* A trickle of tears traveled down her cheek. Zach caught it and swiped at them with his thumb.

"I'm so sorry I hurt you. I'd do anything to take it back. To do it over."

Everything inside of her fought to burst free. Her heart beat too hard, her breath came too fast, her brain spun out of control. He wasn't just here for the clinic. He was here for *her.*

"We can't go back," she said.

"Stella," he said, his voice strained.

Moving closer, she touched her hand to his jaw. "But we can move forward."

When his breath hitched, her heart did the same. He bent his knees, gripping her shoulders. "Together? We can move forward *together.* You and me. Us, right? Tell me there's an us, Stella, because the rest of it doesn't matter. I love you."

Her breath and her heart settled. The pace slowed and the shaky feeling dissipated. Smiling around her tears, she felt steady. Sure. Even though she'd hoped he felt that way, hearing him say it filled her with happiness. With contentment. With hope and trust and all the things she was scared to want. The things she was terrified of losing. But he was standing right in front of her offering it all.

"You love me?"

Pulling her close so their bodies were aligned, the papers crinkled in her hand.

"I love you more than I knew a person could love another person. I feel like you're part of me. A vital part of me, and I can't breathe without you, Stella."

Her chest filled like a balloon and she thought she might float away with the rightness of it.

Cupping her face, he leaned closer. "Say something. Tell me I haven't wrecked everything."

Slipping her arms around his neck, she shook her head. "You did exactly what you said you would."

"What's that?"

"You fixed everything. The clinic, my home. My heart. I love you."

She barely got the last word out before his mouth closed over her own, and he was kissing her like he'd been starved of all of life's necessities. And in a way, maybe they both had been—they'd been without each other and Zach was right about belonging. It wasn't about a place. It was a person. And he was hers. She'd have to work on not being too scared to show him that every day. Even when he stopped kissing her mouth, his hands held her face and he rained kisses all over her face until she laughed.

"I didn't think I'd be the reason for your laughter again."

She rested her head on his chest, held him close. "I didn't think you'd come back."

Kissing the top of her head, he stroked her hair. "I couldn't stay away. You're everything to me. You're *my* reason."

Confused, she tipped her head back. "Reason for what?"

"All of it. Life is short and there were a lot of nights after Travis's death that I wished it was shorter. That I didn't think I'd ever shed the guilt of not going with him to the party. But I got up every day, figuring there was a reason I didn't tag along that night. I needed there to be, you know? I couldn't make sense of it otherwise. I've been roaming around searching for a purpose, trying to understand why I never belonged anywhere else. Why, even though it hurt, I had to come home. Had to come here to this land, to *your* clinic. It's because I was waiting to belong to you."

There were no words to adequately describe how good it felt to look at him and *know* he meant it. Smiling, she gave him what she could. "I love you, and I want to keep being each other's reasons. I want us to belong to each other."

Chapter Thirty-Two

She loved him. He hadn't expected that. He'd hoped. Fuck, he'd even prayed and promised unknown deities, but he hadn't really believed. How the hell had he gotten lucky enough to find her? To have her and be able to call her his? He didn't want to question everything anymore. He didn't know why Travis died, why his dad drank away his life, or what made Andrew wreck his career. That's just what had happened. What he did with each of those things was up to him. But he was done running.

Zach ran his hands over her arms, pulling her in for a hug, just to absorb the heat of her body. He reminded himself not to get distracted by the feel of her body under his hands, the soft, sweet fall of her hair and the vulnerable look he'd seen in her eyes. He'd never give her a reason to doubt him again. They'd fight and disagree, but he'd never withhold anything from her again. Which meant he had several things to tell her. Reluctantly, he pulled back, slid his hand into hers, and led her to the steps.

"We have a lot to talk about," he said.

She sat beside him, her hand still in his, their thighs pressed together. He was having a hard time not hauling her onto his lap just to have her closer.

"You said you paid Andrew back? I'm really sorry he let you down, Zach."

Staring out at the yard, he unclenched his jaw. "I hate what he did and that I brought a piece of that to your home and clinic."

Squeezing his hand, she leaned her head on his shoulder. "I didn't want you to sell the property though. Why didn't you sell the rental?" She straightened and looked at him, her cheeks flushed. "Not that you had to sell either. I really hadn't intended for you to do that."

Cupping her cheek, he placed a kiss on the bridge of her nose then leaned back. "Funny story, actually."

"Oh?"

"I've been renting the place out through an agency, so I didn't know who was in there. When I went by in person to give them notice that I'd be selling, guess who it turned out to be?"

Stella shrugged.

"Colton."

"Oh no." Her lips pressed together, and he knew what she expected. His heart pounded with the eagerness of telling her he'd taken the high road. Because it didn't matter what had happened ten, twenty years ago. What mattered was now.

"He's living there with his girlfriend and her kid. Cute kid. Little boy. Anyway, long story short, they're settled. It's not a rental to them. It's their home. And like you, he was waiting for me to toss him out on his ass."

Stella's smile widened. "Then he doesn't know you at all, does he?"

He grinned. "And you do?"

She nudged her way under his arm so she was cuddled up

to him, and it felt perfect.

"You have some demons, Zach. But you aren't a jerk. You're fair and kind and make the best decisions you know how. Did you tell them they could stay?"

He shook his head and tried not to smile when her mouth opened in surprise.

"Nope. I'm still selling."

"Zach," she whispered.

"I worked out a long-term rent to own with Colton and his girlfriend."

The smile jumped back onto her face and she threw her arms around him.

"I'm proud of you," she whispered. When she pulled back, she lowered her chin, then looked up at him through her lashes. "You're not the only one who's found a way to put the past behind them."

"No?"

Stella shook her head. "Mr. Henley purchased fifteen acres for his son to raise his own dairy cows."

His smile felt like it came up from the depths of his soul. They were on the same page. He'd been dreading telling her there was no way to move forward, even with the two of them and some help, without letting some of it go.

"We're going to be okay," he said.

She scooted closer. "We are. I kept hanging onto the past, like maybe that would keep my dad here with me. But I think the best way to do that is to honor him by pushing this place forward."

"I agree. Which is why I have a present for you, and I don't want any arguments."

Stella laughed. "What makes you think I'd argue over a present?"

Placing a noisy kiss on her lips, he stood up. "You have a bit of a stubborn, independent streak."

Stella stood stretching when he came back around the house to the porch. He'd been bringing the portable ultrasound machine down to the barn, but then he'd heard her and Megan. His eyes tracked the hem of her shirt and his mouth watered at the sliver of skin she exposed with her arms up in the air. Zach had missed everything about her, but fuck, he'd missed touching her. Kissing her. Holding her close.

"That's…" She stopped, looking up at him, her eyes wide with surprise. And gratitude. *Fuck. Finally.*

"This is just the beginning. We need new equipment, Stell. You know we do."

Tears brimmed in her eyes, tweaking the muscles around his heart. "What is it?"

"C.C.'s been acting weird. I think it's a suspensory ligament injury. But I couldn't be sure. I've been pricing these out all week."

He handed her the box, then thought better of it, and set it down on the porch. "Now you don't have to. We're in this together, Stella. I want an extension on the contract."

She sniffed. "Oh yeah?" She laughed. "What time frame were you thinking?"

He stepped into her, took her hand and held it tight. She was his anchor. "I'd like to suggest forever but don't want to scare you. I'll start with twenty-five to fifty years and we'll renegotiate at a later date."

She blinked the tears away and one slipped over. He caught it with his thumb, swiped her cheek gently. "I think that sounds doable."

Taking a step toward her, intending to kiss her until neither of them could breathe, he stopped when he heard the vehicle approach. Before he could turn, Stella stepped into him and put her hands on his biceps, beaming up at him.

"One more thing. I have a present for you, too."

Zach straightened, unable to hide his surprise. "You

didn't even know I'd be here."

"I planned to come to you. I was just trying to gather my courage and get things settled."

The fact that she was going to seek him out, that she'd planned to fight for them, settled every niggling doubt he'd buried.

Curious, he asked, "What is it?" What else could there be? They had money to move forward without sacrificing her desire to not go corporate. They were in love. The hottest girl in town was in love with him. He looked up at the sky and smiled. *Who'd have thought, eh, Trav?*

She gestured to the visitor even as the dogs headed for the drive. He and Stella gave them the stay command at the same time.

He didn't recognize the guy that got out of the aging truck, but obviously Stella did.

The guy, probably a little older than Zach, was wearing a backward baseball cap and his clothes were covered with... wood?

"Hey Stell!" The guy greeted, lifting an arm in the air and then walking to the back of the truck.

"Hi Gary." They walked closer, Stella squeezing his hand. "Gary, this is Zach Mason. Zach, this is Gary, he's a local carpenter."

Gary came over to shake Zach's hand. "Nice to meet you. Heard there was a new vet in town. Mason. Hmm, name sounds familiar." Zach noted that there was no disdain in the man's tone. It wasn't a hey-I-knew-your-dad tone or hey, weren't you the kid who hightailed it outta here ten years ago? Gary snapped his fingers. "Your mom. Sheila, right? She's a riot on karaoke night."

Without realizing it, Zach smiled. Stella looked up at him. "We'll have to check it out. Maybe do a duet."

Gary laughed and walked to the truck bed. Zach lowered

his head so he could whisper in Stella's ear. "Not a chance, babe."

She gave him a mock frown. "But you love me."

He laughed. Yeah, he did. "Damn right I do. But that makes me happy, not certifiably crazy."

She laughed, and his heart seemed to expand, putting pressure on his ribs. The kind of pressure he could definitely learn to live with.

"Thought you'd want to see it before I install," Gary said.

He sensed Stella's nervousness and was about to ask her about it, but she gave him a little push. Curious, he went to see what Gary was gesturing toward in his truck bed. His breath lodged so hard in his lungs, it felt like a bullet had whipped through him. He looked at the massive rectangular sign—beautifully carved—and then back at Stella. His eyes watered again and he couldn't breathe.

Stella rushed forward. "I talked to Travis's mom. I told her I wanted to do something to help you honor him and I knew…no matter what happened between us that we'd find a way to still serve the town. That this," she said, gesturing to the property with an outstretched arm, "would survive. Even if we didn't. I also knew that both of us were struggling with the same thing."

"What's that?" he asked, his throat uncomfortably thick.

Stella took his hands. "Learning how to let go of the past in a way we could still honor the people we loved and lost."

He shook his head, emotions swamping him. The sign read: MACKLEBY LANE STABLES.

"Stella," he whispered.

"I always thought it was weird that our farm didn't really have a name and I thought it should. I figured, what better way to honor what we're building than to pay tribute to two of the people who helped shape us. Are you mad?"

Zach stepped away from the truck and took her face in

his hands. He crushed her mouth under his and channeled everything he felt into kissing her. Jesus Christ, if he could swallow her whole, absorb her into his skin so she was a permanent part of him, he would. Instead, he held her tight and when he finally stopped kissing her, he looked her straight in the eyes and gave her everything.

"Twenty-five to fifty isn't enough. I changed my mind. I want it all, Stella. I want forever. I want everything. I know you're scared and you've been hurt, but I want the same last name and to wake up every day with you and go to sleep every night beside you. I want the good and the bad and everything else in between. But I won't push. You tell me when you're ready. All you need to do is say the word. I'm ready."

Gary cleared his throat with a chuckle. "I'll, uh, go get this hung up."

Stella bit her lip then smiled. "I like the sound of forever."

Pulling her close, Zach realized that he'd come home thinking he had it all together. Now, as he held the woman he loved in his arms, he knew he may not have been right at the time, but no matter what, as long as he had Stella, a woman he'd never expected or planned on, he didn't just have it together. He had it all.

Epilogue

December 31ˢᵗ

It was almost midnight and the twinkling lights were nearly as mesmerizing as the couple dancing under them. Adam said something into Megan's ear, and she looked up at her new husband with such unadulterated adoration, Stella's breath caught. The dress shimmered nearly as much as they did. With a full-bodied skirt and sweetheart bodice, it suited her friend completely. Adam looked every bit the charming prince in his black tuxedo. Stella felt like her heart actually sighed.

She didn't have to believe in miracles or fairy tales to know that magic was real. It was right there in front of her with Adam and Megan. As a hand snaked around her own stomach and she was pulled tight to Zach's body, she acknowledged that it was right behind her as well. His lips touched the outer shell of her ear, which he had easy access to thanks to the fancy upswept hairstyle she was sporting.

"We going to join them out there, Doc?"

Stella shivered. "To dance?"

Zach's rumble of laughter traveled over every inch of her body. She'd laughed more, smiled more with him than she could remember doing in a long time.

"I think we do anything more than that out there, we'd steal the spotlight."

Pressing her hand over Zach's on her stomach, she bit her lip as he swayed softly side to side, his front glued to her back. A perfect fit. She hadn't been thinking about dancing, but more, the idea of first dances and twinkling lights. The thought both excited and terrified her in equal measure.

"Do you want to dance?" he asked, his breath tickling her skin.

Declan walked onto the dance floor holding the hand of a tall blond Stella didn't recognize. She smiled, thinking how not long ago, she'd been as adamant as Adam's best friend about not needing love or promises. Now, she wanted both and she wanted to give them.

Turning in Zach's arms, she pushed her own up around his neck and stared into the eyes that had sucked her in from the moment she saw him.

"I do. I want to dance with you. Tonight, and any other night we can. But mostly..." She went up on her tiptoes and Zach scooped her closer.

"Mostly what, babe?"

He'd taken so many chances on her and too many times, she'd pulled away, scared to want too much. It was her turn to take a chance and give him the truth. And she wasn't even scared.

He ran his nose along hers and she smiled, giving in to her heart. "Mostly, I want to dance with you at our own wedding."

Zach's eyes widened, and his fingers tightened, digging into her skin through her dress. "Don't mess with me, Doc."

His voice was husky and low.

Stella laughed. "I wouldn't."

His fingers loosened, but his hold didn't. The music swelled around them, but everything fell away. All she could see was the hunger and happiness and love in his eyes.

"Just to make sure I'm not misunderstanding, you're asking me to marry you, Doc?"

Her cheeks hurt from smiling. "You did say all I had to do was ask."

"I did, and I meant it. There's nothing I want more."

"That's a yes?" Her heart thundered in her chest.

Zach's forehead lowered to hers and his eyes closed just for a minute. "It's an absolutely-as-soon-as-possible hell yes."

She went on tiptoe to kiss him, but he pulled back slightly. "I didn't bring the ring."

"You have a ring?" A swarm of butterflies took flight in her stomach.

"Damn right I do. I think I fell in love with you about two seconds after I entered the clinic. Even before we straightened things out, I knew I wanted you to be my wife, my partner, my forever."

Tears burned, and she didn't try to stop them. Nodding as one slipped down her cheek, she whispered, "I love you. You're everything I never knew I wanted or needed."

They stayed there, staring at each other, laughter and love surrounding them as they basked in their own happiness. Stella rested her head against his solid chest, listening to his heart for a few minutes, absorbing the feel of his arms around her waist. *This* was home. Pulling back, she looked up at him.

"I thought of something I want more," she said.

His eyebrow arched. "More than marrying me?"

She nodded, and he stared, kept staring while Stella smiled at him, wondering if he'd guess.

"There's only one thing I can think of that I want as badly

as I want you to be my wife."

She grinned. Yeah. They were good partners. She might even say they were meant to be.

His hand slid down her back, across her hip, and he swept the back of it along her belly and his eyes glanced up, full of tenderness, passion, and love. Flutters erupted and her heart spasmed so hard she was surprised she could breathe through it.

"You want to have babies with me, Doc?" His words were whispered, but she heard him just fine.

"I do." She wanted it all. With him. Their very own version of happily ever after.

Acknowledgments

First and foremost, always, to my family who makes me so incredibly happy which makes it easier to write books. There are so many people that take part in helping a story work. People in my own private circle, friends and family, people who let me bounce ideas off of them without wondering why I'm asking such weird questions that I probably don't even phrase properly. Then there's my editors (one of whom I actually got to meet this summer and is every bit as wonderful and adorable in real life as she is online). Cover makers, editors who don't send me angry faces because I still don't know how to use a comma. Twitter pals, the Romance Chicks, new friends, old friends. Writing is solitary but I am definitely not alone.

Thank you to LVD for giving me more information on cows than I wanted to need ;). To everyone at Entangled that helped make this book so much better, thank you. To anyone I forgot to list, I appreciate you: I just have a really bad memory. To my agent, Fran who answers my emails no matter how long they are. To Nicole who has saved me from having to post on social media so I could focus on this story.

To readers—thank you for hanging out with Zach and Stella. Stacey, Cole, Tanya—you're getting a direct shout out this time because no matter what, you're right there encouraging me and stealing book boyfriends from one another. It matters and so do you. Thank you. And thanks to Helen Hoang for not minding that our characters have the same name. I wish our Stellas could spend time together ;)

Thank you to Jennifer Probst for being so kind and approachable. Thank you for writing *Write Naked*. It's made every book struggle I've hit since I read it a little easier to navigate.

About the Author

Jody Holford lives in British Columbia with her family. She's unintentionally funny and rarely on time for anything. She writes multiple genres, but her favorite is romance. Visit her online at http://www.jodyholfordauthor.com or sign up for her newsletter here to stay up to date on all of Jody's new releases.

Discover more Amara titles...

BUTTERFACE
a novel by Avery Flynn

I'm not what most people would call "pretty" and, well, high school was rough. Fast forward ten years and life is good... Until a bunch of jerks put the "butterface" (AKA me) on a wedding Kiss Cam with the hottest cop in Waterbury. But then he kisses me. Then he tells everyone we've been dating for months. Soon everything starts to feel too real. But there's something he's not telling me about why he's really hanging around, and I'm pretty sure it has to do with my mob-connected brothers. Because this is not a make-over story, and Cinderella is only a fairy tale...

ONE NIGHT WIFE
a *Confidence Game* novel by Ainslie Paton

Finley Cartwright is the queen of lost causes. That's why she's standing on a barstool trying to convince Friday night drinkers to donate money to a failing charity. And hot venture capitalist Cal might just be her ticket to success. Professional grifter and modern-day Robin Hood, Cal Sherwood is looking for a partner, and if sexy Fin sticks with him, her charity will thrive, and she'll help him score billions to fund his social justice causes.

WHAT HAPPENS IN VEGAS
a *Girls Weekend Away* novel by Shana Gray

Tough-as-nails detective Bonni Connolly is on a girls' getaway in Vegas with her friends and she splurges on a little luxury, including a VIP booth in an exclusive club. That's when she sees *him*. Professional poker player Quinn Bryant is in town for one of the largest tournaments of the year. What starts as a holiday fling soon turns into something more, as Bonni learns to see the man behind the poker face. Even though Bonni's trip has an end date and there is another tournament calling Quinn's name, their strong connection surprises them both. And by the end of the weekend they start to wonder if what happens in Vegas doesn't have to stay there...

HANDLE WITH CARE
a *Saddler Cove* novel by Nina Croft

First grade teacher Emily Towson always does the right thing. But in her dreams, she does bad, bad things with the town's baddest boy: Tanner O'Connor. But when he sells her grandmother a Harley, fantasy is about to meet a dose of reality. Tanner spent two hard years in prison, with only the thought of this "good girl" to keep him sane. Before either one thinks though, they're naked and making memories on his tool bench. Now Tanner's managed to knock-up the town's "good girl" and she's going to lose her job over some stupid "morality clause" if he doesn't step up.

26564505R00198

Made in the USA
Columbia, SC
18 September 2018